£2.50
19/12

BEFORE I SAY GOODBYE

Nell McDermott is devastated when her husband Adam's cabin cruiser blows up in a New York harbor with him and several close business associates on board. She is also wracked with guilt—for the last time Nell saw Adam alive, she told him to leave and never come back. Their quarrel was caused by Nell's decision to try and win the Congressional seat long held by her grandfather, 'Mac'. Politics is in her blood and Adam had known of her intentions before they got married. Despite her scepticism Nell is persuaded by her great-aunt Gert to see a medium, Bonnie Wilson, to try to make peace with her husband and to come to terms with the tragedy. As Nell searches for the truth about Adam's death, she relies more and more heavily on Bonnie, who claims to be receiving instructions from Adam, which Nell is faithfully carrying out. But what Nell does not know is that she is being closely watched, and the nearer she comes to learning what happened to her husband, the nearer she is to becoming the next victim of a ruthless killer . . .

BEFORE I SAY GOODBYE

Mary Higgins Clark

CHIVERS PRESS
BATH

First published 2000
by
Simon & Schuster
This Large Print edition published by
Chivers Press
by arrangement with
Simon & Schuster UK Ltd
2000

ISBN 0 7540 1491 6

British Library Cataloguing in Publication Data available

Printed and bound in Great Britain by
REDWOOD BOOKS, Trowbridge, Wiltshire

ACKNOWLEDGMENTS

Once again it's time to say—How can I thank thee—Let me count the ways.

My gratitude continues to grow with each passing year to my long-time editor, Michael Korda, and his associate, senior editor Chuck Adams. They always encourage, always persevere, always say the right words along the way.

Blessings on Lisl Cade, my publicist—always my encouraging companion, dear friend and thoughtful reader.

I'm forever grateful to my agents, Eugene Winick and Sam Pinkus. They find answers before I ask the questions. True friends, indeed!

Associate Director of Copy Editing Gypsy da Silva is always there with her eagle eye and heavenly patience. Again and again, thank you, Gypsy.

Bless you Copy Editor Carol Catt and Scanner Michael Mitchell for your careful work.

Thank you Chief Warrant Officer Lionel Bryant of the U.S. Coast Guard for being my giving and thoughtful expert on the likely post events of an explosion in the New York harbor.

Sgt. Steven Marron and Detective Richard Murphy, Ret., NYPD, New York County District Attorney's Office have given marvelous guidance about what police procedure and investigation would unfold if the events depicted here had been actual happenings. Thank you. You're great.

My deep gratitude to architects Erica Belsey and Philip Mahla and interior designer Eve Ardia for being my experts on the architecture and design questions I posed to them.

Dr. Ina Winick is always there for me to answer my psychological queries. Bless you, Ina.

Many thanks to Dr. Richard Roukema for his thoughtful analysis when I asked him hypothetical questions.

Many thanks to Diane Ingrassia, Branch Manager of the Ridgewood Savings Bank, for answering my questions about safe deposit boxes.

Always my thanks to my assistants and friends Agnes Newton and Nadine Petry and my reader-in-progress, Irene Clark.

Thanks to my daughter and fellow author, Carol Higgins Clark, for once again being my sounding board and keeping me from using expressions her generation just plain wouldn't get.

Continuing gratitude to my cheering section, our children and grandchildren. As one of the kids asked, 'Is writing a book like having a lot of homework, Mimi?'

A special loving thank you to my husband, John Conheeney, who continues to survive with great grace and humor being married to a writer on a deadline.

Once again I joyfully quote the fifteenth-century monk. 'The book is finished. Let the writer play.'

P.S. To my friends—I'm available for dinner.

For Michael Korda
Dear Friend
and
Magnificent Editor
with
Many thanks for 25 wonderful years

PROLOGUE

Fifteen-year-old Nell MacDermott turned and began the swim back to shore. Her body tingled with youthful exhilaration as she looked about, taking in the glorious combination of the sun in the cloudless sky, the light, fresh breeze, the salty, foaming whitecaps breaking around her. She had been in Maui only an hour but already had decided that she liked it better than the Caribbean, which for the past several years was where her grandfather had taken the family for their annual post-Christmas vacation.

Actually, 'family' seemed something of an exaggeration. This was the fourth year that their family had consisted of just her grandfather and herself. It had been five years ago when Cornelius MacDermott, legendary congressman from New York, had been called off the floor of the House of Representatives to be given the news that his son and daughter-in-law, both anthropologists on an expedition in the Brazilian jungle, had died in the crash of their small chartered plane.

He immediately had rushed to New York to pick up Nell at school. It was news that she had to hear from him. He arrived to find his granddaughter in the nurse's office, weeping.

'When we were coming in from recess this morning, I suddenly felt that Dad and Mommy were with me, and that they had come to say goodbye to me,' she told him as he held her. 'I didn't actually see them, but I felt Mom kiss me, and then Dad ran his fingers through my hair.'

Later that day, Nell and the housekeeper who took care of her when her parents were away had moved into the brownstone on East Seventy-ninth Street, the place where her grandfather had been born, and where her father had been raised.

Nell flashed briefly on these memories as she began her swim back to shore and to her grandfather, who was sitting in a beach chair under an umbrella, having reluctantly acquiesced to her plea for one quick swim before they unpacked.

'Don't go out too far,' he had cautioned as he opened his book. 'It's six o'clock, and the lifeguard is leaving.'

Nell would have liked to stay in the water longer, but she could see that the beach was almost deserted now, and she knew that in a few minutes her grandfather would realize he was getting hungry and start to get impatient, especially since they hadn't even unpacked. Long ago her mother had warned her that any situation that left Cornelius MacDermott both hungry and tired was to be avoided.

Even from a good distance out, Nell could see that he was still deeply absorbed in his book. She knew though that it wouldn't last much longer. Okay, she thought as she picked up her stroke— 'Let's make waves.'

Suddenly, she felt disoriented, as if she were being turned around. *What was happening to her?*

The shore disappeared from view as she felt herself being yanked from side to side, then pulled under. Stunned, she opened her mouth to call for help, but immediately found herself swallowing salty water. Sputtering and choking, she gasped for breath, struggling to keep afloat.

2

Riptide! While her grandfather was checking in at the front desk, she had overheard two bellmen talking about it.

One of them said that there'd been a riptide on the other side of the island last week, and that two guys had drowned. He said that they died because they fought against the pull instead of letting themselves get carried out until they were beyond it. *A riptide is a head-on collision of conflicting currents.* As her arms flailed, Nell remembered reading that description in *National Geographic*.

Still, it was impossible not to resist as she felt herself being pulled under the churning waves, down, down, and away from shore.

I can't let myself get carried out! she thought in a sudden flash of panic. I can't! If I go out, I'll never get back in. She managed to orient herself long enough to look toward shore and glimpse the candy-striped umbrella.

'Help me!' she said feebly, her effort to scream ending when the salty water filled her mouth, gagging her. The current that was pulling her out and sucking her under was too strong to fight.

In desperation she flipped onto her back and let her arms go limp. Moments later she was struggling again, resisting the horrifying feeling of her body being rushed out away from shore, away from any hope of help.

I don't want to die! she kept saying to herself. *I don't want to die!* A wave was lifting her, tossing her, pulling her farther out. 'Help me!' she said again, then began to sob.

And then, just as suddenly as it had begun, it was over. The invisible foamy chains abruptly released her, and she had to flail her arms to keep afloat.

3

This was what they had talked about in the hotel, she thought. She had been tossed beyond the riptide.

Don't get back into it, she told herself. *Swim around it.*

But she was too tired. She was too far out. She looked at the distant shore. She would never make it. Her eyelids were so heavy. The water was starting to feel warm, like a blanket. She was getting sleepy.

Swim, Nell, you can make it!

It was her mother's voice, imploring her to fight.

Nell, get moving!

The urgent command from her father stung her senses and succeeded in shattering her lethargy. With blind obedience, Nell swam straight out, then began to make a wide circle around the area of the riptide. Every breath was a sob, every movement of her arms an impossible struggle, but she persevered.

Agonizing minutes later, nearing exhaustion, she managed to dive into a swelling wave that grabbed and held her and rushed her toward shore. Then it crested and broke, tossing her onto the hard, wet sand.

Trembling violently, Nell started to get up, then felt firm hands lifting her to her feet. 'I was just coming to call you in,' Cornelius MacDermott said sharply. 'No more swimming for you today, young lady. They're putting up the red flag. They say there are riptides nearby.'

Unable to speak, Nell only nodded.

His face creased with concern, MacDermott pulled off his terry-cloth robe and wrapped it around her. 'You're chilled, Nell. You shouldn't have stayed in so long.'

'Thank you, Grandpa. I'm fine.' Nell knew better than to tell her beloved, no-nonsense grandfather what had just happened, and she especially did not want him to know that once again she had had one of those experiences of being in communication with her parents, experiences that this most pragmatic of men brusquely dismissed as a flight of youthful fantasy.

Seventeen years later
Thursday, June 8

CHAPTER ONE

Nell set off at a brisk pace on her familiar walk from her apartment on Park Avenue and Seventy-third Street to her grandfather's office on Seventy-second and York. From the peremptory summons she had received, demanding that she be there by three o'clock, she knew that the situation with Bob Gorman must have come to a head. As a result she was not looking forward to the meeting.

Deep in thought, she was oblivious to the admiring glances that occasionally came her way. After all, she and Adam were happily married. Still, she knew that some people found a tall woman, with the slim, strong body of an athlete, short chestnut-colored hair that was now forming into humidity-caused ringlets, midnight-blue eyes, and a generous mouth, attractive. While growing up, and frequently attending public events with her grandfather, Nell's rueful observation was that when the media described her, that was usually the word used—'attractive'.

'To me, attractive is like having a guy say, "She's not much to look at, but what a personality!" It's the kiss of death. Just once I want to be described as "beautiful" or "elegant" or "stunning" or even "stylish,"' she had complained when she was twenty.

Typically, her grandfather's comment had been, 'For God's sake don't be so silly. Be grateful you've got a head on your shoulders and know how to use it.'

The trouble was that she knew already what he

9

wanted to discuss with her today, and the way he was going to ask her to use her head was a problem. His plans for her and Adam's objections to them were most decidedly an issue.

*   *   *

At eighty-two, Cornelius MacDermott had lost little of the vigor that for decades had made him one of the nation's most prominent congressmen. Elected at thirty to represent the midtown Manhattan district where he had been raised, he stayed in that spot for fifty years, resisting all arguments to run for the Senate. On his eightieth birthday he had chosen not to run again. 'I'm not trying to beat Strom Thurmond's record as the longest-serving guy on the Hill,' he had announced.

Retirement for Mac meant opening a consulting office and making sure that New York City and State stayed in his party's political fold. An endorsement from him was a virtual laying on of hands for neophyte campaigners. Years ago he had created his party's most famous election commercial on TV: 'What did that other bunch ever do for you?' followed by silence and a succession of bewildered expressions. Recognized everywhere, he could not walk down the street without being showered with affectionate and respectful greetings.

Occasionally he grumbled to Nell about his status as a local celebrity: 'Can't set foot outside my door without making sure I'm camera ready.'

To which she replied, 'You'd have a heart attack if people ignored you, and you know it.'

When she reached his office today, Nell waved

to the receptionist and walked back to her grandfather's suite. 'The mood?' she asked Liz Hanley, his longtime secretary.

Liz, a handsome sixty-year-old, with dark brown hair and a no-nonsense expression, raised her eyes to heaven. 'It was a dark and stormy night,' she said.

'Oh boy, that bad,' Nell said with a sigh. She tapped on the door of the private office as she let herself in. 'Top of the day, Congressman.'

'You're late, Nell,' Cornelius MacDermott barked, as he spun his desk chair around to face her.

'Not according to my watch. Three on the dot.'

'I thought I told you to get here *by* three.'

'I had a column to turn in, and unfortunately my editor shares your sentiments about punctuality. Now, how about showing me the winning smile that melts the voters' hearts?'

'Today I haven't got one. Sit down, Nell.' MacDermott indicated the couch situated beneath the corner window that offered panoramic views of the city east and north. He had chosen that office because it gave him a view of his longtime congressional district.

Nell called it his fiefdom.

As she settled on the couch, she looked at him anxiously. There was an unfamiliar weariness in his blue eyes, clouding his usual keenly observant expression. His erect carriage, even when he was seated, always gave the impression that he was taller than his actual height, but today even that seemed diminished. Even Mac's famous shock of white hair appeared thinner. As she watched, he clasped his hands together and shrugged his

11

shoulders as though trying to dislodge an invisible burden. With sinking heart, Nell thought for the first time in her memory that her grandfather looked his age.

He stared past her for a long moment, then got up and moved to a comfortable armchair near the couch.

'Nell, we've got a crisis, and you've got to solve it. After being nominated for a second term, that weasel Bob Gorman has decided not to run. He's been offered a sweetheart deal to head up a new Internet company. He'll serve out his term till the election but says he can't afford to live on a congressman's salary. I pointed out to him that when I helped him get the nomination two years ago, all he talked about at the time was a commitment to serving the people.'

She waited. She knew that last week her grandfather had heard the first rumors about Gorman not running for a second term. Obviously the rumors had been confirmed.

'Nell, there's one person—and only one, in my opinion—who could step in and keep that seat in the party.' MacDermott frowned. 'You should have done it two years ago when I retired and you know it.' He paused. 'Look, it's in your blood. You wanted to do it from the start, but Adam talked you out of it. Don't let that happen again.'

'Mac, please don't start on Adam.'

'I'm not starting on anyone, Nell. I'm telling you that I know you, and you're a political animal. I've been grooming you for my job since you were a teenager. I wasn't thrilled when you married Adam Cauliff, but don't forget, I helped him to get his start in New York when I introduced him to

Walters and Arsdale, a fine architectural firm and among my most valued supporters.'

Mac's lips tightened. 'It didn't make me look good when, after less than three years, Adam walked out on them, taking their chief assistant, and opened his own operation. All right, maybe that's good business. But from the outset, Adam knew my plans for you, your plans for yourself. What made him change his mind? You were supposed to run for my seat when I retired, and he knew it. He had no right to talk you out of it then, and he has no right to try to talk you out of it now.'

'Mac, I enjoy being a columnist. You may not have noticed, but I get mighty good feedback.'

'You write a darn good column. I grant you that. But it's not enough for you and you know it.'

'Look, my reluctance now isn't that Adam asked me to give up the idea of running for office.'

'No? Then what do you call it?'

'We both want children. You know that. He suggested I wait until after that happens. In ten years I'll only be forty-two. That would be a good age to start running for elective office.'

Her grandfather stood impatiently. 'Nell, in ten years the parade will have passed you by. Events move too fast to wait. Admit it. You're aching to throw your hat in the ring. Remember what you said when you informed me you were going to call me Mac?'

Nell leaned forward, clasped her hands together and tucked them under her chin. She remembered; it happened when she was a freshman at Georgetown. At his initial protest, she had held her ground. 'Look, you always say I'm your best friend, and your friends call you Mac,' she had told him. 'If

13

I keep calling you Grandpa, I'll always be perceived as a kid. When I'm with you in public I want to be considered your aide-de-camp.'

'What's that supposed to mean?' he had responded.

She remembered how she'd held up the dictionary. 'Listen to the definition. In brief, an aide-de-camp is 'a subordinate or confidential assistant.' God knows for the present I'm both to you.'

'For the present?' he had asked.

'Until you retire and I take over your seat.'

'Remember, Nell?' Cornelius MacDermott said, breaking her reverie. 'You were a cocky college kid when you said that, but you meant it.'

'I remember,' she said.

He came and stood right in front of her, leaning forward, his face right in front of hers. 'Nell, seize the moment. If you don't, you'll regret it. When Gorman confirms that he isn't running, there'll be a scramble for the nomination. I want the committee to consider candidates behind you from the get-go.'

'When is the get-go?' she asked cautiously.

'At the annual dinner, on the 30th. You and Adam will be there. Gorman will be announcing his intention to leave when his term is complete; he'll get teary-eyed and sniffle and say that, while it was a difficult decision for him to make, something has made it much easier. Then he's going to dry his eyes and blow his nose, point to you and bellow that *you*, Cornelia MacDermott Cauliff, are going to run for the seat previously occupied by your grandfather for nearly fifty years. It will be Cornelia replacing Cornelius. The wave of the

14

third millennium.'

Obviously pleased with himself and his vision, MacDermott smiled broadly. 'Nell, it'll bring the house down.'

With a pang of regret, Nell remembered that two years ago, when Bob Gorman ran for Mac's seat, she had had a wild sense of impatience, a compulsion to be there, a need to see herself in his place. Mac was right. She was a political animal. If she didn't get into the arena now, it *could* be too late—or at least, too late for a shot at this seat, which was where she wanted to start a political career.

'What's Adam's problem, Nell? He didn't use to pull this stuff on you.'

'I know.'

'Is anything wrong between you two?'

'No.' She managed a dismissive smile to signify the suggestion was absurd.

How long had it been going on? she wondered. At what point had Adam become distracted, even remote? At first her concerned questions, asking him what was wrong, had been brushed off lightly. Now she detected an edge of anger. Only recently she had told him point-blank that if there was a serious problem with their relationship, then she deserved to hear about it. 'I mean *any* kind of problem, Adam. Being in the dark is the worst problem of all,' she had said.

'Where *is* Adam?' her grandfather asked.

'He's in Philadelphia.'

'Since when?'

'Yesterday. He's speaking at a seminar for architects and interior designers. He'll be back tomorrow.'

15

'I want him at the dinner on the 30th, standing by your side, applauding your decision. Okay?'

'I don't know how much applauding he'll do,' she said, a hint of dejection in her voice.

'When you were married he was gung-ho to be the spouse of a future politician. What happened to change his mind?'

You did, Nell thought. Adam became jealous of the time you demanded from me.

When she and Adam were first married, he'd been enthusiastic over the idea that she would continue to be active as Mac's assistant. But that had changed when her grandfather announced his retirement.

'Nell, we now have a chance for a life that doesn't revolve around the almighty Cornelius MacDermott,' Adam had said. 'I'm sick of your being at his beck and call. Do you think that will get better if you campaign for his old seat? I have news for you. He won't give you the chance to breathe, unless he's exhaling for you.'

The children they'd hoped for hadn't arrived, and they became part of his argument. 'You've never known anything except politics,' Adam pleaded. 'Sit it out, Nell. The *Journal* wants you to do a regular column. You might like the freedom.'

His entreaties had helped her make the decision not to pursue the nomination. Now, as she considered her grandfather's arguments, along with his unique combination of ordering and coaxing her, Nell dispassionately admitted something to herself: commenting on the political scene wasn't enough. She wanted to be in on the action.

Finally she said, 'Mac, I'm going to put my cards on the table. Adam is my husband and I love him.

16

You, on the other hand, have never even liked him.'

'That isn't true.'

'Then let's put it another way. Ever since Adam opened his own firm, you've had the shiv out for him. If I run for this office, it will be like the old days. You and I will be spending a lot more day-to-day time together, and if that's going to work you've got to promise me that you'll treat Adam the way you'd want to be treated if the positions were reversed.'

'And if I promise to embrace him to my bosom, then you'll run?'

When she left Cornelius MacDermott's office an hour later, Nell had given her word that she would seek the congressional seat being vacated by Bob Gorman.

CHAPTER TWO

It was the third time Jed Kaplan had passed the ground-floor architectural offices of Cauliff and Associates on Twenty-seventh Street off Seventh Avenue. The window of the converted brownstone contained a display that arrested him: the model of a modern forty-story apartment-office-shopping complex dominated by a gold-domed tower. The starkly postmodern building with its minimal ornamentation and white limestone façade was a striking contrast to the warmth of the brick tower, which radiated light as the dome slowly revolved.

Jed jammed his hands in the pockets of his jeans as he slouched forward until his face was almost pressed against the window. To a casual observer there was nothing either unusual or impressive about his appearance. He was of average height, thin, with short sandy hair.

His appearance was deceptive, however; under his faded sweatshirt, Jed's body was hard and muscular, and his thinness belied his remarkable strength. A close look would have revealed that his complexion had coarsened from long exposure to sun and wind. And actual eye contact would have caused most people to experience an instinctively uneasy reaction.

Thirty-eight years old, Jed had spent most of his life as a loner and a drifter. After five years in Australia, he had returned home for one of his infrequent visits to his widowed mother only to learn that she had sold the small parcel of Manhattan property that had been in the family for four generations, a building which had housed a once-thriving but now barely profitable fur business, with rental apartments above the store.

His reaction had been immediate, and they had quarreled violently about it.

'What'd you expect me to do?' his mother had pleaded. 'Building falling apart; insurance going up; taxes going up; tenants moving out. The fur business is going down the toilet. In case you haven't heard, it isn't good politics to wear fur anymore.'

'Pop intended for me to have that property,' Jed had shouted. 'You had no right to sell it!'

'Pop also wanted you to be a good son to me; he wanted you to settle down, to get married, have children, have a decent job. But you didn't even come when I wrote that he was dying.' She'd begun to weep. 'When was the last time you saw a picture of Queen Elizabeth or Hillary Clinton in a fur? Adam Cauliff paid me a fair price for the property. I have money in the bank. For whatever time I have left, I can sleep at night without worrying about bills.'

With increasing bitterness, Jed observed the model of the complex. He sneered at the legend below the tower: A BEACON OF BEAUTY, SETTING THE TONE FOR THE NEWEST, MOST EXCITING RESIDENTIAL DISTRICT IN MANHATTAN.

The tower was going to be erected on the land his mother had sold to Adam Cauliff.

That land was worth a fortune, he thought. And Cauliff had talked her into believing that you could never do anything to develop it because it was next door to that historical wreck, the old Vandermeer mansion. He knew it never would have occurred to his mother to even *try* to sell it, though, if Cauliff hadn't buzzed around her.

Yes, he'd given her fair market value. But then the mansion had burned, and a big-shot real estate guy, Peter Lang, snapped up that property, and by putting it together with the Kaplans' property they created a prime development site, one now much more valuable as a whole than the two separate parcels had been.

Jed had heard some homeless woman was squatting in the Vandermeer and lit a fire to keep warm. Why didn't that bum burn down the stinking landmark *before* Cauliff got his hands on my property? Jed silently raged. Anger, profound and bitter, rose in his throat. I'll get Cauliff, he vowed. I swear to God I'll get him. If we still had owned that property after they stopped calling that old dump a

19

landmark, we'd have gotten *millions* for it . . .

Abruptly, he turned away from the window. Looking at the miniature of the complex practically made him physically ill. He walked to Seventh Avenue where he stood hesitantly for a minute, then headed south. At seven o'clock he was standing at the marina of the World Financial Center. With envious eyes he viewed the array of small, sleek yachts that bobbed up and down in the rising tide.

An obviously new forty-foot cabin cruiser was the object of his attention. The name written in Gothic script across the stern was *Cornelia II*.

Cauliff's boat, he thought.

Since his return to New York, Jed had been learning everything he could about Adam Cauliff, and he had been at this spot many times with always the same thought in mind: What am I going to do about that jerk and his precious boat?

CHAPTER THREE

After the final session of the architectural seminar in Philadelphia, Adam Cauliff had dinner with two of his colleagues, then quietly checked out of the hotel and drove back to New York.

It was ten-thirty when he started out, and the traffic on the turnpike was reasonably light.

At dinner, Ward Battle had confirmed the rumor that Walters and Arsdale, the architectural firm Adam had worked for until he opened his own company, was being investigated for bid rigging and for accepting bribes from contractors.

'From what I hear, that's only the tip of the

iceberg, Adam, which means, of course, that, as a former employee, you'll probably be asked a lot of questions. Just thought you should know. Maybe MacDermott can make sure they don't put much on you.'

Mac help out? Adam thought scornfully. Forget it. If he believed I was involved in any funny-money deals, he'd boil the pitch for them to throw on me.

He'd remained calm at dinner.

'I don't have anything to worry about,' he had told Battle. 'I was just one of the little guys at Walters and Arsdale.'

He had not known what tonight would hold, and had planned to stay over in Philadelphia. As a result, Nell did not expect him home until tomorrow. When Adam exited the Lincoln Tunnel, he hesitated for a moment, then turned right instead of going left, which would have taken him to his apartment uptown. Five minutes later he pulled into a garage on Twenty-seventh Street.

His suitcase in one hand, his keys in the other, he walked the half block to the office. The window lights had turned off automatically, but even so the silhouette of the miniature Vandermeer Tower was starkly handsome in the glow from the streetlight.

Adam stood observing it, unconscious of the weight of the suitcase in his left hand, unaware that he was restlessly tugging at the key ring in his right hand.

Shortly after they met, Cornelius MacDermott had laughingly observed, 'Adam, you're a prime example of the difference between appearance and reality. You're from a one-horse town in North Dakota, but you look and sound like a preppie from Yale. How do you manage it?'

21

'I manage it because I don't try to pretend to be something I'm not. Maybe you think I should wear overalls and carry a rake?' he had said defensively.

'Don't be so touchy,' Mac had snapped. 'I was complimenting you.'

'Sure you were.'

Mac would have liked Nell to end up with a preppie from Yale, Adam thought, a preppie whose father had clawed his way to the top in New York. Well, Mac may have been a hotshot in Congress, but anything he knows about North Dakota he learned from renting a tape of *Fargo*, he told himself, dismissing all thought of his wife's grandfather.

Then something at the end of the deserted street caught his attention. He glanced to the side and noticed a guy hanging out in a nearby doorway. With three quick steps, he was at the office door and turning the key. He didn't need to get mugged tonight.

He did not relax until he was in his office with the door locked. The handsome oak armoire held a television and a bar. He yanked open the doors, reached for the Chivas Regal and poured a generous amount into a glass. He sat on the couch, slowly sipping the scotch, a man who, to the casual observer, might have seemed to be totally at ease, resting after a long day.

And it was a fact that people did observe Adam. He appeared taller than his six feet because he had taught himself to keep his back ramrod straight, even when sitting. Rigorous exercise had kept his body trim and disciplined. Light hazel eyes and a mouth that curved easily into a smile were the dominant features in his lean face. Darts of gray abundantly sprinkled through his dark brown hair

22

was to him a welcome sight. He knew that without the gray he ran the risk of looking too boyish.

He slid off his jacket, loosened his tie and undid the top button of his shirt. His cell phone was in his pocket. He fished it out and laid it on the table next to his glass. He didn't have to worry that Nell would phone the hotel and be told that he'd checked out. If she tried to reach him at all, she would dial him on this phone, but the odds were that she wouldn't try tonight. They had spoken this afternoon, just before she went to see her grandfather, and if his guess was right, that meeting was one she would wait for the right moment to discuss with him.

So the night is mine, Adam thought. I can do anything I want to do. I can even go downstairs and take the model out of the window, since my design was rejected. Which is something Mac won't be sorry to hear, he thought bitterly. But after an hour of reviewing his options step by step, he decided to go home. The office felt claustrophobic, and he realized he did not want to sleep on the pull-out couch there.

It was nearly two o'clock when, with careful, quiet steps, he entered the apartment and turned on the small foyer light. He showered and changed in the guest bathroom, then methodically laid out his clothes for the morning, after which he tiptoed into the bedroom and slipped into bed. Nell's even breathing told him that he had succeeded in his goal of not waking her, for which he was grateful. He knew that if she had awakened, it might be hours before she would fall asleep again.

He had no such trouble, however: fatigue hit him almost immediately, and he felt his eyes closing.

23

Friday, June 9

CHAPTER FOUR

Lisa Ryan was awake well before the alarm was set to go off at 5:00 A.M. Jimmy had had another restless night, turning and tossing, muttering in his sleep. Three or four times she had reached over and put a soothing hand on his back, hoping to quiet him.

Finally, a few hours ago he had fallen into a heavy sleep, and she knew that now she'd have to shake him awake. She didn't have to get up yet, though, and was keeping her fingers crossed that after he left, she'd be able to doze off until it was time to rouse the kids.

I'm so tired, Lisa thought. I've hardly slept at all, and today's my long day at work. A manicurist, she was booked straight through from nine until six.

Her life didn't used to be this exhausting. Everything had started to go wrong when Jimmy lost his job. He had been out of work for nearly two years before he connected with Cauliff and Associates, and while they had managed to make some inroads, they still had bills that had accumulated during the time he was unemployed.

Unfortunately, the circumstances under which he had lost that previous job had not helped the situation. Jimmy had been fired because the boss overheard him commenting to a coworker on his belief that someone at the company was on the take. The reason for this conclusion: the concrete they were pouring was not nearly the quality listed in the specifications.

After that happened, everywhere he applied he

27

heard the same story: 'Sorry, we don't need you.'

The realization that it had been naïve, stupid and useless ever to have made the comment brought about the beginning of change in him. Lisa was sure he had been on the verge of a nervous breakdown—then the call came from Adam Cauliff's assistant that his application to Cauliff for a job had been passed on to the Sam Krause Construction Company. It had been a great relief that shortly thereafter Jimmy had been hired.

But the emotional turnaround Lisa expected to see in Jimmy after he went back to work didn't come about. She'd even talked to a psychologist who warned her that it sounded as if Jimmy was in a state of depression, adding it probably wasn't something he could get over by himself. But Jimmy had become furious when she suggested that he go for help.

In the last months, Lisa had begun to feel infinitely older than her thirty-three years. The man sleeping next to her no longer seemed to be the man who as her childhood sweetheart had joked that he'd climbed out of his playpen to ask her for their first date. Jimmy's emotional state had become erratic. One minute he would fly off the handle at her and the children, then the next he'd have tears in his eyes as he apologized. He'd begun to drink, usually having two or three scotches every evening—and he didn't handle them well.

She knew this aberrant behavior couldn't be traced to an affair with another woman. Jimmy was home every night now, having even lost interest in going to the occasional baseball game with his buddies. Nor had there been any instances of his infrequent problem of risking too much on a horse

28

or a ball game. On payday he handed his uncashed check to her; the stub showed his accumulated earnings.

Lisa had tried to make him realize that he needn't be depressed about finances anymore, that they were getting caught up with the credit-card charges run up when he was out of work. It didn't seem to make a difference. In fact, nothing seemed to matter to him anymore.

They still lived in the small Cape Cod in Little Neck, Queens, that had been planned as their starter home when they'd married thirteen years ago. But three children in seven years had meant buying bunk beds rather than a larger home. Lisa used to joke about that, but she didn't anymore— she knew it got under Jimmy's skin.

As the alarm finally rang, she reached over and turned it off, then with a sigh turned to her husband. 'Jimmy.' She shook his shoulder. 'Jimmy.' Her voice became louder, although she tried to avoid showing any trace of the concern she felt.

Finally she was able to rouse Jimmy. Listlessly he muttered, 'Thanks, honey,' and disappeared into the bathroom. Lisa got out of bed, went to the window and pulled up the shade. It was going to be a beautiful day. She twisted her light brown hair into a knot, pinned it up and reached for her robe. Suddenly no longer sleepy, she decided to have coffee with Jimmy.

He came down to the kitchen ten minutes later and looked surprised to see her there. He didn't even notice that I'd gotten out of bed, Lisa thought sadly.

She studied him carefully although with caution lest he see the concern in her eyes. There was

29

something terribly vulnerable in the way he looked at her this morning, she thought. He thinks I'm going to start in on him about getting psychological help, she decided.

Careful to keep her voice light, she announced, 'It's too nice a day to stay in bed. Thought I'd join you for a cup of coffee, then go outside and watch the birds wake up.'

Jimmy was a big man, with hair that once had been fiery red and was now a copper brown. Working outdoors had given him a ruddy complexion, but Lisa realized that his face was becoming deeply lined.

'That would be nice, Lissy,' he said.

He did not sit down but stood at the table as he gulped the coffee, shaking his head at her offer of toast or cereal.

'Don't wait dinner for me,' he said. 'The big shots are having one of those five o'clock meetings on Cauliff's fancy boat. Maybe he's going to fire me and wants to do it in style.'

'Why would he fire you?' Lisa asked, hoping her voice didn't convey anxiety.

'I'm kidding. But if it happens, maybe he'd be doing me a favor. How's the painted-nail business? Can you support all of us?'

Lisa went over to her husband and put her arms around his neck. 'I think you're going to feel a lot better when you let me know what's eating at you.'

'Keep thinking that.' Jimmy Ryan's powerful arms pulled his wife close to him. 'I love you, Lissy. Always remember that.'

'I've never forgotten it. And . . .'

'I know—"likewise, I'm sure."' He smiled briefly at the dumb expression that had tickled them when

30

they were teenagers.

Then he turned from her and moved to the door. As it closed behind him, Lisa could not be sure, but she thought Jimmy had whispered, 'I'm sorry.'

CHAPTER FIVE

That morning, Nell decided to make a special breakfast for Adam, then instantly became irritated at the thought that she was using food to try to cajole him into going along with a career choice she had every right to make for herself. That realization did not keep her from going ahead with her preparations, however. With a rueful smile, she remembered a cookbook that had belonged to her maternal grandmother. The book's cover had carried the legend, THE WAY TO A MAN'S HEART IS THROUGH HIS STOMACH. Her mother, a career anthropologist and herself a terrible cook, used to joke about that sentiment to her father.

As she got out of bed she could hear Adam in the shower. Nell had awakened when he came into the apartment last night, but had decided not to let him know that she was awake. Yes, she knew they needed to talk, but two o'clock in the morning did not seem the time to discuss her meeting the afternoon before with her grandfather.

She would have to bring it up at breakfast this morning, though, because they would be seeing Mac that night and she wanted to get the discussion out of the way beforehand. Mac had phoned her last night to remind her that they were

31

expected at the seventy-fifth birthday dinner he was having for his sister, Nell's great-aunt Gert, at the Four Seasons restaurant.

'Mac, you didn't really think we'd forget that, did you?' she had asked. 'Of course we'll both be there.' But she didn't add that she'd rather not have the subject of her possible candidacy raised as a topic of conversation; there was no point, since it was inevitable that it would come up during dinner. So that meant she had to tell Adam this morning about her decision to run. He would never forgive her if he got the word from Mac.

Most mornings Adam left for the office by 7:30, and she tried to be in their study by 8:00 at the latest, working on her column for the next day. Before that, though, they typically had a light breakfast together, albeit a fairly silent one as they both read the morning papers.

Wouldn't it be nice if Adam would just understand how very much I want to try to win Mac's old congressional seat, or at least be a part of the excitement this election year? she thought as she pulled a carton of eggs from the refrigerator. Wouldn't it be terrific if I didn't have to keep walking a tightrope between the only two men in the world who are important to me? Wouldn't it be nice if Adam didn't view my desire to pursue a career in politics as a threat to him and to our relationship?

He *used* to understand, she thought as she set the table, poured fresh-squeezed orange juice and reached for the coffeepot. He used to say that he was looking forward to having a good seat in the Visitors' Gallery on Capitol Hill. That was three years ago. What had happened to change his mind?

32

she wondered.

She tried not to be bothered by Adam's preoccupied air as he hurried into the kitchen, slid onto the bench at the breakfast bar and reached for the *Wall Street Journal*, all with only a nod of acknowledgment.

'Thanks, Nell, but I'm honestly not hungry,' he said, when she offered him the omelet she had prepared. So much for the extra effort, she thought.

She sat across from him and considered what tack she should take. From the closed expression on his face, she could tell this wasn't the right moment to begin any discussion about her possible run for a congressional seat. And that's just too bad, she thought, feeling her irritation begin to mount. I may just have to go ahead without his blessing.

She reached for her own coffee and glanced down at the front page of the *Times*. One of the lead articles caught her eye. 'My God, Adam, have you seen this? The district attorney may press bid rigging charges against Robert Walters and Len Arsdale.'

'I know that.' His voice was controlled, level.

'You worked with them for nearly three years,' she said, shocked. 'Will you be questioned?'

'Probably,' he said matter-of-factly. Then he smirked. 'Tell Mac he has nothing to worry about. The family honor will remain unstained.'

'Adam, that's not what I meant!'

'Come on, Nell, I can read you like a book. You're trying to find a way to tell me that the old man has talked you into running for office. When he opens his newspaper this morning, the first thing he'll do is call you and say that having my name associated with an investigation such as this might well hurt your chances. I'm right, aren't I?'

'You're right about my wanting to run for office, but the possibility of your hurting my chances certainly never entered my mind,' Nell said evenly. 'I think I know you well enough to know that you're not dishonest.'

'There are varying degrees of honesty in the construction business, Nell,' Adam said. 'Fortunately for you, I stick to the highest standards, which is one of the many reasons I left Walters and Arsdale. Do you think that will satisfy Mac the Icon?'

Nell stood up, her irritation flashing. 'Adam, look, I can understand why you're upset, but don't take it out on me. And since you brought it up, I'll tell you. Yes, I've decided I am going to go for Mac's seat, since Bob Gorman is giving it up, and I think it might be nice if you supported me.'

Adam shrugged and shook his head. 'Nell, I've been honest with you. Since we've been married I've seen that politics is an all-absorbing way to spend a life. It can be tough on a marriage. Many don't survive. But it's clearly your decision to make, and clearly you've made it.'

'Yes, I have,' she said, struggling to keep her voice even. 'So please have the good grace to put up with it, if that's what it takes, because I have news for you, Adam: it's a lot worse for a marriage if one spouse tries to keep the other from doing something he or she wants. All along, I've tried to help you in your career. So please give me a break. Help me in mine, or at least don't make it so hard for me.'

34

He shoved his chair back and stood. 'So that's that, I guess.' He moved to leave, then turned back. 'Don't worry about dinner tonight. We've got a meeting scheduled on the boat, and afterward I'll get something to eat downtown.'

'Adam, it's Gert's seventy-fifth birthday. She'll be so disappointed if you're not there.'

He faced her. 'Nell, not even for Gert—whom I like very much. Forgive me, but I just do not want to spend this evening with Mac.'

'Adam, please. Surely you can come after the meeting. It's okay if you're late. Just make an appearance.'

'Make an appearance? Campaign language is starting already. Sorry, Nell.' In quick strides he headed for the foyer.

'Then, damn it, maybe you should skip coming home at all.'

Adam stopped and turned to face her. 'Nell, I hope you don't mean that.'

They stared at each other in silence for a long moment, and then he was gone.

CHAPTER SIX

Sam Krause's newest girlfriend, Dina Crane, was not at all happy when he called on Friday morning to cancel their date that evening.

'I could meet you at Harry's Bar when you finish,' she suggested.

'Look, this is business and I don't know how long it will take,' he said brusquely. 'We've got a lot of stuff to go over. I'll call you Saturday.'

35

He hung up without giving Dina a chance to say anything more. He was seated in his private office at Third Avenue and Fortieth Street, a large, airy corner room, with walls covered by artists' renderings of the skyscrapers built by the Sam Krause Construction Company.

It was only ten o'clock, and his already edgy mood had been exacerbated by a call from the district attorney's office requesting a meeting with him.

He got up and walked to the window, where he stood staring sullenly at the street activity sixteen stories below. He watched a car skillfully weave through the choking traffic, and then smiled grimly as the car became boxed in behind a truck that had stopped suddenly, blocking two lanes.

The smile vanished, though, as Sam realized that in a way he was like that car. He had sidestepped a number of obstacles to get to this point in his life, and now a major hurdle was being thrown in his path, threatening to block it completely. For the first time since he was a teenager, he found himself suddenly vulnerable for prosecution.

He was a fifty-year-old, large-boned man of average height, with weathered skin and thinning hair, and an independent nature. He had never bothered to give much thought to his appearance. What made him attractive to women was his air of absolute self-confidence, along with the cynical intelligence reflected in his slate-gray eyes. Some people respected him. Many more were afraid of him. A very few liked him. For all of them, Sam felt amused contempt.

The phone rang, followed by a buzz on the intercom from his secretary. 'Mr. Lang,' she announced.

Sam grimaced. Lang Enterprises was the third factor in the Vandermeer Tower venture. His feelings about Peter Lang ranged from envy, over the fact that he was the product of family wealth, to grudging admiration of his seeming genius at optioning apparently worthless properties that turned out to be real estate gold mines.

He crossed to his desk and picked up the receiver: 'Yeah, Peter? Thought you'd be on the golf course.'

Peter was in fact calling from his father's waterfront estate in Southampton, which he had inherited. 'I am, as a matter of fact. Just wanted to make sure the meeting is still on.'

'It is,' Sam told him, and replaced the receiver without saying goodbye.

CHAPTER SEVEN

Nell's newspaper column, called 'All Around the Town,' ran three times a week in the *New York Journal*. It contained a potpourri of comments on what was going on in New York City, its subjects ranging from the arts to politics, and from celebrity events to human-interest features. She had started writing it two years ago, when Mac retired and she had declined Bob Gorman's request that she stay on to run the New York congressional office.

Mike Stuart, the publisher of the *Journal* and a longtime friend to both Nell and Mac, had been the one to suggest the column.

'With all the letters you've written to the op-ed

page, you've virtually been working for us for free, Nell,' he had told her. 'You're a damn good writer, and smart too. Why not have a try at getting paid for your opinions for a change?'

This column is another thing I'll have to give up when I run for office, Nell thought as she walked into the study.

Another thing? What am I thinking about? she asked herself. After Adam left that morning, she had gone through her usual routine with anger-fueled energy. In less than half an hour she cleared the table, tidied the kitchen and made the bed. She remembered that Adam had undressed in the guest room last night. A quick check there revealed that he had left his navy jacket and his briefcase on the bed.

He was too busy slamming out of here this morning to remember them, Nell thought. He probably was stopping at a job site; he just had on that light, zip-up jacket. Well, if he needs his jacket and briefcase, let him come back for them, or even better, send someone else to get them. I'm not playing errand girl for him today. She picked up the jacket and hung it in the closet, and she carried the briefcase to his desk in the small third bedroom that had become their study.

But an hour later, sitting at her desk, showered and dressed in her 'uniform'—as she referred to her jeans, oversized shirt and sneakers—it was impossible to ignore the fact that she had done nothing to make this situation easier. Hadn't she as much as told Adam not to come home tonight?

Suppose he takes me up on that? she asked herself, but then refused to consider the possibility. We may be having a serious problem at the

38

moment, but it has nothing to do with the way we feel about each other.

He must be at the office by now, she decided. I'll call him. She reached for the phone, then quickly pulled back. No, I won't call. I gave in to him two years ago when he asked me not to run for Mac's seat, and I've regretted it every day since. If I equivocate now, he will see it as a complete surrender—and there's just no reason why I should have to give it up. There are plenty of women in Congress now—women who have husbands and children they care about. Besides, it's not fair: I'd never ask Adam to give up his career as an architect, or to forego any part of it.

Nell resolutely began to go through the notes she had put together for the column she was going to write this morning, but then, unable to concentrate, she put them down.

Her thoughts went back to last night.

When Adam slipped into bed, he had fallen asleep almost immediately. Hearing his steady breathing, she had moved closer to him, and in his sleep he had thrown his arm around her and murmured her name.

Nell thought back to the first time she and Adam met—it was at a cocktail party, and her immediate impression of him was that he was the most attractive man she had ever met. It was his smile— that slow, sweet smile. They'd left the party together and gone out to dinner. He had told her that he was going out of town on business for a couple of days but would call her when he got back. Two weeks had passed before that call came, and for Nell they felt like the longest two weeks of her life.

Just then the phone rang. Adam, she thought as she grabbed the receiver.

It was her grandfather. 'Nell, I just saw the paper! I hope to God that hotshot Adam hasn't got anything to worry about with this investigation into Walters and Arsdale. He was there during the time they are looking into, so if there was any hanky-panky going on, he must have known about it. He needs to come clean with us; I don't want him hurting your chances of winning this election.'

Nell took a deep breath before she responded. She loved her grandfather dearly, but there were times when he made her want to scream. 'Mac, Adam left Walters and Arsdale precisely because he didn't like some of the things he saw going on there, so you don't have anything to worry about on that front. And by the way, didn't I tell you yesterday to please lay off that 'hotshot Adam' stuff and all that goes with it?'

'Sorry.'

'You don't sound sorry.'

Mac ignored her comment. 'See you tonight. And speaking of which, I called Gert to wish her a happy birthday, and I've got to tell you, I think the woman is nuts. She told me she is spending the day at some damn channeling event. Fortunately, though, she hadn't forgotten about tonight, and she says she is looking forward to the dinner. She also remarked on how much she was looking forward to seeing your husband; said she hadn't seen him in a long time. For some reason, she seems to think the sun rises and sets on him.'

'Yes, I know she does.'

'She asked me if she could bring along a couple of those mediums she hangs out with, but I told her to forget it.'

'But Mac, it *is* her birthday,' Nell protested.

'That may be, but at my age I don't want any of those nuts studying me—even from a distance—to see if my aura is changing, or worse yet, fading away. I've got to go. See you tonight, Nell.'

Nell replaced the receiver in its cradle and leaned back in her chair. She agreed with her grandfather that Gert was a true eccentric, but she wasn't 'nuts,' as he had said. After Nell's parents died, it was Gert who had provided her with a great deal of support, becoming a kind of combination surrogate mother and grandmother. And, Nell reminded herself, it was precisely because of her belief in the paranormal that Gert was able to understand what I meant when I said that I felt that Mom and Dad had been there with me, both on the day they died and when I was caught in the riptide in Hawaii. Gert understands because she gets those feelings too.

Of course, for Gert they are more than 'feelings,' Nell thought with a smile. She is actively involved in psychic research and has been for a long time. No, it wasn't Gert's mind that Nell was concerned about, but her physical health, because her great-aunt had not been well lately. But she's made it to her seventy-fifth birthday with most of her faculties intact, and the least Adam should do is put in an appearance tonight, Nell reflected. His refusal will disappoint her terribly.

That final realization erased any thought Nell might have had of calling Adam to try to put things right between them. It would happen eventually, she was confident of that. But she wasn't going to be the one to take the initiative—at least not

41

right now.

CHAPTER EIGHT

Dan Minor had inherited his father's height and rangy shoulders, but not his face. The sharply sophisticated and handsome features of Preston Minor had been softened and warmed by their genetic blending with the gentle beauty of Kathryn Quinn.

Preston's ice-blue eyes were darker and warmer in his son's face. The mouth and jawline were rounder and more relaxed. The Quinn genes gave Dan the full head of somewhat unruly sandy hair.

A colleague had observed that even in khakis, sneakers and a T-shirt, Dan Minor looked like a doctor. It was an accurate appraisal. Dan had a way of greeting people with genuine interest in his expression—interest that was followed by a second searching glance, as though he were checking to make sure everything was all right with them. Perhaps it was fated that Dan would grow up to be a doctor; certainly it was what he always had wanted. In fact, Dan had not only always known that he would be a doctor, he also had always known that he wanted to be a pediatric surgeon. It was a choice based on very personal reasons, and only a handful of people understood why he had made that decision.

Raised in Chevy Chase, Maryland, by his maternal grandparents, as a young boy he had learned to treat his occasional and infrequent visits from his father with increasing lack of interest, and eventually lack of interest grew into contempt. He hadn't laid eyes on his mother since he was six, although a snapshot of her—smiling, hair windblown, her arms wrapped around him—was always kept in a hidden compartment in his wallet. The photo, taken on his second birthday, was his only tangible memory of her.

Dan had graduated from John Hopkins and then done his residency at St. Gregory's Hospital in Manhattan, so when they asked him to come back and head up their new burn unit, he accepted. By nature somewhat restless at heart, and with the sobering knowledge that a new millennium had begun, he decided it was time for a change in his life. He had established a solid reputation at a Washington hospital as a surgeon, specializing in burn victims. By then he was thirty-six, and his elderly grandparents were moving to a retirement community in Florida. And while he was as devoted to them as ever, he no longer felt the need to be in such close proximity. As for his father, nothing had improved between them. About the same time his grandparents moved to Florida, his father remarried. But Dan had skipped his father's fourth wedding, just as he had skipped his third.

The new assignment in Manhattan began on March 1. Dan wound up his private practice and spent a few days in New York looking for a place to live. In February he bought a condo in the SoHo district of lower Manhattan and shipped to it those few items he wanted to keep from his minimally furnished Washington apartment. Fortunately, he also had his choice of the handsome furnishings from his grandparents' home, so he was able to put together a space with a bit of flair.

Sociable by nature, Dan enjoyed the farewell dinners and gatherings his friends threw for him, including the ones he had with the three or four women he had dated over the years. One of his friends presented him with a handsome new wallet, and when he switched his license and credit cards and money to it, he hesitated, then deliberately removed the old picture and slipped it into the family album that his grandparents were taking to Florida. He knew it was time to put it and all it represented behind him. An hour later he changed his mind and retrieved it.

Then, feeling both nostalgic and unburdened, he saw his grandparents to the Florida-bound train, got in his jeep and drove north. It was a four-hour drive from the railroad station in D.C. to his new home. Arriving at his place in Manhattan, he dropped his suitcases, made several more trips to unload the car, then parked it in the nearby garage. Anxious to see more of the new neighborhood, he set out to look for a place to have dinner. One of the things he had liked best about the SoHo area was that it was alive with restaurants. He found one he hadn't tried on his previous forays, bought a paper and settled at a table near the window.

Over a drink he began to study the front page, but then raised his eyes and began to watch the people passing in the street. With a conscious effort he focused again on the article he had been reading. One of his millennium resolutions had been to try to stop the random search for what he knew would never be found. There were just too many places to look, and the chances of ever finding her were so very dim.

But even as he reminded himself of that

44

resolution, a persistent voice whispered inside his head, reminding him that one of the reasons he had moved to New York was his hope of finding her. It was the last place she was spotted.

Hours later, as he lay in bed listening to the faint sounds of the traffic on the street below, Dan decided to give it one last shot. If by the end of June he had found nothing, then he would give up his search.

Adjusting to a new position and a new environment took up much of his time. Then on June 9th he was delayed with an emergency operation at the hospital and had to wait until the next day to make what he swore would be one of his final attempts to find his mother. This time his destination was the South Bronx, a still-desolate area of New York City, although somewhat improved from what it had been twenty years before. Without any real hope or expectations, he began asking the usual questions, showing the picture that he still carried with him.

And then it happened. A shabbily dressed woman who looked to be in her fifties, her face careworn, her eyes listless, suddenly smiled. 'I think you're looking for my pal Quinny,' she said.

CHAPTER NINE

Fifty-two-year-old Winifred Johnson never entered the lobby of her employer's apartment building on Park Avenue without feeling intimidated. She had worked with Adam Cauliff for three years, first at Walters and Arsdale, and then she had left with him last fall, when he started his own company. He relied on her from the beginning.

Even so, whenever she stopped by his apartment, she couldn't help feeling that one day the doorman would instruct her to use the delivery entrance around the corner.

She knew that her attitude was the result of her parents' lifelong resentment over imagined slights. Ever since she could remember, Winifred's ears had been filled with their plaintive tales of people who had been rude to them: *They use their little bit of authority on people like us who can't fight back. Expect it, Winifred. That's the kind of world it is.* Her father had gone to his grave railing against all the indignities he had suffered at the hands of his employer of forty years, and her mother was now in a nursing home, where complaints of supposed slights and deliberate neglect continued unabated.

Winifred thought about her mother as the doorman smilingly opened the door for her. A few years ago it had been possible for her to move her mother to a fancy, new nursing facility, but even that hadn't stopped the endless flow of complaints. Happiness—even satisfaction—did not seem to be possible for her. Winifred had recognized this same trait in herself and felt helpless. Until I smartened up, she told herself with a secret smile.

A thin woman, almost frail in appearance, Winifred typically dressed in conservative business suits and limited her jewelry to button earrings and a strand of pearls. Quiet to the point that people often forgot she was even around, she absorbed everything, noticed everything and remembered everything. She had worked for Robert Walters and Len Arsdale from the time she graduated from

46

secretarial school, but in all those years neither man had ever appreciated or even seemed to notice the fact that she had come to know everything there was to know about the construction business. Adam Cauliff, however, had picked up on it immediately. He appreciated her; he understood her true worth. He used to joke with her, saying, 'Winifred, a lot of people had better hope you never write your autobiography.'

Robert Walters overheard him and became both upset and unpleasant. But then Walters had always bullied her unmercifully; he never had been nice to her. Let him pay for that, Winifred thought. And he will.

Nell never appreciated him. Adam didn't need a wife with a career of her own and a famous grandfather who made so many demands on her that she didn't have enough time for her husband. Sometimes Adam would say, 'Winifred, Nell's busy with the old man again. I don't want to eat alone. Let's grab a bite.'

He deserved better. Sometimes Adam would tell her about being a kid on a North Dakota farm and going to the library to get books with pictures of beautiful buildings. 'The taller the better, Winifred,' he'd joke. 'When someone built a three-story house in our town, folks drove twenty miles just to get a look at it.'

Other times he would encourage her to talk, and she found herself gossiping with him about people in the construction industry. Then the next morning she would wonder if perhaps she had said too much, her loquaciousness enhanced by the wine Adam kept pouring. But she never really worried; she trusted Adam—they trusted each other—and Adam enjoyed her 'insider' stories about the building world, tales from her earlier days with Walters and Arsdale.

'You mean that sanctimonious old bird was on the take when those bids went out?' he'd exclaim, then reassure her when she became flustered about talking so much. And then he'd promise never, ever to say a word to anyone about what she had told him. She also remembered the night he had said accusingly, 'Winifred, you can't fool me. There's someone in your life.' And she had told him, yes, even giving the name. And that was when she really began to trust him. She confided that she was taking care of herself.

The uniformed clerk at the lobby desk put down the intercom telephone. 'You can go right up, Ms. Johnson. Mrs. Cauliff is expecting you.'

Adam had asked her to pick up his briefcase and his navy jacket on the way to the meeting today. Being Adam, he had been apologetic about the request. 'I left in a hell of a rush this morning and forgot them,' he explained. 'I left them on the bed in the guest room. The notes for the meeting are in my briefcase, and I'll need the jacket if I change my mind and decide to meet Nell at the Four Seasons.' Winifred could sense from his tone that he and Nell must have had a serious misunderstanding, and hearing it only bolstered her certainty that their marriage was heading for the rocks.

As she rode up in the elevator, she thought about the meeting scheduled for later in the day. She was happy that the location for the meeting had been moved to the boat. She loved going out on the water. It seemed romantic, even when the purpose was strictly business.

48

There would be just five of them. In addition to herself, the three associates in the Vandermeer Tower venture—Adam, Sam Krause and Peter Lang—would be attending. The fifth was Jimmy Ryan, one of Sam's site foremen. Winifred wasn't sure why he'd been invited except that Jimmy had been pretty moody lately. Maybe they wanted to get to the heart of the problem and sort it out.

She knew they all would be concerned about the story that broke in today's newspapers, although she didn't feel any concern herself. In fact, she was rather impatient about the whole thing. The worst thing that ever happens in these situations, even if they get the goods on you, is you pay a fine, she told herself. You reach into your back pocket, and the problem goes away.

The elevator opened right onto the apartment foyer, where Nell was waiting for her.

Winifred saw the cordial smile of welcome on Nell's face fade as soon as she stepped forward. 'Is something wrong?' she asked anxiously.

Dear God, Nell thought with sudden alarm, why is this happening? But as she looked at Winifred, she could almost hear the knowledge filtering through her being: *Winifred's journey on this plane is completed.*

CHAPTER TEN

Adam reached the boat fifteen minutes before the others were due to arrive. Entering the cabin, he saw that the caterer had been there and left a selection of cheeses and a plate of crackers on the

49

sideboard. The liquor cabinet and the refrigerator would have been checked and stocked at the same time, so he didn't even bother to look.

He had found that the casual atmosphere of the boat, combined with the social tone drinks gave a meeting, served to loosen tongues—those of his associates as well as of potential clients. On these occasions, Adam's favorite drink, vodka on the rocks, was often plain water instead, a fact he skillfully hid.

Throughout the day he had been tempted to phone Nell, but then finally had decided against it. He hated to quarrel with her almost as much as he had begun to hate the sight of her grandfather. Nell simply refused to acknowledge the fact that Mac wanted her to run for his former seat for only one reason: he intended to make her his puppet. All that pious mouthing about retiring at eighty rather than be the oldest member of the House was a lot of baloney. The truth was that the guy the Democrats were putting up against him at the time was strong and might have staged an upset. Mac didn't want to retire; he just didn't want to go out a loser.

Of course, he didn't want to go out, period. So now he'd get Nell, who was high profile, smart, very attractive, articulate and popular, to win the seat— and the power—back for him.

Frowning at the mental image of Cornelius MacDermott, Adam crossed to look at the boat's fuel gauge. As he'd expected, the tank was full. After he had taken the boat out last week, the service company had checked it over and refueled it.

'Hello. It's me.'

Adam hurried out on deck to give Winifred a hand as she stepped down to the boat. He was pleased to note that she had his briefcase and jacket under her arm.

Something was obviously distressing her, though he could tell by the way she moved and held her head back. 'What's wrong, Winifred?' he asked.

She tried to smile, but it was a failed effort. 'You can look right through me, can't you, Adam?' Clutching his hand, she made the long step onto the deck. 'I have to ask you, and you have to be completely honest,' she said earnestly. 'Did I do something to make Nell angry at me?'

'What do you mean?'

'She wasn't at all like herself when I stopped by the apartment. She acted as though she couldn't wait to get me out.'

'You shouldn't take any of that personally. I don't think it was you who caused her to act differently. Nell and I had a disagreement this morning,' Adam said quietly. 'I would guess that's what's on her mind.'

Winifred had not released his hand. 'If you want to talk about it, I'm here for you.'

Adam pulled free from her grasp. 'I know you are, Winifred. Thank you. Oh, look, here's Jimmy.'

Jimmy Ryan was obviously ill at ease on the boat. He had made little attempt to clean up his appearance after spending the day at the job site. His work boots left dusty imprints on the cabin carpet as he silently followed Adam's suggestion to fix himself whatever he'd like to drink.

Winifred watched as he poured himself a particularly heavy scotch, thinking that she should probably talk with Adam about Jimmy later.

Still inside the cabin, Jimmy Ryan sat at the table as though ready for the meeting to start. When he realized, however, that Adam and Winifred seemed to have no intention of coming in from the deck, he got up and stood there awkwardly, but made no effort to join them.

Sam Krause arrived ten minutes later, fuming at the traffic and at the incompetence of his driver. As a result, he got on the boat in a sour mood and went directly into the cabin. With a curt nod at Jimmy Ryan, he poured straight gin into a glass and went out on the deck.

'Lang's late as usual, I see,' he snapped.

'I spoke to him just before I left the office,' Adam told him. 'He was in his car and on his way into the city then, so he should be along any minute.'

A half-hour later the phone rang. Peter Lang's voice was clearly strained. 'I've been in an accident,' he said. 'One of those damn trailer trucks. Lucky I wasn't killed. The cops want me to go to the hospital and get checked out, and I guess I'd better, just to be on the safe side. You can either call off the meeting or go ahead without me—it's your decision. After I see the doctor, I'm heading back home.'

Five minutes later *Cornelia II* sailed out of the harbor. The light breeze had stiffened, and clouds were beginning to pass over the sun.

CHAPTER ELEVEN

'I don't feel good,' eight-year-old Ben Tucker complained to his father as they stood at the railing of the tour boat that was returning from a visit to the Statue of Liberty.

'The water's getting choppy,' his father acknowledged, 'but we'll be on shore soon. Pay attention to the view. You won't get back to see New York again for a long time, and I want you to remember everything that you see.'

Ben's glasses were smudged, and he pulled them off to clean them. He's going to tell me again that the Statue of Liberty was given to the United States by France, but it wasn't until that lady, Emma Lazarus, wrote a poem to help raise money for a base that it got put up here. He's going to tell me again that my great-great-grandfather was one of the kids who helped collect the money. 'Give me your huddled masses yearning to be free . . .' All right. Give me a break, Ben thought.

He actually had liked going to the Statue of Liberty and Ellis Island, but now he was sorry he'd come because he felt as though he was going to barf. This tub smelled of diesel fuel.

Longingly he gazed at the private yachts around them in New York harbor. He wished he were on one of them. Someday, when he made money, that was the first thing he'd do—buy a cabin cruiser. When they started out a couple of hours ago, there had been a couple of dozen boats in the water. Now that it was getting overcast, there weren't so many out.

Ben's eyes lingered on the really keen yacht way over there: the *Cornelia II*. He was so farsighted that with his glasses off he could read the letters.

Suddenly his eyes widened. 'No-o-o-o . . . !'

He didn't know that he had even spoken aloud, nor was he aware that his word—half protest, half prayer—had been echoed by virtually everyone on the starboard side of the tour boat, as well as by all the observers in lower Manhattan and in New Jersey who at that moment happened to be looking in that direction.

As he had been watching it, *Cornelia II* had exploded, suddenly becoming an immense fireball, sending shiny bits of debris shooting high into the air before falling all over the waterway that led from the Atlantic Ocean to the harbor.

Before Ben's father had spun him around and clutched him against his side, and before merciful shock had blunted the vision of bodies being blown to bits, Ben registered an impression that settled immediately in his subconscious, where it would stay, to become the source of relentless nightmares.

CHAPTER TWELVE

And I even told him not to come home, Nell reflected, as she agonized over the terrible day that was ending. Adam had replied, 'I hope you don't mean that,' and I didn't answer him. I thought about calling him later, trying to put it right, but I was too stubborn and too proud. Dear God, why didn't I call him? All day that awful feeling was hanging over me, an awareness that something was terribly, terribly wrong.

Winifred—when I saw her, I sensed she was going to die! How is it possible that I knew that?

It was like the feeling I had about my mother and father. I remember I was walking in from the playground after recess, and suddenly I knew that they were with me. I even felt Mom kiss my cheek, and Daddy ran his fingers through my hair. They were gone by then, but they came and said goodbye to me. Adam, she thought, please say goodbye to me. Let me have a chance to tell you how sorry I am.

'Nell, is there anything I can do?'

She was vaguely aware that Mac was talking to her, vaguely aware that it was after midnight. Gert's birthday dinner had gone ahead as planned, none of them aware of what had happened. Nell had made the lame excuse that Adam couldn't be there because of an important meeting. She had said it with as much conviction as possible, but the disappointment on Gert's face and the forced festivity of the evening had built up in her a new head of steam against him.

By the time she arrived home at ten o'clock, she had decided that she would have to work things out with Adam that night, assuming, of course, that he didn't accept her challenge to not come home. She would reason with him, listen to his objections, see what compromises they could make—but she just could not stand more days of uncertainty and irritation. Being a good politician was all about being able to negotiate and, when necessary, come to a compromise. It struck Nell that maybe the same qualities were necessary in a good wife.

When Nell walked into the lobby of her building,

however, she realized that the sense of foreboding that had troubled her all day had reached its culmination. Waiting there for her were Mac's assistant, Liz Hanley, and NYPD Detective George Brennan. Instantly Nell had known that something was terribly wrong, but they insisted on not talking until they were inside the apartment.

Then, as gently as he could, Detective Brennan told her about the accident, and with an apology said he needed to ask her some questions.

There were witnesses who had seen her husband getting on his boat, he told her, followed by at least three more people. Did she know the names of his companions? he asked.

Too stunned yet for reality to sink in, Nell had told him that she understood it was to be an associates' meeting, and that Winifred Johnson, Adam's assistant, was also going to be there. She told him the names of the associates, even offered to look up phone numbers, but the detective demurred. He told her he would take it from there for the night, and that she should go to bed and try to get some sleep. The media blitz would start tomorrow, and she would need all her strength.

'I'll be back to talk with you in the morning, Mrs. Cauliff. I'm so terribly sorry,' he said, then walked with Liz Hanley to the door.

As the detective left, both Mac and Gert arrived at the apartment, having been called by Liz.

'Nell, go to bed,' Mac said immediately.

Mac's voice always has had a peculiar ability to sound both brusque and concerned at the same time, Nell thought objectively.

'Mac's right, Nell. The next few days aren't going to be easy,' Gertrude MacDermott coaxed, taking a seat on the couch next to Nell.

Nell looked at these two people, the only family she had now. With a slight smile, she remembered how one of her grandfather's aides had commented once, 'How can Cornelius and Gertrude look so much alike, yet be so different?'

It was true. Both of them had a shock of unruly white hair, vivid blue eyes, thin lips and a jutting chin. But the expression in Gert's eyes was tranquil rather than fierce like Mac's; her demeanor was as retiring as her brother's was combative.

'I'll stay with you tonight,' Gert volunteered. 'You shouldn't be alone.'

Nell shook her head. 'Thank you, Aunt Gert. But I need to be alone tonight,' she said.

Liz came back to say good night, and Nell got up and walked her to the door. 'Nell, I'm so sorry. When I heard the news on the radio tonight, I came right over. I know you mean more to Mac than anything else in the world, and I know he feels terrible about Adam too, even though he was always a little hard on him. If there is anything I can do . . .'

'I know, Liz. Thanks for coming so quickly. Thanks for taking care of so many things already.'

'Tomorrow we'll talk about arrangements,' Liz said.

Arrangements? Nell thought with a start. Arrangements. A funeral. 'Adam and I never really discussed what he would want if something happened to him,' Nell said. 'It was just not something that seemed necessary. But I do remember that one time in Nantucket, when he'd been out fishing, he said that when his time came he'd like to be cremated and have his ashes spread

57

over the ocean.'

She looked at Liz and understood the surge of sympathy in her eyes. Nell shook her head and forced herself to smile. 'I guess it looks like he got his wish, doesn't it?'

'I'll call you in the morning,' Liz said, taking Nell's hand and squeezing it gently.

When Nell returned to the living room, her grandfather was standing up and Gert was looking for her pocketbook. As Nell walked Mac to the door, he said gruffly, 'You're smart not to have Gert stay. She'd be going on all night in that channel-babble nonsense of hers.' Mac stopped and faced Nell, putting a gentle hand on each of her arms. 'I'm more sorry than I can express, Nell. After what happened to your mother and father, you certainly don't deserve to lose Adam this way.'

I especially don't deserve to lose him after a quarrel, Nell thought, feeling a surge of resentment rise in her. Mac, you were the root of the problem, she told herself. Your demands on me—they do sometimes get to be too much. Adam was wrong about not wanting me to run for office, but he was right about that.

When she did not answer, after a moment her grandfather turned away from her.

Gert appeared and took both of Nell's hands. 'I know there is little anyone can say at a time like this that will offer any real consolation, but Nell, I want you to remember that you haven't really lost him. He's on a different plane now, but he's still your Adam.'

'Come on, Gert,' Mac said, taking his sister's arm, 'Nell doesn't need to listen to that kind of talk now. Try to get some sleep, Nell. We'll talk in the morning.'

They were gone. Nell walked back into the living room, aware that she was half listening for the sound of Adam's key in the lock. She moved about the apartment as though in a trance, arranging some magazines on a side table, straightening the decorative pillows on the deep, comfortable couch. The room had northern light, and the couch had been reupholstered last year in a warm red fabric that Adam at first questioned, then approved.

She looked about the room, noting the eclectic combination of furnishings. Both she and Adam had strong likes and dislikes. Some things from her parents' home—wonderful artifacts from their travels—had been kept in storage for her. Other items she had bought—most of them at hole-in-the-wall antique shops or at obscure auctions found by Aunt Gert. Many things had been purchased only after a period of negotiation. Negotiation and compromise, Nell thought again, another pang of sorrow gripping her. Adam and I would have worked everything out, I just know we would have.

She crossed to a three-legged table that Adam had found one day when she was off at a party fund-raiser, and he had accompanied Gert on one of her foraging expeditions. Adam and Gert had hit it off from the beginning. She will miss him tremendously too, Nell thought sadly. She knew Gert encouraged him to buy the table for her.

Sometimes she worried about Gert, concerned lest someone take advantage of her. She is so trusting, Nell thought, letting all those psychics and channelers influence virtually every decision she makes. Yet when it came to bargaining over things like this sofa, Gert was amazingly sharp. Her own apartment on East Eighty-first Street was a cheerful, somewhat dusty hodgepodge of furniture and artifacts she had either inherited or accumulated over the years, and which now had the pull of sentimental ties and cozy familiarity.

Adam, on his first visit there, had laughingly commented that Gert's apartment was like her mind: busy, eclectic and somewhat fey. 'No one else would have art deco lacquer cheek by jowl with rococo fantasy,' he said.

Aunt Gert's furniture! The stuff in this room! What in the name of God was her mind doing, thinking about tables and chairs and carpets at a time like this? When would it finally register, she wondered, when would she finally get it through her head that Adam was dead?

But it *was* difficult, and it would continue to be. It was because she needed him to be alive, needed him to open the door and come in and say, 'Nell, let me say it first: I love you and I'm sorry about the blowup.'

The blowup. First they had had an explosive fight, and then Adam's boat had blown up. Detective Brennan had said it was too soon to know if it was a fuel leak that caused the explosion.

Adam named both his boats after me, Nell thought, but I hardly ever went out on either one with him. I've been so afraid of water ever since the time I was caught in that riptide in Hawaii. He begged me to come out on the boat with him. He promised he'd stay near shore.

She had tried to overcome the fear of the ocean, but she never really succeeded. She restricted her swimming now entirely to a pool, and while she could travel on an ocean liner—although, in truth,

60

she was never completely comfortable there—she just could not stand to be on a smaller boat, where the feeling of the undulating water made her relive the certainty that she was going to drown.

But Adam loved boats, loved being on them. In a way, what could have been a problem became a plus for us, Nell thought. So many weekends, when Mac wanted me to go to political affairs with him, or when I needed to work on my column, Adam would go sailing or fishing.

And then he would come home, and I would come home, and we'd be together. Compromises and accommodations, she thought again. We would have worked it out.

Nell turned off the living room lights and went into the bedroom. I wish I could feel something, she thought. I wish I could cry or grieve. Instead, I feel like all I can do is wait.

But wait for what? Wait for whom?

She undressed, taking care to hang up the green silk Escada pants suit she had been wearing. It was new. When it was delivered, Adam had opened the box, taken it out of the tissue and examined it carefully. 'That's gotta be great on you, Nell,' he had said.

She had worn it tonight because in her heart she'd been hoping that he would feel as rotten about the quarrel as she did and would join them, even if only in time for dessert. She had visualized him coming in just as they brought over the spun-sugar confection topped by a candle that was a birthday tradition at the Four Seasons.

But, of course, Adam didn't come. I'd like to think he was planning to join us, Nell thought as she took a cotton nightgown from the drawer.

61

Automatically, she washed her face and brushed her teeth. The image she saw in the bathroom mirror was that of a stranger, a pale woman with wide, blank eyes and dark chestnut hair that framed her face in damp ringlets.

Was it too warm in here? she wondered, noticing the perspiration on her forehead. If so, then why did she feel so cold? She got into bed.

Last night she hadn't expected Adam to come home from Philadelphia, and when she heard his key, she hadn't even acknowledged his presence. I was so reluctant to get into a discussion about running for Mac's old seat that I pretended I wasn't awake, Nell thought, angry with herself again.

Then, after he fell asleep, he had thrown his arm over her and had murmured her name. Now she said his aloud: 'Adam. Adam. I love you. Please come back!'

She waited. The faint hum of the air conditioner and the wail of a police siren were the only sounds she could make out.

Then in the distance she heard the screeching cry of an ambulance.

There must have been police boats and ambulances at the marina, she reasoned. They had looked for survivors, although Detective Brennan had reluctantly explained that it would have been more than a miracle if there were any. 'It's like most plane crashes,' he had explained. 'A plane usually disintegrates on the way down. We know there's no hope for anyone to live through such an occurrence, but we have to give it a shot.'

Tomorrow, or at least in the next few days, they should be able to piece together the exact reason the boat exploded. 'It was a new boat,' Brennan had said. 'They'll look for a mechanical problem, a fuel leak, something like that.'

'Adam, I'm sorry.' Again Nell spoke quietly into the darkened room. 'Please, somehow let me know that you can hear me. Mom and Daddy said goodbye to me. So did Grammy.'

It had been one of her earliest memories. She'd been only four when her grandmother died. Her mother and father had been teaching at a seminar in Oxford, and she with her au pair had been staying in Mac's house. Her grandmother was in the hospital. During the night, Nell had awakened and smelled her grandmother's favorite scent, Arpège. She wore it just about all the time.

I remember it so well, Nell thought. I was very sleepy, but I remember thinking how glad I was that Grammy was home and that she was all better.

The next morning Nell had rushed down to the dining room. 'Where's Grammy? Is she up yet?'

Her grandfather was sitting at the table; Gert was with him. 'Grammy is in heaven,' he had said. 'She went there last night.'

When I told him that she had come into my room last night, he thought I'd been dreaming, Nell remembered. Gert believed me, though. She understood that Grammy had come to say goodbye. And then later, so did Mom and Dad.

Adam, please come to me. Let me sense your presence. Please give me the chance to tell you how sorry I am before I say goodbye to you.

For the rest of the night, Nell waited, lying awake, staring into the darkness. As dawn broke, she was at last able to weep—for Adam, for all the years they would not spend together, for Winifred and Adam's associates, Sam and Peter, who had

63

been on the boat with him.

And she was able to weep for herself, because once again she had to become used to living without someone she loved.

CHAPTER THIRTEEN

Safely ensconced in the backseat of the limousine, Peter Lang reflected on the collision that had taken place earlier between his car and the trailer truck. He had been on his way into Manhattan for a meeting with Adam Cauliff, cruising along on the Long Island Expressway, just about to enter the Midtown Tunnel, when *bang*! Collision!

Five hours later, Lang, with a cracked rib, his lip cut and head bruised from the impact, was picked up at the hospital by a limousine service and driven through teeming rain to his home in Southampton.

His oceanfront estate, in the most exclusive section of that exclusive community, had been given to him by his parents when they decided to divide their time between Saint John's in the Caribbean and Martha's Vineyard.

The house was a turn-of-the-century, sprawling white colonial, with hunter-green shutters. The two-acre gated property also contained a swimming pool, tennis court and cabana, and was enhanced by a velvety green lawn, flowering shrubs and meticulously pruned trees.

Married at twenty-three and amicably although expensively divorced at thirty, Lang had cheerfully settled into the role of what was once known as a man-about-town. Blessed with blond good looks, sophisticated charm, reasonable intelligence and a quick sense of humor, he also had inherited an uncanny instinct for acquiring land that would someday become valuable.

That instinct had originally motivated his grandfather, prior to World War II, to buy hundreds of acres in rural Long Island and Connecticut, and his father to invest heavily in Third Avenue property in Manhattan when the elevated railroad tracks were about to be taken down.

As his father proudly boasted when he talked about his forty-two-year-old son, ' "Shirtsleeves to shirtsleeves in three generations" doesn't apply to our family. Peter's turning out to be the smartest of the lot of us.'

With his usual casual generosity, Lang tipped the limousine driver and let himself into the house. He had long ago pensioned off the couple that had been employed there from the time he was born. In their place he had hired a daily housekeeper and used a small catering firm to take care of the extra demand when he had guests.

The house was dark and cool. Whenever he found it necessary to be in the city for a meeting with his real estate partners—typically held on a Friday afternoon—he usually spent the night in his Manhattan apartment and drove to Southampton early the next morning. That was what he would have done if he had met Adam and the others on the boat today, but the accident on the way in had made that impossible.

Now Peter found himself glad to be in this house, glad to be able to fix a quiet drink and take stock of his aching body. His head throbbed. He

65

ran his tongue over his lip and grimaced at the realization that the swelling there was increasing.

The driver of the tractor-trailer—Peter could still feel the moment when he knew the crash was inevitable.

The message light on the phone was flashing, but Peter ignored it. The last thing he wanted to do right now was to get into a conversation with anyone about the accident. And it probably was a reporter. Since he had become something of a 'man-about-town,' he reflected, everything he did had become fodder for the gossip columns.

Carrying his drink, he walked across the room, opened the door to the porch and stepped outside. On the drive from the hospital the rain had been getting steadily heavier. Now it was pouring down and driven by the force of the wind. Even the porch's long overhang did not fully protect him from the downpour. It was so dark that he could not see the ocean, but there was no doubting its presence, as the crescendo of the waves broke forcefully around him. The temperature was dropping sharply, and the sunny afternoon he had spent on the golf course seemed now to have been something in the distant past. Shivering, he went back inside, locked the door and headed upstairs.

Fifteen minutes later, and feeling somewhat better after a hot shower, he got into bed. Remembering to turn off the ringer on the telephone, he flipped on the radio and set the timer for fifteen minutes, just long enough for him to catch the eleven o'clock news.

He fell asleep, however, before he heard the lead story about the explosion of *Cornelia II* earlier that day in New York harbor, and among the facts

66

he missed was that he, Peter Lang, prominent New York real estate entrepreneur, was one of the people presumed lost in the tragedy.

CHAPTER FOURTEEN

At 7:30, Lisa began to listen for Jimmy's car. She was looking forward to surprising him with the chicken-and-rice dinner that was his favorite meal.

Her last appointment at the salon had been canceled, and she'd been able to leave early, in time to do grocery shopping and still have the kids fed by 6:30. She'd decided to wait and eat with Jimmy. She had set the dinette table for the two of them and even had wine chilling in the refrigerator, a special treat. The vague uneasiness she had felt all day demanded that she take action. Jimmy had looked so lost, so defeated, when he left the house this morning. She hadn't been able to get that image out of her head all day, and she felt an urgent need to put her arms around him, to show him how much she loved him.

Now the kids, Kyle, Kelly and Charley, were at the kitchen table, doing their homework. Kyle, the oldest, was twelve, and as usual needed no urging; he was a good student. Kelly was ten and a dreamer. 'Kelly, you haven't written a word in five minutes,' Lisa prodded.

Charley, the seven-year-old, was elaborately copying his spelling words. He knew he was in hot water because of the note from the teacher he had brought home saying that he had been talking in class again.

'Don't even *think* about television for a week,' Lisa had warned him.

As usual the house seemed empty without Jimmy. Even though he just wasn't himself these days—too quiet, sometimes too edgy—he was always a powerful and protective presence in their lives, and the rare evenings he wasn't with them felt odd and uncomfortable.

Maybe I've been bugging him, Lisa thought, always asking if he's feeling better or nagging him to talk to me about what's bothering him or begging him to go to a doctor. I'm going to back off on that, she promised herself as she checked the dinner keeping warm in the oven.

He had looked so troubled when he went out this morning, she thought. Was it possible that I heard him right, that he said, 'I'm sorry,' just as he was leaving?

Sorry, for *what*? she wondered.

By 8:30 she was starting to worry. Where was Jimmy? Certainly he was not still on the boat. The weather was changing fast. Overcast skies had turned into a storm. It wouldn't be safe to get caught out on the water in this.

He's probably on the way home, she told herself. Traffic was always terrible on Friday evenings.

An hour later Lisa shooed the two younger children up to shower and put on pajamas. Kyle, homework completed, went into the den to watch television.

Jimmy, where are you? Lisa agonized as the hands on the clock approached 10:00 P.M. Something's wrong. Maybe you *did* get fired. Well, if so, then I don't care. You'll find something else. Maybe you should get out of construction. You

68

always said there was a lot of stuff going on in that business that was downright crooked.

At 10:30 the front doorbell rang. Sick with fear, Lisa rushed to open it. Two men were standing there. They held up identification for her to see under the overhead light—and police badges.

'Mrs. Ryan, may we come in?'

Without thinking, the question came to her lips. Her voice dull with pain, Lisa sobbed, 'Jimmy committed suicide, didn't he?'

CHAPTER FIFTEEN

Cornelius and Gertrude MacDermott shared a taxi when they left Nell's apartment. They sat in silence, each deep in thought, not noticing when the cab stopped in front of Gert's building at Eighty-first Street and Lexington Avenue.

Gert felt rather than saw the driver's almost contemptuous, over-the-shoulder glance in her direction. 'Oh. I didn't realize,' she said. With an awkward motion she turned and saw that the doorman was already holding the door for her. The rain was now pouring down in drenching, windswept sheets. Even with the protection of an umbrella, she could see that the doorman was getting soaked.

'For God's sake, Gert, get a move on,' her brother barked.

She turned to him, ignoring his brusque tone, aware only of the terrible concern they shared. 'Cornelius, Nell *adored* Adam. I got the feeling tonight that she's not going to be able to handle this. She's going to need all the support we can give her.'

'Nell's strong. She'll be all right.'

'You don't really believe that.'

'Gert, that poor guy's gonna drown waiting for you. Don't worry—Nell will be fine. I'll call you tomorrow.'

As she moved to leave the taxi, one word that Mac had said suddenly stuck in her mind. *Drown*, Gert thought, did Adam drown or was he blown to bits in the explosion? She realized her brother had the same thought, because he took her hand and leaned over and kissed her cheek.

She felt the familiar stabs of pain in her knees as she stepped out of the cab and straightened up. My body is wearing out, she thought. Adam was so strong, so healthy. This is a terrible shock.

Suddenly she felt infinitely weary and gladly accepted the doorman's hand under her arm as she walked the short distance from the curb to the building's entrance. A few minutes later, at last safely in the quiet of her own apartment, she sank into a chair. She leaned back and closed her eyes. They welled with tears as Adam's face filled her mind.

He had a smile that would warm even the hardest heart. She thought back to the first time Nell had brought him to meet her. Nell had been radiant, so obviously in love. Gert felt a lump forming in her throat as she thought of the contrast between the happiness in Nell's eyes that afternoon and the confusion and heartbreak that was so evident in them tonight.

It was as though a light went on in Nell's soul when she met Adam, Gert thought. Cornelius never really understood how devastating it was for Nell to lose her mother and father when she was so young.

Cornelius did everything he could for her, of course, and spent every possible minute with her, but no one can replace two parents like Richard and Joan, Gert thought sadly.

With a sigh, she got up and went into the kitchen. She reached for the kettle and smiled to herself as she remembered how, soon after she met him, Adam had asked her why with all the tea she drank she didn't just fill the kettle so that there was always warm water in it that would reheat quickly.

'It doesn't taste the same if the water is reheated,' she had explained.

'Gert, I have to tell you that's pure imagination,' he had responded with a hearty, affectionate laugh.

We laughed together a lot, Gert thought. He wasn't like Cornelius, who gets so impatient with me. Adam even came here a few times when our psychic group met. He was genuinely *interested*. He wanted to know why I believe so devoutly that it's possible to contact people who have passed on.

Well, it *is* possible, she thought. Unfortunately it's not a gift that I have, but some of the others truly *can* become channels between those of us who are here and those who have left this plane. I've *seen* how comforted people are after they've contacted someone they loved who isn't with us anymore. If Nell has trouble accepting Adam's passing, I'm going to insist that she try to reach him through channeling. She will feel much better if she can find closure after this terrible loss. Adam will tell her that it was time for him to go, but that she mustn't cling to grief, because he is *here*; it will make everything much easier for her.

That decision made, Gert felt comforted. The kettle was whistling, and she turned it off quickly as she reached for a cup and saucer. Tonight the usual cheery sound of the steam forcing its way through the narrow passageway in the cover over the spout had become a mournful wail. It was almost like a lost soul shrieking for surcease, she thought uneasily.

CHAPTER SIXTEEN

As a kid growing up in Bayside, Queens, Jack Sclafani had always wanted to be the cop when the neighborhood kids played cops and robbers. At school, he was a serious and quiet student, winning first a scholarship to St. John's Prep, and then a second one to Fairfield College, where a Jesuit education honed his already logical mind.

Eschewing an academic career, his next step was to earn a master's degree in criminology. Then, with his formal education behind him, Jack joined the NYPD as a rookie cop.

Now, some eighteen years later, at age forty-two, living in Brooklyn Heights, married to a successful real estate broker and the father of twin boys, Sclafani was a detective first class on the district attorney's elite squad, an assignment in which he took great pride. In his time on the force, he had worked with many fine men, but the one he had known the longest and still liked the best was his partner, George Brennan. This was Sclafani's day off, but he roused himself from his pre-bedtime

72

nap when he heard Brennan being interviewed on the eleven o'clock news, fielding reporters' questions about the cabin cruiser that had exploded in the harbor early that evening.

Using the remote, he turned up the volume and leaned forward, fully alert now, his attention riveted to the scene he was watching. Brennan was standing outside a modest house in Little Neck, only a fifteen-minute drive from Bayside.

'Mrs. Ryan has confirmed that her husband, Jimmy, an employee of the Sam Krause Construction Company, was planning to be at a meeting today on the boat, *Cornelia II'*, Brennan was saying. 'A man of his description was seen boarding the boat before it sailed out into the harbor, so we are assuming that Mr. Ryan was one of the victims.'

Jack listened intently as questions were thrown at Brennan.

'How many people were on the boat?' an off-camera voice asked.

'We've learned that in addition to Mr. Ryan, four other people were expected to attend the meeting,' he replied.

'Isn't it unusual for a diesel-fueled boat to explode?'

'We're investigating the explosion,' Brennan said, his words clipped, giving nothing away.

'Isn't it true that Sam Krause was about to be indicted for bid rigging?

'No comment.'

'Any hope of survivors?'

'There's always hope. Search and rescue is still under way.'

Sam Krause! Jack thought. You bet he was about

73

to be indicted. So he was on that boat! Son of a gun! The guy was a blueprint for everything rotten in the construction business. When they start looking into it, there'll be a laundry list of people who might have wanted to get rid of him.

'I'm home. Does that make anybody's heart beat faster?' The voice came from the doorway just behind him.

Jack looked around. 'I didn't hear the door open, honey. How was the movie?'

'Wonderful—except for being about an hour too long and totally depressing.' Nancy dropped a kiss on her husband's cheek as she passed the couch. Petite, with short blond hair and hazel eyes, she exuded warmth and energy. She glanced at the television screen and stopped as she recognized Brennan. 'What's George up to?'

'The boat that blew up near the Statue of Liberty is in his bailiwick, although during this interview he must have been visiting the home of one of the apparent victims, out in Queens.' The segment was over, and Jack clicked off the set. Diesel fuel doesn't cause explosions, he thought. I'll bet anything that if that boat was turned into confetti, it was because somebody planted a bomb on it; you can bet on *that*.

'Are the boys upstairs?' Nancy asked.

'Watching some movie in their room. I'm ready to pack it in.'

'Me too. Will you close up?'

'Sure.' As Jack turned off lights and checked to be certain the front and back doors were securely locked, he continued to mull over the news of the boat explosion. If indeed it was confirmed that Sam Krause was on that boat, that the explosion was no

74

accident would have to be considered a definite possibility. It was no wonder someone would want to get rid of him before he was brought in for questioning. Krause knew too much—and he wasn't the kind of guy to view a long prison sentence as an option.

Too bad, though, that four other people had to die just to get rid of Krause; surely whoever did it could have found a more economical way to waste him, Jack thought. Whoever did it must have been hard as nails. He knew of more than a few people who fit *that* description.

Wednesday, June 14

CHAPTER SEVENTEEN

'Nell, I can't tell you how sorry I am. I still can't believe any of this—it's just inconceivable.'

Peter Lang was seated opposite Nell in the living room of her apartment. His face was bruised and his lip swollen. He looked genuinely shaken, and his demeanor was far different from the supremely confident persona he usually projected. Nell realized that for the first time she actually felt some empathy for this man. In the past, she always had been put off by Peter's manner. 'Cock of the walk,' as Mac scornfully called it.

'I was so banged up that when I got home that night, I just turned off the phone and went to bed. The media called down to Florida and reached my parents. It's damn lucky my mother or father didn't have a heart attack. Mom couldn't stop crying when she realized I was okay. She still doesn't believe it. She called me four times yesterday alone.'

'I can understand that,' Nell said, as she considered what her own reaction might have been had Adam phoned and said that he hadn't been on the boat, that something had delayed him and he had told Sam to run the meeting without him. Suppose . . .

But that would never have happened. There was nothing to suppose. The others wouldn't have gone out on Adam's boat without him, she reminded herself. Adam's boat—named after me. Something I never even wanted to set foot on that he named after me—and it became his casket, Nell thought.

79

No, *not* his casket! Sunday they had found body parts that had been positively identified as being Jimmy Ryan's. As of now, only he would have a funeral with a casket. The odds of finding and identifying any more bodies, or parts, were almost negligible. Adam, Sam Krause and Winifred must have been blown to bits or incinerated. Whatever pieces of them still existed probably had by now been swept by the strong tides past the Verrazano Bridge and out into the Atlantic.

'Not incinerated; cremated, or buried at sea. Try to think of it that way, Nell.' That was what Monsignor Duncan had told her when she had arranged with him for Adam's memorial Mass.

'There'll be a Mass for Adam on Thursday,' she told Lang, breaking the silence that had fallen between them.

Lang said nothing for a moment, then began speaking softly. 'There are a lot of rumors flying about, Nell. Have the police confirmed that it was a bomb that destroyed the boat?'

'Not confirmed it officially, no.'

But she knew that a bomb was suspected, and it was a thought that wouldn't let go. Why would anyone do that? Was it a random act of violence, like when people randomly attack strangers on busy streets? Or maybe it was a case of a 'have-not' person, jealous of the owner of the sleek new boat, wanting to punish him. Whatever the reason, it was something she needed to know, needed to get out of the way before she could find closure to this terrible thing.

Jimmy Ryan's wife needed an answer too. She had phoned the day after the tragedy, looking for some understanding as to why her husband was dead. 'Mrs. Cauliff, I feel as though I know you,' she said. 'I've seen you on television, and I read your column, and over the years I have read about you and how your grandfather brought you up after your parents died. I feel terribly sorry for you. You've had a lot of grief in your life. I don't know what they're telling you about my husband, but I don't want you to think someone I loved caused your husband's death.

'*Jimmy did not do this.* He was a victim the same as your husband. Yes, Jimmy was depressed. He'd been out of work a long time, and we had run up a lot of bills. But things were getting better—in great part because of your husband. I know Jimmy was grateful to him or to whoever it was in his firm who passed his application to the Krause Construction Company. But now the police are insinuating that Jimmy caused that explosion. I want you to know that even if Jimmy *was* suicidal—and as much as it pains me to admit it, he may have been—he would never, ever have caused another human being's death. *Never!* He was a good man, as well as being a wonderful father and husband. I knew him, and he would never have done something like that.'

Pictures of Jimmy Ryan's funeral had been on page three of the *Post* and on page one of the *News*. Lisa Ryan, with her three children huddled beside her, was shown walking behind the casket that held the shattered remains of a husband and father. Nell shut her eyes.

'Nell, next week sometime I'd like to go over some business matters with you,' Lang said softly. 'There are a few decisions that have to be made, and I need your input. But there's time enough for that.' He stood up. 'Try to get some rest. Are you able to sleep at night?'

'A fair amount, all things considered.'

She was glad to close the door behind Peter Lang, ashamed of the resentment she felt that he was the one who had been spared. His bruises would fade. The swelling on his lip would be gone in a few days.

'Adam,' she said aloud. 'Adam,' she repeated quietly, as if he were listening.

Of course there was no answer.

The storm Friday night had broken the warm spell. Now it was unseasonably cool for early June. The heating system in the building had been switched over to air conditioning, and even though she had turned that off, the apartment still felt chilly. Nell hugged her arms and went into the bedroom to get a sweater.

The wonderful Liz had shown up at the apartment Saturday morning, carrying a grocery bag. 'You're going to eat,' she had said briskly. 'I didn't know what you had in the house, so I brought grapefruit, bacon and fresh-from-the-oven bagels.'

Over second cups of coffee she had said, 'Nell, I know it's none of my business, yet it is my business. Mac is heartbroken for you. *Don't shut him out.*'

'He shut Adam out, and right now I'm having trouble forgiving him for that.'

'But you know he had your best interests at heart. He felt that what was right for you— meaning running for office—was ultimately the right thing for your marriage as well.'

'Well, I guess we'll never know, will we?'

'Think about it.'

Since that morning, Liz had been over every day.

82

This morning she had commented sadly, 'Mac still hasn't heard from you, Nell.'

'I'll see him at the service. We'll go to lunch here with the others afterward. Right now I need to adjust without him bullying me.'

Adjust here in the home I shared with Adam for the past three years, she thought. Adjust to being alone.

She had bought the apartment eleven years ago, after she graduated from Georgetown, using money that had been held in trust for her until she was twenty-one. It was a time when the volatile real estate market in New York was in one of its lean periods, when sellers far outnumbered buyers, and the spacious co-op had turned out to be an excellent investment.

'Whatever little nest I carry you off to won't be in this league,' Adam had joked when they began to talk of marriage. 'Give me ten years, though, and I promise the picture will change.'

'Why not spend those ten years right here? I happen to love this place.'

She had cleared one of the two large bedroom closets for him, and taken from Mac's brownstone the antique chest-on-chest dresser that had belonged to her father. She went over to that dresser now and picked up the oval-shaped silver tray that lay next to their wedding picture. The tray was where Adam always put his watch and keys and change and wallet when he undressed at night.

I hadn't realized how alone I'd always felt until we were married and he was here with me all the time, she thought. Thursday night he changed in the guest room. He didn't want to wake me up. And I didn't let on that I was awake because I didn't want to have to talk about my day and tell him that I had decided to run for Mac's old seat.

Suddenly it seemed fiercely important and disturbing that she had missed that last night of watching him go through his familiar bedtime ritual. Liz had suggested that she come over sometime next week and help Nell pack up Adam's clothing and personal effects. 'You keep saying his death doesn't feel real to you, Nell, and I don't think you'll start to heal until it does. Perhaps it will feel more real when all the reminders aren't there.'

Not yet, though, Nell thought. *Not yet!*

The phone rang. Reluctantly she picked it up. 'Hello.'

'Mrs. Cauliff?'

'Yes.'

'This is Detective Brennan. Would it be convenient if my colleague Detective Sclafani and I came over to talk with you?'

Not now, Nell thought. I need to be alone now. I need to hold something that was Adam's and feel close to him.

Aunt Gert had taught her about contacting a lost loved one by having her hold an object that had belonged to her mother. She remembered that it was six months after their deaths; she was upstairs in her room in Mac's house, curled up in a chair, clutching a book on which she was supposed to write a report. She didn't hear Aunt Gert come in. And she wasn't reading.

I was just sitting there, staring out the window, Nell thought. I loved them both so much, but at that moment it was my mother I wanted. I needed my mother.

Gert came in and knelt beside me. Her voice was

84

so soft. 'Say a name.'

I whispered, 'Mommy.'

'I sensed that,' she said, 'and I brought something for you. One of the things that your grandpa didn't think worth keeping.' It was that ivory box that Mom kept on her dresser when I was little. It had a special woodsy scent that I loved. When Mom and Dad were on a trip, I would go into their room and get it, and whenever I opened that box, I felt so close to Mom.

It happened again that day. The little box hadn't been opened in so long that the woodsy scent was very pungent. And at that moment, I felt as though Mom were there, in the room with me. I remember I asked Aunt Gert how she knew to bring that particular item.

'I just knew,' she said. 'And remember, your mother and dad will be around as long as you need them. You'll be the one to free them, whenever you are able to let them go.'

Mac hates it when she talks like that, Nell thought. But Gert was right. And after my parents saved me in Maui, I could let them go. And I did. But I'm still not ready to let Adam go. I want to hold on to something that will make me feel he is still close to me. I have to have him with me for at least a little while longer—before I say goodbye.

'Mrs. Cauliff, are you all right?' the detective asked, breaking the long silence.

'Oh, yes. I'm sorry. I'm still having a little trouble adjusting,' she said, her voice halting.

'Look, I don't like to press you at this time, but it really is important that we meet with you now.'

Nell shook her head, a gesture she had picked up from Mac, his unconscious sign of displeasure when he didn't want to give voice to his objection to something. 'All right. Come over if you must,' she told Brennan crisply, and then hung up.

CHAPTER EIGHTEEN

On Wednesday afternoon, Lisa's next-door neighbor, Brenda Curren, and her seventeen-year-old daughter, Morgan, arrived to pick up the Ryan kids, Kyle, Kelly and Charley, and take them to a movie and then out to dinner.

'Go get in the car with Morgan,' Brenda ordered, 'I want to talk to your mom for a minute.' She waited until the three were outside before saying, 'Lisa, don't look so worried. You know they'll be fine with us. You were right to keep them home from school today, but now you need some time to yourself.'

'Oh, I don't know,' Lisa said dully, 'all I see stretching out ahead of me is time. When I think about it, I wonder what in God's name I'm going to do with all of those hours and days.' She looked at her neighbor, saw the look of concern in her eyes. 'But you're right, of course. I do need some time alone. I have to go through Jimmy's desk. I have to file for Social Security for the children. At least that will offer some income while I figure out what I'm going to do.'

'You do have insurance, don't you Lisa?' Brenda's pleasant face creased with worry. 'I'm sorry,' she added hastily. 'It's none of my business, of course. It's just that Ed is so insurance conscious that it's the first thing I think of.'

'We have some,' Lisa said. Enough to bury Jimmy, she thought, but that's about it. She kept the thought to herself, though; she would not admit that even to a good friend like Brenda.

Keep your business to yourself—that was a warning she had heard all her life from her grandmother: *It's nobody's affair what you have or don't have, Lisa. Keep them guessing.*

Only there's not much to guess about, Lisa thought, feeling the weight over her pressing harder. We still owe $14,000 on credit cards, computed at 18 percent interest a month.

'Lisa, Jimmy always kept up this place so well. Ed isn't nearly as handy as Jimmy was, but he asked me to tell you that if anything comes up that needs fixing, he'll do his best to take care of it for you. You know what I mean. Plumbers and electricians cost a fortune.'

'Yes, they do.'

'Lisa, we're all so sorry about Jimmy. He was a great guy, and we love you both. We'd do anything to help you out. You know that.'

Lisa saw the tears Brenda was trying to blink back and tried to will herself to smile. 'I know you would. And you are helping me. Go ahead now and take my kids off my hands.'

She walked Brenda to the door, then headed back down the narrow hallway. The kitchen was large enough for a table and chairs, small enough to feel perpetually cramped. The writing desk was built in, a feature the real estate agent seemed to consider a stunning addition when they had first looked at the house all those years ago.

'You just don't get built-ins in this price range,' the agent had gushed as she pointed it out.

Lisa looked at the stack of envelopes on the desk. The mortgage, gas and phone bills were already almost a week overdue. If Jimmy had come home, they would have sat there together and paid them over the weekend, to avoid late charges. My job now, Lisa thought, something I get to do alone with all the time I have.

She wrote those checks and with a sinking heart pulled out another stack of envelopes, this one held together with a rubber band. The credit-card bills; so many of them. She didn't dare to make more than a minimum payment on any of them this month.

She debated about cleaning out the one desk drawer. Deep and wide, it had become a catchall for the junk mail that should have been thrown out immediately. Here are coupons we never got around to using, Lisa thought. And even when we didn't have any extra money, and no way to afford them, Jimmy tore pictures of tools out of catalogs—all things he'd want someday, when we got caught up.

She grasped a handful of loose papers and caught sight of an envelope with columns of figures. She didn't need to examine it to know what it was. How often had she seen Jimmy sitting at this desk, adding up the bills, agonizing as they mounted? It had become a familiar sight these last years.

And then he would go downstairs and sit at his workbench for a couple of hours, pretending to be fixing something, Lisa thought. He didn't want me to see how worried he was.

Why didn't he stop worrying once he went back to work? Lisa wondered, asking herself once more the question that had plagued her over these last months. Almost without thinking, she crossed the room and opened the door to the basement. As she walked down the stairs, she tried not to think about how hard Jimmy had labored to transform the dreary space below into a comfortable family room and a workroom for himself.

She went to the workroom and turned on the light. The kids and I almost never came in here, she thought. It was like a sanctuary for Jimmy. He said he was afraid that someone would pick up a sharp tool and get hurt. It hurt Lisa now to see that the space was painfully neat, unlike the times when the broad table had been cluttered with the tools necessary for whatever had been Jimmy's current project. Now they were all in place, all lined up on the Peg-Board over the table. The saw horses that often held sheets of beaverboard or plywood were standing together in a corner next to the file cabinet.

The file cabinet—Jimmy used it for income tax records and papers he thought worth keeping. It was one other thing that she'd have to examine carefully eventually. Lisa opened the top drawer, glanced at the carefully labeled manila folders. As she had expected, they contained sequentially numbered income tax statements.

Opening the second drawer, she saw that Jimmy had taken out the dividers. Neatly folded blueprints and specification sheets were piled on top of each other. She knew what they were: they were his plans—plans for finishing the basement, plans for the built-in bunks in Kyle's room, for the screened-in porch off the living room.

Maybe even the plans for our dream house, she

89

thought, the one we were going to have someday. He made them for me as a Christmas present two and a half years ago, before he lost his job. He asked me to tell him exactly what I wanted to have in a house, and he drew plans to accommodate everything I asked for.

Thrilled at the prospect, Lisa had given full vent to her imagination. She asked for a kitchen with a skylight, and she wanted that room to flow into a family room with a raised-hearth fireplace. She also had asked for a dining room with window seats, and a dressing room off the master bedroom. From what she had described, he'd made a model to scale.

I hope he kept those plans, Lisa thought. She reached into the drawer and lifted out the stacks of papers. There weren't as many of them as it had appeared, however, and under them, at the bottom of the drawer, she saw a bulky box—no, two—sealed with brown wrapping paper and twine. They were wedged in tightly, though, and she had to kneel on the floor and slip her fingers underneath to wrench them loose.

She placed the boxes on the table, then reached for a sharp-edged tool from the Peg-Board, slashed the twine, unwrapped the heavy brown paper and lifted the lid from the first box.

Then, with a mixture of fascinated horror and disbelief, she stared down at stacks of currency lying in neat rows inside the box: twenties, fifties, a few one hundreds—some worn, some mint new. The second box was mostly fifties.

An hour later, after a careful count, followed by an even more careful recount, Lisa dazedly acknowledged that $50,000 had been hidden in this basement room by Jimmy Ryan, the beloved husband who had suddenly become a stranger.

CHAPTER NINETEEN

In the two years since she had moved to New York from Florida, Bonnie Wilson, psychic and medium, had developed a solid clientele she met with regularly in her West End Avenue apartment.

Thirty years old, slender, with black hair worn straight and full across her shoulders, pale skin and enviable features, Bonnie perhaps looked more like a model than a master of psychic phenomena, but, in fact, she had become quite well established in her profession and was especially sought after by all those anxious to be in touch with a loved one who had passed on.

As she would explain to a newcomer, 'We all have psychic ability, some more than others. It can be developed in all of us; however, mine came already finely tuned when I was born. Even as a child, I had the ability to sense what is going on in other peoples' lives, to intuitively hear their concerns, to help them find the answers they are seeking.

'As I studied, as I prayed, as I joined groups of others who share these special gifts, I found that when people came to consult me, the ones they loved, now on the higher plane, began to join us. Sometimes their messages were specific. At other times they simply wanted to let the grieving know that they are happy and well and that their love is eternal. Over time, my ability to communicate has become more and more precise. Some people find what I tell them to be disturbing, but most draw from it only the greatest comfort. I am anxious to assist all those who come to me, and I request only that they treat me and my abilities with respect. I want to be of help, for God has given me this gift, and it is my obligation to share it with others.'

Bonnie regularly attended the New York Psychic Association meetings, held on the first Wednesday of every month. Today, as she had expected, Gert MacDermott, a regular attendee of these sessions, was not present. In hushed tones, the members discussed the terrible tragedy that had befallen her family. Gert, a loquacious person to begin with, was almost uncommonly proud of her successful young niece and frequently spoke of her psychic abilities. She had even talked of having her join their group but so far had not coaxed her to one of these meetings.

'I met the niece's husband, Adam Cauliff, at Gert's house at one of her cocktail parties,' Dr. Siegfried Volk told Bonnie. 'Gert seemed extremely fond of him. I don't think he had much interest in our studies and our psychic efforts, but he certainly pleased her by showing up for the party. A charming man. I sent Gert a note expressing my sympathy, and I plan to call on her next week.'

'I'm going to visit her too,' Bonnie said. 'I want to help her and her family in any way I can.'

CHAPTER TWENTY

Earlier that day, Jed Kaplan had set off on his favorite walk, starting at his mother's apartment at Fourteenth Street and First Avenue, and ending up on the Hudson River at the North Cove Marina at the World Financial Center, where Adam Cauliff had kept his cabin cruiser. It was the fifth day in a row that Jed had made this journey, a walk that usually took him a little over an hour, depending on distractions along the way, and each time he enjoyed it more.

And now, just as he had on the previous days, Jed sat staring out over the Hudson, a slight smile on his lips. The thought that *Cornelia II* was no longer arrogantly bobbing in the water there sent a thrill throughout his body so pleasurable it was almost sensual. He savored the image of Adam Cauliff's body being blown to bits, starting with the startling, instantaneous recognition that must have registered in Cauliff's brain, the knowledge that he was indeed dying. Then he thought of the body being torn to pieces, hurtling into the air before dropping into the water—it was an image he relived over and over in his mind, relishing it more each time.

The temperature had been dropping all day, and now that the sun was going down, the breeze from the river had become cold and penetrating. Jed glanced around, noticing that the outdoor tables in the plaza, which had been crowded each of the last four days, were now all but empty. The passengers he saw arriving on the ferry boats from Jersey City and Hoboken walked quickly toward shelter. A bunch of sissies, Jed thought contemptuously. They should try living in the bush for a couple of years.

He observed a cruise liner being piloted toward the Narrows and wondered where it was heading. Europe? he thought. South America? Hell, maybe he should try going to one of those places. Clearly it was time for him to push off. The old lady was driving him crazy, and he could only guess that he must be driving her crazy too.

When she had fixed him breakfast this morning, she said, 'Jed, you're my son and I care about you a lot, but I can't put up with you upsetting me all the time. You've got to get beyond all this. Despite everything you believe, Adam Cauliff was a nice man, or at least *I* thought so. Now, unfortunately, he's dead, so you have no reason to keep hating him. It's time for you to get on to something else. I'll give you money to make a fresh start somewhere.'

Initially she had suggested giving him five thousand bucks. By the time he finished his breakfast, he had gotten her up to twenty-five thousand, plus she had let him see her will, which showed that she was leaving everything to him. Before he finally had agreed to leave town, he made her swear on his father's soul that she would never change the will.

Cauliff had paid her $800,000 for the property. Chances were, given the way his mom scrimped, most of that money would still be there when she turned up her toes.

It certainly wasn't the amount he had hoped for—that property was worth ten times that—but it was the best he could do, now that she had practically given his inheritance away. Jed shrugged and went back to visualizing Adam Cauliff's death.

A witness to the explosion who had been on a boat coming back from the Statue of Liberty had been quoted in the *Post* as saying, 'The boat wasn't moving. I figured they'd dropped anchor and were having a couple of drinks or something. The water was getting choppy, and I remember thinking that the party wouldn't last much longer. Then all of a sudden *boom*. It was like an atomic bomb hit it.'

Jed had cut out that account of the explosion and kept it in his shirt pocket. He enjoyed rereading it, enjoyed visualizing bodies and debris hurling into the air, carried by the force of the explosion. His only real regret was that he hadn't been there to see it.

It was too bad about the other people who got killed, of course, but then they couldn't have been worth much, because they worked with Cauliff, he told himself. They were probably in on his trick of finding senile widows who they could talk into selling off the property they owned for only a fraction of its value. Well, at least there won't be a *Cornelia III*, he exulted.

'Excuse me, sir.'

Startled out of his reverie, Jed sprang up, on the defensive, ready to tell whoever was bothering him to get lost. But instead of the homeless beggar he had expected to confront, he found himself staring into the knowing eyes of a grave-faced man.

'Detective George Brennan,' the man said as he held up his badge.

Too late, Jed acknowledged to himself that hanging around the marina may well have been the stupidest mistake of his whole life.

95

CHAPTER TWENTY-ONE

Dan Minor's search for his mother finally promised to yield some results. The woman at the shelter who recognized the picture of her, and even called her 'Quinny,' had provided him with the first ray of hope he'd had in a long, long time. He had been searching for his mother for so long—without *any* success—that even a glimmer of hope was enough to energize him.

Today, in fact, he was so energized that once he was finished at the hospital for the afternoon, he had quickly changed and raced off to Central Park to continue his search there.

It seemed as though he had been searching for his mother all his life. His mother had disappeared when he was six years old, right after the accident that almost took his life.

He had a clear memory of waking to find her kneeling by his hospital bed, sobbing. Later, he learned that as a result of the accident—she had been drunk when it happened—she was indicted for criminal negligence, and rather than face a terrible public trial, and almost certainly losing custody of her son, she had fled.

Occasionally, on his birthday, he would get an unsigned card that he knew was from her. But for much of his life, it was the only confirmation that he had that she was still alive. Then, one day seven years ago, he had been sitting in the family room at home with his grandmother when he had turned on the television and started surfing through the channels, stopping with casual interest when he saw a documentary on homeless people in Manhattan.

Some of the interviews had been filmed in shelters, others on the street. One of the women interviewed was standing on a street corner on upper Broadway. Dan's grandmother was in the room at the time, reading, but when that woman spoke, his grandmother had jumped up, her eyes suddenly riveted to the screen.

When the interviewer asked the homeless woman her name, she had replied, 'People call me Quinny.'

'Oh, God, it's Kathryn!' his grandmother shrieked. 'Dan, look, look! *It's your mother!*'

Did he actually remember that face, or was it because of all the pictures of her he had devoured over the years that he was sure this woman was indeed his mother? The face on the television screen was careworn, the eyes dulled; still, there were traces of the pretty girl she once had been. The dark hair was generously sprinkled now with gray, and it was worn too loose and full on her shoulders to look anything but unkempt. Still, to his eyes, she was beautiful. She was wearing a shabby wraparound coat that was too big for her. Her hand rested protectively on a shopping cart filled with plastic bags.

She was fifty years old when I saw that program, Dan often thought. She had looked much older.

'Where are you from, Quinny?' the interviewer had asked.

'From here, now.'

'Do you have a family?'

She had looked straight into the camera. 'I had a wonderful little boy, once. I didn't deserve him. He was better off without me, so I left.'

97

The next day Dan's grandparents had hired a private investigator to try to track her down, but Quinny had vanished. Dan did manage to learn something about the way she had lived, and about her frame of mind—facts that saddened him and broke his grandparents' hearts.

Now, several days after finding someone who could identify his mother's photograph, he was more determined than ever to locate her. She's in New York, Dan thought. I will find her. I *will*! But when I *do* find her, what will I say? What will I do?

Of course, he didn't have to worry—he had been rehearsing this reunion for so long. Maybe he would limit his comments to only those words that might mean something to her: 'Stop punishing yourself. It was an accident. If I can forgive you, why can't you forgive yourself?'

He had given his card to Lilly Brown, the woman he had met in the shelter. 'If you see her, just phone me,' he told her. 'Please don't tell her I'm looking for her. She might disappear again.'

Lilly had assured him, 'Quinny will be back. Knowing her, it should be about now. She never stays away from New York for too long at a time, and in the summer she likes to sit in Central Park. She says it's her favorite place in the world. I'll ask around for you. Maybe someone's seen her lately.'

For now I'll have to be content with that, Dan thought as he jogged the paths of Central Park, the sky still light with the setting sun, but the air getting steadily cooler and the wind chilling his damp back and legs. Now that summer is almost here—but please, he thought, don't let this evening be any indication of what summer in New York will be, because she'll freeze—there was always the chance that the woman who called herself 'Quinny' might be found sitting on one of the park benches.

CHAPTER TWENTY-TWO

Cornelius MacDermott arrived at Nell's apartment promptly at six o'clock. When she opened the door for him, they stood apart for a few moments, silently looking at each other. Then he reached out and put his arms around her.

'Nell,' he said, 'remember what the old Irish guys say to the bereaved at wakes? They say, 'I'm sorry for your trouble.' You used to think it was the dumbest remark in the world. In your most smart-alecky voice, you'd say, "You're not sorry for someone's *trouble*. You're sorry they're *experiencing* trouble."'

'I remember,' Nell said.

'And what did I tell you?'

'You said that what the expression means is, "*Your* trouble is *my* trouble. I share your grief."'

'That's right. So just think of me as one of those old Irishmen. In a very real way, your trouble *is* my trouble. And that's why you have to know how very, very sorry I am about Adam. I'd do anything to keep you from having to go through the hurt I know you are experiencing right now.'

Be fair to him, Nell told herself. Mac is eighty-two years old. He has loved me and cared for me as long as I can remember. Maybe he couldn't help being jealous of Adam. There were plenty of women who would have loved to marry Mac after Gram died. I was probably the reason he didn't get involved with any of them.

'I know you would,' she told him, 'and I'm glad you're here. I guess I just need some time to let everything sink in.'

'Well, unfortunately, Nell, you don't have time,' Mac told her abruptly. 'Come on. Let's sit down. We've got to talk.'

Not knowing quite what to expect, she obeyed, following him into the living room.

As soon as she was seated, Mac began: 'Nell, I realize that this is an awful time for you, but there are some things that we have to talk about. You haven't even had Adam's memorial Mass yet, and here I am about to start lobbing some tough questions at you. I'm sorry to move on you like this. Maybe you'll want to throw me out, and if you do, I'll understand. But some things simply can't wait.'

Nell knew now what he was going to say.

'This isn't just *any* election year. It's a presidential election year. You know as well as I do that anything can happen, but our guy is ahead big time, and unless he does something really stupid, he's going to be the next president.'

He probably *is* going to be president, Nell thought, and he'll make a good one. For the first time since she heard the news of Adam's death, she felt a stirring within her—a first sign that life was returning. She looked at her grandfather and realized that his eyes seemed brighter than she had seen them in a while. Nothing like a political campaign to get the old war horse up and running, she thought.

'Nell, I just learned that a couple more guys are about to throw their hats in the ring for my old seat. Tim Cross and Salvatore Bruno.'

100

'Tim Cross has been nothing but a wimp on the council, and Sal Bruno has missed more Senate votes in Albany than the mother of ten kids has missed periods,' Nell snapped.

'That's my girl. You could have won that seat.'

'*Could have* won? What are you talking about, Mac? *I am going to go for it.* I *have* to.'

'You may not get the chance.'

'I repeat: what are you talking about, Mac?'

'There's no easy way to say it, Nell, but Robert Walters and Len Arsdale came to see me this morning. A dozen building contractors have signed statements saying they paid bribes in the millions of dollars to the Walters and Arsdale firm in order to land the big jobs. Robert and Len are two fine men. I've known them all my life. They never pulled that stuff. They never took any bribes.'

'What are you trying to tell me, Mac?'

'Nell, I'm telling you that Adam was probably on the take.'

She looked at her grandfather for a moment, then shook her head. 'No, Mac, I don't believe that. He wouldn't do it. It's also much too easy to lay blame on a dead man, not to mention convenient. Did anyone say they actually handed Adam the money?'

'Winifred was the go-between.'

'*Winifred!* For heaven's sake, Mac, that woman didn't have the gumption of a sunflower. What makes you think she'd be capable of putting together a bribery scheme?'

'That's exactly it. While Robert and Len agree that Winifred knew the business inside out and would have known how to do a scam, they also agree that she'd never try to do something like that

101

on her own.'

'Mac,' Nell protested, 'listen to what you're saying. You're taking the word of your old buddies that they're pure as the driven snow and that my husband was a thief. Isn't it entirely possible that by dying, he has provided them the perfect scapegoat for their own misdeeds?'

'Well, let me ask you this: where did Adam get the money to buy that property on Twenty-eighth Street?'

'He got it from me.'

Cornelius MacDermott stared at her. 'Don't tell me you invaded your trust fund.'

'It was mine to invade, wasn't it? I lent Adam the money to buy that loft property and to open his own firm. If he'd actually been taking money as you imply, would he have needed to borrow from me?'

'He would if he didn't want to leave a paper trail. Nell, get this straight—if it comes out that your husband was involved in a bribery scandal, you can kiss your chance of being a congresswoman goodbye.'

'Mac, at the moment I'm much more interested in protecting Adam's memory than I am in worrying about my own political future.' This isn't real, Nell thought, putting her hands over her face for a moment. In a few minutes I'll wake up from a bad dream and Adam will be here and none of this will have happened.

Nell stood suddenly and crossed to the window. Winifred, she thought. Quiet, timid Winifred. I saw her step off that elevator and immediately I knew she was going to die. Could I have prevented it? she wondered. Could I have warned her?

From what Mac says, Walters and Arsdale are

102

sure she was cheating. I can't believe Adam would have taken her with him into his company if he had thought she was dishonest.

It's obvious, she decided. If there was bribery going on, Adam didn't know anything about it.

'Nell, you realize that this throws a whole new light on the explosion,' Mac said, intruding upon her thoughts. 'It couldn't have been accidental, and almost certainly it was intended to make sure that someone on that boat wouldn't talk to the district attorney's office.'

It's like the riptide, Nell thought, turning back to her grandfather. Wave after wave keeps crashing into me, and I can't stay afloat. I'm getting drawn farther and farther out to sea.

They talked a few minutes more about the explosion, and about the bribery scheme described by Walters and Arsdale. Sensing that Nell was drawing further and further away, Mac tried to persuade her to go out with him for dinner, but she turned him down.

'Mac, I couldn't swallow anything right now. But soon, I promise. Soon I'll be able to talk about all this,' she said.

When he left, Nell went into the bedroom and opened the door of Adam's closet. The navy-blue jacket he had worn home from Philadelphia was on the hanger where she had hung it the next morning. When Winifred came by on Friday afternoon, I must have given her his other one, she thought, just like this one except it had silver buttons. Then this was the one he wore the day before he died.

Nell took it off the hanger and slipped her arms through the sleeves. She had expected to feel comforted, almost as though Adam's arms were around her, but instead she had a chilling sense of alienation, following a sudden, startling remembrance of the angry outburst between them that last morning that had caused him to rush away without it.

Still wearing the jacket, she walked restlessly around the room. A premise, unbidden and unwelcome, was insinuating itself into her mind. Adam had been on edge for months. Besides the normal pressure of opening a new firm, had there been something else upsetting him? Was it possible that there really was something going on that she had not caught wind of? Did he have anything at all to fear from an investigation?

She stopped for a moment and stood still, weighing what Mac had told her. Then she shook her head. No. No, I'll never believe that, she thought.

Thursday, June 15

CHAPTER TWENTY-THREE

After getting the call from his partner about the guy he had picked up at the marina the day before and brought in for questioning, Jack Sclafani rushed downtown to meet George Brennan.

'It's almost too easy,' Brennan told him. 'If you look at the way it's shaping up, this guy not only did it, but then just sat around waiting for us to pick him up.'

He gave Jack a rundown on Jed Kaplan: 'Thirty-eight years old. Raised in Manhattan, over in Stuyvesant Town, off East Fourteenth Street. Always in trouble. His juvenile court record is sealed, but as an adult he served a couple of brief terms on Riker's Island for beating up guys in bars. Apparently he gets really mean when he hits the booze or gets into any drugs.'

Brennan shook his head in disgust as he continued: 'Father and grandfather were well-respected furriers. Mother's a nice old lady. Family owned a loft building on Twenty-eighth Street. Adam Cauliff bought it from Kaplan's mother at a fair enough price last year. Kaplan got back to New York last month, after five years in Australia. From what the neighbors say, he went berserk when he heard his mother had sold the building.

'What apparently has him nuts is that the lot more than tripled in value because the Vandermeer mansion, an old building next door to it that was a historical landmark, burned down last September. You can't be a historical landmark if you're a pile of ashes, so that property was sold to Peter Lang, the hotshot real estate entrepreneur, who, if you remember, was the guy who was supposed to be on the boat when it blew up, but who didn't make it to the meeting because of an accident on the way into the city.'

Brennan looked down at his desk and reached for the container of coffee he had allowed to get cold. 'Adam Cauliff was involved in a deal with Lang to build a fancy apartment-office-shopping complex on the combined parcels. He designed a tower to stand on the exact spot where the Kaplans used to hang their furs. So we've got motive— young Kaplan was furious that the lot had been sold for a price less than it proved to be worth— and opportunity. But is that enough to arrest and convict him? Absolutely not, but it's a good start. Come on with me. He's inside.'

Kaplan looked up at him and sneered.

Jack did not need more than one glance at Kaplan to know they were dealing with a small-time hood. Everything about his appearance said bad news: the furtive eyes; the sneer that seemed etched on his face; the way he sat at the table in a crouched position, as though he might spring up to attack—or escape. Plus the faint, sweet odor of pot clung to his clothes.

I'll bet he has a rap sheet in Australia too, Jack thought.

'Am I under arrest?' he demanded.

The two detectives looked at each other. 'No, you are not,' George Brennan said.

Kaplan pushed back his chair. 'I'm out of here.'

George Brennan waited until they were gone, then turned to his old friend and asked reflectively, 'What do you think?'

108

'Of Kaplan? He's a bum,' Jack Sclafani said. 'And do I think he's capable of blowing up that boat? Yes, I do.' He paused. 'What bothers me, though, is that if he did blow those people to kingdom come, I don't think he'd be stupid enough to hang around the marina. He may be sleazy, but is he an idiot?'

CHAPTER TWENTY-FOUR

In the hours shortly before dawn, Ken and Regina Tucker were startled from their sleep by shrieks of terror coming from the bedroom of their son, Ben. It was the second time since their ill-fated trip to New York City that Ben had experienced frightening nightmares.

They both sprang from bed and raced down the hall, pushed open the door to their son's room, flipped on the light and rushed in. Ken grabbed the little boy and held him tightly against him.

'It's all right, guy, it's all right,' he said soothingly.

'Make the snake go away,' Ben sobbed. 'Make it go away.'

'Ben, it was just a bad dream,' Regina said as she smoothed his forehead. 'We're here with you; you're safe.'

'Tell us about it,' Ken urged.

'We were floating on the river, and I was looking out over the railing. And then the other boat . . .' Ben's eyes were still closed as his voice faltered and trailed off.

His parents looked at each other. 'He's

trembling all over,' Regina whispered.

It took almost half an hour before they were sure Ben had settled back into sleep. When they returned to their own bedroom, Ken said quietly, 'I think we'd better get Ben to a counselor. I'm sure no expert on the subject, but from what I've read and picked up on TV, this looks like a case of what I believe they call post-traumatic stress syndrome.'

He sat on the edge of the bed. 'What a lousy break. You try to give your kid a memorable day in New York, and he has the hard luck to be looking straight at a boat that explodes with four people on it. I wish we'd just stayed home.'

'Do you think he actually saw those people blown apart?'

'With his kind of vision, he might have, the poor kid. But he's young, and resilient. With a little help, he'll be fine. I know it's almost time to get up, but let's try to get a few minutes' more sleep. I've got a busy day ahead of me, and I don't want to be dozing out right in the middle of it.'

Regina Tucker turned off the light and lay down, moving close to her husband for comfort. Why would Ben be dreaming of snakes? she wondered. Maybe it's because he knows I've always been afraid of them, she thought. I've probably talked about it too much around him. But that still doesn't explain why he's tied my fear of snakes into the nightmare about the boat.

Feeling wretched and guilty, she closed her eyes and willed herself to sleep, even while every sense strained to be alert for the first sound of Ben crying out in terror again.

CHAPTER TWENTY-FIVE

At the memorial Mass for Adam Cauliff, held late on that Thursday morning, Nell sat in the first pew of the church, her grandfather and great-aunt on either side of her. She felt detached, almost like an outsider observing the ceremony. As the ritual progressed, memories washed over her, and random thoughts rushed through her mind.

She had sat here in this same pew twenty-two years ago at exactly the same kind of Mass—for her mother and father. *Their* bodies, like Adam's, had been lost in the explosion and fire when their plane crashed.

Adam had been an only child, the son of two only children.

I was an only child, the daughter of two only children.

His father had died when he was in high school, his mother shortly after he finished college.

Was that part of what drew her to him? she wondered. A shared sense of isolation?

She remembered that on their first date, Adam had said, 'I don't go back to North Dakota anymore. I don't have relatives there, and I feel a lot closer to the friends I made in college then I do to kids I grew up with.'

Since Adam's death, she hadn't heard from any of those college friends. She didn't think any of them were there at the Mass.

My life was so full, she thought. So busy. There was always so much going on. I just fit Adam into my routine the way I would any new assignment or

111

responsibility. I took him for granted in so many ways. I never pushed him to talk about his childhood. I never once asked if he'd like to have any of his old friends visit us.

On the other hand, did Adam ever suggest that they be invited?

I would have said yes in a minute, Nell told herself.

The church was packed with her friends, with Mac's friends, with the constituents who considered them family.

Mac's hand was under her arm, urging her to stand. Monsignor Duncan was reading the Gospel.

Lazarus, who came back from the dead.

Come back, Adam, please come back, she pleaded.

Monsignor talked about the senseless violence that had taken the lives of four innocent people. Then he turned back to the altar.

The pause before the final blessing, Nell thought, then realized that Mac had stepped into the aisle and was walking up the sanctuary steps.

Mac stood at the lectern. 'Adam was my grandson by marriage,' he began.

Mac is eulogizing Adam, Nell thought. He didn't tell me he was going to do that. Then she had the disturbing thought that perhaps no one else had volunteered to speak; no one else either knew Adam well enough or cared for him enough to eulogize him.

For a moment she felt herself on the verge of hysterical laughter, as she remembered a joke Mac sometimes told at political rallies when he was poking fun at an opponent: 'Pat Murphy is dead, and at the Mass, the priest gets up and asks for a

112

few kind words about him. Now Pat, for sufficient reason, didn't have a friend in the world, so no one stands up to speak for him. The priest again asks for a volunteer to say a few words and again no one comes forward. The third time he asks, the priest is pretty upset, and he practically shouts, 'We'll not be leaving this church until someone speaks for Pat Murphy.' Hearing that, one fellow gets up and says, 'His brother was worse.'

Adam, why isn't there someone here to speak for *you*? Nell thought. Why did someone hate you enough to kill you?

Mac had returned to the pew. Next came the final blessing, then the closing music. The Mass was over.

As Nell walked with Mac and Gert from the church, a woman reached out and stopped her. 'Could I talk to you?' she asked. 'Please. It's very important.'

'Of course.' Nell stepped away from Mac and Gert. I know this woman, she thought. But from where?

The woman appeared to be about Nell's own age, and, like Nell, was dressed in black. Her eyes were puffy, and lines of grief were etched in her face. It's Lisa Ryan, Nell thought, remembering her finally from the picture she had seen in the newspaper. Her husband Jimmy was on the boat with Adam. She phoned me after the stories came out suggesting that the explosion may have been an act of suicide, and that he may have been responsible for the deaths. When she phoned, she acknowledged that her husband had been depressed, but she insisted that he never would have deliberately hurt anyone else.

'Mrs. Cauliff,' Lisa began hurriedly, 'I wonder if I can meet with you privately. And soon. It's very important.' She glanced around nervously. Suddenly her eyes widened, and a look of sheer panic came over her. 'I'm sorry I bothered you,' she said abruptly, as she turned and rushed down the steps of the church.

She's *terrified*, Nell thought. But of what? And what was that all about?

She looked back and recognized Detective Brennan, who along with another man was coming out of the church and approaching her. Why, she wondered, would the sight of those two men terrify Jimmy Ryan's widow?

CHAPTER TWENTY-SIX

On that Thursday afternoon, Bonnie Wilson phoned Gert MacDermott and asked if it would be convenient for her to stop by for a brief visit.

'Bonnie, in all honesty, today isn't the best for me,' Gert said. 'The memorial Mass for Adam Cauliff was this morning, and afterward my brother had arranged for people to go to the Plaza Athenée for lunch. I just got home. It's been a long day.'

'Gert, I just feel I should come by. I can be there in twenty minutes, and I promise I won't stay more than half an hour.'

Gert sighed as the phone clicked in her ear. After the emotional seesaw of the day, she had looked forward to simply putting on a robe and making a cup of tea.

I wish that somewhere along the way I'd learned

to be a little more assertive, more forceful, she thought. On the other hand, Cornelius is probably forceful enough for both of us, she decided.

It was good of him to speak so beautifully about Adam, she thought. She had told him that after the service.

'Any politician worth a damn can speak beautifully about anyone, Gert,' he had responded gruffly. 'After all these years of listening to me throw the baloney, you should know that.'

Irritated at his bluntness, she had warned him not to dare say that to Nell, and to his credit he kept his mouth shut when Nell thanked him.

Oh, poor Nell, she reflected, remembering her demeanor at the service this morning. If only she had shown some emotion. Instead she just sat there, as though in a daze. It was almost the way she reacted to the Mass for Richard and Joan all those years ago.

That day Cornelius had cried silently throughout the Mass. It had been ten-year-old Nell who had patted his hand and tried to comfort him. Then, as today, she had been dry-eyed.

I wish she would let me stay with her for a little while, Gert thought. She's not accepting Adam's death, just not dealing with it at all. At lunch after the Mass, she had said, 'It still feels so unreal.'

Gert sighed as she crossed her bedroom and opened a closet. Dear God, I wish Bonnie hadn't insisted on coming over right now, but at least I can change into something a little more comfortable before she gets here.

She slipped into some slacks and a cotton cardigan, and put on comfortable slippers. She splashed water on her face and brushed her hair.

115

Feeling somewhat refreshed, Gert went back to the living room just as the intercom buzzed and the doorman asked if she was expecting Miss Wilson.

*   *   *

'I know you would have preferred that I didn't come,' Bonnie said as she came into the apartment, 'but I felt it was necessary.' Her intense gray eyes studied Gert's face. 'Don't worry so much,' she said calmly. 'I think I can help your niece. I have a feeling you were just about to make yourself a cup of tea. Why don't we both have one?'

A few minutes later the two women sat across from each other at a small table in the kitchen.

'I remember my grandmother used to read tea leaves,' Bonnie said. 'She was amazingly accurate. I'm sure she had natural psychic powers that she didn't understand. After she correctly predicted that a cousin would become very ill, my grandfather begged her to stop reading for people. He convinced her that the power of suggestion was the reason her cousin was sick.'

Bonnie's long fingers were wrapped around the cup. A few tea leaves had slipped through the strainer, and she stared down at them reflectively. Her black hair fell forward, shielding her face. Gert studied the younger woman with growing uneasiness. *She knows something*, she thought. She's going to give me bad news. I can tell.

'Gert, you know what independent-voice phenomena are, don't you?' Bonnie asked suddenly.

'Yes, of course. Or I should say I've heard about it. From my understanding, it's very rare.'

116

'Yes, it is. A new client came to me for a consultation yesterday. I was able to communicate with her mother on the other side, and I think I helped her to accept her mother's death. But then, just as her mother told me she was tired and had to leave us, I felt that there was someone else who was trying to reach me.'

Gert put down her cup.

'My client left, and I sat quietly for a little while, waiting to see if I was supposed to receive a message. Then I heard it—a man's voice. But it was so soft that at first I couldn't understand what he was saying. I waited and could feel his effort, his struggle to get through to me, and then I realized he was saying a name over and over: *"Nell. Nell. Nell."*'

'Was it . . . ?' Gert's voice trailed off.

Bonnie's eyes had widened, become almost luminous. The dark gray iris had deepened to jet black. She nodded. 'I asked him to give me his name. His energy was almost gone, so he was barely able to communicate with me. But just before he left me, he said, 'Adam. I am Adam.'

CHAPTER TWENTY-SEVEN

When the luncheon ended, Nell had insisted on walking home alone from the Plaza Athenée. She knew the ten-block walk back to her apartment would do her good, and she wanted the time to herself, just to think.

'Mac, I'm fine,' she had said to her grandfather, reassuring him. 'Please stop worrying about me.'

117

She finally slipped away while he was still holding court with the last of the luncheon guests, old friends who also happened to be movers and shakers in the party. Several of them had barely finished offering their condolences before they started talking bluntly with her about politics.

Mike Powers, for example, had confided, 'Nell, to say it straight, Bob Gorman hasn't accomplished diddley-squat in the two years he's had Mac's seat. We're glad he's going to go work for one of those dot-com Internet outfits. Good riddance to him, I say. With you on the ticket, we can win.'

Can I win? Nell wondered as she walked up Madison Avenue. Will you still feel that way when you find out Adam's former employers are trying to throw the blame for their own bid rigging and bribery on Adam and Winifred?

It's so easy to blame two people who aren't around to defend themselves, she thought angrily. And so convenient.

Still, Nell realized that a persistent thought had been rattling around in her subconscious: Was it possible that Adam and Winifred were dead because they knew too much about the bribery scandal that the district attorney was investigating?

If Adam was in any way involved, even minimally, she could lose the seat for the party, assuming it came out after she announced her candidacy.

And what was that scene at the church this morning? Why did Lisa Ryan panic when she saw the detectives who were investigating the explosion of the boat? Was it possible her husband was responsible for the explosion? Or could he perhaps have been the target? According to the

118

newspapers, he had been out of work for quite some time, and his wife had said it was because he had complained about substandard material being used on a job. Was there something *else* he knew that made him dangerous?

As she walked, Nell became aware of the sun on her face. Finally lifting her head enough to look around, she realized it was a picture-perfect June afternoon. Adam and I used to walk along Madison Avenue all the time, she thought sadly. They both liked to look in the shop windows, though only rarely did either of them buy anything. Occasionally they would treat themselves to a meal at one of the restaurants there; more often they would stop for coffee at one of the cafés.

She never failed to marvel that so many restaurants managed to survive in New York. She passed two of the smallest, both with tiny wrought-iron tables and chairs on the sidewalk.

As she watched, two women settled at one table, dropping their packages beside them. 'Sidewalk cafés make me feel as though I'm in Paris,' one of them said.

Adam and I spent our honeymoon in Paris, Nell remembered. It was his first time there. I loved showing him around.

Mac had been upset that she and Adam had known each other such a brief time before they were married. 'Give it a year,' he had counseled. 'Then I'll throw you a wedding that will be the talk of the town. Good publicity too.'

He couldn't understand why she had never wanted a big wedding, but to her it was obvious. Big weddings were for people who had lots of family. She would have needed cousins to be

119

bridesmaids; grandmothers to give sentimental presents; nieces to be flower girls and steal the show.

She and Adam had talked about that. All the friends in the world don't quite make up for having your own immediate family around at one of those big bashes, and since that was something that neither of them had, except for Mac and Gert, of course, they had agreed to keep it very simple.

'Let's have a really small, private wedding,' Adam had said. 'We don't need a lot of reporters popping flashbulbs in our faces. And if I start asking my friends, there's no drawing the line.'

Where were those friends today? Nell wondered.

Mac had exploded when she told him she and Adam had set the date.

'Who the hell is this guy? Nell. You hardly know him. Okay, so he's an architect from North Dakota who came to New York with a lousy starter job. What else do you know about him?'

Mac—being Mac—had him checked out. 'That college he attended is a cockamamie factory, Nell. Trust me, this guy is no Stanford White. And the places he's worked at are mom-and-pop operations, small-time builders of shopping centers, senior-citizen housing. That kind of stuff.'

But Mac—being Mac—was all bark and no bite where I was concerned—as always, Nell thought. Once he accepted the fact that she had made up her mind, he introduced Adam to his friends Robert Walters and Len Arsdale, and they gave him a job.

She arrived at the door of her own building. Eleven years ago when she bought her co-op, she had been fresh out of college. Mac couldn't understand why she just didn't continue to live with

120

him in his brownstone.

'You're going to run the New York office for me and go to law school at night. Save your money,' he said.

'It's time, Mac,' she had insisted.

Carlo, the doorman, had been new to the building then. She remembered that he had helped her unload the car, carrying the few things she brought from Mac's house. Today he wore an expression of concern as he opened the door for her. 'Pretty rough day for you, Ms. MacDermott,' he said, sympathy showing in his eyes.

'I'd say so, Carlo.' Nell felt oddly comforted by the concern in the man's voice.

'Hope you can just take it easy for the rest of the day.'

'That's exactly what I'm going to do.'

'You know, I was thinking about that lady who worked for Mr. Cauliff,' Carlo said.

'You mean Winifred Johnson?'

'Yeah, that one. She was here last week, the day of the accident.'

'That's right.'

'She was always so nervous when she was here; I mean she seemed so timid.'

'That's right,' Nell said again.

'Last week, just when I was letting her out, her cell phone rang. She stopped to answer it. I couldn't help but overhear. It was her mother. I guess she's in a nursing home?'

'Yes, she's in Old Woods Manor up in White Plains. The father of a friend of mine was there. It's about as nice as those places get.'

'I could tell Ms. Johnson's mother was complaining that she felt depressed,' Carlo said. 'I

121

hope the old lady has someone to visit her now that Ms. Johnson is dead.'

*   *   *

An hour later, showered and changed into a denim jacket and slacks, Nell took the elevator down to the garage level and got into her car. She felt ashamed that it had not occurred to her all week to contact Winifred's mother, at least to offer sympathy, and to see if there was anything she could do for her.

But as Nell drove up the always-crowded FDR Drive, she acknowledged to herself that there was a second reason for this sudden visit to Old Woods Manor. The friend whose father had been a resident there had told her it was a very expensive facility. As she thought about it, Nell had begun to wonder how long Mrs. Rhoda Johnson had been living at the manor, and how had Winifred managed to pay for it?

She remembered that Adam had remarked that there was nothing Winifred didn't know about the ins and outs of deal making in the construction business. And Mac had suggested that Winifred might not be as much a mouse as everyone thought.

Now Nell wondered if the needs of an ailing mother might not have given Winifred the impetus she needed to cash in on her knowledge of under-the-table deal making. Maybe she did know something about the bribes Walters and Arsdale mentioned to Mac. And maybe *she* was the reason the boat had exploded—and Adam had been killed.

122

CHAPTER TWENTY-EIGHT

Peter Lang had fully intended to attend the memorial Mass held for Adam Cauliff, but at the last minute he received a call from Curtis Little, an officer of Overland Bank, one of the potential investment partners in the Vandermeer Tower project. Little wanted him to give his associate John Hilmer an update on the status of the negotiations. The only available time for the meeting conflicted with the Mass.

They met in the boardroom of Peter's spacious offices on Forty-ninth Street and Avenue of the Americas.

'My father never stopped complaining when they changed the name of Sixth Avenue to Avenue of the Americas,' Peter said to Hilmer as they took their places at the conference table. 'These were his offices originally, and to the day he retired he always told people he worked on Sixth Avenue. He was a very down-to-earth man.'

Hilmer smiled slightly. It was his first meeting with the legendary Peter Lang, and it was apparent that there was nothing particularly 'down-to-earth' about *him*. Even with the cuts and bruises from his accident still showing, Lang was a handsome man who exuded self-confidence and wore his expensive clothes with casual grace.

The slightly bantering tone disappeared as Lang pointed to a cloth-covered structure on the table. 'Curt, in a few minutes you and John are going to see a model of an apartment-office-shopping complex that was designed by Ian Maxwell. As you

123

may know, Maxwell just completed an award-winning, fifty-five story residential and business building on Lake Michigan. It's considered by many to be one of the most imaginative and beautiful structures constructed in Chicago in the last twenty years.'

He paused, and the others saw an expression of pain come over his face.

With an apologetic smile Lang reached for a pill and washed it down with a quick sip of water.

'I know I look as though I've been mugged, but my real problem is the cracked rib,' he explained.

Curtis Little, fiftyish, silver-haired, and exuding nervous energy, said dryly, 'I'm sure under the circumstances you're happy to settle for the bruises and the cracked rib, Peter. I know I would be.' Restlessly his fingers tapped the tabletop. 'Which brings us to the point of this meeting. Where do we stand with Adam Cauliff's estate?'

'Curt, you've been in on this from the start,' Peter said, 'but let me fill you in, John. As you know, the blocks between Twenty-third and Thirty-first Streets on the West Side are the next area in Manhattan ripe for renovation. As a point of fact, the renovation is already well under way. I had been trying for some time to get the Vandermeer mansion removed from designated landmark status. We all agree that it is an outrage that vital Manhattan property is being held hostage because of sentimental attachments to useless, broken-down structures that should have been razed many years ago. The Vandermeer place was a particularly egregious example of bureaucracy run amuck—not only had it become an eyesore, but it hadn't been a particularly interesting building in the first place.'

124

Lang leaned back in his chair, trying to find a more comfortable position. 'Despite my conviction that the building was undeserving of landmark status, I confess that I didn't actually think I'd ever be successful in having the Board of Estimate remove the mansion from its list of protected structures. That's why I never did go after the Kaplan property adjacent to it. I kept pressuring the board, though, and finally I succeeded. The irony, of course, is that the mansion burned down—with that unfortunate woman in it—only hours after the Board of Estimate voted to declassify it.' He flashed a quick, sad smile.

Lang reached again for the water glass. He let the water linger on his swollen lip before he continued. 'As you know, while I was working to free up the Vandermeer place, Adam Cauliff bought the Kaplan property. I offered him twice what he paid for it, but that wasn't what he wanted. He proposed instead that he be the architect of the complex we planned to build, and he wanted to involve Sam Krause in the construction.'

Curtis Little stirred restlessly. 'Peter, we are not prepared to provide funding for the building Adam Cauliff proposed to erect. It is imitative, pedantic, unexciting and a hodgepodge of architectural styles.'

'I happen to agree,' Lang said promptly. 'Adam thought he could tie the sale of the property in to a contract for himself as architect. He thought we'd do anything to get our hands on the Kaplan parcel. He was mistaken. Which is what brings me to Ian Maxwell's design. Several of my associates have worked with Ian in the past. At their suggestion, I called him.'

125

Peter leaned forward and pulled the cloth off the structure on the table, revealing a scale model of a building with a postmodern, art deco façade.

'Ian was in town two weeks ago. I took him to the site and explained the problem. This is a tentative idea of how he believes he can erect the kind of tower complex we want without using the Kaplan property Adam Cauliff owned. I conveyed to Adam last week the fact that we had developed an alternative plan.'

'Cauliff knew we weren't going along with his proposal?' Little asked.

'Yes, he did. He'd opened his own office on the expectation that we couldn't do without him, but he was wrong. I saw his wife—or widow, I should say—yesterday. I told her it was important that I see her on a business matter next week. At that time I'll explain that we don't need her parcel—let's call it the Kaplan parcel for clarity—but that we'll pay fair market value for it if she is willing to sell.'

'Then if she goes along . . .' Curtis Little began.

'If she goes along with us, Ian Maxwell will design our building with the tower to the side as we'd originally hoped to have it. Otherwise, as I explained to Adam, the tower will be in the rear of the structure, which will work perfectly well, if not *as* well.'

'Would Adam Cauliff have gone along with fair market value for the Kaplan property?' John Hilmer asked.

Peter Lang smiled. 'Of course he would have. Adam had an inflated ego and an unrealistic opinion of his own potential, both as an architect and as a businessman, but he wasn't stupid. That's not to say that he was particularly happy that I offered to take the Kaplan site off his hands for a modest profit. But I suggested to him that if he didn't accept our proposal to sell, the best use of the property would be to donate it to the city for a pocket park.' He gave a thin, grim smile at his own joke.

Curtis Little was studying the scale model. 'Peter, you *could* put the tower at the back of the structure, but you'd lose most of the aesthetic value of the building and a hell of a lot of rentable footage. I'm not at all sure that we'd be putting our money into it if that were the case.'

Peter Lang smiled. 'Of course you wouldn't. But Adam Cauliff didn't know that. He was just a small-town guy playing in a league in which he didn't belong. Trust me, he would have sold us the property—and at our price.'

John Hilmer, newly appointed as vice president in charge of venture capital and investment for Overland Bank, had himself come up the hard way. As he studied Peter Lang across the table, and thought about how he had been handed everything in life, he felt a growing distaste for the man.

A minor traffic accident had kept Lang from being killed in the fatal explosion of Cauliff's boat. But not once in talking about the poor guy had Lang expressed even the slightest suggestion of regret that Adam Cauliff and three other people had lost their lives on that boat.

Lang is *still* furious that Adam Cauliff was shrewd enough to beat him to snapping up the Kaplan property, Hilmer thought. He had found a way to make Cauliff believe he could get his funding for the building without that parcel, and now that the guy is dead, he's licking his chops because he's sure he'll get the Kaplan property at his price. *Not* a nice guy, even in a hardball business.

As Hilmer got up to leave, another thought hit him. His son, a defensive tackle on his college football team, often came out of a game looking a heck of a lot worse than Peter Lang, who had tangled with a trailer truck.

CHAPTER TWENTY-NINE

Carrying hot pastrami sandwiches and containers of steaming coffee, Jack Sclafani and George Brennan went back to Jack's office after the memorial Mass. They ate quietly, both men deep in thought.

Then, in sync, they stuffed the aluminum foil, napkins and uneaten garlic pickles into the plastic lunch bags and tossed them in the wastebasket. As they sipped the last of the coffee, they looked at each other.

'What's your take on the Widow Ryan?' Jack Brennan asked.

'Scared. Worried like crazy about something. She ran like a rabbit caught in Farmer McGregor's cabbage patch when she saw us.'

'What's she got to be afraid of?'

'Whatever it is, she wants to get it off her chest.'

Brennan smiled. 'Catholic guilt? The need to confess?'

Both men were practicing Catholics, and they had long ago agreed that anyone raised Catholic had been bred to confess sins and ask forgiveness. They joked that sometimes it made their job easier.

Outside the church after the Mass, Jack Sclafani had been closer to Lisa Ryan than his partner when she looked past Nell MacDermott and saw him approaching. She was panicky, he thought. That was fear I saw in her eyes. I'd give a lot to know what she was saying—or, more likely, *would have said*—to the MacDermott woman if she hadn't spotted us first. 'I think we should pay her a visit,' he said slowly. 'She knows something that scares her, and she doesn't know what to do about it.'

'You think she may have some proof that her husband *did* cause that explosion?' Brennan asked.

'She has proof of *something*. Too soon to know what it is, though. Any report from Interpol on Kaplan?'

Brennan reached for the phone. 'I'll call downstairs and see if anything came in since I left.'

Jack Sclafani's pulse quickened at the sudden tension he saw in Brennan's face as he inquired about the Interpol response. He's got something, Sclafani thought.

Brennan finished his call and replaced the receiver. 'Just as we suspected, Kaplan has a rap sheet in Australia as long as the Barrier Reef. Most of it is petty stuff—except one conviction that put him away for a year. Now, get this: he was nabbed carrying explosives in the trunk of his car. He was working for a demolition company at the time and had stolen the explosives from the job site. Fortunately, they did catch him. But unfortunately, they never did find out what he intended to do with the stuff. They suspected that he'd been paid to blow up something, but they were never able to prove it.'

Brennan stood up. 'I think it's time to take another look at Kaplan, don't you?'

'Search warrant?'

'You bet. With his record and his open hostility to Adam Cauliff, I think the judge will go along with it. We could have our search warrant later this afternoon.'

'I still want to talk to Lisa Ryan,' Jack Sclafani said. 'Even if I saw Kaplan with a stick of dynamite in his hand, my hunch would still be that whatever is bugging *her* is the key to what happened on the boat that night.'

CHAPTER THIRTY

Old Woods Manor was only a few blocks off busy Route 287 in Westchester County, just north of New York City, but when Nell turned up the long driveway that led to the facility, the setting changed dramatically. All traces of suburbia disappeared. The handsome stone edifice ahead of her might have been the country residence of a wealthy landowner somewhere in England.

When her grandfather was a congressman, she had often accompanied him on fact-finding missions. At his side, she had observed the entire spectrum of nursing homes, from facilities that obviously should be closed, to modest but adequate extensions of small hospitals, to well-run, carefully planned—sometimes even luxurious—facilities.

As she parked her car, went inside and was greeted by a clerk in the expensively furnished reception room, her impression solidified that this place was the crème de la crème of assisted-living facilities.

An attractive woman who appeared to be in her early sixties escorted Nell to the elevator and rode with her to the second floor.

She introduced herself as Georgina Matthews. 'I volunteer here a few afternoons a week,' she explained. 'Mrs. Johnson is in suite 216. Her daughter's death has been such a blow to her. We're all trying to help her any way we can, but I warn you—she's in an emotional state in which she's angry at the world.'

Well, that makes two of us, Nell thought.

They got out of the elevator on the second floor and walked down the tastefully carpeted hallway. On the way, they passed several elderly people using walkers or in wheelchairs. Georgina Matthews had a smile or quick word for each of them.

With a practiced eye, Nell registered the fact that all of the elderly people she saw looked well cared for and exquisitely well groomed. 'What is the ratio of attendants to residents?' she asked.

'A good question,' Matthews responded. 'There are two for every three residents. Of course, that includes RNs and therapists.' She stopped. 'This is Mrs. Johnson's apartment. She's expecting you.' She tapped on the door, then opened it.

Rhoda Johnson was resting in a recliner, her eyes closed, her feet up, a light blanket covering her. Her physical appearance surprised Nell. She appeared to be in her late seventies, a broad-shouldered woman with luxurious salt-and-pepper hair.

131

Nell was momentarily startled by the contrast between mother and daughter. Winifred had been painfully thin. Her hair had been straight and fine textured. Nell had expected that she would have resembled her mother. But obviously Rhoda Johnson had been fashioned from a different mold.

She opened her eyes as they entered the room, and she fixed her gaze on Nell. 'They told me you were coming. I guess I should be grateful.'

'Now Mrs. Johnson,' Georgina Matthews cautioned.

Rhoda Johnson ignored her. 'Winifred was doing just fine working at Walters and Arsdale all those years. They'd even given her enough of a raise so she could move me here. I hated the last nursing home. I told her over and over to stay put instead of going with your husband when he opened his own firm, but she wouldn't listen. Well, was I right?'

'I'm very, very sorry about Winifred,' Nell said. 'I know this is awful for you too. I wanted to see if I could help you in any way.' She could sense the quick side glance from Mrs. Matthews. She has to know about Adam, Nell thought, but they didn't connect what happened to Winifred with me when I phoned.

In a gesture of spontaneous sympathy, Georgina Matthews touched Nell's arm. 'I didn't realize,' she murmured. 'I'll leave you two to chat.' She turned to Rhoda Johnson. 'You be nice.'

Nell waited until the door closed behind her. 'Mrs. Johnson, I understand how sad and frightened you must feel. I feel the same way myself. That's why I wanted to see you.'

She pulled a chair close and impulsively kissed

132

Rhoda Johnson's cheek. 'If you'd rather, I won't stay. I do understand,' she said.

'I guess it's not your fault.' Mrs. Johnson's tone was only mildly belligerent. 'But why did your husband keep after Winifred to give up her job? Why didn't he open his own place first, see if it worked out? Winifred had a good job with a good income and lots of security. Did she think of *me* when she took a chance and gave it up to work for your husband? No, she did *not.*'

'Perhaps she had an insurance policy that might take care of your expenses here,' Nell suggested.

'If she did, she never told me. Winifred could be pretty closemouthed. How am I supposed to know about insurance?'

'Did Winifred have a safe-deposit box?'

'What would she have to put in it?'

Nell smiled. 'Then where did she keep her personal records?'

'In her desk in her apartment, I believe. A good apartment, too. Still rent controlled. We lived there from the time she was in kindergarten. I'd be there now if it weren't for the arthritis. I'm crippled with it.'

'Perhaps we could arrange for a neighbor to go through the desk for you and send up any papers.'

'I don't want any neighbors going through my business.'

'Well, do you have a lawyer?' Nell asked.

'Why would I need a lawyer?' Rhoda Johnson looked intently at Nell, taking her measure. 'Your grandfather is Cornelius MacDermott, isn't he?'

'Yes, he is.'

'A good man, one of the few honest politicians in the country.'

'Thank you.'

'If I let you go into the apartment and look for any records, would he go with you?'

'If I asked him, he would. Yes.'

'When Winifred was a baby and we lived in his district, we voted for him. My husband thought he was tops.'

Rhoda Johnson began to cry. 'I'm going to miss Winifred,' she said. 'She was a good person. She didn't deserve to die. She just didn't have enough gumption—that was her problem, poor girl. Always trying to please people. Like me, she was never appreciated. Worked her fingers to the bone for that firm. At least they finally gave her the raise she deserved.'

Maybe, Nell thought. And maybe not. 'I know my grandfather would go with me to your apartment, and if you can think of anything else you'd like us to bring to you, we'll take care of that too.'

Rhoda Johnson fumbled in the pocket of her sweater for a handkerchief. Watching her, Nell realized for the first time that Mrs. Johnson's fingers were almost deformed from arthritis. 'There are some framed pictures,' she said. 'Bring them along. Oh, and yes, would you see if you can find Winifred's swimming medals? She took all the prizes when she was growing up. A coach told me that if she had stayed at it she could have been another Esther Williams. But with my arthritis getting the best of me, and her father out of the picture, I couldn't have her running all over the country, could I?'

134

CHAPTER THIRTY-ONE

After Bonnie Wilson left, Gert agonized about how to tell Nell what she had just learned. How should she break the news to Nell that Adam was trying to contact her?—for Gert was certain that what Bonnie Wilson had told her was genuine. She knew that Nell would resist. She refuses to understand that some people have genuine psychic gifts, Gert thought, powers that they use to help other people. She's also frightened of the fact that she has psychic gifts herself. And it's no wonder, given all Cornelius's talk of 'flights of fantasy.'

Gert's eyes filled with tears as she remembered how ten-year-old Nell had sobbed in her arms: 'Aunt Gert, Mommy and Daddy *did* so say goodbye to me. You know how Daddy always ran his fingers through my hair? I was at recess, and he came to me and did that. And then Mommy kissed me. I felt her kiss me. I started to cry. I knew then that they were gone. *I knew it.* But Grandpa says it didn't happen. He says that I imagined it.'

I asked Cornelius how he explained the fact that Nell had that experience at precisely the same moment her parents' plane went off the radar screen, Gert thought. I asked him how he could be so certain that Nell only imagined a visit from her parents. His answer was that I was filling Nell's head with nonsense.

And, Gert thought, even before that terrible time, Nell had known when Madeline, her grandmother, had died. She was only four years old, but I was there when she came running

135

downstairs. She was so happy because 'Grammy' had come into her room during the night, and she thought that meant Grammy was home from the hospital. Typically, though, Cornelius had dismissed that as a dream as well.

I wouldn't dare let him know what Bonnie Wilson told me, Gert thought. Whether or not Nell talks to Bonnie herself, I'll make her promise not to tell Mac about it, she vowed.

At eight o'clock that evening, she called Nell. The answering machine was on and picked up after the third ring. She probably wants to be left alone tonight, Gert thought. She tried not to sound nervous when she left her message: 'Nell, just anxious to see how you are,' she began. Then, after a moment of hesitation, she blurted out, 'Nell, it's very important that I talk to you. I—'

She heard a click as the phone was picked up. 'Aunt Gert, I'm here. Is something wrong?'

From the thickness of her voice, Gert could sense that Nell had been crying. She threw caution to the winds: 'Nell, there's something I have to tell you. Bonnie Wilson, a psychic friend of mine, came to see me today. She puts people who have passed on in contact with their loved ones here.

'Nell, I can refer you to people who have absolute faith in her. She is the real thing, I'm sure of it. When Bonnie was here today she told me that Adam has contacted her from the other side and wants to talk to you. Nell, please let me take you to see her.'

She had rushed every word, anxious to get it out before either Nell hung up or she lost her courage and changed her mind about telling her grandniece about Bonnie's visit.

136

'Gert, I don't believe in all that stuff,' Nell said softly. 'You know that. I know that it means a lot to you, but it just doesn't work for me. So please don't bring it up again—especially not anything having to do with Adam.'

Gert winced at the click as Nell broke the connection. She was tempted to redial Nell's number and apologize for intruding in such a way, and at such a terrible time.

What Gert did not know was that when Nell hung up the phone, she was trembling with fear and uncertainty.

I happened to catch Bonnie Wilson on that bizarre television program last year, Nell thought, the one where they invited people to call in and test the psychic powers of the experts. Unless it was a complete sham, she was astonishing in the way she related to some people in the audience. Nell remembered in particular the vivid picture Bonnie had conjured up when the woman asked the psychic about her husband, who had died in an automobile accident.

'You were waiting for him in the restaurant where you became engaged,' she had said. 'It was your fifth wedding anniversary. He wants you to know he loves you and that he's happy, even though he feels cheated of all the years he'd hoped to spend with you.'

Dear God, Nell thought, is it possible that Adam really *is* trying to reach me? I know that Mac hates for me to talk of it, but I do believe that the dead have a real presence in our lives. After all, I *know* that Mom and Dad came to say goodbye to me when they died, and I *know* they were with me, guiding me to safety when I almost drowned in

Hawaii. Why, then, should it be so improbable for Adam to try to reach me now? And why did he contact someone else instead of coming directly to me as Mom and Dad and Grammy did?

Nell looked at the phone, struggling to resist the urge to call Gert and confess to her just how confused she was.

CHAPTER THIRTY-TWO

By the time he had returned home after his daily run in Central Park, a sense of unease had replaced Dan Minor's previous feeling of euphoria. He admitted to himself that it was grasping at straws to hope that he would spot his mother, Quinny, as Lilly Brown had called her, sitting on a park bench, or that Lilly would phone one day soon and say, 'She's here in the shelter.'

A long shower, however, helped to revive his spirits somewhat. He dressed in chinos, a sport shirt and loafers and went to the bar refrigerator. He wasn't sure yet where he wanted to have dinner, but he did know a glass of chardonnay with cheese and crackers was in order.

He settled on the couch in the sitting area of the spacious, high-ceilinged room, deciding that after three and a half months the place was finally beginning to shape up. Why do I feel so much more at home in a condo in Manhattan than I ever did living on Cathedral Parkway in Washington? he asked himself, although he knew the answer.

Some of Quinny's genes, he guessed. His mother had been born in Manhattan, and according to

Lilly Brown, New York City was 'her favorite place in the world,' although his grandparents moved back to Maryland when she was about twelve.

How much of her do I actually remember, and how much of what I know of her comes from the things I have heard about her? Dan asked himself.

He knew that his father had fallen in love with another woman when Dan was three years old, so he had no memory of ever living with him. The only really positive thing I can say about dear old Dad, Dan thought, is that he didn't fight for custody of me after Mom disappeared.

He knew his grandparents despised his father, but they had been careful not to show that to him when he was growing up. 'Unfortunately, a lot of marriages break up, Dan,' they told him. 'The one who doesn't want the marriage to end can be badly hurt. After a while, people get over the pain. In time, I'm sure, your mother would have gotten over the divorce, but she couldn't get over what happened to *you*.'

Why do I think that after all these years my mother and I could have any kind of relationship? Dan asked himself.

But we *could*, he thought. I *know* we could. The private investigator they had sent to find her after they glimpsed her on that television documentary had been able to glean some information about her. 'She's worked as an aide to old people,' he told them, 'and apparently she is very good at it. But when depression hits her, she starts drinking again, and then it's back to the streets.'

The investigator had found a social worker who reported once having a long talk with Quinny. Now, as he sipped his wine, Dan mulled over one

139

thing in particular that social worker said: 'I asked Quinny what she would like most to have in this life. She looked at me for what seemed like a long time, then whispered, *"Redemption."*'

The word echoed in his mind.

The phone rang. Dan walked over to it and checked the Caller ID. His eyebrows raised when he saw that the call was from Penny Maynard, the fashion designer who lived on the fourth floor of his loft building. They had chatted a few times in the elevator. She was about his own age and sleekly attractive. He had been tempted to ask her out, but then decided he didn't want to have any kind of close friendship with someone he would be seeing regularly in the elevator.

He decided to let the answering machine take a message.

The machine clicked on. 'Dan,' Penny said firmly. 'I know you're home. A couple of the other people in the building dropped by, and we all agreed it was time we got to know our resident pediatrician. So come on up and join us. You don't have to stay more than twenty minutes, unless, of course, you decide to partake of one of my thrown-together pasta suppers.'

In the background, Dan could hear murmured conversation. Suddenly heartened at the prospect of being with other people, he picked up the phone. 'I'd be delighted to come,' he said.

Finding the people at Penny's gathering to be pleasant, and feeling relaxed and cheered, he stayed for the pasta and got back to his loft just in time to catch the ten o'clock news. There was a brief segment covering the memorial Mass for Adam Cauliff, the architect who had been killed in the boating accident in New York harbor.

Rosanna Scotto of Fox News was reporting: 'The explosion that killed Cauliff and three others continues to be under investigation. Former congressman Cornelius MacDermott is escorting Adam Cauliff's widow, his granddaughter, Nell, from the church. Rumors are rampant that Nell MacDermott may run for the congressional seat her grandfather held for almost fifty years, since Bob Gorman, the incumbent, is believed to be retiring from public life.'

There was a close-up of Nell on the screen. Dan Minor's eyes widened—she looked very familiar. Wait a minute, he thought. I met her four or five years ago. It was a reception at the White House. She was with her grandfather, and I was escorting Congressman Dade's daughter.

He remembered that he and Nell MacDermott had chatted for a few minutes and discovered they were both graduates of Georgetown. It was hard to believe that since that chance meeting, she had been married, widowed and now might be setting off on a political career of her own.

The camera lingered on Nell's face. The rigidly composed features and pain-filled eyes were a startling contrast to the sparkling and smiling young woman Dan remembered.

I'll write her a note, he thought. She probably won't remember me at all, but I'd like to do it. She looks so grief stricken. Adam Cauliff must have been quite a guy, he decided.

Friday, June 16

CHAPTER THIRTY-THREE

Winifred Johnson had lived in a building at the corner of Amsterdam Avenue and Eighty-first Street. At ten o'clock on Friday morning, Nell met her grandfather in the lobby there.

'Faded grandeur, Mac,' she said when he arrived.

He looked around the lobby, which obviously had seen better days. The marble floor was stained, the lighting dim. The furniture consisted of two shabby armchairs.

'Winifred's mother phoned the manager this morning to tell him we were coming,' she explained as the handyman, who seemed to double as doorman, waved them to the single elevator.

'Nell, I think it's a big mistake coming here,' Cornelius MacDermott said as the elevator lumbered upward toward the fifth floor. 'I don't know where the district attorney's investigation is going to lead, but if Winifred was either involved in or had any knowledge of bribery, or if . . .' He stopped.

'Don't *think* of suggesting that Adam was involved in bribery or bid rigging, Mac,' she said fiercely.

'I'm not suggesting anything other than the fact that if the police at any point are able to get a search warrant for these premises, it won't look good that you and I beat them to it.'

'Mac, *please*.' Nell tried to cover the catch in her voice. 'I'm just trying to help. I came here primarily to see what kind of financial provisions Winifred may have made for her mother; I'm looking for insurance policies and that sort of thing. Mrs. Johnson is worried sick that she'll have to leave Old Woods Manor nursing home. She's happy there. I don't think she's a particularly easy person, but it's obvious she has terrible rheumatoid arthritis. If I were in pain all the time, I don't think I'd be oozing charm either.'

'What has oozing charm got to do with our snooping around in Winifred's apartment?' Mac asked as they stepped off the elevator. 'Come on, Nell. We used to be honest with each other. You're not a Girl Scout doing a good deed. If there was bribery going on at Walters and Arsdale, you're hoping to find something that will tie Winifred to the problem and leave Adam as clean as the driven snow.'

They walked down the dingy hallway. 'Winifred's apartment is 5E,' Nell said. She reached into her shoulder bag for the keys Mrs. Johnson had given her.

'Double lock and safety lock,' Mac observed dourly. 'A professional could bust them with a can opener.'

When Nell opened the door, she hesitated for a moment, then stepped inside. Winifred was here only a week ago, she thought, but already the place has a feeling of being neglected, abandoned.

They stood for a moment in the foyer, getting their bearings before venturing farther into the apartment. A table to the left of the door held a vase of wilting flowers, the kind of stingy arrangement sold in grocery stores. The living room was directly in front of them, a long, narrow, cheerless space with a threadbare Persian-style carpet, an aging red velour-covered sofa and

146

matching chair, an upright piano and a library table.

A lace runner covered the table. On it were several precisely placed framed pictures and a pair of matching lamps with fringed shades. It was so old-fashioned that it made Nell think of movies she had seen that were set in the Victorian era.

She walked to the table and studied the pictures. Most of them showed a young Winifred, wearing a bathing suit and receiving an award. In a more recent photograph, she seemed to be in her early twenties, a thin, eagerly smiling, waiflike creature. 'These have to be the pictures her mother said she wants,' she told Mac. 'I'll collect them on the way out.'

Nell went back to the foyer and glanced into the kitchen, which was to the left. Then she turned right and walked down the hall, her grandfather closely behind her. The larger of the two bedrooms off the dark corridor contained a double bed, a dresser and a chest. The chenille spread on the bed reminded her of one her grandmother had when she was a child.

She went on to the next room, clearly used by Winifred as both den and office. Crowded into the small space were a couch, a television set, a basket of magazines and a computer desk. Two rows of bookshelves over the desk and rows of framed medals over the couch added to Nell's growing sense of claustrophobia. The whole place is so depressing, she thought. Winifred spent most of her life here, and I'll bet, except for this room, she hasn't changed a thing about it since her mother went into a nursing home.

'Nell, if we've finished the grand tour, I would
147

suggest you try to find what it is you're looking for, and we get out of here.'

Nell knew that when Mac sounded his most curmudgeonly it was a signal that he was worried. She admitted to herself that it had not occurred to her that going into Winifred Johnson's apartment might be misinterpreted by the district attorney's office, but since her grandfather had pointed it out, she had become concerned as well.

'You're right, Mac,' she said. 'Sorry.' She went over to the desk, and, feeling uneasy about what she was doing, opened the center drawer.

It was as though she had discovered another world. The drawer was stuffed with pieces of paper of every size and description, from sticky-backed notepads to architectural plans. On every one of them, in print, in handwriting, in large letters, or letters almost too small to be read, Winifred had written four words: WINIFRED LOVES HARRY REYNOLDS.

CHAPTER THIRTY-FOUR

The Manager of the salon at which Lisa Ryan worked told her to take the whole week off. He said to her, 'You need a little time to yourself, honey, so you can start the healing process.'

'The healing process,' Lisa thought scornfully as she looked at the piles of clothing on the bed. Those must be the stupidest three words ever uttered. She remembered how contemptuous Jimmy had been whenever he heard them used by some newscaster after the report of a plane crash or an earthquake.

'The relatives have just been notified, the bodies haven't been found and some yo-yo with a mike in his hand is talking about the healing process beginning,' he would say to her, shaking his head in irritation.

Someone had told her it would be therapeutic if she kept moving, kept busy, and one of the activities suggested was cleaning out Jimmy's closet and drawers. So here she was, sorting Jimmy's clothes and putting them in boxes to be given away. Better they help some poor soul than rot in the closet like Grandpa's did, she thought.

Her grandmother had kept everything her grandfather had ever owned, almost—or so it seemed at the time—creating a kind of shrine to his memory. As a child she remembered seeing his jackets and coats hanging neatly from hangers next to her grandmother's dresses.

I don't need Jimmy's clothes to remind me of him, she thought as she folded the sport shirts the children had given him this past Christmas—there isn't a moment I'm *not* thinking about him.

'Change your routine,' the funeral director had urged. 'Don't sit at the same place at the table. Move the furniture around in your bedroom. You'd be surprised how little things can help you get through the first year after a loss.'

When she had finished clearing out Jimmy's dresser, she was going to put it in the boys' room. She already had moved the model of her dream house into the living room. She couldn't bear to look at it when she was lying alone in the bed she had shared with Jimmy.

Tomorrow I'll move the bed and put it between

the windows, she thought, although she doubted that all the changes in the world would really help. She couldn't imagine that she ever would have a day in which she didn't at some point think about Jimmy.

She glanced at the clock and was dismayed to see that it was quarter of three, which meant the children would be home in twenty minutes. She didn't want them to see her sorting through their father's things.

The money—suddenly it flashed into her mind.

She had managed all day not to think about it. Yesterday, after Adam Cauliff's Mass, when she saw the two cops coming out of the church, she was sure they were going to want to talk to her. Suppose they find out about the money, she thought. Or suppose they suspect something, and get a search warrant and find it here. And suppose they think I know how Jimmy got it, and they arrest me. What would I do then?

She could no longer force that fear from her mind. I don't know what to do, she thought. Oh dear God, *I don't know what to do.*

The sudden sound of the door chimes shattered the quiet of the house. With a startled gasp, Lisa dropped the shirt she was holding and hurried downstairs. It's Brenda, Lisa reassured herself. She said she would stop over later.

But even before she opened the door she knew with fatalistic certainty that instead of Brenda she would find one of the detectives standing at her door.

*   *   *

150

Jack Sclafani felt a tug of genuine compassion as he observed the swollen eyes and blotchy complexion of Jimmy Ryan's widow. She looks as though she's been crying all day, he thought. This has got to be a terrible shock. Also, at thirty-three she is awfully young to be left with three kids to raise alone.

He had first met her when he came with Brennan to tell her that her husband's body had been positively identified—or rather, *pieces* of her husband's body, he corrected himself mentally—and he was certain she had recognized him outside the church at the Cauliff Mass.

'Detective Jack Sclafani again, Mrs. Ryan. Remember me? I'd like to talk to you for a few minutes, if you don't mind.'

As he watched, naked fear replaced the intense grief in her eyes. This won't be hard, he thought. Whatever is on her mind is going to be on the table fast.

'May I come in?' he asked politely.

She seemed immobilized, unable to either speak or move. Finally she whispered, 'Yes. Of course. Come in.'

Bless me, Father, for I have sinned, Jack thought as he followed her into the house.

They sat stiffly across from each other in the small but pleasant living room. Jack made a point of studying the large framed family portrait that was hanging over the couch.

'That was taken in happier times,' he observed. 'Jimmy looks as though he's got the world by the tail, every inch the proud husband and father.'

The words achieved the desired effect. As tears welled in Lisa Ryan's eyes, some of the tension he

151

had seen in her expression seemed to relax.

'We did have the world by the tail,' she said quietly. 'Oh, you know what I mean. We lived from payday to payday like most people in our circumstances, but that was okay. We had a lot of fun and we had plans. And dreams.'

She pointed to the table. 'That's a scale model of the house Jimmy was going to build for us someday.'

Jack got up and walked over to inspect it closely. 'Very, very nice. Is it okay if I call you Lisa?'

'Yes, of course.'

'Lisa, your first reaction when you heard Jimmy was dead was to ask if he had committed suicide. That has to mean something was pretty wrong in his life, but what? I have a feeling it wasn't a problem between you two.'

'No, it wasn't.'

'Was he worried about his health?'

'Jimmy was never sick. We used to joke that it was a shame to pay for health insurance for a guy like him.'

'If it's not a marital problem, and if it's not health, then it's usually a money problem,' Jack suggested.

Bingo, he thought as he saw Lisa Ryan's hands clench.

'It's easy to run up bills with a family. You put something you need on the credit card. You're sure you're going to pay it off in a couple of months, but then suddenly you need tires for the car or a new roof for the house or one of the kids has to go to the dentist.' He sighed. 'I'm married; I'm a father. It happens.'

'We never ran up bills,' Lisa said defensively. 'At

152

least not until Jimmy lost his job. Do you know why he lost it?' she burst out. 'It was because he was honest and decent and he was outraged that the contractor he was working for was using substandard concrete on the job. Oh, sure, some contractors cut corners. That's the way it is in the building industry, but Jimmy said this guy was putting lives in danger.

'Well, for his conscientiousness he was not only fired, he was also *blackballed*,' she said, 'unable to get work anywhere. *That's* when we started having financial problems.'

Be careful, Lisa warned herself. You're talking too much. But the understanding in Detective Sclafani's eyes was balm to her soul. It's been only a week, she thought, and already I'm hungry to talk things over with an adult man.

'How long was Jimmy out of work, Lisa?'

'Almost two years. Oh, he managed to get a little work here and there, off the books, but they were not the kind of long-term jobs that pay decent money. The word was out that he had a big mouth, and they tried to destroy him for it.'

'He must have felt pretty relieved then, when he got a call from Adam Cauliff's office. How did Jimmy happen to contact him? Cauliff only opened his own place recently.'

'Jimmy contacted everybody,' Lisa said. 'Adam Cauliff happened to see his résumé. He had his assistant pass it on to Sam Krause, and Krause took Jimmy on.'

Suddenly, a possibility occurred to Lisa. Of course, she thought, that must be what happened. Jimmy had told her that Krause was known to cut corners. So in working for Krause, maybe he had

153

been forced to go along with it or lose his job.

'It seems as though something was bothering Jimmy pretty badly even though he was working,' Sclafani suggested. 'Certainly it had to have been if you thought he might be contemplating suicide. I think you know something about that, Lisa. Why don't you talk it over with me? Maybe there's something Jimmy would want us to know, now that he's not here to tell it himself.'

That's what happened, Lisa thought, barely hearing the detective's words. I'm sure of it. Jimmy saw something on one of Krause's jobs that he knew was wrong. He was given his choice of being fired or being paid to look the other way. He felt he had no choice, but he also knew that once he took money under the table, they had him.

'Jimmy was a good, honest man,' she began.

Sclafani nodded at the family portrait. 'I can see that,' he agreed.

This is it, he thought. She's going to talk about it.

'The other day, after the funeral . . .' Lisa began, but her words trailed off when she heard the sound of the kitchen door being opened and then the tramping of feet as the children ran into the house.

'Mom, we're home,' Kelly called.

'I'm in here.' Lisa sprang up, suddenly aghast that she had been about to tell a member of the police department that hidden downstairs was a packet of what could only be called 'dirty money.'

I have to get rid of it, she thought. I was right when I tried to talk to Nell MacDermott yesterday. I feel as though I can trust her. Maybe *she* can help me to get that money returned to whomever it should go to in Krause's company. After all, it was her husband who sent Jimmy to him.

The children were beside her, reaching up to kiss her. Lisa looked at Jack Sclafani. 'Jimmy was mighty proud of these three,' she said, her voice steady, 'and they were mighty proud of him. As I said, Jimmy Ryan was a good and decent man.'

CHAPTER THIRTY-FIVE

'So Winifred had a boyfriend?'

'I'm shocked,' Nell admitted to her grandfather. They were in a cab on the way home from Winifred's apartment. 'I used to tease Adam by saying that she had a crush on him.'

'She had a crush on him the way women had a crush on the Beatles or Elvis Presley,' Cornelius MacDermott said tartly. 'Adam buttered her up so she'd leave Walters and Arsdale and go with him when he opened his own firm.'

'Mac!'

'Sorry,' he said hastily. 'What I mean is, Adam was a much younger man, married to a beautiful woman. Whatever Winifred was, she wasn't a dope. She was obviously involved with—or at least crazy about—some guy named Harry Reynolds.'

'I wonder why he doesn't come forward?' Nell said. 'I mean it's as though Winifred just disappeared off the face of the earth. According to her mother, no one contacted her except the building manager, who called to say that unless she was planning to move back home, he hoped she would give up the apartment. Meaning that she shouldn't plan on trying to sublet it.'

'I still say we made a mistake going into her home. Especially since it turns out she didn't keep any records there,' Mac said. 'You should have gone to the office first.'

'Mac, I went to Winifred's apartment at the *specific* request of her mother.'

The package of framed photographs Nell had gathered was on her lap. Cornelius MacDermott eyed it. 'Want me to have Liz mail that stuff to the nursing home?'

Nell hesitated. I may visit Mrs. Johnson again, she thought, but not soon. 'Okay, have Liz send it,' she agreed. 'I'll call Mrs. Johnson and tell her it's on the way. And that we'll look in the office for Winifred's records.'

The cab was slowing down in front of Nell's building. She felt Mac's arm go around her. 'I'm here for you,' he said quietly, giving her a gentle hug.

'I know that, Mac.'

'If you need to talk it out, just pick up the phone, day or night. Don't forget—I've been through some grieving time myself.'

Yes, you have, Nell thought. Your wife, your only son, your daughter-in-law—all taken so suddenly. No one has to tell you about grief.

As she turned, Carlo was opening the cab door for her. Then she heard Mac's voice.

'Nell, just one thing.'

Mac's tone was hesitant, which was not like him. As Nell put one foot outside the cab, she turned to look at him and waited.

'Nell, you never filed a joint income tax return with Adam, did you?'

She was about to flare at him when she saw the

156

deeply worried look on his face. With a pang of concern, she realized that with every passing day Mac was more and more showing his age.

She remembered that when she married Adam, Mac had warned her to file income tax returns separately. 'Nell,' he had said at the time, 'you intend to have a career in government service. That means the vultures will be circling around you every inch of the way, looking for some misstep on your part. You can't afford to give them any opportunity to smear you. Let Adam file his own income tax. He might innocently claim something that later could be used to hurt you. You do your own return and make it simple. Don't play around with complicated tax dodges.'

'Yes, Mac, I filed separately,' she said tightly. 'So stop worrying.' She started once more to step outside, then turned back again. 'But level with me. Is there anything you know—hear me out—and I mean *know* that would suggest Adam wasn't on the up and up?'

'No,' he said somewhat reluctantly, shaking his head. 'Nothing.'

'Then it's a combination of rumor, and Walters and Arsdale's denial, and that famous gut-level instinct of yours that has you so sure Adam was involved in whatever it is the district attorney is investigating?'

He nodded.

'Mac, I know you're trying to protect me, and I guess I should love you for it, but . . .'

'I don't feel very loved by you at the moment, Nell.'

She managed a smile. 'Truthfully, you're not; and then again, of course you are. Trust me, it's

157

both.' With an apologetic glance toward Carlo, she finally stepped out of the cab. By the time she was in the elevator and on the way up to the blessed sanctuary of her apartment, Nell had made a decision.

She didn't begin to understand her own psychic ability to discern certain events. She also didn't understand—or accept—the idea of a medium communicating with the dead. But if Bonnie Wilson claimed to be in touch with Adam, Nell knew she had to investigate that claim.

I have to do it, she told herself, if not for my sake, then for Adam's.

CHAPTER THIRTY-SIX

Each day since the explosion of *Cornelia II*, the search and recover Coast Guard team had continued the tedious process of searching for any remains of the boat and its passengers, and trying to collect the many bits of debris. On Friday afternoon, for the first time in four days, a significant find was made. In the area of the Verrazano Bridge, a three-foot section of splintered wood bobbed through the water and onto the shore. Pieces of a stained blue sport shirt with fragments of human bone were caught in the splinters.

The somber and macabre find confirmed to the search team that minute remains of one more victim might well have been recovered. Sam Krause's secretary had been asked to describe what he was wearing when he left the office to go to the meeting on the boat. She was absolutely certain that it had been a long-sleeved blue sport shirt and khaki slacks.

George Brennan got the news of the find as he was leaving to meet Jack Sclafani at 405 East Fourteenth Street. In his pocket he had a warrant that gave them permission to search the residence of Ada Kaplan, whose son, Jed, had now become an active suspect in the explosion of the yacht.

They met in the lobby of the building, and Brennan filled Jack in on the newest find. He said, 'You know, Jack, whoever did this used enough explosive to blow away half an ocean liner. Last Friday was a perfect boating day. From what I hear, there were a lot of small craft in the harbor. It's just lucky that most of the others had headed back toward their marinas before Cauliff's boat blew up. No telling how many other injuries there might have been if someone had been really near.'

'Do you suppose there was a remote control or maybe a timing device? Whoever did the job had to be pretty careful setting it up.'

'Pretty careful, yeah, if it was someone experienced with explosives like Jed Kaplan, or pretty damn lucky if it was an amateur. Otherwise he easily could have killed himself putting the components together.'

*   *   *

A distraught Ada Kaplan wept with embarrassment at the thought of what her neighbors were saying as her four-room apartment was searched inch by inch. Her son Jed sat at a table in the small dining area, an expression of contempt on his face.

159

He's not worried, Jack thought. If he did blow up that boat, he never had anything that could be evidence here.

They did have one small victory—the discovery of a bag of marijuana in a duffle bag in the closet. 'Come on, you can tell that stuff is old,' Jed protested. 'I never even saw it, and anyhow, the last time I was here was five years ago.'

'It's true,' Ada Kaplan protested. 'I put his old bags in that closet in case he ever wanted them, but he hasn't touched them since he got home. I swear it.'

'Sorry, Mrs. Kaplan,' Brennan told her. 'And I'm sorry for you too, Jed, but there's enough smoke here to book you for possession with intent to sell.'

*   *   *

Three hours later, Sclafani and Brennan left Jed in the lockup at the precinct station house. 'His mother'll put up the bond money, but at least the judge agreed to lift his passport,' Brennan observed. He didn't sound happy.

'He must have learned a lesson when he got caught in Australia with explosives in his car,' Jack Sclafani said. 'There was zilch in the apartment to tie him to what happened on that boat.'

They walked toward their cars. 'Any luck with your visit to Lisa Ryan?' Brennan asked.

'Unfortunately, no. But I'm sure she was on the verge of spilling something when her kids came in from school.' Jack shook his head as he pulled out his ignition key. 'I swear, two minutes more and I would have heard whatever it is she knows. I even hung around, talked to the kids.'

160

'Did you have milk and cookies with them?'

'Then coffee with her when they went out. Believe me, I tried. She just wasn't buying any more "trust me" talk.'

'Why did she clam up?'

'Impossible to be sure,' Sclafani said, 'but my guess is it's because she doesn't want to tell me something that, if it came out, could hurt Jimmy Ryan's memory in his kids' eyes.'

'You know, I bet you're right. Okay, see you tomorrow. Maybe then we'll get a break.'

Before they reached their cars, George Brennan received a call on his cell phone informing him that a woman's pocketbook had been found washed ashore in the same area near the Verrazano Bridge as the splintered wood and stained sport-shirt fragment.

Inside the water-soaked wallet they'd found the credit cards and driver's license of Winifred Johnson.

'They say it was hardly even scorched,' Brennan said when he had clicked off. 'Crazy how that happens. It must have flown straight up, then landed in the water.'

'Unless it wasn't on the boat when that bomb went off,' Sclafani suggested after a thoughtful pause.

CHAPTER THIRTY-SEVEN

Nell spent the afternoon responding to the sympathy notes that had been piling up on her desk all week. When she was finished, it was nearly five

161

o'clock. I've *got* to get out of here for a while, she thought. I haven't exercised all week.

She changed to shorts and a T-shirt, put a credit card and a ten-dollar bill in her pocket and jogged the three blocks to Central Park. At Seventy-second Street she turned in to the park and began to run south. I used to run three or four times a week, she thought. How did I let myself stop doing it?

As she slowly eased herself into the old routine and enjoying the feeling of freedom that came with such open, unrestricted movement, Nell thought of the many cards of condolence she had received.

'You seemed so happy with Adam . . .'

'We're so sorry about your tragedy . . .'

'We're here for you . . .'

Why didn't I read one *single* letter saying what a terrific guy Adam was, and that he'll be missed?

Why do I feel so numb? Why can't I cry?

Nell picked up the pace, but she couldn't get the questions out of her mind. Where was it she had read that you can't outrun your thoughts? she asked herself.

*   *   *

Dan Minor looped around Central Park South and re-entered the park, beginning the run northward. A perfect day for running, he thought. The late afternoon sun was pleasantly warm, the breeze refreshing. The park was filled with joggers, Rollerbladers and pedestrians. Most of the benches were occupied by people either enjoying the passing scene or engrossed in reading.

Dan felt a stab of pain as he passed a bench

occupied by an unkempt young woman wearing a threadbare dress. No one is sitting near *her*, he thought, observing the overflowing plastic bags at her feet.

Is this the way Quinny spent most of her life? he wondered. Was she also avoided or ignored?

Odd that it was easier for him to think of her as 'Quinny.' 'Mom' was someone else—Mom was a pretty, dark-haired woman, with loving arms, who used to call him Danny-boy.

She was also a woman who night after night began drinking after I was in bed, he thought. Sometimes I'd wake up and bring a blanket down to cover her after she passed out.

As he ran, he had a fleeting impression of a tall woman with chestnut hair jogging past him.

I know her, he thought.

It was an immediate reaction, the kind of sensation one gets when something familiar triggers a memory reflex. Dan stopped and turned. But who is she, and why do I remember her?

He knew he had seen that face in the last twenty-four hours.

Of course, he thought. It was Nell MacDermott. I saw her on the ten o'clock news last night. There had been a clip showing her standing outside the church after the memorial Mass for her husband.

A compulsion he did not understand made Dan turn and jog back toward Central Park South, following Nell MacDermott's cascading chestnut hair.

*   *   *

As she approached Broadway, Nell slackened her

163

pace. Coliseum Books was on the corner of Broadway and Fifty-seventh Street. When she left the apartment, she had thought to bring cash and credit card in case she decided to stop in there on her way home. Now was the time to make up her mind.

She decided. If I am indeed going to see Bonnie Wilson and deal with her claims of being in touch with Adam, then I need to know a lot more about psychic phenomena than I do, she thought. I know Mac would ridicule the idea and tell me that only simpletons and dotty old women—meaning Aunt Gert, of course—give any credence to the 'babbling' of psychics. In fact, it's really only because of him that I rejected Gert's earlier suggestion. But if what I saw Bonnie Wilson do on that television program was legit, then maybe she actually *can* be in contact with Adam. At the very least, if I'm going to see her, I want to be prepared. I want to know what to look out for and what to ask.

*   *   *

Dan followed Nell down Broadway until she disappeared into the bookstore. Undecided about what to do, he stood on the sidewalk and stared at the window, pretending to be absorbed in the display. Should he follow her in? He didn't have a cent on him, so there was no way he could pretend he was shopping. Besides, he had been running pretty hard before he spotted her, and he knew he must look like he needed a shower and a change of clothes. He was hardly fit for shopping.

Lifting the bottom of his shirt, he mopped

perspiration from his forehead. Maybe I should just write her a note, he thought.

But I'd really like to talk to her now. Her phone number probably isn't listed, and at a time like this, she's got to be getting too much mail to deal with. I'll go inside, he finally decided.

Through the window he caught a glimpse of her as she walked between the racks of books. Then, with a combination of relief and uneasy anticipation, he saw her walk to the checkout counter.

When she came out of the store, she took two long strides to the corner and raised her hand to signal a cab coming down Broadway.

It's now or never, Dan thought. Then he took the plunge.

'Nell.'

Nell stopped. The tall, sandy-haired jogger in the long-sleeved sweatshirt was vaguely familiar.

'Dan Minor, Nell. We met at the White House. It was a few years back.'

They both smiled. 'You have to admit, that line certainly beats, "Haven't we met before?"' Dan said, then quickly added, 'You were with your grandfather. I was Congressman Dade's guest.'

I'm sure I know him, Nell thought as she studied his pleasant face. Then it came back to her. 'Oh, yes, I remember. You're a doctor,' she said, 'a pediatric surgeon. You went to Georgetown.'

'That's right.' Now what do I say? Dan asked himself. He watched as the spontaneous smile faded from Nell MacDermott's lips. 'I just wanted to tell you how terribly sorry I am about your husband's death,' he said quickly.

'Thank you.'

'Lady, do you want this cab or not?' The taxi Nell had signaled had pulled over to the curb.

'Yes, wait, please.' She put out her hand. 'Thanks for stopping to say hello, Dan. It was good to see you again.'

Dan stood watching as the taxi cut across Broadway and made a turn east on Fifty-seventh Street. How do you ask a woman who's been widowed for exactly a week if she would like to go out to dinner? he wondered.

CHAPTER THIRTY-EIGHT

On Friday afternoon, in Philadelphia, Ben Tucker was taken to the office of clinical child psychologist Dr. Megan Crowley.

He sat alone in the reception room while his mother went into another room to talk to the doctor. He knew that he was going to have to talk to her too, and he didn't want to, because she was sure to ask him about the dream. It was not something he wanted to talk about.

He had it every single night now, and sometimes even during the day he was sure he would turn a corner and the snake would be there and jump straight at him.

Mom and Dad tried to tell him that what he was seeing wasn't real, and that he was upset. They said that it was very hard for a little kid to see a terrible explosion where people died. They said that the doctor would help him to get over it.

But they didn't get it—it wasn't the explosion. It was the *snake*.

166

Dad said when Ben thought about that day in New York, he should think about the visit to the Statue of Liberty. He should think about how much fun they had climbing all those steps, and about the view from the statue's crown.

Ben had tried to do all that. He'd even made himself think about Dad's boring story of how his great-great-grandfather was one of the kids who collected pennies so that the Statue of Liberty could be put up in the first place. He thought about all the people who had come from other countries, had sailed by the statue and looked up at it, excited to be coming to the United States. He thought about all those things, but they didn't help—he just couldn't stop thinking about the snake.

The door opened and his mother came out with another lady.

'Hi, Ben,' she said, 'I'm Dr. Megan.'

She was young, not like Dr. Peterson, his pediatrician, who was real old.

'Dr. Megan would like to talk with you now, Benjy,' his mother said.

'Will you come with me?' he asked, starting to be afraid.

'No, I'll wait right here. But don't worry. You'll be fine. And you'll be back here with me in no time, and we'll go get a treat.'

He looked at the doctor. He knew he was going to have to go with her. But I'm not going to talk about the snake, he promised himself.

Dr. Megan surprised him, though. She didn't seem to want to talk about the snake. She asked him about school, and he told her he was in the third grade. And then she asked about sports, and he told her he liked wrestling best, and he told her

167

how the other day he won his match because he pinned the other kid in thirty seconds. Then they talked about music class, and he said he knew he didn't practice enough, and he told her that he hit a real clinker when he was playing the recorder today.

They talked about a lot of things, but she never once asked him about the snake. She just said that she would see him again on Monday.

'Dr. Megan's nice,' he told his mother when they were going down in the elevator. 'Can we go for ice cream now?'

Saturday and Sunday
June 17 and 18

CHAPTER THIRTY-NINE

Nell had spent all Friday evening reading the books about psychic phenomena she had purchased that afternoon after her run in the park.

By Saturday afternoon she had gotten through all the sections of each book that dealt with the aspects of the phenomena she wanted to explore. What do I believe about all this? she kept asking herself as she read, and then reread, many of the passages.

I knew the exact moment when Gram and Mom and Dad died, she thought, and I know that when I was in Hawaii, Mom and Dad made me keep swimming when I wanted to give up—these are my own personal experiences with psychic phenomena.

Nell noted that in some of the books the author wrote about a person's 'aura.' That last day, she thought, the day of the explosion, when I saw Winifred, there seemed to be a kind of blackness around her. According to what I've read here, I was seeing her aura. That blackness, according to these books, is a symbol of death.

Nell thought about the time she had seen Bonnie Wilson on television. She was positively startling in the way she talked to that woman about the circumstances of her husband's death, she remembered.

The skeptics say that these people who claim to have psychic powers are just making lucky guesses, based on information they have been clever enough to trick the subject into revealing. Well, I admit to being a skeptic, Nell thought, but I confess that if

Bonnie Wilson is a trickster, then she's fooled me too.

Do the people who claim to be in touch with the dead really just make lucky guesses? she wondered. Bonnie Wilson could *not* have guessed everything she told that woman that day Nell had watched her on television. But what about synchronicity? Nell wondered. That's what they call it when you're thinking of someone and a minute later that person calls you. It's as though one person is sending a fax, and the other is receiving it. They're in synch.

That would go a long way toward explaining the phenomenon she had seen when watching Bonnie Wilson. Maybe the psychics who claim to be in touch with the dead are actually fax machines for the thoughts of the people who consult them, she decided.

Oh, Adam, why did I tell you not to come home that day? Nell agonized. If only I hadn't done that, would I be able to accept that you're gone?

But even if we had never had that misunderstanding, your death would have left so many questions unanswered. Who did this to you, Adam? And why?

I thought poor Winifred had a crush on you, but now I know that there was someone else in her life. I'm glad I learned that, and I hope that she knew what it was to be loved.

Mac is so worried that your name is going to be dragged into the bribery and bid rigging inquiry that is going on at Walters and Arsdale. Even though these things may have been going on while you were there, is it fair that they blame everything on you now, when you're not here to defend yourself?

172

You worked for Walters and Arsdale for over two years, yet neither one of the principal partners came to your memorial Mass. I know they were furious with you because you bought the Kaplan property and then left them to open your own firm. But wasn't that just ambition on your part? I was raised to believe that ambition was good, Nell thought.

Was the person who blew up your boat someone who wanted you out of the way? Were *you* the target? Or was it Sam Krause? Or maybe Winifred? Jimmy Ryan's widow started to talk to me after the Mass, but then something made her run away. Was she about to tell me something I should know about the meeting on the boat? Could Jimmy Ryan have been the one who knew something dangerous to someone else? Could he have been the target?

That last morning, Adam had said there were different degrees of honesty in the construction business. What had he meant by that? Nell wondered.

For most of Saturday night Nell lay sleepless. I feel as though at any moment Adam might come in, she thought. Finally she dozed off, but she awoke again at six. It was going to be another beautiful June morning. She showered and dressed and went to the seven o'clock Mass.

'May Adam's soul and the souls of the faithful departed rest in peace . . .' Her prayer was the same as the week before. And it would be the same for many Sundays to come. She had to find some answers, some explanation to all that had happened.

But if Adam is trying to get in touch with me,

173

Nell thought, there must be some reason why he can't find rest.

She thought of the teachings of the Church. The Curé of Ars, who is the patron saint of priests, was said to have a remarkable understanding of the afterlife. Padre Pio was a mystic.

I don't know what to believe, Nell thought.

On the way home from Mass, she stopped to buy a bagel. It was still hot from the oven. I love New York on Sunday morning, she thought as she walked down Lexington Avenue. On mornings such as this, it's like a small town just waking up. The streets are empty and quiet.

This part of Manhattan had been Mac's electoral district, his streets. Will it be *my* district, *my* streets? she wondered with a quickened heartbeat.

Without Adam there would be no more agonizing about running for office.

She hated the realization that, for a brief instant, she felt a flicker of relief, knowing that at least that problem no longer existed.

CHAPTER FORTY

Peter Lang spent the weekend alone in Southampton, having turned down the half-dozen invitations he'd had from friends to join them for golf or cocktails or dinner. All his energy and thoughts were concentrated on the situation he faced in financing his projected new Vandermeer project, and his now compelling need to have Nell MacDermott sell to him the parcel of land her husband had bought from the Kaplan woman.

I never considered that there was even a prayer of getting the Board of Estimate to overturn the designation of the Vandermeer mansion as a landmark, he thought, berating himself for such a careless miscalculation. Then, when it was in the air that that was going to happen, it was too late—Cauliff had beaten him to Ada Kaplan.

Without the Kaplan parcel, the complex they could erect would be serviceable, but nothing special. With it, however, he could finally be the force behind the creation of a masterpiece of architecture, a grand addition to the Manhattan skyline.

He had never put the Lang name on one of his buildings. He had waited, knowing that eventually he would find the perfect combination of location and design worthy of carrying his family's name. The result would be a building that would stand as a monument to three generations of Langs.

As he had feared, when he approached Adam Cauliff with an offer to buy the Kaplan property from him, Cauliff had told him in so many words that he would see him in hell before he sold that parcel to him, thus the forced partnership.

Well, it looks like Adam will be showing up in hell before me, Peter thought with grim satisfaction.

And now he had to figure out the best way to deal with Cauliff's widow and to convince her to sell him that property. He had learned enough about her to know that at least for the immediate future she could not be induced to sell the parcel out of need—she seemed to be financially well off on her own, independent of her late husband. He

175

had one card up his sleeve, however, one trump he could play that was almost guaranteed to carry the day.

It was an open secret that Cornelius MacDermott had been intensely disappointed that his granddaughter hadn't run for his congressional seat when he retired two years ago.

She has the credentials, Peter Lang mused as, late Sunday afternoon, he walked down the flower-bordered path that led from his house to the ocean. Too bad she didn't run last time, he thought. Gorman was a waste, and if he does quit, she's going to have to work to get back voters who were dissatisfied by his performance.

Nell MacDermott is a chip off the old block, though, and like her grandfather, she's politically very savvy. She's also smart enough to know that I can do a lot to help her get elected, and that it would be wise to get me on her side. Not only can I help her, I suspect that when the courts start looking into some of the practices Adam was involved in, she'll be begging me to come to her aid as a defender of her husband's character.

Peter Lang dropped the towel he was carrying, and with long, decisive strides raced though the breaking surf and threw himself into the Atlantic.

The water was numbingly cold, but once he had gone a few yards his body began to adjust. As he swam with swift, expert strokes, Lang thought about his missed date with destiny, and wondered if Adam Cauliff had still been alive and aware of what was happening when the water closed over him after the boat exploded.

CHAPTER FORTY-ONE

Bonnie Wilson had told Gert to call her at any time if Nell MacDermott decided that she wanted a consultation. She fully understood that even if Nell were anxious to see her, she still might hesitate. As a popular newspaper columnist, with high public visibility, to be known to be consulting a psychic might bring her more publicity than she wanted. And there was also talk of her possibly running for Congress—the press were always looking for ways to discredit a candidate, so any hint of a visit with a noted psychic such as Bonnie might well be used against her.

The media had scoffed at the report that Hillary Clinton had used a medium in an effort to contact Eleanor Roosevelt, and Nancy Reagan had been endlessly criticized for consulting an astrologer.

But then on Sunday evening, at ten o'clock, Bonnie received the call from Gert MacDermott that she had hoped for. 'Nell would like to meet you,' Gert said, her voice subdued.

'Something's wrong, Gert. I don't have to be a psychic to hear the stress in your voice.'

'Oh. I'm afraid my brother is terribly upset with me. He took Nell and me to dinner tonight, and I let slip that you and I talked, and I even said a little about what you had told me. Then he got all riled up and made the mistake of forbidding Nell to see you.'

'Which of course means that she *is* going to see me.'

'Maybe she would have anyhow,' Gert said,

'although I don't think even she is sure of that. But now she absolutely wants to consult you, and she wants to do it as soon as possible.'

'Fine, Gert. Ask her to be here tomorrow at three.'

Monday, June 19

CHAPTER FORTY-TWO

The salon was closed today; it was always closed on Mondays. In a way, Lisa Ryan was grateful for the extra day; it gave her a little more time to get herself emotionally prepared to go back and face the world. In another way, she wished she were already back at work. She dreaded getting through that first week, when all her steady clients would express their sympathy and then want to hear the inside details of the explosion that had taken Jimmy's life.

Many of them had come to the funeral parlor. Others had sent flowers and notes of sympathy.

Lisa knew, though, that the novelty of the event was already over, at least for everyone but her. By now, all of her clients were going about their own lives, only fleetingly conscious of Lisa's loss. Maybe for a while each of them would remain grateful that she could anticipate the sound of her own husband's car pulling into the driveway at night. Soon, though, that too would become routine. Oh, they were all sorry for her, genuinely sorry, but each of them was also happy not to be the one receiving the sympathy.

Lisa had felt that way herself, last year, when the husband of one of her clients had been killed in a traffic accident.

She had talked about that to Jimmy at the time. I'll never forget what he said, Lisa thought: 'Lissy, we're all a little superstitious. We all have a feeling that if something terrible happens to someone else, it may satisfy the gods for a time and they'll leave us alone.'

*   *   *

By nine o'clock she had straightened up the house. There were still plenty of notes from friends and well-wishers to answer, but Lisa simply could not make herself get into them now.

So many old friends who had moved away from the area had written to express shock and sorrow. One of her favorite notes was from a guy she and Jimmy had grown up with who was now a big shot at a movie studio in Hollywood.

'I remember Jimmy when we were in the seventh grade,' he wrote. 'We once had one of those science-project assignments that, as a parent, I now know teachers give just to cause trouble in the family. The night before the projects were due, I still hadn't done mine, but as usual Jimmy had his own all worked out and was willing to lend me a hand as well. He came over and helped me put together a Lego bridge and then to write a composition on why it had a degree of sway built into it. He was one terrific guy.'

And I almost handed his good reputation to a cop, Lisa thought, remembering the Friday visit from Detective Sclafani. But not telling about the money didn't solve the problem—she still had to return it. She knew with absolute certainty that Jimmy hadn't taken the money willingly; she knew without a doubt that he had been forced to accept it. There simply was no other explanation. Jimmy had been given a choice of losing his job or closing his eyes to something wrong on the job site. Then he'd been forced to accept money he didn't want—

that way they would have a hold over him.

Even though she didn't really know her, Lisa sensed that Nell MacDermott was someone she could trust. She also thought that Nell might know something about whatever it was Jimmy was working on. After all, it was someone from Nell's husband's firm who had called Jimmy in for an interview in the first place, then had passed his application along to Sam Krause Construction. What began as an apparent act of kindness, had ended up with Jimmy dead.

Somehow the money in that box was tied to it all. And even though she needed it—needed it to pay the bills and to keep food on the table—she knew she could never spend a penny of it. It was tainted, soiled now with Jimmy's blood.

*   *   *

At ten o'clock, Lisa tried to phone Nell MacDermott. She knew that Nell lived in Manhattan, somewhere on the East Side, in the Seventies. Her phone, however, proved to be unlisted.

Then Lisa remembered reading in the newspaper that Nell's grandfather, former congressman Cornelius MacDermott, now had a consulting firm. Getting that number from information, she decided to call there; maybe someone would be able, and willing, to put her in touch with Nell.

Almost immediately, she was put through to a pleasant-voiced lady who said she was Liz Hanley, former congressman MacDermott's assistant.

Lisa made it simple: 'My name is Lisa Ryan. I'm
183

Jimmy Ryan's widow. I must speak to Nell MacDermott.'

Liz Hanley asked her if she could put her on hold. Two minutes later Liz was back on the line. 'If you call right away, you can reach Nell at 212-555-6784. She's expecting your call.'

Lisa thanked her, broke the connection and immediately dialed the number. The call was answered on the first ring. Five minutes later, at twenty past ten, Lisa Ryan was on her way to meet Nell MacDermott, the other woman made a widow by the boat explosion.

CHAPTER FORTY-THREE

During his thirty-eight years of life, Jed Kaplan had been in trouble with the law enough to know when he was under surveillance. He had developed a kind of sixth sense about having somebody on his tail.

I can smell a cop two miles away, he thought bitterly that Monday morning, as he slammed out of the apartment house and began walking downtown. Hope you got comfortable shoes on. We're going to take one of our nice long walks.

Jed wanted to get out of New York. He couldn't stand living with his mother another minute. When he woke up an hour ago, his back felt almost paralyzed from sleeping on the crummy mattress of that lousy sofa bed. Then he had gone into the kitchen to get a cup of coffee and found his mother sitting at the table, crying her eyes out.

'Your father would have been eighty years old

today,' she told him, her voice breaking. 'If he were still alive, I'd be having a party for him. Instead, I'm in here, alone, hiding, ashamed to look any of my neighbors in the face.'

Jed had tried to dismiss her concerns, asserting his innocence once more. There'd been no shutting her up, however, and she had continued on in the same vein.

'You remember seeing old movies with Edward G. Robinson in them, don't you?' she said. 'When his wife died, the only thing she left their son was his highchair. She said the only time he'd ever given her happiness was when he sat in it.'

Then she shook her fist at him. 'I could say the same about you, Jed. Your behavior is a disgrace to me. You disgrace your father's memory.'

He had taken all he could stand and quickly left the apartment and its feeling of hopeless claustrophobia. He had to get away, but to do that he needed his passport. The cops knew that the trumped-up charge on the grass they found in his duffle bag would be thrown out of court, so they had confiscated his passport, just to make sure he didn't go anywhere.

I never admitted that grass was mine, Jed thought, congratulating himself. I told them truthfully that I hadn't touched that bag in five years.

But even after that charge was dropped, he wouldn't be out of trouble with the cops. They'd cook up something else to force him to hang around.

The trouble is, Jed thought, as he stopped for coffee at a deli on Broadway, the one tip I *could* give the cops also could be used to help them nail

185

me for the explosion.

CHAPTER FORTY-FOUR

'I'm sorry I'm late,' Lisa Ryan apologized to Nell as she was shown into the apartment. 'I should have known I wouldn't be able to find a parking spot. I finally ended up going into a garage.'

She hoped she didn't sound as nervous and flustered as she felt. Manhattan traffic always unnerved her, and then having to put the car in a garage—at so much expense; the minimum charge was twenty-five dollars—had left her both irritated and disoriented.

Twenty-five dollars was an awful lot of money to Lisa, an amount equal to the tips she would receive for doing between five and eight manicures. All that money wasted just to keep a ten-year-old car off the streets—if it hadn't been so important that she see Nell MacDermott, she might have just driven right back to Queens.

When she left the garage and was walking toward the apartment building, she had felt tears of frustration welling behind her eyes, forcing her to stop and fish for a handkerchief to wipe them away. She refused to make a spectacle of herself on the streets of Manhattan.

Always before, Lisa had felt well dressed when she wore her navy-blue pants suit, but looking at the woman in front of her, she knew her outfit must look bargain basement compared with the beautifully tailored tan slacks and cream-colored blouse Nell MacDermott was wearing.

Her pictures don't do her justice, Lisa thought. She's so pretty. And not surprisingly, she looks much better today than when I saw her right after the memorial Mass for her husband.

Nell MacDermott's greeting to her had been kind and warm. She told Lisa right away to call her Nell, and instinctively Lisa felt that she could be trusted, a quality that was very important under the present circumstances.

There was something else reassuring about her as well—Nell MacDermott had an air of quiet confidence about her. As Lisa watched her, she could tell Nell had grown up accustomed to living in a nice place like this.

As she followed Nell into the living room, she thought once more of Jimmy, and of how he used to kid her about the way she would pore over interior-design magazines. Lisa thought of the many hours she had spent mentally furnishing their dream house. Sometimes she envisioned it with a formal décor, including antique furniture and Persian carpets. At other times she saw it as decorated in English country style, and occasionally even in art deco or modern, although she knew those styles were out because Jimmy didn't like them. Sadly she remembered how she used to tell him that when the kids were grown up, she wanted to go back to school and learn interior design. That would never be an option now.

'You have a beautiful home,' she said quietly, looking about the room at the eclectic yet perfectly matched furnishings.

'Thank you. I love it,' Nell said almost wistfully. 'My mother and father traveled a great deal. They were anthropologists. They brought home some

187

unusual pieces from all over the world. Add to them a couple of really comfortable couches and chairs, and the whole thing works. I can tell you, it certainly has been a haven for me this last week.'

As she spoke, Nell MacDermott studied her visitor. Base makeup could not conceal the fact that Lisa Ryan's eyes were puffy, and her complexion still showed the blotches that came from crying. Nell had the feeling that it would not take much to open a floodgate of tears.

'I made a fresh pot of coffee,' she said. 'Would you join me?'

A few minutes later, they were sitting across the kitchen table from each other. Lisa knew it was up to her to break the silence. I'm the one who asked to come here, she thought, so I should begin. But where? she wondered.

Taking a deep breath, she started: 'Nell, my husband was out of work for nearly two years. He applied for a job at your husband's firm, and then, out of the blue, got hired by your husband's business partner, Sam Krause.'

'I think Sam Krause was more of a business associate than a partner,' Nell said. 'Adam was working on projects with several people, but he didn't really consider any of them to be partners. When Adam was with Walters and Arsdale, he was the architect in charge of some building renovations, and Sam Krause was the building contractor. Then Adam opened his own firm and was planning to work with Krause on the Vandermeer project.'

'I know. Jimmy had been reconstructing old apartment houses, but recently he told me they expected to start a big job, a tower apartment building, he said, and that he would be head foreman.'

Lisa paused. When she spoke again, she said only 'Nell,' and then her voice faltered. After another moment, she burst out, 'Nell, Jimmy lost his job a couple of years ago because he was an honest man and spoke up about substandard materials being used by the outfit he was working with. He got blackballed for it and was out of work for a long time. So when he got the call about the job with Sam Krause, he was so happy to go to work. Looking back, though, I realize that the minute he started to work for him, something must have happened. I loved Jimmy so much and was so close to him, I couldn't help but notice—he changed, almost overnight.'

'What do you mean by "changed"?' Nell asked quietly.

'He couldn't sleep. He lost his appetite. He seemed almost to be in another world.'

'What do you think was the reason for that?'

Lisa Ryan put down her coffee and looked directly at the woman across the table from her. 'I think Jimmy was forced to look the other way when he saw something at work that was terribly wrong. He would never have done anything bad himself, but at that point in his life, he was so beaten down that if he had to make a choice between being out of work again, or of simply looking the other way, I think he would have chosen the latter. But of course it was the wrong decision, especially for him. Jimmy was too good a man to be able to live with himself after doing something like that. I know that's what must have happened, and it was driving him crazy.'

189

'Did Jimmy talk to you about this, Lisa?'

'No,' Lisa said, hesitating. When she spoke again, her words were rushed and nervous. 'Nell, you're a stranger, but I've got to tell somebody, so I'm trusting you. I found money hidden in Jimmy's workroom in our basement. I think it was money he was given to keep his mouth shut. The way it was packed up, I can tell he never touched a nickel of it. But that was like him; he was honest and knew that he could never use that money.'

'How much money was it?'

Lisa's voice dropped. 'Fifty thousand dollars,' she whispered.

Fifty thousand dollars! Jimmy Ryan clearly was in on something big, Nell thought. Would Adam have suspected or known about it? she wondered. Was that why Ryan had been invited to the meeting on the boat?

'I want to give the money back,' Lisa said. 'And I want to do it quietly. Even if Jimmy had to lose his job again, he should never have taken it, but as I say, he knew that. That's why those last months, even though he was working, he was so terribly depressed. He can't make retribution now, but I can do it for him. That money had to have come from someone at Krause Construction. I need to get it back to them. That's why I've come to you.'

Drawing on a supply of courage that was greater than she knew she possessed, Lisa leaned forward and reached across the table, taking the other woman's hand. 'Nell, when Jimmy applied for that job with your husband's company, they had never met—I'm sure of that. Then, right after your husband got Jimmy on Sam Krause's payroll, something happened, something terrible. I don't

190

know what it was, but I believe it had to do with whatever Jimmy and your husband both were working on. You have to find out what it was and then help me find a way to make it right.'

CHAPTER FORTY-FIVE

George Brennan and Jack Sclafani were both present when Robert Walters, senior partner of Walters and Arsdale Design Associates, accompanied by the firm's chief counsel, arrived at the office of Assistant District Attorney Cal Thompson. Thompson was the member of the D.A.'s staff in charge of the city's recently launched investigation into bribery and bid rigging in the construction industry.

All the parties in attendance knew that Walters was there under a 'Queen for a Day' agreement, which granted him limited immunity for anything he disclosed in the discussion.

His chief counsel had already issued a pro forma statement to the press: 'Walters and Arsdale and its principals deny any wrongdoing and are confident they will not be charged with any criminal activity.'

Behind the façade of disdain and casual indifference, it was clear to both Brennan and Sclafani that Robert Walters was nervous and agitated. Everything he did was just a little too precise, too perfect to be anything other than a well-rehearsed act.

I'd be nervous too, Brennan thought. The big guys in almost two dozen firms just like his already had copped a plea, choosing the easy way out of this investigation. He knew that as a result, most of them would end up with a slap on the wrist, getting off by paying fines. Big deal. So you pay a million bucks while your company is raking in half a billion. Sometimes, if the prosecutor really had the goods on them, some of these guys ended up doing community service. In a couple of cases, a few of the big shots actually had gone to jail for a couple of months. But then they come out—and guess what? It starts all over again.

It's a simple racket, he thought. The powerhouse builders agree among themselves who's going to get the job. The lowest bid is still padded, but the architect or planner accepts it—and gets a kickback in return. Then the next big project comes along, and bingo!—it's the turn of the next powerhouse guy to give the low bid. It's all a trade-off. Everything is rigged, and oh so civilized.

Despite the apparent futility of the effort, Brennan believed in pursuing these cases. If we hold the feet of some of these top dogs to the fire, then the smaller companies at least will have a chance to get some of the good jobs, Brennan thought. Sometimes, though, he wondered if perhaps he weren't too much of an optimist.

'This is an industry in which legitimate sales commissions have been misconstrued,' Walters was saying.

'What my client meant to say . . .' Walters' counsel interrupted.

The questioning finally got around to what George Brennan and Jack Sclafani had come wanting to hear: 'Mr. Walters, was the late Adam Cauliff a member of your firm?'

Oh, he doesn't like that name, Sclafani thought

192

as he watched the face of Robert Walters flush with anger at the question.

'Adam Cauliff was in our employ for about two and a half years,' Walters responded. Walters' voice remained clipped and cold, as if he were disdainful of the subject.

'In what capacity did Mr. Cauliff work for Walters and Arsdale?'

'He began as a staff architect. Later he was put in charge of what we would consider midlevel reconstructions and renovations.'

'What do you consider midlevel?'

'Projects that will bill less than one hundred million dollars.'

'Was his work satisfactory?'

'I would say so.'

'You say that Cauliff was with you for more than two years. Why did he leave you?'

'To open his own firm.' Robert Walters smiled coldly. 'Adam Cauliff was a detail-oriented man and very practical. We sometimes encounter architects who simply will not face the reality of the fact that office space is rented by the square foot. Despite their awareness that economies are important—sometimes paramount—considerations, they will plan unnecessary, space-wasting effects, such as extremely wide corridors, which, multiplied by thirty or forty stories, may dramatically reduce the space that will produce income.'

'I gather then that Adam Cauliff was a valued employee, one who didn't make that kind of mistake.'

'He was efficient. He got the jobs done. And he learned quickly. He was smart enough to purchase the parcel of land adjacent to the Vandermeer

193

mansion, which was then a historic landmark. When the mansion was removed from landmark status, the Kaplan property Adam purchased became infinitely more valuable.'

'The mansion burned down, did it not?' the assistant D.A. asked.

'Yes, that's true. But not before it had already lost its landmark status. Even if there had not been a fire, the mansion would have been razed soon. Peter Lang bought the property and had begun plans to erect a combined apartment-office building.'

Walters smiled grimly. 'Adam Cauliff thought Lang would so desperately want the Kaplan parcel, which he now owned, that he would accept Cauliff's design for the proposed building. It was not working out that way, however. If Adam had stayed with us and allowed our gifted architects to work with him, he would have had a chance to land the job.'

'Meaning your firm would have landed the job?'

'Meaning a team of visionary, award-winning architects, capable of creating a structure that would be on the cutting edge of urban design, would have worked with him. Cauliff's design was pedestrian and imitative. The investors wouldn't touch it, and I understand that Lang told him so.

'Cauliff was in something of a bind. He would have had to sell the Kaplan parcel to Lang at more or less whatever price he was offered. Otherwise Lang might well have constructed a much less ambitious building, independent of Cauliff. Had that happened, the Kaplan parcel would have been so hemmed in as to be virtually useless. So you see, Cauliff was definitely in a tough spot.'

'You weren't sorry to see Adam Cauliff in that bind, were you, Mr. Walters?' the attorney asked.

'I gave Adam Cauliff a job because of my great personal friendship with former congressman Cornelius MacDermott, into whose family he had married. Cauliff rewarded me for my effort by walking out on the firm and taking with him Winifred Johnson, who had been my assistant for twenty-two years, and who had become my virtual right arm. Am I sorry he's dead? Yes, as a decent human being, I regret his passing. He was the husband of Nell MacDermott, whom I've known all her life. Nell is a wonderful young woman, and I regret the pain she must be experiencing.'

The door to the office opened, and Joe Mayes, an assistant D.A., came in. From the expression on his face, Brennan and Sclafani could see that something big had happened.

'Mr. Walters,' Mayes asked abruptly, 'is your firm in the process of inspecting an office building on Lexington and Forty-seventh that you renovated several years ago?'

'Yes, this morning we received notice that several bricks in the façade seemed loose. We immediately sent an inspection team to the site.'

'I'm afraid the bricks are more than loose, Mr. Walters. The entire façade collapsed onto the street this morning. Three pedestrians were seriously injured, one of them critically.'

George Brennan watched as the flushed face of Robert Walters became sickly pale. Was it a matter of substandard material? he wondered. Or perhaps shoddy workmanship? If so, whose pockets had been lined to ignore it?

CHAPTER FORTY-SIX

At precisely three o'clock that afternoon, Nell rang the doorbell at Bonnie Wilson's apartment on Seventy-third Street and West End Avenue. Hearing the faint sound of approaching footsteps on the other side of the door, she thought for a moment of making a dash for the elevator while there still was time.

What in the name of God am I doing here? she asked herself. Mac was right. All this talk of mediums and of messages from lost loved ones is nothing more than hocus-pocus, and I'm an idiot to put myself in the position of being ridiculed if it ever comes out that I fell for this kind of thing.

The door opened.

'Nell, come in.'

Nell's immediate impression was that Bonnie Wilson was more attractive in person than she had seemed on television. Her midnight black hair was a startling contrast to her porcelain complexion. Her large gray eyes were fringed with heavy lashes. The two women were about the same height, but Bonnie was rail thin, almost undernourished in appearance.

Her smile was apologetic. 'This is something I've never done before,' she explained as she led Nell from the foyer, halfway down a long hallway into a small study. 'It has happened that, occasionally, when I am in touch with someone on the other side, another person there will communicate with me. But this is a different situation altogether.'

She gestured to a chair. 'Please sit down, Nell.

Please understand, if, after we've chatted for a few minutes, you want to get up and walk out, I won't be offended. From what your aunt tells me, you're very uncomfortable with the whole concept of contact with those who have passed on.'

'Truthfully, I *may* walk out, and I'm glad you realize that,' Nell said stiffly. 'After what Aunt Gert told me, though, I felt I had to come. In my own life, I've had several instances that I suppose could be called psychic experiences. Gert may have told you about them.'

'Actually, no, she has not. Over the last few years I have seen her at some of our Psychic Association meetings, and I was at a gathering in her apartment once, but I never had any discussion with her about you.'

'Bonnie, I feel like I have to be very up front with you,' Nell said. 'I simply don't buy the concept of your being able to do something that sounds to me suspiciously like picking up a phone and contacting a dead person. Nor do I accept that someone on the "other side," as the books I've read put it, in essence picks up a phone and contacts *you*.'

Bonnie Wilson smiled. 'I appreciate your honesty. Nevertheless I, and other people all over the world with psychic powers—for reasons beyond our ken—have been chosen to be the mediators between people who have passed over and their loved ones here. Usually someone comes to me who is grief stricken and wants to try to be in touch with the person who has gone ahead.

'But sometimes, infrequently, it works in a different way. For example, one day when I was helping a husband who had passed over give a

197

message to his wife, I was contacted by a young person named Jackie who had died in an automobile accident. I didn't understand how I could help him. Then, less than a week later, I received a phone call from a woman I had never met.'

It seemed to Nell that Bonnie Wilson's eyes darkened as she spoke. 'That woman had seen me on television and wanted to make an appointment for a private meeting. It seems her son, Jackie, had died in an automobile accident. She was the mother of the young man who had spoken to me from the other side.'

'But there is much less coincidence in my being here now. To begin with, you knew Gert,' Nell protested. 'Then the newspapers were filled with the story of the explosion on the boat, and virtually every article reported that Adam was married to Cornelius MacDermott's granddaughter.'

'Which is precisely why, when Adam contacted me during a channeling, gave me his name and asked for Nell, I knew to go to Gert.'

Nell stood up. 'Bonnie, I'm sorry, but I'm just not a believer. I'm afraid I've wasted too much of your time already. I should go.'

'You haven't wasted my time if you'll just give me the chance to see if Adam wants to convey a message to you.'

Reluctantly, Nell sat down again. I suppose I owe her that much, she thought.

Minutes passed. Bonnie's eyes were closed, her cheek resting on her hand. Then suddenly she tilted her head as though straining to hear someone or something. A long moment later she lowered her hand, opened her eyes and looked directly at

Nell.

'Adam is here,' she said quietly.

In spite of her disbelief, Nell felt a chill pass through her body. Be sensible, she told herself fiercely. This is nonsense. She tried to make her voice sound both crisp and calm. 'Can you see him?'

'In my mind's eye. He's looking at you with so much love in his expression, Nell. He's smiling at you. He's saying that of course you don't believe he's here. You're from Missouri.'

Nell gasped. 'I'm from Missouri' was an expression she had used jokingly whenever Adam tried to convince her that she could learn to enjoy boating.

'Does that make sense to you, Nell?' Bonnie Wilson asked.

Nell nodded.

'Adam wants to apologize to you, Nell. I'm getting from him that you two quarreled the last time you were together before he passed over.'

I didn't tell anyone that we had quarreled, Nell thought. Not one single soul.

'Adam is telling me that the quarrel was his fault. I'm getting a sense that there was something you wanted to do, and that he was making it difficult for you.'

Nell felt burning tears well up in her eyes.

Bonnie Wilson sat very still. 'I'm starting to lose contact. But Adam doesn't want to leave yet. Nell, I see white roses over your head. They're a sign of his love for you.'

Nell did not believe her own words as she spoke: 'Tell him I love him too. Tell him I'm so sorry we quarreled.'

199

'Now I see him a little more clearly again. He looks so pleased, Nell. But he is saying that he wants you to begin the new chapter in your life. Is there a situation that will take all your energy and time?'

The campaign, Nell thought.

Bonnie did not wait for her to reply. 'Yes, I understand,' she was murmuring. 'He says, 'Tell Nell to give away all my clothes.' I see a room, with racks and bins . . .'

'I always take the clothes we give away to a thrift shop connected to a church in our neighborhood,' Nell said. 'It has a room like the one you describe where they sort clothes.'

'Adam said that you should give them away now. By helping others in his name, you help him to achieve higher spiritual fulfillment. And he says you must pray for him. Remember him in your prayers, he says, but then let him go.'

Bonnie paused, her eyes staring straight ahead but not seeming to actually see anything. 'He is leaving us,' she said softly.

'*Stop him!*' Nell cried. 'Someone blew up his boat. Ask him if he knows who did that to him.'

Bonnie waited. 'I don't think he's going to tell us, Nell. That means he either doesn't know, or that he has forgiven his assailant and does not want you to be unforgiving.'

After a moment, Bonnie shook her head and looked directly at Nell. 'He's gone,' she said with a smile. Then suddenly she clutched her chest. 'No wait, what he is thinking is coming to me. Does the name 'Peter' mean anything to you?'

Peter Lang, Nell thought. 'Yes,' she said quietly.

'Nell, blood is dripping around him. I can't be

sure if that means this person named Peter was the assailant. I *can* be sure, though, that Adam is trying to warn you about something involving him. He begs you to be on your guard against this Peter, to be careful . . .'

CHAPTER FORTY-SEVEN

On Monday afternoon, Dan Minor arrived home to find a message from Lilly Brown on the answering machine. But when he played it back, it was not what he had hoped to hear.

Lilly's voice sounded nervous, and her speech was rapid. 'Dr. Dan,' she began, 'I've been asking and asking around about Quinny. She has a lot of friends, but nobody has seen or heard from her in months. That's just not right. There's a group she stays with sometimes who live on East Fourth Street, in some of the old tenements there. They're wondering if maybe she's sick and got locked up in a hospital somewhere. Sometimes when Quinny got one of her big-time depressed attacks, she wouldn't talk or eat for days.'

Is that where I'll find her? Dan wondered, his heart sinking. Locked in a psychiatric ward—or worse? The past winter had been bitterly cold in New York. Suppose she hadn't left the city last fall? If Quinny had been in a protracted depression and not been forced into a shelter, anything might have happened to her.

What made me so convinced I'd find her? he asked himself, for the first time really feeling a loss of resolve. It's not over yet, though, he thought. It's just that I can't sit back any longer and wait for her to show up. Tomorrow I'll start checking out hospitals. He forced himself to acknowledge that he would also have to find out which city agency might list the unidentified dead.

Lilly had talked to homeless people who squatted in abandoned buildings around East Fourth Street. Next weekend I'll walk around there and try to talk to some of them myself, he decided.

There was something else he could do. Lilly had described how Quinny looked now. She said that her hair had turned completely gray and was long enough to reach her shoulders. 'She's even thinner than she is in that old picture you have,' Lilly had said. 'Her cheekbones stick out. You still can tell she might have been really pretty when she was young.'

There are places that will do computer aging, if that's what they call it, Dan thought. I know the police department can do it.

Dan decided it was time to actively pursue other ways to find Quinny, or, even if it was bad news, to find out exactly what had happened to her.

As Dan changed to shorts and a long-sleeved sweatshirt, preparing to go to the park for another run, he found himself hoping that he would luck into another chance encounter with Nell MacDermott.

That possibility helped to relieve the growing anxiety that he was now feeling about Quinny. I became what I am for her sake, he thought. *Please let me be able to tell her that*, he prayed.

CHAPTER FORTY-EIGHT

Cornelius MacDermott had a visit on Monday afternoon from Tom Shea, the party chairman for New York City. He had come because he needed to know one way or the other about Nell's decision on making a run for the congressional seat being vacated by Bob Gorman.

'I don't have to tell you it's a presidential election year, Mac,' Shea said. 'A strong candidate for this seat is going to help get out the overall vote we need to put our guy in the White House. You're a legend in this district. Your presence at Nell's side during the campaign will be a constant reminder to the voters of what you did for them.'

'You ever hear about the advice they give to the groom's mother before a wedding?' Mac snapped. 'It's "Wear beige and keep your mouth shut." That's what I intend to do if Nell runs. She's smart, good looking, fast on her feet, knows what the job entails and is capable of doing it better than anyone else I know. Best of all, she cares about people. That's why she should run. That's why people should vote for her—not because I'm considered some kind of legend.'

Liz Hanley was in the office with them, taking notes. Good God, is he prickly today! she thought. But she understood why. Mac had confided in her his concern about Nell's emotional state, and he was paralyzed with worry that her visit to a psychic might somehow become known and then be leaked to the press.

'Oh come on, Mac, you know what I mean,' Tom

Shea said good-naturedly. 'People fell in love with Nell when they saw that picture of her as a ten-year-old, trying to dry your tears at her parents' memorial Mass. She grew up in the eye of the public. We can hold off the announcement till the dinner on the 30th, but we have to be sure that the effect of her husband's death won't make it too tough for her to campaign.'

'Nothing is too tough for Nell,' Mac snapped. 'She's a pro.'

But when Shea left, Mac's façade of bluster crumbled. 'Liz, I blew up at Nell last night when I realized she was going to go to that psychic. Call her up and help me make peace. Tell her I want to have dinner with her.'

'Blessed are the peacemakers,' Liz said dryly. 'For they shall be called the children of God.'

'You've told me that before.'

'That's because I've done this before. Where shall I tell her to meet you for dinner?'

'Neary's. Seven-thirty. You come too, okay?'

CHAPTER FORTY-NINE

On Monday afternoon, at her second meeting with Ben Tucker, Dr. Megan Crowley skillfully maneuvered the conversation around to the day the young boy had observed the boat blow up in New York harbor. She would have preferred to wait for another session or two before bringing it up, but Ben had experienced nightmares again over the weekend, and she could see they were taking a heavy toll on him.

She began the session with him by talking about ferryboat rides. 'When I was little, we used to go to a place called Martha's Vineyard,' she said. 'I loved to go there, but boy, was that a long trip, at least from here. Six hours in the car, and then over an hour on the ferry.'

'Ferries stink,' Ben said. 'The one I was on made me want to barf. I don't ever want to go on one again.'

'Oh, where did you go on one, Benjy?'

'In New York. My dad took me to see the Statue of Liberty.' He paused. 'That was the day the boat blew up.'

Megan waited.

Ben's expression became reflective. 'I was looking right at the boat. It was cool. I was wishing I was on it instead of on that stupid ferry, but now I'm glad I wasn't on it.' He frowned. 'I don't want to talk about it.'

Megan saw the look of fear settle over him. She knew he was thinking about the snake, but she still had no real idea how the two things were connected. 'Ben, sometimes it helps to talk about something if it's bothering you. It's pretty awful to see a boat blow up.'

'I could see the people,' he whispered.

'Ben, you know something? If you would draw a picture of what you saw, I bet it would help you to get it out of your mind. Do you like to draw?'

'I really like to draw a lot.'

Megan had sheets of sketching paper, Magic Markers and crayons waiting. A few minutes later, Ben was bent over the worktable, deep in concentration.

As Megan watched, she realized that he must

have seen the accident in closer detail than even his father had realized. The sky in the drawing became filled with brightly colored debris, some of it in flames. Other objects resembled pieces of broken furniture and dishes.

Ben's face became pinched and tight as he drew in what was clearly a human hand.

He laid his crayon down. 'I don't want to draw the snake,' he said.

CHAPTER FIFTY

At the appointed hour, Nell was settled at a corner table, sipping a glass of wine and nibbling on a breadstick when her grandfather and Liz arrived at Neary's on East Fifty-seventh Street.

Noting her grandfather's surprised expression, she said airily, 'Just thought I'd play your game, Mac. Arrange to meet at seven-thirty. Arrive at seven-fifteen. Then tell the other guy he's late so he'll be thrown off balance.'

'Too bad that's the only thing you've learned from me,' Mac barked as he slid in next to her.

Nell kissed his cheek. When Liz had called her earlier, she had laid it on the line to her. 'Nell, I don't have to sell you on the way Mac operates. He calls it as he sees it. He's bleeding because he knows what Adam's death means to you. He can't stand to see you hurt. He'd kill for you. God help him, he'd even have taken Adam's place on that boat to spare you pain.'

Listening to Liz earlier, Nell had felt ashamed of herself. Yes, they had their differences, but Mac was a rock for her, always there, always ready to help if she needed it. She simply could not stay mad at him. 'Hi, Grandpa,' she said now.

Their fingers interlocked. 'Still my best girl, Nell?'

'Of course I am.'

Liz had settled across the table from them. 'Shall I leave while you two make up?'

'No. The special tonight is sliced steak, your favorite. My favorite too.' Nell smiled at Liz and gestured with her head toward her grandfather. 'Of course, only the mind of God knows what the Legend here will have.'

'In that case, I'll stay. But do you think we could possibly talk about the weather or the Yankees until I have a chance to eat?'

'We'll try,' Cornelius and Cornelia MacDermott said in unison, then smiled at each other. Inevitably, over shrimp cocktail, they began to discuss the election. 'It's never over till it's over, Nell,' Mac said. 'In an election year, New York, both city and state, is always unpredictable. That's why every congressional district is important. People who feel strongly about one candidate will pull the lever down for everyone else on that same slate. You are a candidate who can make them do that.'

'Do you really think so?' she asked.

'I know so,' Mac replied. 'I haven't been doing this all my life for nothing. Let us put your name on that ballot, and you'll see.'

'You know I probably will, Mac. Just let me have another couple of days to get my head together.'

The issue of the election temporarily out of the way, she knew what the next subject would be.

207

'You go to that psychic?'

'Yes, I did.'

'Did you get to speak to Jesus Christ and the Blessed Mother?'

'*Mac*,' Liz warned.

He can't help himself, Nell reminded herself. She chose her words carefully: 'Yes, Mac, I did go. She told me that Adam was sorry he had opposed my decision to do something I wanted to do. I'm sure, of course, that what that meant was my decision about going into politics. She said that Adam wants me to go on with my life and to pray for him. She told me he said to give away his clothes so that other people can be helped.'

'If that's what you heard, it was pretty good advice.'

'I'd say it wasn't much different from what Monsignor Duncan might have told me if I'd spoken to him. The only difference,' she added deliberately, 'is that *Bonnie Wilson hears it directly from Adam.*'

Nell was aware that both her grandfather and Liz were staring at her. 'I know it sounds incredible,' she said, 'but when I was there with her, I believed it too, absolutely.'

'Do you believe it now?'

'I believe the advice. But Mac, there was something else. Peter Lang's name came up. Again, I don't know what to think, but, if I can believe Bonnie Wilson, Adam—from the other side, as they put it—is warning me about him.'

'Nell, for God's sake! You're taking all this much too seriously.'

'I know. But Adam and Peter Lang *were* working together to develop that property on Twenty-eighth

208

Street. Adam was designing the building that was to go up there. Peter called me late this afternoon, saying he had important business to discuss with me. He's coming over tomorrow morning.'

'Look,' Mac said, 'Lang didn't get to where he is now without pulling a few fast ones, so chances are he's not lily white. I'll get someone to nose around.' He paused, hesitating to bring up one more problem over dinner. Then he plowed ahead. 'But he's not the only cause for concern right now. Nell, you must have heard about that building façade that collapsed on Lexington Avenue this afternoon?'

'Yes, I caught it on the six o'clock news.'

'It's just one more problem, Nell. Right before I left the office tonight, I got a call from Bob Walters. Sam Krause was the builder who did the actual work on that Lexington Avenue building. But Adam was the architect on record at Walters and Arsdale who designed the renovation. If corners were being cut—you know, the kind of thing that you hear about, with inferior supplies being used and a slackening of standards—then arguably Adam was the one to have known about it. Several pedestrians were hurt in the collapse, and one is in critical condition and may not make it.' He paused. 'What I'm saying is that Adam's name may come up in another criminal investigation.'

Mac saw the glimmer of anger flash in his granddaughter's eyes. 'Nell,' he said, his voice almost a plea, 'I have to warn you about all this. It's not easy for me. I just don't want to see you hurt.'

Nell flashed back to earlier in the day, when Bonnie Wilson was communicating with Adam:

209

He is looking at you with so much love . . . she had said; . . . *he has forgiven his assailant* . . .

'Mac, I want to know every single thing they are saying about my husband, because even if it kills me, I'm going to get to the truth of all this. Somebody put a bomb on that boat and took Adam's life. I swear this to you: one way or another, I'm going to find out who it was, and when I do, that person will wish he were already burning in hell. As for Walters and Arsdale, I'll sue them for every penny they've got if they keep trying to make Adam the scapegoat for all their own misdeeds and mistakes. And when you speak to those old pals of yours, you can just tell them that for me.'

In the silence that followed, Liz Hanley cleared her throat and said softly, 'The steak is coming. Could we discuss something else, the Yankees' lineup, maybe?'

Tuesday, June 20

CHAPTER FIFTY-ONE

As his driver threaded the car through the tortuous morning traffic on Madison Avenue, an edgy Peter Lang mentally reviewed the approach he would take in presenting to Nell MacDermott his offer to purchase her late husband's property. He sensed that he would have to proceed with care, because when he had phoned to set up the meeting, he thought he detected a note of hostility in her voice.

Funny, she seemed friendly enough when I saw her last week, he thought. Nell had talked about how Adam had been looking forward to working on the project, and how proud he had been of his design.

If Cauliff never told her that he was off the job, then surely there's no point in telling her now, Lang reasoned. I'll offer her a better than fair price, he decided; that way she won't have any reason not to take it. As he considered his options, however, he realized he felt no reassurance in his rationale. Every instinct told him this meeting would not go well.

The car continued to move at a snail's pace. He looked at his watch; it was ten of ten. He leaned forward and tapped his driver on the shoulder. 'Is there any particular reason why you insist on staying in this lane?' he snapped.

*   *   *

As she opened the door to Peter Lang, Nell could not help wondering just how bad the traffic

213

accident had been that kept him from attending the fatal meeting on Adam's boat. Less than a week had passed since she'd seen him, yet she could not detect the trace of a bruise on his face. Even his lip, which had been badly swollen, seemed completely healed.

Urbane. Handsome. Polished. A real estate visionary. Those were the words used to describe Lang in the gossip and society columns.

Blood is dripping around him . . . Adam is trying to warn you. The psychic's words suddenly flashed into Nell's mind.

He kissed her cheek. 'I think about you a lot, Nell. How have you been?'

'I guess I've been about as well as you would expect,' she responded, a distinct chill in her voice.

'You certainly look very well,' he said, taking both her hands in his. He smiled disarmingly. 'I feel odd saying that—but it *is* a fact.'

'Nothing like keeping up appearances, is there, Peter?' Nell replied, freeing her hands and leading him into the living room.

'Oh, I suspect you're a very strong woman who takes pride in keeping up appearances.' He looked around. 'This is a beautiful apartment, Nell. How long have you had it?'

'Eleven years.' The answer was automatic— dates had been on her mind so much lately. I was twenty-one when I bought this place, Nell thought. I had income from Mom's trust, and the insurance money from both Mom and Dad. I had been living with Mac all through college, but once I graduated, I wanted a bit of freedom. Mac had talked me into managing his New York office, and I was about to start Fordham Law at night. Mac tried to talk me

214

out of buying the co-op, but even he agreed that I got a steal.

'Eleven years ago, huh?' Lang said. 'The real estate market in New York was in a real slump back then. I'm sure that now it's worth at least three times what you paid for it.'

'It's not for sale.'

Lang could hear the coldness in her voice and could sense that she did not intend to indulge in small talk.

'Nell, Adam and I were in a business venture together,' he began.

'I'm aware of that.'

How much does she know? Lang wondered, pausing for a moment. He decided to take a chance. 'As you no doubt know, Adam had created the design for the tower complex we planned to build.'

'Yes, he was very excited about the project,' Nell said quietly.

'We were delighted with the preliminary work Adam had done. He was a creative and exciting architect. We will miss him terribly. Unfortunately, now that he isn't with us, I'm afraid we have to start all over. Another architect doubtless will have his own concept.'

'I can understand that.'

So Adam hadn't told her, Lang thought triumphantly. He looked at her, sitting across from him, her head down. Maybe he had been wrong about sensing hostility from her. Maybe she was just strung out emotionally.

'As I'm sure you know, last August Adam purchased a downtown building and lot from a Mrs. Kaplan, for which he paid a little under a

215

million dollars. It adjoins a lot I have since purchased, and it was part of the equity he brought to the construction deal we had worked out. The assessed value of that property as of last week was eight hundred thousand dollars, but I'm prepared to offer you three million dollars for it. I think you'll agree that represents a nice return on an investment of only ten months.'

For a moment, Nell studied the face of the man sitting opposite her. 'Why are you willing to pay so much money for it?' she asked.

'Because with it, we will have room to give our building complex a more impressive presence. It will enable us to include a number of aesthetic additions, such as a curving driveway and more elaborate landscaping, which will in turn enhance the value of our venture. I might add that when our tower complex goes up, it will have such a dominant presence that your property, assuming you retain it, may actually lose some of its present value.'

You're lying, Nell thought. She remembered that Adam had said something about the Kaplan parcel being necessary to Lang if he was to actually erect the structure he planned. 'I'll think about it,' she said, giving him a slight smile.

Lang smiled in return. 'Of course. I understand. Obviously you'll want to discuss this with your grandfather.' He paused, then added, 'Nell, I may be out of line, but I'd like to think we're friends and that you can be up front with me. As you must be aware, there have been a lot of rumors around town about you.'

'Are there? What kind of rumors?'

'The rumors I hear, and I hope they're true, are

that you're planning to announce that you're running for your grandfather's congressional seat.'

Nell stood, indicating that their meeting was finished. 'I never discuss rumors, Peter,' she said, her face showing no expression.

'Meaning that *if* you announce, you'll choose your own time to do it.' Lang followed her lead and stood as well. Before Nell could stop him, he had reached out and taken her hand. 'Nell, I just want you to know that you have my wholehearted support, in every way possible.'

'Thank you,' she said, pulling her hand back. And you're about as subtle as a sledgehammer, she thought.

The door had barely closed behind Lang when the phone rang. It was Detective Jack Sclafani requesting that Nell agree to admit him and his partner, Detective Brennan, to Adam's office, and to allow them to examine the contents of Winifred Johnson's desk and files.

'We can probably get a search warrant,' Sclafani explained, 'but it would be much easier to do it this way.'

'I don't mind. I'll meet you there,' Nell told him. Carefully she added, 'I should tell you that, at her mother's request, I went to Winifred's apartment and went through her desk. She had asked me to look for insurance policies or any other personal financial information that might indicate what steps Winifred had taken to secure her mother's financial future. Since I found nothing helpful there, I was planning to see if she perhaps had left personal papers in the office.'

*   *   *

217

The detectives arrived on Twenty-seventh Street a few minutes before Nell. Together they stood in front of the office building and studied the architectural model in the window.

'Pretty fancy,' Sclafani observed. 'You must get big bucks for dreaming up something as fancy as this.'

'If Walters was right in what he said yesterday,' George Brennan replied, 'it looks better to us than it does to people who know about architecture. According to him, the design was being turned down.'

Nell had gotten out of a taxi and come up behind the two detectives just in time to hear Brennan's remark.

'What?' she demanded. 'Did you say they were turning down Adam's design?'

Sclafani and Brennan spun around. Seeing Nell's shocked expression, Sclafani realized that she didn't have a clue that her husband had been taken off the project. How long did Cauliff know it himself? he wondered.

'Mr. Walters was at the district attorney's office yesterday, Ms. MacDermott,' he said. 'That was what he told us.'

Her expression hardened. 'I wouldn't trust anything Mr. Walters said.' With that, Nell turned abruptly, walked to the door of the building and rang the bell for the building superintendent. 'I don't have a key,' she explained crisply, 'and Adam probably had his with him on the boat.'

She waited with her back to the two men, trying to calm herself. If what they had said about Adam's design was true, why did Peter Lang lie to me less

218

than an hour ago? she wondered. And if it was true, why didn't Adam tell me about it? Was that why he'd been so preoccupied, so on edge those last weeks? He should have told me. I might have been able to help him, she thought. I would have understood his disappointment.

The superintendent, a burly man in his late fifties, appeared and opened the door for them. In the process he offered his sympathy to Nell and told her he had had inquiries about the space. Would she be giving it up? he wondered.

Jack Sclafani could tell from his partner's expression that George Brennan had the same reaction to Adam Cauliff's business quarters as he did: well-enough furnished, but surprisingly small. Basically it consisted of a reception area and two private offices, one large, the other a hole in the wall. To him, the space had a cold, impersonal feeling. Certainly it was not an inviting place and didn't go far in giving one confidence in the creativity of the people who worked there. The only picture on the wall of the reception area was an artist's rendering of the proposed edifice, and in this context even it had a shabby look about it.

'How many people did your husband employ?' Sclafani asked.

'He only had Winifred here with him. Today, so much of the work of an architect is done on computer that when you're starting out on your own you don't need to take on a big overhead. Adam could farm out segments of the work on his project to others, such as structural engineers, for example.'

'So the office has been closed since the . . .' Brennan hesitated. 'Since the accident?'

219

'Yes.'

Nell realized that she had spent much of the past ten days trying to sound calm and self-controlled. *Well, now the winch has been turned up another notch*—that was the thought that had run through her head all night, as once again she lay sleepless till dawn. Presenting an outward appearance of calm was becoming more and more difficult.

What would these detectives think if they knew about Lisa Ryan's challenge to her? she wondered. Because, for all practical purposes, that's what it had been—a challenge: *Find out where and why someone made my husband take fifty thousand dollars to keep his mouth shut, and help me find a way to make it right.* How do I begin to even attempt to do that? she kept asking herself.

What would these practical, no-nonsense detectives think of Bonnie Wilson? she wondered. An hour after I got back to the normality of my own home, I had begun to doubt everything she had told me, including that she actually had been talking to Adam. I really do believe that she can read my thoughts, Nell decided. On the other hand, I certainly wasn't thinking about 'I'm from Missouri' when Bonnie talked about it. And I told absolutely no one that Adam and I had quarreled.

And what about the collapse of the building façade on Lexington Avenue? Can they blame that in some way on Adam? There were so many questions out there, so many different forces pulling at her. She needed time to think, time to put all the pieces together. At the moment, she didn't know which way to turn.

She realized suddenly that the two detectives were looking at her with an expression of

220

speculative interest mixed with concern. 'Sorry,' she said. 'Woolgathering, I guess. Being here is more difficult than I had thought.'

She did not realize, of course, that the understanding and sympathy in their faces masked a sudden certainty in both Brennan and Sclafani that, like Lisa Ryan, Nell MacDermott knew something that she was afraid to discuss with them.

Winifred's desk was locked, but George Brennan produced a ring of keys, and one of them fit the master lock. 'Her purse was recovered,' he told Nell, 'and these were inside. Oddly enough, the purse was hardly scorched. That's the amazing thing about these explosions.'

'A lot of amazing things have happened in these last ten days,' Nell said. 'Including the attempt of Walters and Arsdale to suggest that any irregularities you find in their company should be blamed on my husband. This morning I spoke to Adam's accountant. He assures me that there is absolutely nothing in his affairs that won't bear the closest scrutiny.'

I hope so, George Brennan thought. Because somebody from Walters and Arsdale had to have been working hand-in-glove with Sam Krause Construction, considering the kind of inferior materials they used in constructing the building façade that collapsed yesterday. When things like this happen, they aren't just mistakes—somebody had to be in the know and on the take.

'I don't want to keep you,' Brennan said to Nell. 'Why don't we take a quick look through Ms. Johnson's desk, and then we can all leave.'

It took only minutes to ascertain that there was nothing out of the ordinary to be found there. 'It's

221

exactly the same as her desk at home,' Nell told them. 'All routine bills and receipts and memos, except here we did at least find an envelope with some insurance policies and the deed to her father's grave.'

The top two drawers of the filing cabinet next to the desk held files. The bottom drawer contained boxes of paper for the copier and printer, sheets of heavy brown wrapping paper and rolls of twine.

Jack Sclafani skimmed through the files. 'Run-of-the-mill correspondence,' he said. He thumbed through Winifred's address book. 'Do you mind if we borrow this?' he asked Nell.

'No, of course not. It probably should go to her mother anyway.'

There is one difference from the desk in her home, Nell thought—there's nothing here about Harry Reynolds. I wonder who he was? Perhaps he was helping Nell to keep her mother in that expensive home.

'Ms. MacDermott, this safe-deposit key was found in Ms. Johnson's wallet.' As he spoke, George Brennan took a key from a small manila envelope and laid it on Winifred's desk. 'It has a number on it, 332. Would you know if it came from this office, or was it a personal key belonging to Ms. Johnson?'

Nell examined it. 'I have no idea. If it came from this office, then I knew nothing about it. I've had my own safe-deposit box for years, and as far as I know, Adam didn't have one, either personal or for business. Can't you take it to the bank and find out there?'

Brennan shook his head. 'Unfortunately all safe-deposit keys look alike, and there is no bank

222

identification on them. The newer ones don't even carry numbers. We'll only be able to try to trace this one by going into the bank that issued it, and figuring which one that might be could take a while.'

'It sounds a little like trying to find a needle in a haystack.'

'Not unlike it, Ms. MacDermott. But chances are it will turn out to be issued by a bank within a ten-block radius of either Winifred Johnson's apartment or this building.'

'I see,' Nell said, then paused, hesitating as though unsure of what she was going to say next. 'Look, I don't know whether this is relevant or not, but Winifred apparently was involved with a man named Harry Reynolds.'

'How do you know that?' Brennan asked quickly.

'When I looked through the desk in her apartment, one drawer was stuffed with papers of every imaginable kind, from architectural plans to the backs of envelopes to Kleenex. On every one of them she'd written 'Winifred loves Harry Reynolds.' My impression when I saw it was that they'd been written by a fifteen-year-old girl with a terrible crush on someone.'

'To me, that sounds more like an obsession than a crush,' Brennan observed. 'From what I understand, Winifred Johnson was a quiet woman who lived with her mother all her life until the mother went into a nursing home.'

'That's right.'

'Invariably, that's the kind of woman who falls like a ton of bricks for the wrong guy.' He raised an eyebrow. 'We'll follow up on Harry Reynolds.' With a decisive shove, Brennan closed the file drawer.

223

'Ms. MacDermott, we're about finished here and then we're going for a cup of coffee. How about joining us?'

Nell hesitated for a moment, then decided to accept. For some reason she did not want to be alone in this office. As she had traveled there in the cab, she had thought she might take the time to go through Adam's desk, but looking about her, she knew instinctively that this was not the day. She still felt such a sense of unreality about Adam's death. And for some reason that she still had not quite assessed, if anything, the visit to Bonnie Wilson had enhanced rather than detracted from that feeling.

How long had Adam known that they were not going to accept his design for Vandermeer Tower? she wondered. She remembered how confident he had been when he first told her about it. He'd said Peter Lang had come to see him, that Lang had bought the Vandermeer property and wanted to buy the Kaplan parcel. Adam had told him he'd sell it, but only on the condition that he go along with it as the architect. 'Lang's investors have commissioned me to prepare plans and a model,' he'd said.

I asked him at the time what would happen if they didn't accept his design. I remember his exact words: *The Kaplan property is indispensable to the kind of complex Lang wants to erect. They'll accept it.*

'Thank you, yes. I would like to have coffee,' she said. 'I had a meeting with Peter Lang this morning that I want to tell you about. When I'm finished, you may begin to understand—and perhaps even to share—my feeling that he is both a liar and a manipulator, and he was definitely someone who

224

stood to benefit from my husband's death.'

CHAPTER FIFTY-TWO

Like his granddaughter, Cornelius MacDermott had spent a sleepless night. On Tuesday he did not go to the office until nearly noon, and when he arrived there, Liz Hanley was startled to see that his normally ruddy complexion had faded to an unhealthy gray.

He soon made clear to her why he was showing such signs of stress, and though he argued a convincing case as to why his granddaughter was in danger of irreparably damaging any chance she had of running for elected office, it was Liz's concern for his health that convinced her she should go along with his plan to prove to Nell that celebrity psychic Bonnie Wilson was nothing but a charlatan.

'Call for an appointment,' he told her. 'Use your sister's name, just in case Gert ever mentioned you to this Wilson woman. I don't trust her, and I want your slant on what she's all about.' His voice was tense, not at all like his usual tone.

'If I phone from here and she has Caller ID, she'll know perfectly well who I am,' Liz pointed out.

'Good thinking. Your sister lives on Beekman Place, doesn't she?'

'Yes.'

'Pay her a visit now and call from there. This is very important.'

Liz got back to the office at three o'clock.

'I, in my new identity as Moira Callahan, am

225

seeing Bonnie Wilson tomorrow at three o'clock,' she announced.

'Good. Now if you happen to talk to Nell or Gert . . .'

'Mac, you weren't seriously going to warn me not to let on what I'm doing, were you?'

'I guess not,' he said somewhat sheepishly. 'Thanks, Liz. I knew I could count on you.'

CHAPTER FIFTY-THREE

Lisa Ryan went back to work at the salon on Tuesday. She endured the response she expected from her coworkers and clients—a mixture of genuine sympathy and avid curiosity about the details of the explosion that had claimed Jimmy's life.

She arrived home at six o'clock to find her closest friend, Brenda Curren, in the kitchen. The enticing aroma of roasting chicken was in the air. The table had been set for six, and Brenda's husband, Ed, was working with Charley on his second-grade reading assignment.

'You're too good to be true,' Lisa said quietly.

'Forget it,' Brenda said briskly. 'We thought a little company might be welcome after your first day back on the job.'

'It is.' Lisa went into the bathroom and splashed water on her face. You haven't cried all day, she told herself fiercely. Don't start now.

Over dinner, Ed Curren brought up the subject of the equipment in Jimmy's workroom. 'Lisa, I know a little about what Jimmy was doing down there, and I know he had some sophisticated tools. I think you should sell them right away. Otherwise they'll lose their value very quickly.'

He began to carve the chicken. 'If you'd like, I'll be glad to go through Jimmy's workroom and sort out everything that's down there.'

'No!' Lisa said. Then, when she saw the expressions on the faces of her friends and her children as they sat staring at her, she realized how vehemently she had refused what was merely a kind, neighborly offer.

'I'm sorry,' she said, 'it's just that the thought of selling Jimmy's things makes me realize that he really isn't coming back. I just don't feel up to dealing with it right now.'

She saw the look of sadness coming over her children's faces and tried to turn it into a joke. 'Can you imagine if Daddy came back and found his workroom cleaned out?'

But later, when the Currens were gone and she knew the children were asleep, she crept downstairs, opened the file drawer and stared at the package of money. It's like a time bomb, she thought; I *have* to get it out of here!

CHAPTER FIFTY-FOUR

Dan Minor reaaranged his Tuesday afternoon schedule in order to have time to go downtown to the Bureau of Missing Persons at One Police Plaza, the headquarters of the NYPD.

It did not take long, however, to realize how hopeless it was to attempt to get information about

Quinny there.

The detective he spoke to was sympathetic but laid out the facts in a very convincing and realistic way. 'I'm awfully sorry, Doctor Minor, but you don't know if your mother was even in New York at the point you started looking for her. You're not even certain that she's 'missing'—you just know that you haven't been able to find her. Have you any *idea* how many people are reported missing in this city each year?

He left the building and took a cab home with a feeling of total hopelessness. His best chance, he decided, was to walk around the East Fourth Street area.

He wasn't sure exactly how he would go about contacting the clusters of homeless people who were living in the abandoned buildings. I can't just walk in on them, he reasoned. I guess I'll just have to try to get friendly with anyone I see outside, and then I'll mention Quinny's name to them and see what happens. Just showing an old picture worked with Lilly, he reminded himself, somewhat reassured. And at least now I know what her friends called her.

He changed into a light sweat suit and sneakers. Just as he was leaving his building, he ran into Penny Maynard, who was just coming in.

'Drinks at seven, my place?' she said, flashing him an inviting smile.

She was very attractive, and he had enjoyed himself when he had been to her apartment a few nights earlier with some other neighbors for drinks and pasta. Without any hesitation, however, Dan declined, saying that he already had made plans for the evening. I don't want to fall into a drop-in pattern with someone who lives so close, he told himself as he walked rapidly across town.

As he began to accelerate his pace, Nell MacDermott's face floated through his mind—a frequent occurrence since the day he had run into her in the park. She wasn't listed in the phone book; he knew because he had checked. But her grandfather's consulting firm was listed, and he had thought of trying to reach her through someone there.

I could phone and ask MacDermott for her number, Dan thought. Or maybe it would be smarter to actually stop in and see him. I *did* meet him once, at that White House reception. At least he would see that I'm not some kind of stalker or romantic phony.

The thought of seeing Nell MacDermott again cheered Dan during the next two hours as he walked, block after block, in the area of East Fourth Street, begging for information about Quinny.

He had fortified himself with a stack of his cards with his phone number, which he handed out to just about everyone he talked to. 'Fifty bucks for anyone who can give me a lead to her,' he promised.

Finally, at seven o'clock he gave up, took a cab back uptown to Central Park and began to jog. At Seventy-second Street he once again ran into Nell.

CHAPTER FIFTY-FIVE

After leaving Nell MacDermott, Jack Sclafani and George Brennan drove directly to headquarters. By unspoken mutual consent, they waited until they were back in their offices before discussing what she had told them.

Jack settled at his desk and began drumming his fingers on the arm of the chair. 'MacDermott as much as said she thinks Lang may have had something to do with the explosion on the boat. Yet when we took a look at him, his story about the traffic accident seemed to check out.

'As I remember it, he claimed he was using a cellular phone and that the sun got in his eyes. He had a fender bender with the trailer truck. When we saw him, his face did look pretty banged up.'

'Maybe, but he was the one who hit the truck. The truck didn't hit him,' Brennan said. 'It could have been intentional. Anyway, Nell MacDermott raised a lot of interesting questions.' He pulled out a pad and began to jot down notes. 'Here's one right off the top of my head that I think might be worth looking into: Exactly what kind of building did Lang *really* want to put up on that Vandermeer property, and how essential was the Kaplan parcel to him if he was going to realize his goal? That question goes to motive.'

'Add this one,' Sclafani said. 'When did Lang tell Cauliff that his design had been rejected?'

'Which leads to *my* next question, Jack. Why didn't Cauliff tell his wife that Lang had dumped him? That would be the normal thing to do, assuming they were a close couple.'

'Talking about close—what do you think is going on with Winifred's boyfriend, Harry Reynolds?' Sclafani asked.

'I'll throw another suggestion on the table,' Brennan said. 'Let's dig around and see if we can't find a connection between Lang and our old friend, Jed Kaplan.'

Sclafani nodded, pushed back his chair, got up and walked over to the window. 'A nice day,' he observed. 'My wife thinks it would be a great idea if we spent a long weekend at her folks' place in Cape May. Somehow, though, I don't think that's going to happen anytime soon.'

'It isn't,' Brennan assured him.

'Since we're making work for ourselves, I have one more name to add to the list.'

'I can guess who it is: Adam Cauliff.'

'Exactly. Kaplan hated him. His former employer, Robert Walters, hated him. Lang rejected his design. He doesn't exactly come through as prince of the city. I wonder who else may have thought it would be a good idea if his boat didn't make it back to the marina?'

'Okay. Let's get busy,' Brennan said. 'I'll start by making some background calls on Cauliff.'

A couple of hours later, Brennan poked his head into Sclafani's office. 'Got some preliminary feedback from a guy I called in North Dakota. It seems Cauliff was about as popular with his former employer out there as ants are at a church picnic. This could be leading somewhere.'

CHAPTER FIFTY-SIX

As they jogged together along the paths of Central Park, Nell realized that there was something very comforting about having Dan Minor running beside her. He seemed to exude an innate strength, a power that showed in the firm line of his jaw, in the disciplined way he moved, and in the firm grasp of his hand on her arm when she started to trip and he reached out to steady her.

They ran as far north as the reservoir, then circled back until they were on the East Side at Seventy-second Street.

Panting, Nell stopped. 'This is where I get off,' she announced.

Having serendipitously run into her again, Dan had no intention of letting her go until he knew where she lived and had extracted her phone number. 'I'll walk you home,' he said promptly.

On the way, he said casually, 'I don't know about you, Nell, but I'm getting hungry. I also know that I'll be a lot more presentable after I shower and change. Would you consider meeting me for dinner in about an hour or so?'

'Oh, I don't think—'

He interrupted her. 'Do you have specific plans?'

'No.'

'Don't forget—I'm a doctor. Even if you don't feel hungry, you have to eat.'

After a few more minutes of gentle persuasion, they parted, having agreed to meet later at Il Tinello on West Fifty-sixth Street. 'Better make that an hour and a half,' Nell suggested. 'Unless, of course, all the traffic lights turn green when they see you coming.'

*   *   *

Earlier that day, after she had returned home from Adam's office, Nell had spent several hours sorting and folding Adam's clothing. Now the bed and the chairs in the guest room were covered with stacks of socks and ties, shorts and undershirts. She had moved all his suits and slacks and jackets into the closet there as well.

Unnecessary work, she said to herself as she went back and forth carrying the hangers, but once she started to take Adam's things out of the master bedroom, she wanted to complete the job.

When the dresser was empty, she had the building maintenance men take it down to the storage room. Then she had rearranged the furniture in the bedroom to where it had been before her marriage.

Now, as she returned from the park and hurried into the bedroom, where she began to peel off her jogging shorts and T-shirt, Nell realized that the room seemed in some way to have a renewed familiarity—that it was again giving her a sense of sanctuary.

I guess it's just that looking at Adam's dresser and opening the closet and seeing his clothes made me think of how he died—so suddenly, she thought, without any chance to say goodbye. It also reminded me of those last angry moments we spent together before he stalked out of the house, and out of my life forever.

233

Now, with all those reminders gone, she at least knew that when she got home from dinner, she would at last be able to sleep.

After a quick shower, she looked into her now more spacious-seeming closet and decided to wear a periwinkle-blue silk pants suit that she had bought at the end of the season last year and had forgotten about. She had come across it when she was rearranging the closet and remembered how much she had liked it when she tried it on.

Best of all, though, was the fact that it didn't have any link to Adam, who noticed everything she wore.

*   *   *

Dan Minor was waiting for her at the table when Nell arrived at Il Tinello. He was so deep in thought, though, that he didn't see her until she was almost upon him. He looks as if he's worried about something, Nell thought, but then as the maître d' pulled out a chair for her, Dan sprang to his feet and smiled.

'All the traffic lights must have turned green for you,' Nell said.

'Almost all of them. You look lovely, Nell. Thanks for joining me. I'm afraid I bullied you into saying yes. That's the trouble with being a doctor. We expect people to do exactly what we tell them.'

'You didn't bully me. I'm glad you persuaded me to get out, and, to be honest, I'm actually hungry.'

It was true. The enticing smell of wonderful Italian food filled the restaurant, and as she looked about the room, Nell realized it emanated from the pasta the waiter was carrying to the next table. She turned to Dan and laughed. 'I almost pointed over there and said, 'I want that.'

Over a glass of wine they discovered the mutual friends they had in Washington. Over prosciutto and melon they talked about the upcoming presidential election and realized they would be canceling out each other's vote. When the pasta arrived, Dan told her about his decision to move to New York, and the reasons behind it.

'The hospital is becoming a major pediatric burn center, and since that's my area of specialization, it's a great opportunity for me to help make it happen.'

He also told her about his search for his mother.

'You mean she just dropped out of your life?!' Nell exclaimed.

'She was suffering from massive clinical depression. She had become an alcoholic and felt I'd be better off with my grandparents.' He hesitated. 'It's a very long story,' he said. 'Someday, if you're interested, maybe I'll tell you the whole thing. The bottom line is that my mother is getting older. God knows, her body has been abused and neglected all these years. Moving to New York makes it possible for me to search for her myself. I thought I had a lead on her for a while there, but now I can't find her, and no one has seen her since last fall.'

'Do you think she wants you to find her, Dan?'

'She left because she blamed herself for an accident in which I was nearly killed. I want to show her how that accident turned out not to be a bad thing, and, in fact, proved to be of enormous value to me.'

He told about going to the missing persons
235

bureau, and added, 'I have absolutely no faith that anything will come of that.'

'Mac might be able to help,' Nell told him. 'He's got a lot of pull, and I know they'd search the records if he made a few calls. I'll talk to him, but I also think you should drop in to his office yourself. I'll give you his card.'

When the demitasse came, Dan said, 'Nell, I've talked your ear off about me. Say that you don't want to discuss it, and we're off the subject, but I have to ask: How is it *really* going for you?'

'*Really* going for me?' Nell dropped the sliver of lemon peel into her cup of espresso. 'I don't know how to answer that. You see, when someone dies but you don't have a body and a casket and a procession to the graveyard, there's a lack of closure about the death. It's almost like that person is still out there somewhere, even though you know he isn't. That's the way I feel, and I'm almost haunted by a sense of unreality. I keep saying to myself, 'Adam is dead, Adam is dead,' but they keep sounding like just meaningless words.'

'Did it feel that way when you lost your parents?'

'No, I knew they were gone. The difference is that they died in an accident. Adam did not—I'm sure of that. Think about it. Four people died on that boat. Someone needed to get rid of one of them, maybe all four of them, who knows? That person is still walking around, enjoying life, maybe having a late dinner right now, just as we are.' She paused, looking first at her hands and then back up into his face. 'Dan, I am going to find out who did this—and I'm not doing it just for myself. Lisa Ryan, a young woman with three little kids, needs answers too. Her husband was one of the four

236

people on the boat.'

'You realize, Nell, that anyone who can so calculatingly take four lives is a very dangerous human being.'

Across from him, Nell MacDermott's face contorted into a grimace, and her eyes widened and filled with an expression of near panic.

Dan immediately became alarmed. 'Nell, what is it?'

She shook her head. 'No, it's all right,' she said, as much to convince herself as to convince him.

'It's *not* all right, Nell. What is it?'

For an instant she had felt just as she had in those terrible moments when she was caught in the riptide. She had felt trapped and as though she were fighting for air. But this time, instead of trying to swim, she had been struggling to open a door. And instead of the cold water, she had sensed heat. Burning heat—and an awareness that she was going to die.

Wednesday, June 21

CHAPTER FIFTY-SEVEN

'The Vandermeer site is only *one* of many properties under development by Lang Enterprises,' Peter Lang said coldly.

He clearly did not relish the Wednesday morning visit of Detectives Jack Sclafani and George Brennan to his office on the top floor of 1200 Avenue of the Americas.

'For example,' he continued, his tone condescending, 'We own *this* building. I could drive you all over Manhattan and show you the scope of the other properties we own, as well as those we manage as realtors. But before you waste any more of my time, I have to ask, gentlemen, what is your point?'

Our point, Buddy, Sclafani thought, is that you're starting to look like the prime suspect in four murders, so don't get on your high horse with us.

'Mr. Lang, we appreciate how busy you are,' George Brennan said soothingly. 'But I'm sure you can understand our need to ask you a few questions. You went to see Nell MacDermott yesterday, didn't you?'

Lang raised an eyebrow. 'Yes, I did. What of it?'

He didn't like having that brought up, Sclafani thought. Up till now, he's been on his own turf and feeling pretty sure of himself. But all his money and looks and background won't be worth a plugged nickel if we can hang a quadruple murder on him, and he *knows* it.

'What was the purpose of your visit to Ms.

MacDermott?'

'Purely business,' Lang said, looking at his watch. 'Gentlemen, I'm afraid you'll have to excuse me. I have to leave for a meeting.'

'You're *having* a meeting, Mr. Lang.' Brennan's voice had become steely. 'When we spoke to you some ten days ago, you said that you and Adam Cauliff were discussing a kind of joint venture on which he might be architect.'

'Which is and was true.'

'Will you explain that venture to us?'

'I believe I have already explained it in our previous meeting. Adam Cauliff and I owned adjoining parcels of real estate on Twenty-eighth Street. We were considering joining them for the purpose of building a structure that would have both co-op apartments and offices.'

'Mr. Cauliff would have been the architect on this project?'

'Adam Cauliff was invited to submit a design for that purpose.'

'When did you reject his design, Mr. Lang?'

'I would not say it was rejected. I would say that it needed considerable rethinking.'

'That's not what you told his wife, is it?'

Peter Lang stood up. 'I have tried to be cooperative. I see my efforts are wasted and that it is not possible to talk with you on a strictly friendly basis. I resent your tone and attitude. If this is to continue, I must insist on calling my lawyer.'

'Mr. Lang, just one more question,' Detective Sclafani said. 'You made a peremptory bid for the Vandermeer property after the mansion was removed from landmark status, didn't you?'

'The city desperately wanted other land I owned.

242

I traded. The city got the better deal.'

'Just a moment more, please. If you had *not* engaged Adam Cauliff as the architect on your project, would he have sold his property to you?'

'He would have been very foolish had he not sold it to us. But, of course, he died before any transaction could be completed.'

'And I assume that was the reason for your visit to his widow. Suppose Nell MacDermott refuses to sell the property to you?'

'That, of course, would be her decision to make.' Peter Lang stood. 'Gentlemen, you'll have to excuse me. If you have any further questions, you can call my lawyer.' Lang switched on the intercom. 'Mr. Brennan and Mr. Sclafani are ready to leave,' he told his secretary. 'Please show them to the elevator.'

CHAPTER FIFTY-EIGHT

Gert MacDermott called Nell on Wednesday morning. 'Are you going to be home?' she asked. 'I made a crumb cake this morning, and I know it's one of your favorites.'

Nell was at her desk. 'Was and is, Aunt Gert. Sure—come on over.'

'Now, if you're too busy . . .'

'I'm doing my column, but it's almost finished.'

'I'll be there by eleven.'

'I'll have the kettle whistling.'

At quarter of eleven, Nell turned off the computer. The column was almost right, she decided, but she wanted to let it sit a while longer

243

before she gave it a final polish.

I've enjoyed doing the column for these two years, she thought as she filled the kettle. But it's definitely time to move on.

Although, move *back* is more like it, she admitted to herself as she got out the teapot. Back to the world that was second nature to her, campaigning and election night—and Capitol Hill, assuming she won, of course. Also back to long hours and commuting between Manhattan and D.C.

At least I know what I'll be getting into if I win, she thought. People like Bob Gorman can't take it. Or perhaps Mac was right, and Gorman was only using the position as a stepping stone to other things . . .

*   *   *

At precisely eleven, the doorman phoned to say that Ms. MacDermott was on the way up. Mac taught both Gert and me to be prompt, Nell thought. Adam, though, was always late. It was a trait that used to drive Mac crazy.

She felt disloyal remembering that.

'You look better,' were Gert's first words, as she kissed her. Gert held a cake tin in her hands.

'I had my first decent night's sleep in nearly two weeks,' Nell said. 'That helps.'

'Yes, it does,' Gert agreed. 'I tried to phone you last night, but you were out. Bonnie Wilson called to see how you were doing.'

'That was nice of her.' Nell took the cake from her great-aunt. 'Come on. Let's have that tea.'

As they sipped, Nell noticed that Gert's hands
244

were trembling slightly, something that was not uncommon for someone her age, she thought, but, dear God, I don't want anything to happen to her or Mac for a long time.

She remembered what Dan Minor had said at dinner: 'I wish I'd had siblings. I may never find my mother, and once my grandparents are gone, that's it for my family.' Then he had added, 'I don't count my father. Unfortunately, he's incidental to my life. We haven't been in touch in some time.' Then he had smiled, 'of course, I do have a very pretty stepmother, and two former ones.'

She made a mental note to call Mac and tell him to expect a call from Dan.

Promptly at 11:30, Gert got up. 'I've got to be on my way. Nell, a quick thought. Anytime you're really down and want company, you know who to call.'

Nell hugged her. 'You.'

'That's right. And listen, I hope you've followed up on giving away Adam's clothing. Bonnie thinks it's important.'

'I've started to pack his things.'

'Do you need help?'

'Not really. The superintendent is getting me some boxes. I'll load them in the car and drop them off Saturday morning. That's still the day they accept donations, isn't it?'

'That's right. And on Saturday, I'll be there. It's my day to check in whatever we get.'

A small church on First Avenue and Eighty-fifth Street ran the thrift shop at which Gert volunteered, and where Nell left all her discarded clothes. It accepted only what it called 'gently worn' garments, and sold them at minimal cost.

With a stab of emotion, Nell remembered how, on the Saturday before Thanksgiving, she had gone through her closet and gathered up all the stuff she never wore anymore, and then she had bullied Adam into doing the same. Afterward they had packed everything up and taken it to the thrift shop.

Then, feeling virtuous about having done a good deed, they had lunch at a new Thai restaurant on Second and Eighty-first. Over lunch Adam had admitted how difficult it was for him to give away clothing that was still wearable. He said he got that from his mother, who never parted with anything, saying that she would 'keep it for a rainy day.'

'I'm kind of like her in that respect, I guess,' he had admitted. 'If you hadn't prodded me, that stuff would have been in my closet until the hangers collapsed.'

It was not Nell's favorite memory of him.

CHAPTER FIFTY-NINE

In one gesture, Liz Hanley tapped on and opened the door of Cornelius MacDermott's private office. 'I'm on my way,' she told him.

'I was just going to remind you to get started. It's 2:30.'

'And I'm due at three.'

'Now, Liz, I feel a little guilty asking you to do this, but it *is* important.'

'Mac, if that woman puts a hex on me, it's *your* fault.'

'Come straight back here when you get finished

with her.'

'Or she gets finished with me.'

*   *   *

Liz gave the address of Bonnie Wilson's West Side apartment to the cabbie, then she leaned back and tried to calm her nerves.

The problem, she admitted to herself, was that she actually believed that some people *do* have genuine psychic ability—or ESP, or whatever they wanted to call it. She had shared this misgiving with Mac, and, as usual, he had an answer.

'My mother didn't think she had psychic ability, but she was darn sure she could read psychic signs,' he had told her. 'Three raps at the door in the middle of the night, or if a picture fell off the wall, or a pigeon flew in the window, and she would get the rosary out. She swore that any one of those events was a sure sign of impending death.' He paused, obviously enjoying his monologue.

'Then, if six months later she got a letter from the old country saying that her ninety-eight-year-old aunt had died, she'd say to my father, "Now, Patrick, didn't I tell you when I heard those three raps that night that we'd be getting bad news?"'

Mac *is* convincing, and he *does* make it sound ridiculous, Liz thought, but there are hundreds of documented cases where, as people died, they visited their loved ones to say goodbye. Years ago there was a story in *Reader's Digest* about Arthur Godfrey, the old-time television star. When he was a kid on a navy ship during World War II, he dreamed that his father was standing at the foot of his bunk. The next morning he learned his father

247

had died at that exact moment. I'm going to look up that article and show it to Mac, Liz thought. Maybe he'll at least believe Arthur Godfrey.

Not that that would do any real good, she admitted to herself as the cab pulled up to the curb. Mac will find some clever way to dismiss anything I say.

*   *   *

Her first reaction to Bonnie Wilson was similar to the one Nell had described over dinner at Neary's. Bonnie was a startlingly attractive woman and younger than Liz had anticipated. However, the atmosphere in the apartment was more in keeping with her expectations. The gloomy foyer made a startling contrast to the brightness of the June afternoon she had just left outside.

'The air-conditioning is being repaired,' Bonnie apologized, 'and the only way to keep the apartment from being impossibly warm is to keep the sun out. These buildings have wonderful big rooms, but they are aging, and it shows.'

Liz was about to say that she lived in a similar type building on York Avenue, when she remembered just in time that she had made the appointment as Moira Callahan of Beekman Place. I've never been a good liar, she thought nervously, and at nearly sixty-one, it's too late to start learning how to be one.

Meekly she followed Bonnie Wilson the short distance from the foyer to a study on the right side of the long hallway.

'Why don't you sit on the couch?' Bonnie said. 'That way I can pull up my chair. I'd like to hold your hands for a few moments.'

Feeling increasingly nervous, Liz sat down and obeyed.

Bonnie Wilson closed her eyes. 'You're wearing your wedding band, but I sense you've been a widow for a long time. Is that true?'

'Yes.' My God, can she *really* pick that up so quickly? Liz wondered.

'You've just passed what would have been a special anniversary. I see the number forty. You've been rather nostalgic the past few weeks because you would have celebrated your fortieth wedding anniversary. You were a June bride.'

Dumbfounded, Liz could only nod.

'I hear the name 'Sean.' Was there a Sean in your family? I don't think it's your husband. It's more like a brother, a younger brother.' Bonnie Wilson raised her hand to the side of her head. 'I feel the most intense pain here,' she murmured. 'I believe it means Sean was killed in an accident. He was in a car, wasn't he?'

'Sean was only seventeen,' Liz said, her voice thick with emotion. 'He was speeding, and the car went out of control. His skull was fractured.'

'He is on the other side, along with your husband and all the members of your family who have passed over. He wants you to know they all send you their love. You are not destined to join them for a long time. However, that does not mean that we are not constantly surrounded by our loved ones, or that they do not become our spirit guides while we are here. Be comforted, knowing that is true.'

Later, almost in a daze, Liz Hanley followed Bonnie back down the shadowy hallway. A table with a mirror over it was against the far wall at the turn that led back to the foyer. A silver dish on the table held Bonnie's business cards. Liz paused and reached to take one of them. Suddenly her blood went cold, and she froze in her tracks. She was looking into the mirror, but there was another face there, a face behind her own image, staring back at her. It was only an impression, of course, and it was fleeting, gone almost before she caught it.

But on the ride back to the office in the cab, a shaken and troubled Liz acknowledged to herself that she was positive Adam Cauliff's face had materialized in that mirror.

She was equally positive that she would never, never, never even *hint* to anyone that she had seen that apparition.

CHAPTER SIXTY

Ben Tucker had nightmares again on both Monday and Tuesday nights, but they weren't as scary to the young boy as the ones he had had earlier. Ever since he had drawn the picture of the boat exploding, and he and Dr. Megan had talked about how *any* kid would be upset and frightened after seeing something that bad happen to people, he had begun to feel a little better.

He didn't even mind the fact that coming here today meant that he would be late for his Little League game—and they were playing the second-best team in their league. When he walked into Dr. Megan's office, he told her so.

'Hey, you make me feel pretty good, Benjy,' she

said. 'Do you feel like drawing any more pictures for me today?'

This time he found it was easier, because the snake didn't seem so scary. In fact, Ben realized that the 'snake' didn't even really look like a snake. In the dreams last night and the night before, he hadn't been so afraid, and he had been able to see it more clearly.

As he drew, his concentration was so intense that he bit his tongue. Sputtering at the oddly unpleasant sensation, he told Dr. Megan, 'My Mom laughs at me when I do that.'

'She laughs at you when you do what, Ben?'

'When I bite my tongue. She said her dad always did that when he was concentrating hard.'

'It's nice to be like your granddad. You just keep concentrating.'

Ben's hand began to move with quick, sure strokes. He liked to draw and was very good at it, something he took pride in. He was not like some of the kids in his class who made a joke out of everything, and who kept drawing dumb things instead of trying to make something that looked real. He thought they were real jerks.

He was glad that Dr. Megan was off to the side, writing on some papers, and not paying attention to him at all. It was a lot easier this way.

He finished the drawing and put the pen down. Sitting back, he looked closely at his creation.

He thought it looked pretty good, although what he had drawn surprised him. He could see now that the 'snake' wasn't a snake at all. That was just what it had looked like to him at the moment of the explosion. He had been mixed up just then, because everything had been so scary.

251

It wasn't a snake he saw sliding off the boat. It looked more like someone in a tight, shiny black suit and mask who was holding onto something that looked like a lady's pocketbook.

CHAPTER SIXTY-ONE

At work on Wednesday afternoon, Lisa Ryan received a phone call from Kelly's guidance counselor, Mrs. Evans. 'She's grieving terribly for her father,' Evans said. 'She started to cry in class today.'

Instantly heartsick, Lisa said, 'But of the three, I thought she was doing the best. At home, she seems to be just fine.'

'I tried to talk to her, but she wouldn't say very much,' Mrs. Evans said. 'She is, however, very mature for a ten-year-old. I get the feeling that she's trying to spare you, Mrs. Ryan.'

It's not Kelly's job to spare me, Lisa thought despairingly. It's *my* job to spare *her*. I've been too wrapped up in myself, and I've been too worried about that damn money. Well, I'm going to do something about that before another day goes by.

She fished around in her purse, found the number she wanted, and went to the pay phone. Then, while her client looked pointedly at her watch, she hurried into the office and told the manager she had to cancel her last two appointments.

As he voiced his protest, she told him flatly, 'I have some business to take care of tonight, and it is absolutely necessary. Before I do it, though, I have

252

to give my kids dinner.'

'Lisa, we gave you a week off to get your affairs settled. Don't make this a habit.'

She hurried back to her station and smiled apologetically at her client. 'I'm so sorry. I had a call from school. One of the kids was upset in class.'

'That's a shame, but Lisa, can you please finish me up. I've got a million things to do myself.'

*   *   *

Morgan Curren was coming to baby-sit at seven o'clock. At 5:30 Lisa had dinner on the table. She had followed the funeral director's advice and moved the chairs around. Because there were only four of them now, she had taken the extra leaf out of the center, so the table was again a circle. It had been that way until Charley was out of his high chair. With a pang, she remembered how they had made a big event of moving him to a 'big-boy chair.'

With senses newly attuned to the pain her children were experiencing, she saw the troubled expression on Kyle's face, as well as the deep grief in Kelly's eyes, and she understood the unnatural silence of little Charley.

'How was school today?' she asked, trying to sound cheerful, not talking to anyone in particular.

'It was okay,' Kyle said stiffly. 'You know that overnight trip the guys are going on next weekend?'

Lisa's heart sank. The trip he was referring to was a father-and-son outing to the Greenwood Lake home of one of Kyle's friends. 'What about it?' she asked.

'I know Bobby's father is going to call and say he really wants me to be with him and Bobby, but I just don't want to go. Please, Mom, don't make me.'

Lisa wanted to cry. Kyle would be the only boy at the outing without a father. 'It wouldn't be much fun for you,' she agreed. 'I'll tell Bobby's dad that you'd rather skip it this time.'

She remembered another bit of advice from the funeral director: 'Give the children something to anticipate,' he had said. Well, thanks to Brenda Curren, she could do that.

'Good news,' she said brightly. 'The Currens are renting a bigger house at Breezy Point this year because they want us to stay with them every weekend. And are you ready for the best part? This house is *right on the ocean*!'

'Really, Mom! That's awesome,' Charley said with a big sigh.

Charley the water rat, Lisa thought, rejoicing as she watched an ecstatic smile brighten his face.

'That's really good, Mom.' Kyle, now visibly relaxed, was obviously pleased.

Lisa looked at Kelly. She seemed indifferent to the good news; it was almost as though she weren't listening. The plate of pasta before her was barely touched.

It wasn't the time to press her, though. Lisa knew that. She needed more time to come to terms with the loss. There also wasn't time to deal with any of this right now, since Lisa knew she had to clear the table, get the homework started and be in Manhattan at 7:30.

'Kyle,' she said, 'as soon as we finish dinner, I want you to help me bring up a couple of packages

254

from Daddy's workroom downstairs. They belong to someone he worked for, and I'm dropping them off with a lady who's going to figure out to whom they should be returned.'

CHAPTER SIXTY-TWO

After he left the hospital on Wednesday afternoon, Dan Minor went directly to Cornelius MacDermott's office. When he had called for an appointment, he learned that Nell already had told her grandfather about him, so his call was expected.

MacDermott greeted him cordially. 'You and Nell are both Georgetown graduates, I hear.'

'Yes, although I was ahead of her by some six or seven years.'

'How do you like living in New York?'

'Both my grandmothers were born here, and my mother was raised in Manhattan and lived here until she was about twelve. Then they moved to the D.C. area. I've always felt that genetically I had one foot here and the other in Washington.'

'So do I,' MacDermott agreed. 'I was born in this house, and in those days, this wasn't a fancy neighborhood. In fact, the joke was that you could get a buzz just from smelling the fumes coming out of Jacob Rupert's brewery.'

Dan smiled. 'Cheaper than buying a six-pack.'

'But in the end not quite as satisfying.'

As they chatted, Cornelius MacDermott realized that he very much liked Dr. Dan Minor. Fortunately, he's no chip off the old block, he

255

thought. Over the years, he had met Dan's father at various affairs in Washington and had found him to be pretentious and boring. Dan was obviously made from fairly sturdy stuff. Another guy would have written off a mother who deserted him, especially one who was known to be a homeless drunk. This son, though, wanted to find her, and to help her. My kind of guy, MacDermott thought.

'I'll see if I can't get some of these bureaucrats off their duffs and have them put on a real search for Quinny, as you call her,' he said. 'You say the last time she was seen was in the squats south of Tompkins Square, back in September, about nine months ago?'

'Yes, although her friends there thought she might have gone out of town,' Dan explained. 'From the little bit I've been able to glean, when she was last seen she was in one of her terribly depressed moods, and whenever that happened, she didn't want to be with people. Apparently she would just find her own space and crawl into it.'

With every word he spoke, Dan felt with a growing certainty that his mother was no longer alive. 'If she's alive, I want to take care of her, but I know she may well be dead,' he told Cornelius. 'If she is, and if she's buried in potter's field, I want to find her and bring her to the family grave in Maryland. Either way, it would give great peace to my grandparents to know that she isn't still wandering the streets, sick and maybe delusional.' He paused. 'And it also would give me great peace,' he admitted.

'Got any pictures of her?' Cornelius asked.

Dan opened his wallet and took out the picture he always carried. He handed it to Nell's grandfather.

As Cornelius McDermott studied the picture, he felt a lump forming in his throat. The look of love captured there between the pretty young woman and the young boy in her arms seemed to leap from the well-worn black-and-white photo. Both of them were windblown, their faces pressed together, and his small arms were wrapped tightly around her neck.

'I also have a picture of her taken from the documentary film on the homeless that aired on PBS seven years ago. I had it aged digitally on the computer, and then the technician adjusted it to conform to the description her friend gave of her appearance last summer.'

MacDermott knew that Dan's mother would be about sixty years old. In this picture, the gaunt woman with shoulder-length gray hair looked eighty. 'We'll get some duplicates and put posters around town,' he promised. 'And I'll get some of those guys with nothing better to do to go through the files to see if any unidentified woman buried in potter's field since September matches this description.'

Dan stood. 'I should go. I've taken enough of your time, Congressman. I'm very grateful to you.'

MacDermott waved him to a seat. 'My friends call me Mac. Look, it's 5:30, which means the cocktail flag is up. What's your choice?'

Liz Hanley walked into the office unannounced as the two men were companionably sipping very dry martinis. It was clear to both of them that she was upset.

'I stopped home after I left Bonnie Wilson's apartment,' she said quietly. 'I was pretty shaken.'

257

MacDermott jumped up. 'What happened to you, Liz? You're so pale!'

Dan was already on his feet. 'I'm a doctor. . .' he began.

Liz shook her head and sank into a chair. 'I'll be fine. Mac, pour me a glass of wine. That'll help. It's just . . . Mac, you know I went there pretty much as a skeptic, but I have to tell you that she has changed my mind. Bonnie Wilson is on the level. I am convinced that she is a genuine psychic—which means that if she warned Nell about Peter Lang, then she's got to be taken seriously.'

CHAPTER SIXTY-THREE

After Gert left the apartment, Nell had gone back to her desk and reread the column she had drafted earlier for the Friday edition of the *Journal*, a piece about the long and frenzied campaigns that increasingly characterize presidential elections in the United States.

Her next—and, if all went according to plan, her final—column would be both a farewell and an announcement of her intention to view the campaign frenzy firsthand by becoming a candidate for her grandfather's former congressional seat.

I made the decision two weeks ago, Nell thought as she edited the work she had done earlier, but only now does it seem as though all the confusion and doubt and self-questioning are over. Inspired by Mac, she always had known that public office was something she wanted to pursue, but for so long she had harbored many fears and misgivings.

Had all the negativity come from Adam? she wondered. As she sat in her study, she thought back to many discussions they had had about her possibly running for office. I just don't understand what changed him, she thought. When we were first married three years ago, he was gung-ho for me to take over Mac's seat, but then he not only cooled to the idea, he became downright hostile. Why the radical turnaround?

It was a gnawing question that she acknowledged had begun to take on added significance since his death. Was there something going on in Adam's life that made him nervous about our having to face public scrutiny? She got up from her desk and began to walk restlessly around the apartment, pausing at the bookshelves that flanked the fireplace in the living room. Adam had a habit of pulling out a book he hadn't read, glancing through it briefly, then putting it back willy-nilly in the shelves. Her eyes and hands moving in synch, Nell rearranged the shelves so that the books she especially enjoyed again and again were all once more within easy reach of her comfortable club chair.

I was sitting in this chair, reading a novel, when he phoned me that first time, she recalled. I'd gotten a little depressed after not hearing from him. We had met at a cocktail party and been attracted to each other. We had dinner, and he said he would call. But then, two weeks later, I was still waiting. I was disappointed.

I remember I'd just come back from Sue Leone's wedding in Georgetown. Most of the others in our crowd were married and swapping baby pictures. I was very ready to meet someone. Gert and I even joked about it. She said that I had developed an acute nesting instinct.

Gert warned me not to wait too long. '*I* did,' she said. 'And I look back and think of a couple of the men I could have married, and I wonder what in the name of God I thought I was waiting for.'

And then Adam phoned. It was about ten o'clock at night. He said his out-of-town business had taken him longer than he expected. He had missed me, he said, but he hadn't been able to call because he had left my number in his apartment in New York.

I was so ready to fall in love, and Adam was so appealing. I was working for Mac; Adam was starting on his first job in New York, with a small architectural firm. There was so much ahead. Life for us was just beginning. It was a whirlwind courtship, she remembered. We were married three months later, in a quiet wedding, with only my family in attendance. It didn't matter, though, Nell thought. I never wanted a big splash anyhow.

As she sat now, in her favorite chair, she thought back to that heady, special time. It had all happened so fast, but it had been exciting. What had attracted her so totally to Adam? Nell wondered, as she reminisced, sadly thinking of the man she had loved and then lost so abruptly. I know what it was, she thought: he was so absolutely charming. He made me feel special.

And of course there was more, Nell told herself, so say it straight. Adam was in some ways the antithesis of Mac. I know how Mac feels about me, she thought, but he would choke on the word 'love.' I was hungry for someone to tell me instantly, passionately that I was loved.

But in other ways, Adam and Mac were very similar, and I liked that too. He didn't so much have the take-no-prisoners mentality that Mac had, but he had the same moral stamina. Adam, like Mac, was very independent, having worked his way through college and graduate school.

'My mother wanted to pay my way, but I wouldn't have it,' Adam had said. 'I told her that *she* was the one who taught me to neither a borrower nor a lender be. And it took.'

I admired that, Nell thought. I believed that Adam, like Mac, would give you the shirt off his back, while at the same time harboring a horror of borrowing money himself. 'Make do, or do without, Nell.' That was the lesson Mac preached to me.

All that changed later, though. Adam had no trouble asking me to invade my trust fund to lend him more than a million dollars, Nell thought. What happened to his staunch stand against borrowing? she wondered. But of course she hadn't questioned him at the time.

As soon as they were married, Adam had asked Mac to help him get a better job. That was how he happened to go to work for Walters and Arsdale.

Then he left them to open his own firm, using the rest of the money he borrowed from me.

The last two weeks had been so terrible. First she had lost her husband, and then came all the suggestions that he wasn't the man she thought him to be. I don't want to believe he was in on that bid rigging and kickback scheme, Nell told herself. Why *would* he have been involved? He didn't exactly need the money. The boat was his only extravagance. He wouldn't have had to borrow money from me if he was also getting paid off

261

under the table, she reasoned.

But why didn't he tell me that his design had been rejected by Peter Lang? That was a question for which she would have to find an answer.

And why did he do such a complete turnaround when I began to talk seriously about wanting to run for Mac's seat? He blamed his anger on Mac. He said Mac would never let me be my own person, not so long as he held any sway over me, and that I would just end up being a puppet for my grandfather. Well, I fell for it, but now I have to wonder if I wasn't really just being manipulated by Adam.

What reason—other than his disdain for Mac, and perhaps politics in general—would Adam have to keep me away from the glare of the media? she wondered.

As she looked back over what she had learned in the past few days, an answer to the questions that were plaguing her began to form in Nell's mind, one that made sense and that chilled her to the bone. Adam knew that if I ran for that office, then the media and my opponents would dig deep and hard into our personal histories to see if there were any skeletons in either of our closets. I'm confident I'm clean, she thought. So what was he afraid of?

Could there be some truth to the suggestion that he had been taking kickbacks? Was he in any way to blame for that defective renovation job on Lexington Avenue, where the façade collapsed the other day?

Anxious to put these questions out of her mind, Nell decided to tackle one of the chores she had been putting off. The maintenance men had brought up to the apartment a pile of boxes for her to use in packing Adam's clothes. She went into the guest room and put the first box on the bed. The neat piles of underwear and socks disappeared into it.

Questions beget questions, Nell thought. As she continued to pack away Adam's clothes, she allowed herself to face the one question that she had been most determinedly avoiding these past few days: *Was I truly in love with Adam, or did I merely* want *to be in love with him?*

If I hadn't rushed so quickly into marriage with Adam, would the initial attraction have worn off? Did I see in him what I wanted to see? Wasn't I always denying the truth to myself? The truth is, it wasn't a great marriage—at least, not for me. I resented having to give up my career goals for him. I also wasn't sorry when Adam would take off for the weekend on his boat, fishing and cruising. I enjoyed the time alone, and it gave me time to spend with Mac as well.

Or could all my doubts be something else? Nell asked herself as she closed a box, set it on the floor and picked up another one. Is it simply that I have grieved enough in my life, and that now I am trying to find a reason not to grieve deeply again?

I've read that people are often angry at the loved one who has died. Is that what's happening to me? she wondered.

Nell carefully folded sports clothes—chinos and jeans and short-sleeve shirts—placing them in boxes; ties and handkerchiefs and gloves were the last items to be packed away. The bed was now clear. She had no heart to start in on the closet. That can wait till another day, she thought.

The Ryan woman had called earlier in the afternoon and insisted that she had to see Nell that evening. The call had been abrupt, almost rude, and Nell had been tempted to tell the woman where to get off. Still, she knew that Lisa Ryan was in great pain, and she deserved to be given time to come to terms with her loss.

Nell looked at her watch. It was after six. Lisa Ryan had said she would be there by seven-thirty; that gave Nell enough time to freshen up and relax for a few minutes. A nice glass of chardonnay would also help, she decided.

*   *   *

The elevator operator helped Lisa carry the two heavy packages into Nell's apartment. 'Where shall I put these, Ms. MacDermott?' he asked.

It was Lisa who answered. 'Just put them there.' She was pointing to the round table under the window that overlooked Park Avenue.

The elevator operator glanced at Nell, who nodded.

When the door closed behind him, Lisa said defiantly, 'Nell, I have nightmares that the cops will come in with a search warrant, find this cursed money and arrest me, right in front of my children. They'd never do that to *you*. That's why *you've* got to keep it here until you can give it back to someone.'

'Lisa, that is absolutely impossible,' Nell told her. 'I respected your confidence, but there's no way under the sun I can hold on to or send back money that was given to your husband because he went along with something illegal.'

'How do I know your husband wasn't involved in this?' Lisa demanded. 'There was something very strange in the way Jimmy got his job in the first
264

place. He sent a résumé to everyone in the building trade, but only your husband responded. Was Adam Cauliff in the habit of being a bleeding heart for a guy who was blackballed because he was honest? Or did he get him a job with Sam Krause precisely because he thought poor Jimmy might just be desperate enough to be useful? That's what *I* want to know.'

'I don't know the answer,' Nell said slowly. 'I do know that no matter who gets hurt, it's important to find out just how and why Jimmy was useful to someone.'

Lisa Ryan's face drained of color. 'Over my dead body will Jimmy's name come into this,' she cried. 'I'll take that damn money and throw it in the river first. That's what I should have done the minute I found it.'

'Lisa, listen to me,' Nell pleaded. 'You've read about the building façade that collapsed on Lexington Avenue. Three people were injured, and one of them may die.'

'My Jimmy never worked on Lexington Avenue!'

'I didn't say he did, but he worked for Sam Krause, and it was his company that did that renovation. If Krause did shoddy work on that building, then chances are he did the same on others. Maybe there's another job that Jimmy was on, in which corners were cut and inferior materials were used. Maybe there is another structurally unsound building, an accident waiting to happen. Jimmy Ryan hid that money away and never spent it, and from what you tell me, he was terribly depressed. I have a feeling that he was the kind of man who would now want you to do whatever you could to help avoid another tragedy.'

The defiant anger in Lisa's face faded, and she collapsed into deep, wracking sobs. Nell put her arms around her. She's so thin, she thought compassionately. She's only a few years older than I am, yet here she is, faced with the responsibility of raising three kids with basically no money. And still she'd throw fifty thousand dollars into the river rather than feed and clothe her children with money that was dirty.

'Lisa,' she said. 'I know what you're going through. I also have to face the fact that my husband may have been involved in bid rigging, or at the very least guilty of closing his eyes to the use of substandard materials. True, I don't have children to protect, but if knowledge of Adam's complicity in anything illegal comes out, it could cost me my political career. And having said that, I want your permission to talk to the detectives investigating the explosion.

'I'll ask them to do whatever they can to keep Jimmy's name out of the investigation, but Lisa, do you realize that if Jimmy knew too much, *he* may well have been the target in the explosion that blew up the boat?'

Nell paused, then went ahead and said what had been in the back of her mind ever since Monday, when Lisa first told her about the money. 'Lisa, if someone is worried that Jimmy told you what he did to get that money, you also might be considered a threat. Had you considered that?'

'But he *didn't* tell me!'

'You and I are the only ones who know that.' Nell gently touched the other woman's arm. 'Now do you understand why the detectives need to be told about the money?'

Thursday, June 22

CHAPTER SIXTY-FOUR

On Thursday morning, Jack Sclafani and George Brennan were once again at Fourteenth Street and First Avenue, visiting the apartment of Ada Kaplan.

'Is Jed home?' Sclafani asked.

'He's not up yet.' Ada Kaplan was once again on the verge of tears. 'You're not going to search my house again, are you? I can't take any more. You've got to understand that.' The dark circles under her eyes accentuated the extreme whiteness of her face.

'No, we're not going to search your house again, Mrs. Kaplan,' Brennan said soothingly. 'We're sorry we have to inconvenience you at all. Would you just tell Jed to get dressed and get out here. We want to talk to him, that's all.'

'Maybe he'll talk to *you*. He hardly says a word to *me*.' She looked at them appealingly. 'What would he have to gain by hurting Adam Cauliff?' she asked. 'Sure, he was mad because Cauliff talked me into selling my building—and Jed thinks for too little money—but truthfully, if I hadn't sold it to him, I'd have sold it to that big-shot realtor, Mr. Lang. I *told* Jed that.'

'Peter Lang?' Brennan asked. 'Did you speak with him about your property?'

'Sure I did. Right after that fire in the mansion, he came to see me. Had a check in his hand.' Her voice sank to a whisper. 'He offered me *two million dollars*, and only the month before, I'd sold it to Mr. Cauliff for less than *one* million! It broke my

269

heart to have to tell him I didn't own it anymore, and I didn't dare let Jed know how much more I could have gotten for it.'

'Was Lang upset when he learned you'd sold the property?'

'Oh, my, yes, he was. I think if Mr. Cauliff had been standing there, he'd have strangled him with his bare hands.'

'Are you talking about me, Mom?'

All three people turned to see an unshaven Jed Kaplan standing in the doorway.

'No, I wasn't,' Ada Kaplan said nervously. 'I was just telling the gentlemen that Peter Lang had been interested in buying my property too.'

Jed Kaplan's expression became ugly. '*Our* property, Mom. And don't you forget it.' He turned to Brennan and Sclafani. 'What do you two want?'

They got up. 'Just the chance to make sure you're as charming as ever,' Sclafani remarked. 'We also don't want you to forget that until we say it's okay, you shouldn't be planning any vacations or anything like that. While this investigation is ongoing, we need to know where you are. So don't be surprised if we drop in again for a little visit.'

'It's been a pleasure talking to you, Mrs. Kaplan,' Brennan said.

On the way down in the elevator, Sclafani spoke first. 'You thinking the same thing I am?'

'Yeah. I'm thinking that Kaplan's nothing but a two-bit hood, and that we're wasting our time on him. Lang, on the other hand, deserves a little closer scrutiny. He had motive in wanting Adam Cauliff out of the way, and he very conveniently saved his own life by missing the meeting on the boat.'

270

They arrived back at headquarters at eleven o'clock to find an unexpected visitor waiting for them. The receptionist explained: 'His name is Kenneth Tucker. He's from Philadelphia, and he wants to speak to whoever is handling the investigation into that boat explosion a couple of weeks back.'

Sclafani shrugged. There's never a high-profile case that doesn't get its share of loonies with hot tips or crackpot theories, he thought. 'Give us ten minutes to get some coffee.'

He tried not to raise his eyebrows when Tucker was escorted into the office. He looked like the typical young executive, and his first words, 'I may be wasting your time,' convinced both men that that was exactly what he would be doing.

'I'll get right to the point,' Tucker said. 'My son and I were on a boat in New York harbor when that boat exploded two weeks ago. He has been having nightmares ever since.'

'How old is your son, Mr. Tucker?'

'Benjy is eight.'

'And so you think that these nightmares are related to that explosion?'

'Yes, I do. Both Benjy and I witnessed it. We were returning from a visit to the Statue of Liberty. Truthfully, the whole episode was kind of a blur to me, but Ben saw something that I believe may be significant.'

Sclafani and Brennan exchanged glances. 'Mr. Tucker, we spoke to a number of people who'd been on the ferry at the time. Some of them witnessed the explosion, but they all agree that the ferry was too far away for them to see anything distinctly. I can understand why a little boy might

271

have nightmares if he happened to be looking at that boat when it blew up, but I can assure you that from that distance, he did not see anything significant.'

Kenneth Tucker flushed. 'My son is unusually far-sighted,' he said with quiet dignity. 'He wears glasses to correct his vision so that he can read, but he had taken them off just before the explosion. And as I told you, it was right after that that he began having nightmares. He kept saying that in his dreams, when the boat blew up, a snake would leap off it and start coming at him. We took him to a child psychologist. After several visits, she got him to draw what he had seen.'

He handed them Ben's latest sketch. 'He now believes he saw someone in a wet suit and carrying a woman's pocketbook dive off the boat at the moment it exploded. It may indeed be a child's fantasy, but I felt you should at least see the sketch. I am aware that you get many crank calls after an incident such as this, and I figured that if I sent it to you by mail, then it would be ignored, and I didn't want that to happen. The drawing may not help at all, but I felt I had to bring it to your attention.'

He stood up. 'Obviously the face mask prevented Ben from having even the faintest idea of what the person in the wet suit looked like. If you put any credence in this drawing, I hope you realize there is no point in questioning him. He slept through the night last night for the first time in two weeks. And of course, we want no media attention.'

Brennan and Sclafani again exchanged glances.

'Mr. Tucker, we're very grateful,' George Brennan said. 'I can't be sure without more

272

investigation, but your son's drawing could have significance. Ben's name will not be mentioned, I promise you, and I'm going to ask you not to reveal to anyone else what you've just told us. Even if someone did get off that boat, we know that at least two people, and probably a third, died in the explosion. We're dealing with a multiple homicide, and whoever was responsible has to be considered extremely dangerous.'

'Then we understand each other.'

When the door closed behind Kenneth Tucker, Sclafani whistled. 'It was never leaked to the media that our guys found Winifred Johnson's pocketbook,' he said. 'So there's no way the guy could have known that.'

'Absolutely.'

'That would explain why it was hardly singed. Whoever got off the boat was carrying it.'

'And probably lost it in the water when the boat exploded. If the kid was right, whoever jumped off the boat barely got away in time.'

'Then who do you think it was?' Sclafani asked.

Without knocking, Cal Thompson, the assistant District Attorney who had interviewed Robert Walters, opened the door and poked his head in. 'Thought you guys might be interested in the latest development. We've got ourselves another Queen for a Day. Sam Krause's top assistant came in with his lawyer. He admits they've been using substandard materials on many of their jobs and consistently overbilling on jobs they got from Walters and Arsdale.'

'Does he say who over at Walters and Arsdale was making the deal with them?'

'No. He said he assumed it was Walters and

273

Arsdale themselves, but he can't swear to that. The contact for these transactions was Winifred Johnson. He said they even had a name for her: "Winnie the bag lady." '

'She also seems to be one hell of a swimmer,' Brennan said.

Thompson raised his eyebrows. 'Unless I'm mistaken, her swimming days are over.'

'Maybe yes. Maybe no,' Sclafani replied.

CHAPTER SIXTY-FIVE

On Thursday morning, Nell had gotten up at dawn. Whatever sleep she had known during the night had been disturbed by bad dreams, and several times she had awakened, startled by imagined sounds in the night. More than once she also had awakened to feel her face wet with tears.

Were they for Adam? she wondered. In truth, she could not be sure. I'm not sure of anything, she admitted to herself that morning, as she pulled the covers closer around her. When she had gone to bed, the night air was cool, so she had turned off the air-conditioning and opened the windows wide.

As a result, the sounds of New York had been with her all night—the traffic, the occasional wail of a police siren or ambulance, the faint strains of music from the apartment below her, whose owner played the stereo almost nonstop.

But the room embraced her, filling her with the sensation of having come home. Without the tall dresser that had been Adam's, the room felt spacious again, her own dresser back in its original place, positioned so that with the tiny night-light she could see the picture of her mother and father whenever she woke.

The picture evoked memories, but fortunately they were happy ones. Before she was old enough to begin school, her parents had taken her on some of their field trips to South America. She had vague memories of them talking to natives in remote villages, of herself playing with other small children. The game was often one of teaching each other the words for parts of their bodies, such as the nose and ears and eyes and teeth.

Nell realized that she was reminded of that time because she had something of the same sensation now, that of being in a strange land and having to try to learn the language. The difference this time, she thought, is that I don't have a mother and father hovering around me to make sure I don't get into trouble.

Several times when Nell had awakened, Dan Minor's face floated across her mind. She found the image a reassuring sight, since he was a fellow traveler, another survivor of a broken childhood, another person on a quest for answers.

That morning, over a cup of coffee, she decided to open the packages and count the money Lisa Ryan had thrust on her the night before. She had said it was fifty thousand dollars. It might be wise for me to verify that figure, Nell thought.

The packages were heavy, and it was a struggle for her to haul them to the dining room table. With meticulous care she opened the knots on the twine, making a mental note of the strand of green in the twist. The brown wrapping paper also brought back childhood memories, those of her parents sending packages to the friends they had made all over the world.

Twine and wrapping paper.

Nell ignored a troubling sensation that settled into her subconscious, as she went ahead and opened the first box and looked down at the neat stacks of bills held together with rubber bands.

Before she began to count, she examined the box carefully. It was about two-thirds the size of a box a department store might have used to pack a woman's suit. There was no company or product identification of any kind displayed on the sides. She was sure the box had been chosen with care. Clearly someone did not want to have it traced back to its source.

She poured herself more coffee and got out her calculator. As she counted and recounted each stack, she entered the figure. The first box contained twenty-eight thousand dollars in mostly fifty-dollar bills.

She opened the second one and began to count, noting that this one had well-worn, smaller bills, including fives and tens and twenties as well as fifties. Few hundreds, she thought. Whoever did this was smart enough to realize that Jimmy Ryan flashing hundreds might draw attention.

The total in the second box was exactly twenty-two thousand dollars. The total was not one cent less than the fifty thousand Jimmy must have been promised for whatever it was he had to do to earn it, she thought. But why didn't he spend any of it? she wondered. Was he so guilt ridden that he couldn't bear to touch it?

Reflecting on what Jimmy Ryan must have felt, Nell remembered that in the Bible, after the

Crucifixion, Judas, overwhelmed with guilt, had tried to return the thirty pieces of silver he had been paid for betraying Jesus.

And then he hanged himself, Nell thought as she replaced the money in the second box. Was it possible that Jimmy Ryan was suicidal? she wondered.

As she began to fold the brown wrapping paper back around the first package, she suddenly realized what it was that had been bothering her all morning about these packages. She had seen this same kind of heavy paper before, as well as the twine with the green thread running through it.

In Winifred's file drawer.

CHAPTER SIXTY-SIX

During the night, Lisa Ryan had tossed and turned, listening to the familiar sounds from outdoors that punctuated the night. Some of the sounds were reassuring, almost comforting, like the breeze rustling the maple trees in their front yard. But there also had been the sound of their next-door neighbor, a bartender, parking his car in the driveway sometime in the very early hours, and then only a little later she had heard the rumbling of the freight train as it passed on nearby tracks.

By five o'clock she had given up trying to sleep. She got out of bed and put on her chenille robe. As she tied the belt, she was reminded that she had lost considerable weight in the short time since Jimmy's death.

One way to do it, she thought grimly.

There wasn't the slightest doubt in Lisa's mind that after Nell MacDermott talked to the detectives assigned to investigate the case, they would rush to talk to her again. In the months he had worked for Sam Krause, Jimmy had been involved with a number of different building projects. She wanted to try to figure out which sites he had been working on and when. Perhaps that way she might be able to tell them exactly where he had been working when his intense depression started.

She was sure that location was the key to whatever it was that he had done, or had *not* done, to be paid the bribe.

As she had headed downstairs, Lisa looked in on the children. Kyle and Charley were fast asleep in their bunk beds.

In the faint early morning light, she studied their faces. Kyle's jaw was showing the first hint of firming into adolescence. He will always be lean, like my side of the family, she thought.

Charley had a sturdier build. He would be a big man, like Jimmy. Both boys had inherited their father's red hair and hazel eyes.

Kelly was in the smallest bedroom—a glorified closet, Jimmy had called it. Her slender body was curled in the fetal position. Strands of her long, light blond hair covered her cheek and spread over her shoulders.

Her journal was half hidden under the pillow. She wrote in it every night, something she had begun as a school project but then kept up on her own. 'It's very private,' she had said solemnly, 'and the teacher said that our families should respect our privacy.'

278

They all had pledged never to read it, but Jimmy, made suspicious by the mischievous glance Kyle and Charley exchanged, had made Kelly a strongbox that sat on top of her dresser. The box had two keys. One Kelly wore on a chain around her neck. The other Lisa kept hidden in her own dresser, in case the first one was ever lost.

Kelly had exacted a 'cross my heart, I hope to die,' promise that Lisa would never use that key to open the box, and she never had. But now, looking down at her sleeping child, Lisa knew she was going to break that promise.

It was not only because she needed to know what Kelly, who had been the ultimate 'Daddy's girl,' was thinking and feeling now. It was also because of what Kelly—always observant and sensitive to moods—might have written about Jimmy at the time when he plunged into depression.

CHAPTER SIXTY-SEVEN

Dan Minor had arrived at the hospital early on Thursday morning. He had three operations back to back, and the first of them was at seven o'clock. Then he had the pleasure of discharging a five-year-old patient who had been in the hospital for a month.

With easy good humor he cut off the parents' outpouring of gratitude. 'You'd better get him out of here fast. The nurses are signing a petition to adopt him.'

'I was so sure he'd be disfigured,' the mother said.

'Oh, he'll have a few reminders, but it won't be enough to hurt him with the girls in ten or twelve years.'

It was one o'clock before Dan was able to grab a sandwich and coffee in the physicians' lounge. He also used the time to call Cornelius MacDermott's office to see if they possibly had learned anything about his mother. He knew it was unlikely—it had been less than a day—but still he couldn't resist calling. He's probably at lunch, though, Dan thought as he dialed the number.

Liz Hanley answered on the first ring. 'He's in his office, Doctor,' she told him, 'but I have to warn you. The good Lord barreling down Fifth Avenue on a tricycle wouldn't get a smile out of him today, so if he bites your head off, don't take it personally.'

'Maybe I'd better skip trying to talk to him now.'

'No, not at all. But I hope you don't mind hanging on for a bit. He's on the other line. It should be only a minute more, though. I'll put you through as soon as he's done.'

'Before you get off, Liz, tell me how you feel today. I don't know whether you realize it, but you were in mild shock yesterday.'

'Oh, I'm all right now, but what I experienced yesterday was definitely a shock to my system. Doctor, you *have* to believe me when I tell you that Bonnie Wilson is a gifted psychic. That's why I'm absolutely *sure* I saw . . . Well, I won't go into all that.'

Dan was aware from the abrupt change in Liz Hanley's tone that there was something disturbing about what she had experienced, and she was not going to tell him what it was. 'Okay, so long as you feel all right now,' he said.

'I really do. Oh, hold on, Doctor. The Presence has just graced my office.'

Dan heard her say, 'It's Dr. Dan, Congressman.'

There was a moment's pause as he heard the receiver changing hands, then he heard Cornelius MacDermott's booming voice. 'Liz is like Nell. When she calls me Congressman, it means she's mad at me. How are you today, Dan?'

'I'm okay, Mac. I was phoning to thank you for being so kind yesterday.'

'Well, I made some calls first thing this morning, and I've got my people working on the records. If there's anything to be found about your mother, they'll find it. I don't know if Liz told you, though, that I've got a problem.'

'She said you were upset about something,' Dan said cautiously.

'That's a mild word. You had dinner the other night with Nell. Did she talk about running for my old seat?'

'Yes, she did. She's obviously looking forward to it.'

'Well, she phoned half an hour ago to tell me to let the party bosses know she doesn't intend to run.'

Dan was stunned. 'What changed her mind? She's not sick, is she?'

'No, but she's beginning to believe that what I've been telling her about her late husband's business dealings is possible. Adam Cauliff, or at least his assistant, may have been involved in the bribery scandal you've been reading about.'

'But that has nothing to do with Nell.'

'In politics, everything has to do with everything.
281

I told her not to make up her mind yet, though, and that she had to hold off her decision until next week at least.'

Dan decided to take a chance. 'What was Adam Cauliff like, Mac?' he asked cautiously.

'He was either a smart—perhaps even ruthless—businessman, or he was a hick trying to play in the big time who got in way over his head. We'll probably never really know which. But one thing I *do* know. He wasn't the man for my granddaughter.'

CHAPTER SIXTY-EIGHT

After she called Mac, Nell immediately began to dial Detective Sclafani, but then abruptly broke the connection. Before she called him, she decided, she would go to Adam's office and get the twine and wrapping paper she had seen in Winifred's office.

She showered and dressed, putting on white chinos, a short-sleeve blouse, a lightweight blue denim jacket and sandals.

It's almost time for a cut, she decided as she brushed her hair into a French twist. Then she paused suddenly, as something in the mirror struck her as odd. It was the face—the face she saw there seemed almost to be that of a stranger, the expression strained and anxious. This ordeal has definitely taken its toll, she realized. Something had better be resolved soon, or I will be a total wreck.

I really don't want to give up my chance to run for Congress, she admitted to herself, and I'm glad

Mac bullied me into waiting until next week to make a final decision. Maybe by then I'll have some answers. Maybe Adam was simply naïve and didn't realize something corrupt was going on under his nose.

The wrapping paper and twine were in Winifred's file—she remembered that clearly. She also knew that Winifred was involved with someone named Harry Reynolds, although she still had no clue as to who he was. Winifred had been at Walters and Arsdale for over twenty years, long before Adam went there. When she began working closely with Adam, had she taken advantage of his trust? Nell wondered. He would have been the new man on the job, untried and untested, while she knew the construction business, including the seamy side, backward and forward.

As she was leaving the apartment, Nell thought about the money Lisa Ryan had forced her to keep. I can't just leave it out on the table, she thought. She knew she probably was being paranoid, but it seemed to her that anyone who came into the room would be able to merely glance at the packages and guess that they contained cash.

I'm starting to understand how Lisa felt having this stuff under her roof, she thought as she carried the boxes into the guest room and put them on the floor of the closet.

Adam's suits and jackets and slacks and coats were still hanging there. She stood in the doorway of the closet and looked at them, many of them items she had helped him select. Now they seemed to be reproachful reminders that she was questioning the integrity of the man who had worn and enjoyed them. They seemed to chide her for

283

doubting the man who had been her husband.

Nell promised herself that before the day was over, all the clothes would be packed and ready to take to the thrift shop first thing on Saturday morning.

*   *   *

The cabbie turned right onto Central Park South and then left down Seventh Avenue as it headed south to Adam's office. A block before reaching it, they passed the construction fence that had been put up around the ruins of the Vandermeer mansion. The shabby, narrow building next to it was the one she now owned, the one Peter Lang wanted so badly.

The one *Adam* had wanted so badly, Nell thought suddenly. 'Let me off here,' she said to the driver.

Getting out at the corner, she walked back and stood in front of the property she owned. Most of the buildings in this immediate area were old, but she could see the beginning of change in the neighborhood. An apartment complex was going up across the street, and a sign announced the forthcoming erection of another one farther down the block. When he borrowed the money from her to buy this property, Adam had said that this was turning into the hottest new real estate section in the city.

The Vandermeer mansion had been on a fairly large parcel of land, whereas the parcel she owned was a narrow strip. All the tenants were gone from the building, and it had a deserted, shabby look. Graffiti added to the dismal effect of the dark stone exterior.

What did Adam think he was going to do with this property? she wondered. How much money would he have needed to be able to pull it down and build something in its place? As she studied the location, she realized fully for the first time that its only real value derived from its possibilities as an addition to the Vandermeer property.

So why was Adam so anxious to buy this parcel? she wondered. It was especially odd since at the time of the purchase, the Vandermeer mansion was still standing and still had its landmark status.

Could Adam have had inside information that the Vandermeer mansion's landmark status was being removed?

It was another troubling possibility.

She turned and walked the block and a half to Adam's office. When she had left there with the detectives on Tuesday, the superintendent had given her a spare key to the front door. She let herself in and once again experienced a sense of deep disquiet when the door closed behind her.

She went into Winifred's cubbyhole and could visualize her sitting at that desk, smiling meekly whenever a visitor came in.

Nell stood facing the desk, remembering. It was the expression in Winifred's eyes that she remembered most, she thought. Always anxious, almost pleading, as if she were afraid she was going to be criticized.

Had that been an act?

She opened the bottom drawer of the file and took out the brown wrapping paper and twine. She had brought a shopping bag in which to carry them. Even before comparing side by side, she knew that

285

the pattern of the twine was identical to the pattern of the twine around the boxes of money.

She had been there only a few minutes, but in that time she had become aware that the temperature was becoming increasingly warmer. It's happening again, she thought, as she felt a sense of disorientation overtaking her.

I have to get outside, she told herself.

Nell slammed shut the file drawer, grabbed the shopping bag and rushed from Winifred's cubbyhole back through the reception area and to the outer door.

She grabbed the doorknob and pulled, but nothing happened. The door was stuck. The handle felt hot to the touch, and suddenly she was coughing. Frantically she kicked the door as she felt her hands begin to blister.

'Something wrong, Ms. Cauliff? That door sticking again?' The building superintendent was there suddenly, calmly shoving open the door with his shoulder. Nell stumbled past him to the steps outside. Her legs gave way as she sat on the bottom step and covered her face with her hands.

It's happening again, she thought. It's a warning. The coughing began to subside, but she was still gasping for air. She looked at her hands. The blisters she had felt forming there did not exist.

'I guess it's kind of emotional to go into your husband's office,' the superintendent said sympathetically, 'I mean knowing that he and Ms. Johnson are never coming back to it.'

*   *   *

Nell returned to her apartment to find there was a

message from Dan Minor on the answering machine. 'Nell, just spoke to Mac,' he said. 'We're getting to be old friends. He's got his people checking the records for me for information about my mother. I'll call you later to see if you're free for dinner tonight.'

Still shaken by the bizarre experience in Adam's office, Nell played the message again, soothed by the undertone of concern in Dan's voice. He probably got an earful about me from Mac, she thought.

She noticed Jack Sclafani's card lying next to the phone. Once again she dialed the number, but this time she did not break the connection. He answered on the first ring.

'It's very important that I see you, and I have to ask you to come here, to my apartment,' she told him. 'I'd rather not go into it over the phone.'

'We'll be there in an hour,' he promised.

Trying to banish from her mind the frightening memory of those moments in Adam's office, Nell went into the guest room and began to empty the closet. As she removed the jackets and suits and slacks from the hangers, she reflected on how Adam, though still quite youthful, had been a very conservative dresser. Navy and charcoal and tan were his inevitable choice of colors. She remembered that a year ago she had urged him to buy a dark-green summer jacket that she had seen in the window at Saks, but instead he had once again bought a navy blazer.

I told him it looked exactly like another one he had, Nell thought as she took a navy jacket from the closet. In fact, it looked just like this one.

But as she held it, she realized she was mistaken.

287

This one was the newer of the two—she could tell from the weight. Puzzled, Nell held it in her hands. *This is the one I meant to give Winifred to take to him that day. This is the one he laid out. The other one would have been too warm.*

Oh, of course! she thought, as suddenly she remembered the sequence of events. *That last night, Adam changed in here and laid out on this bed the clothes he intended to wear in the morning. Then he rushed out after we quarreled in the morning, and I put his briefcase in his study and hung his jacket in his closet and later in here. The one I gave Winifred was the wrong jacket, the heavier one.*

If he had lived, he probably would have been glad of the mistake, she thought. *The temperature dropped a lot during the day, and it was raining hard that night.*

Nell started to fold the jacket to place it in the box, then hesitated. She remembered how a few days after his death, feeling bereft, she had put on this blazer, wanting to have some sense of his presence. *Now I'm acting as if I can't wait to get rid of it,* she thought.

There was a buzz from the intercom in the foyer. She knew that had to mean the detectives, Jack Sclafani and George Brennan, were on their way up.

Nell hung the navy jacket over the back of a chair. *I can decide later whether or not to keep it,* she told herself, as with increasing trepidation she hurried to let the detectives in.

CHAPTER SIXTY-NINE

When he talked to Dr. Dan Minor, Cornelius MacDermott did not tell him that one of the calls he had Liz make in trying to trace Dan's mother's whereabouts had been to the Medical Examiner's office.

Liz had learned from the call that in the last year, fifty unidentified bodies had been buried in potter's field—thirty-two men and eighteen women.

At the request of the M.E.'s clerk, Liz faxed the computerized picture of Quinny that Dan had given them, as well as the vital statistics he had furnished.

In midafternoon, she received a call from the morgue. 'We may have a match,' a laconic-voiced clerk told her.

CHAPTER SEVENTY

Jack Sclafani and George Brennan sat with Nell in the dining room. They had carried the boxes of cash to the table, opened them and confirmed the count.

'You don't get fifty thousand dollars for looking the other way when the right concrete isn't used,' Sclafani said. 'For this amount of money, Jimmy Ryan was on the take for something bigger than that.'

'I thought as much,' Nell said quietly. 'And I

think maybe I know who gave it to him.'

She had left the shopping bag in the kitchen and went to retrieve it. Returning, she dumped the ball of twine and the sheets of wrapping paper on the table next to the money. 'These came from Winifred Johnson's file drawer,' she explained. 'I noticed them on Tuesday, when I was there with you.'

Brennan held the twine used to wrap the packages of cash against a strand he unraveled from the ball. 'The lab can verify it, but I'd swear that what was on the packages was cut from here,' he said.

Sclafani was comparing the brown wrapping paper. 'I'd say this is a match too, but that's up to the lab to determine for sure.'

'I hope you understand that if Winifred Johnson passed on a bribe to Jimmy Ryan, it does not necessarily mean that my husband was in any way involved,' Nell said, with a conviction she knew she did not feel.

Sclafani studied Nell as they sat across from each other. She doesn't know what to believe, he thought. She's playing straight with us, and she convinced Lisa Ryan that turning the money over was the only way to go. We should be straight with her as well.

'Ms. MacDermott, this may be farfetched, but we have a witness, an eight-year-old kid, who may have seen someone in a wet suit dive off your husband's boat just before the explosion.'

Nell stared at him. 'Is that possible?'

'Ms. MacDermott, *anything* is possible. Is it probable? No. The currents in that part of the harbor are pretty vicious. Could a strong swimmer make it to shore in either Staten Island or Jersey City? Maybe.'

'Then you believe this child *did* see someone?'

'The detail that hits home is that in the picture the kid drew, the diver is carrying a woman's pocketbook. The truth is, we did find Winifred's purse, but we never released that detail to the press, so there is no way this kid could have known unless he really *did* see something—or is just very good at guessing. There are a few other facts we have that you may or may not be aware of.' Sclafani paused; he knew the next part was going to be difficult. 'We know from DNA tests we have run on remains that have turned up that both Sam Krause and Jimmy Ryan are dead. There are two people, however, whose deaths we haven't been able to verify.' He paused. 'Winifred Johnson and Adam Cauliff.'

Nell sat in stunned silence, a look of confusion in her eyes.

'There's also another possibility, Ms. MacDermott,' Brennan said. 'Someone else—a fifth person—may have been on the boat, perhaps hiding in the engine room. We know from tests that's where the bomb was set.'

'But even if that child was right about what he saw,' Nell said, 'I still don't understand why anyone would want Winifred's pocketbook.'

'We're not completely sure either,' George Brennan told her, 'although we think we have the answer. The only object that we found in that purse that has any potential value is a safe-deposit key that carries the number 332.'

'Can't you just take it to the bank that issued it and find out what is in the lock box?' Nell asked.

291

'Perhaps, but we don't know which bank issued it. The key has no other designation, and the task of going to every bank in the area is going to take time. But that's what we're doing, and we plan to keep looking until we find it.'

'I have a safe-deposit box,' Nell said. 'If I lost the key, couldn't I just call the bank and ask them to make me another one?'

'You *could*,' Sclafani said promptly. 'But you'd need proper identification. Your signature would need to be on file at the bank, of course. And it would cost you about one hundred and twenty-five bucks to have the locksmith come and open the box for you and make another key.'

'Then the key in Winifred's pocketbook is only useful to the owner?'

'That's right.'

She looked at them. 'It was Winifred's pocketbook. And Winifred was a champion swimmer, or at least she was once upon a time. The walls of her apartment are covered with gold medals and photos of her winning swimming meets. I realize that was a long time ago, but maybe she kept at it.'

'We're already checking out that angle. We know she was a member of a health club and that she swam in the club's pool every day, either before or after work.' He hesitated. 'I'm sorry, but I have to ask you another question, and I'm sure you can understand why: Was your husband a good swimmer?'

Nell thought for a moment, stunned to realize that she didn't know the answer. It was not something she had ever thought about, but it disturbed her not to be able to answer the question.

That is one more thing I don't know about Adam, she thought.

After a long pause, she spoke: 'I nearly drowned when I was fifteen. Since then, I've never completely gotten over my fear of water. I went out on the boat with Adam only a few times, and I was miserable. I can handle a cruise ship, but not a small boat, where I'm conscious of the water being so close. All this is a long way of saying that I can't really answer your question. I *know* Adam could swim, but as for how well, I'm just not sure.'

The two detectives nodded to each other and then stood up. 'We'll be going to see Ms. Ryan; I'm sure you realize that it is necessary to try to get to the source of this money. But if you talk to her, please assure her we'll do our best to keep her husband's name out of this part of the investigation, at least as far as the press is concerned.'

'Can you just tell me this?' Nell stood and faced the men. 'Do you have any hard evidence that my husband was involved in the bribery or the bid-rigging scandals?'

'No, we do not,' Brennan replied promptly. 'We *do* know that Winifred Johnson was the conduit for the transfer of a lot of money, perhaps millions of dollars. Based on the evidence you've given us here, it now appears that she was the one who prepared the money for Jimmy Ryan's payoff. The people who paid Winifred money have come forward, and they apparently had the impression it was all going to Walters and Arsdale themselves, but so far there's no proof of that.'

'And am I right that so far there's also no proof that Adam was receiving any payoff money?' Nell asked.

Sclafani paused, then answered. 'Yes, you're right. We don't know what role, if any, your husband played in all of the stuff that was going on at Walters and Arsdale. Winifred could have been working on her own, and she may have concocted a scheme to feather her own nest. Or she may have been working with the mysterious Harry Reynolds.'

'What about Peter Lang?' Nell asked.

Sclafani shrugged. 'Ms. MacDermott, this investigation remains wide open.'

In a way, what she had learned today was a comfort, Nell thought as she closed the door behind the detectives. In another way, though, it was unsettling. What Sclafani was saying basically was that no one had been cleared, including Adam.

Earlier in the day, Nell had noticed that her plants were in need of attention. Now she collected them from the foyer and living and dining rooms and brought them into the kitchen. With swift, expert movements she stripped away the dry leaves, turned up the soil and sprayed the leaves and buds.

She could almost see the plants begin to perk up. You were bone dry, she thought. A flash of memory came to her. Just before I met Adam, I was doing this job one day, and I realized I felt like one of these plants. Emotionally I was dry. Mac and Gert had just gotten through really rough cases of the flu. I'd realized then that if something happened to them, I would be absolutely alone.

I knew I needed to be loved the way those plants needed water just now.

And so I fell in love. But with what? she asked herself. Maybe I just fell in love with love . . . Wasn't there a song with those words?

I've always felt condescending toward Winifred, Nell thought. I was nice to her, but I thought of her as a faithful little drudge. But I'm coming to believe that underneath that meek and submissive exterior there lurked an entirely different person. If she had been heart-hungry, and had met someone who made her feel loved, who knows to what lengths she might have gone in order to please him—and to keep him?

I gave up my political career to please Adam, she thought. That was my sacrifice for love.

She finished working with the plants and started returning them to their posts around the apartment. Abruptly she took one and set it back on the kitchen counter. It was something she had never fully acknowledged, not even to herself, but the truth was, she had never liked the spider plant Adam gave her on her birthday two years ago. Impulsively, she took that one and put it out by the incinerator. One of the maintenance men will be glad to have it, she told herself.

The other plants she put back on the windowsills, the coffee table and the Bombay chest in the foyer. When she was done, she stood in the foyer and looked into the living room.

As an anniversary surprise, Adam had had their wedding picture copied by an artist. The portrait, too large for her taste, was hanging over the fireplace.

Nell walked up to it, took the frame in her hands and lifted it off the wall. The artist had been, at best, pedestrian. There was something lifeless in her smile, and Adam's smile seemed flat as well. Or perhaps the artist actually was very good, one who caught what the camera missed? Nell pondered the possibilities as she carried the portrait to the storage closet and exchanged it for the watercolor of the village of Adelboden she had bought years ago while skiing in Switzerland.

When the picture was hung, she once again stood in the foyer and looked around. She suddenly realized that all traces of Adam had been expunged from the living and the dining rooms.

Then she remembered the clothes and decided she was going to finish that job. She went back to the guest room. It took only fifteen minutes more to complete packing the suits and jackets in the boxes. She closed and marked them.

Then she noticed the navy jacket, still hanging on the back of the chair, and she was hit with another sudden memory. Last summer, she and Adam were out to dinner. The air-conditioning in the restaurant had been bone chilling, and she'd been wearing a sleeveless dress.

Adam had stood up, taken off this jacket and draped it over her. 'Go ahead, put your arms through,' he had urged.

But he was wearing short sleeves, and I told him that now *he'd* be cold; then he said that as long as I was warm, he'd be fine.

He was the master of the small courtesies, of the tender phrase, Nell thought as she picked up the jacket and slipped her arms into it. She wrapped it around her, trying to evoke once more the feeling of comfort and warmth she had felt when Adam gave it to her that day.

It was this jacket that he wore home that last night, she remembered. She held the lapel to her face, wondering if she could pick up any trace of the scent of Polo, the eau de cologne he used.

Perhaps there was the faintest trace there, she decided, although she could not be sure.

Bonnie Wilson had told her that Adam wanted her to give his clothing away to help other people. She wondered if the fact that he had not been generous with his unused garments until he met her had been a reproach to him after his death.

She decided she definitely would give the jacket away with his other clothing. She put her hands in the side pockets to be sure he had not left anything in them. He had always cleaned out his pockets when he undressed, but he had planned to wear this jacket again that last day, so Nell knew she should check it thoroughly just to be sure.

There was a pristinely ironed handkerchief in the lefthand pocket. The right pocket was empty. She put her finger in the breast pocket. That too was empty.

Nell folded the jacket, reopened the last box she had filled and put it in. She had begun to close the top when she remembered that this jacket had several inside pockets as well. Just to be on the safe side, she decided to check them too.

Within the inside pocket on the right side of the jacket there was a small sac that buttoned for security. It was flat, but Nell thought she could feel something under her fingers. She opened the button, reached in and withdrew a tiny manila envelope.

From it, she removed a safe-deposit key. It was stamped with the number 332.

CHAPTER SEVENTY-ONE

At three o'clock, Lisa Ryan received a phone call at work that she had been both anticipating and dreading.

Detective Jack Sclafani said it was necessary for him and Detective Brennan to have a meeting with her when she got home from work.

'We just left Ms. MacDermott,' Sclafani told her.

Lisa had to take the call in the manager's office. 'I understand,' she replied. She turned her back, not wanting to see the naked curiosity in her boss's eyes.

'We'll need to talk frankly,' Sclafani warned. 'I know that wasn't possible for you last week once the children came home.'

'I have a friend who will take the children out for dinner. Would 6:30 be all right?'

'That would be fine.'

Feigning a lightness of spirit she did not feel, Lisa somehow got through the rest of the afternoon.

*   *   *

When the two detectives arrived, she opened the door, and gesturing with a cup of coffee in her hand, said, 'I just made a fresh pot. Would you like some?'

It was a perfunctory offer, but Jack Sclafani accepted even though he didn't care about having coffee without a meal. He could sense that despite the cordial way in which she had greeted them, Lisa

Ryan was clearly frightened and on the defensive. He needed to get her to relax, because he wanted her to feel as if they were her friends.

'I wasn't going to say yes, but it smells good,' Brennan responded, smiling.

'Jimmy liked my coffee,' Lisa said as she took mugs from the shelf. 'Said I had a magic touch. It sounds silly, of course. We all make coffee the same way. I guess he was just prejudiced.'

They took their coffee into the living room. Sclafani noticed immediately that the model of the dream house was no longer on the table.

Lisa followed his glance. 'I packed it away,' she told him. 'It was kind of hard, seeing it every time the kids and I were in this room.'

'I can understand that.'

It was what Kelly wrote in her diary that made me put it away, she thought.

Every time I look at Mommy's dream house, I think of how Daddy let me see it when he was making it. He said that it was our secret, that it was his present to Mommy for Christmas. I never told a single soul. I miss Daddy so much. I miss looking forward to living in the dream house, especially the room he was going to build for me.

There was another secret Kelly had written about in her diary that Lisa knew she was going to have to share with the detectives. She decided not to wait for them to ask questions. 'I believe you both said you have children,' she began. 'If something happened to you, I don't think you'd want them, or anyone else for that matter, to judge you by one mistake that you felt had been forced upon you.'

She looked at the detectives. Their eyes were
299

sympathetic. Lisa prayed that they weren't just pretending, that this wasn't a professional trick, designed to make her believe they understood what must have happened to Jimmy.

'I'll tell you everything I know,' she continued, 'but I am pleading with you to keep Jimmy's name out of this investigation. Those boxes with the money were sealed. For all I know, someone asked him to hold them for them and he never even knew what was in them.'

'You don't believe that, Lisa,' Jack Sclafani said.

'I'm not sure *what* to believe. I *am* sure that if Jimmy knew anything about substandard construction on a job that might later cause a tragic accident, he would have come forward eventually. And I know also that since he is not here to speak for himself, it has to come out now.'

'You told Ms. MacDermott that you found the sealed packages in your husband's file,' Brennan said.

'Yes. The file cabinet is in his workshop. I was going through it, looking for any records I might need to keep, like income tax statements.' A hint of a smile touched Lisa's lips. 'I grew up listening to the story of how my great-aunt found an insurance policy in my great-uncle's desk that she never knew he had. It was for twenty-five thousand dollars, which in 1947 was big bucks.' She paused and looked at her hands, clenching and unclenching them as they lay in her lap. 'I didn't find an insurance policy downstairs. Instead, I found the packages.'

'You have no idea where they came from?'

'No. But I think I can pinpoint when he did something to be given them. It was this past

300

September 9th.'

'How can you be sure of that?'

'My daughter's diary.' Lisa's voice faltered. She twisted her hands together. 'Oh, God, what am I doing?' she cried. 'I *swore* to Kelly I'd never read her diary.'

She's going to clam up again, Jack Sclafani thought. 'Lisa,' he said, 'you're right that we've both got kids. We don't want to hurt a child any more than you do. But please, tell us what she wrote that pertains to September 9th, and why you think it is important. After that, we'll get out of here, I promise.'

At least for now, Brennan thought as he looked at his partner. Jack is good. He's acting like Lisa Ryan's big brother. What's better is that he means it.

Lisa kept her head down as she spoke. 'After reading the diary, I remembered that on Thursday, September 9th, Jimmy came home late. He was working at a site on the Upper West Side, at about One Hundredth Street. I think it was a renovation project on an apartment building. Before he got home, I had a phone call from someone who asked to talk to Jimmy and said it was urgent, even wanted to know if he had a cell phone. Jimmy didn't believe in those things. I asked if I could take a message.'

'Was it a man or a woman who called?'

'Man. He had a low, nervous voice.'

Lisa got up and walked to the window. 'The message he asked me to give Jimmy was, 'The job is canceled.' I was so afraid it meant that Jimmy was out of work again. He finally got home around nine-thirty, and I told him about the call. He was

301

terribly upset.'

'What do you mean by "upset"?'

'He turned almost ghostly pale and began sweating. Then he grabbed his chest. For a moment there, I thought he was having a heart attack. But then he pulled himself together and said that the owner had demanded some changes that he'd already made and now couldn't undo.'

'Why do you remember this episode so clearly?'

'Only because of something Kelly wrote in her diary. At the time, I thought that Jimmy was just terrified that something would happen to make him lose the job. After that night, I didn't think anything more about it. I remember that I went to bed about an hour after Jimmy got home. He said he wanted to have a beer and unwind, that he'd join me in a little while. Kelly wrote in her diary that she woke up and heard the television on. She went downstairs because she'd been asleep when Jimmy came home and she wanted to say good night to him.'

Lisa crossed to a desk and took a piece of paper out of a drawer. 'I copied this from her diary, dated September 9th.

' "I sat on Daddy's lap. He was so quiet. He was watching the news. Then, all of a sudden, he began to cry. I wanted to run and get Mommy, but he wouldn't let me. Then he said that he was all right, and it was our secret that he felt sad. He said he was just tired out and had had a very bad day at work. He brought me back up to bed, and he went into the bathroom. I could hear him throwing up, so I guess he just had a flu bug or something." '

Deliberately, Lisa folded and then tore up the paper she was holding. 'I don't know much about

302

law, but I do know that in a court, this is not considered evidence. If you have any decency in you, you'll never refer to it publicly. But I would suggest that whatever the job was that Jimmy described as 'too late to cancel' is at the center of this whole issue about the money and a payoff. I think the apartment building renovation Jimmy was working on last September 9th may need to be inspected.'

The detectives left a few minutes later. Once they were in the car, Sclafani said, 'You're thinking what I'm thinking?'

'You bet I am. We need to get a tape of all the September 9th late-night news broadcasts and see if there's anything reported on one of them that might be connected to Jimmy Ryan's big payoff.'

CHAPTER SEVENTY-TWO

'Ms. Nell MacDermott on the phone, sir.' The secretary's voice was apologetic. 'I told her you were not available, but she's quite insistent that you accept her call. What shall I tell her?'

Peter Lang raised an eyebrow and thought for a second, looking across the desk at his corporation counsel, Louis Graymore, with whom he had been meeting. 'I'll take it,' he said.

His conversation with Nell was brief. When he replaced the receiver, he said, 'That's quite a surprise. She wants to see me immediately. How do you figure that one, Lou?'

'When you saw her the other day, didn't you say she practically threw you out? What did you tell

303

her?'

'I told her to come ahead. She'll be here in about twenty minutes.'

'Want me to wait?'

'I don't think that's necessary.'

'I could gently remind her that your family has been supporting her grandfather's campaigns since before either you or she was born,' the lawyer offered.

'I don't think so. I tried a gentle hint that I'd be happy to support her candidacy if she runs for his seat. I never got the freeze so fast in my life.'

Graymore got up. Silver-haired and urbane, he had been chief legal advisor on real estate matters to Lang's father, as well as to Peter. 'If I may offer you a word of advice, Peter, you made a tactical mistake when you were less than honest about your proposed use of the Kaplan parcel.' He paused. 'With some people, straight talk works.'

Lou may be right, Peter thought as, not long after that, his secretary ushered Nell into his office. Though she was dressed casually, in a denim jacket and chinos, she had a bearing that bespoke class. He also found her very attractive, noticing the way loose tendrils of hair framed her face.

Even his most sophisticated visitors usually commented on the superb view and his exquisitely furnished office. He had the feeling that Nell, however, was totally unaware of any of it—the view, the furnishings, the expensive art on the walls.

With a nod, he indicated to his secretary that she should escort Nell to the chairs at the window that looked out toward the Hudson River.

'I have to talk to you,' Nell said abruptly as she

304

sat down.

'That's why you're here, isn't it?' he said, smiling.

Nell shook her head impatiently. 'Peter, we don't know each other well, but we have met any number of times over the years. I'm not interested in any of that now, though. What I *am* interested in is how well you knew my husband and why you lied to me the other day about your proposed use of the property Adam bought from the Kaplans.'

Lou was right on target, Peter Lang thought. Dissembling was not the way to go with this woman. 'Nell, let me put it this way. I met Adam a number of times while he was with Walters and Arsdale. My firm has been involved in construction projects with that firm for many years.'

'Would you have called yourself Adam's friend?'

'No. Frankly, I would not. I knew him—period.'

Nell nodded. 'What did you think of him as an architect? The way you spoke the other day, one might have thought that the world had lost a genius.'

Lang smiled. 'I don't think I went *that* far, did I? What I was trying to convey was that we could not use his design for the Vandermeer project. Quite frankly, it was just a courtesy to you to suggest that we would have used it if he had lived. Since he obviously did not tell you that he was off the job, I saw no point in delivering that rather negative news after his death.'

'You also lied when you said you only wanted the property I now own for additional landscaping,' Nell said flatly.

Without responding, Lang went over to the wall and pushed a button. A hidden screen rolled down and was illuminated. On the screen was a panoramic view of Manhattan. In it, buildings and projects, numbered and outlined in blue, dotted the landscape from north to south, and from east to west. A gold-lettered legend on the right listed the names and locations of the various properties.

'The ones marked in blue are the Lang holdings in Manhattan, Nell. As I told the detectives, who all but accused me of setting the bomb that blew up Adam's boat, I would like to acquire the Kaplan property because we now have a stunning design we'd like to go ahead with, but it is one that requires that extra bit of land.'

Nell walked over to the illustration he indicated and studied it closely. Then she nodded.

Peter Lang pushed the button that retracted the screen. 'You're absolutely right,' he said quietly. 'I wasn't truthful with you, and for that I apologize. I would like to couple the Kaplan property with the Vandermeer land because my grandfather settled almost on that exact spot when he was an eighteen-year-old immigrant, just off the boat from Ireland. I would like to erect a magnificent tower of a building that would be a kind of monument to what three generations of Langs—my grandfather, my father and myself—have accomplished. To achieve that, in that particular spot, I need the Kaplan land.'

He looked directly at her. 'However, if I don't get it, I will move on. Another opportunity will present itself in that area, sooner or later.'

'Why didn't you buy the Kaplan property yourself?'

'Because I had no use for it unless the landmark status was removed from the Vandermeer mansion,

306

and when that happened, it was totally unexpected.'

'Then why do you think Adam bought it?'

'Either he had extraordinary foresight, or someone on the Board of Estimate spoke out of turn about the status of the mansion. And by the way, don't think that isn't being investigated.'

'I noticed that the Lang Tower was already listed as part of your landscape.' She pointed to the wall where the screen had been. 'You must have been pretty sure you'd be able to build it in that location.'

'Pretty *hopeful*, Nell, not sure. In this business, you always assume you're going to get what you go after. It doesn't always turn out that way, of course, but real estate developers tend to be optimists.'

She had one more question before she left. 'Do you know someone named Harry Reynolds?' Nell watched Peter Lang carefully, observing his reaction.

Lang looked puzzled, then his face brightened. 'I knew a *Henry* Reynolds at Yale. He taught medieval history. But he died ten years ago. No one ever called him Harry. Why do you ask?'

Nell shrugged. 'It's not important.'

He walked with her to the elevator. 'Nell, what you do with your property is up to you. I'm like a ballplayer who gets fired up when he goes to bat, but if he strikes out, he doesn't waste too much time regretting it. If he wants to keep his batting average up, he starts thinking about his next time at the plate.'

'That's not the tune you sang the other day.'

'Some things have changed since the other day. No piece of land is worth having the police

307

questioning me as if I'm a murderer. Look, my offer to buy it is on the table. To show you I mean business, I'm taking my offer off the table as of Monday evening.'

Peter Lang, you do *not* get the Boy Scout award for sincerity, Nell thought as the elevator plunged from the penthouse to the lobby. You've got an almost maniacal ego. As far as that property goes, I don't believe for a single minute that you'd walk away from it. In fact, I believe you want it so much it hurts. But that isn't important, and it isn't even the real reason I came here. I needed an answer, and I believe I have it.

In some deep part of her being, Nell was sure she now knew all she needed to know about Peter Lang. The sensation was akin to the certainty she felt the several times in her life she had heard her dead parents speak to her.

She was the only passenger in the elevator. As it rushed down, she said aloud, 'Peter Lang, you *do not* have blood on your hands.'

CHAPTER SEVENTY-THREE

Dan Minor both anticipated and dreaded checking his answering machine at the end of the day. For some reason, the very act of aggressively searching for his mother was accompanied by the feeling that if her whereabouts *were* discovered, the news would not be good.

When he arrived home on Thursday, the message he found waiting was from Mac: 'Give me a call, Dan. It's important.'

From the somber tone of Cornelius MacDermott's voice, Dan knew that the search for Quinny was over.

He was a surgeon whose fingers held the most delicate instruments, whose slightest miscalculation could cost a life. But those fingers trembled as Dr. Dan Minor dialed Cornelius MacDermott's office.

It was quarter of five, just the time Dan had told Mac he usually got home from the hospital. When the phone rang, Mac did not wait for Liz to put the call through but picked it up himself.

'I have your message, Mac.'

'There's no easy way to say this, Dan. You'll make the final identification in the morning, but the picture you gave me matches the picture they took of a homeless woman who died last September. The vital statistics are right, and pinned to her bra she had the same picture you carry.'

Dan swallowed over the choking lump that had formed in his throat.

'What happened to her?'

Cornelius MacDermott hesitated. He doesn't have to know everything now, he thought. 'The place where she was staying caught fire. She suffocated.'

'Suffocated!' Dear God, Dan thought, anguished. Couldn't she have been spared that?

'Dan, I know how tough this is. Why don't you meet me for dinner?'

It was an effort to speak. 'No, Mac,' he managed to say. 'I think I kind of need to be by myself tonight.'

'I understand. Then call me at nine o'clock tomorrow morning. I'll meet you at the M.E.'s

309

office. We'll make the arrangements.'

'Where is she now?'

'Buried. In potter's field.'

'They're sure of the location where they put her body?'

'Yes. We can arrange to have it exhumed.'

'Thanks, Mac.'

Dan replaced the receiver, took out his wallet, threw it on the coffee table and sat down on the couch. From the wallet, he took the photo he had carried around with him ever since he was six years old. He propped the picture up.

Minutes, an hour, an hour and a half went by as he sat immobilized, straining for every memory of her, however vague, he could recall.

Oh, Quinny, why did you have to die like that? he asked.

And why, Mother, did you blame yourself for what happened to me? It wasn't your fault. *I* was the stupid little kid who caused the accident.

But it turned out all right, actually better than all right. I wanted you to at least know that, he thought.

The doorbell rang. He ignored it. It rang again, this time persistently.

Damn! Leave me alone, he thought. I don't want to have a drink with the neighbors.

Reluctantly, he got up, walked across the room and opened the door. Nell MacDermott was standing there. 'Mac told me,' she said. 'I'm so sorry, Dan.'

Wordlessly he stepped aside and let her in. He closed the door, put his arms around her and began to cry.

Friday, June 23

CHAPTER SEVENTY-FOUR

On Friday morning, a messenger was sent to collect tape cassettes of the September 9th, late-evening newscasts from each of New York City's six major television stations. Once gathered, they were to be delivered to the district attorney's office.

Detectives Sclafani and Brennan were waiting for the messenger, and when he arrived they took the tapes to the tech room on the ninth floor. Making their way through the maze of equipment and wires, they selected a VCR and television off to one side of the room. Brennan pulled up chairs, while Sclafani dropped the tape from the CBS station into the player.

'Showtime,' he told his partner. 'Get out the popcorn.'

The lead story was about the fire that had engulfed the landmark Vandermeer mansion on Twenty-eighth Street and Seventh Avenue.

Dana Adams was the CBS reporter on the scene, broadcasting live at the time. 'The Vandermeer mansion, erected on one of the oldest original Dutch farms in the city, and a landmark building that had been standing empty for the past eight years, was engulfed in flames tonight. The fire, which was called in to the local fire station at 7:34, spread rapidly through the building, at one point engulfing the entire roof. On reports that homeless people had occasionally been seen in and around the premises, firefighters risked their lives to search the structure. Tragically, in an upstairs bathroom they discovered the body of a homeless woman who apparently had died of smoke inhalation. She is believed also to have started the fire that consumed the building. Authorities say they have made a tentative identification but will not release the victim's name until it has been confirmed and the next of kin can be located and notified.'

The news segment ended and a commercial began.

'The Vandermeer mansion!' Sclafani exclaimed. 'Lang owns that, doesn't he?'

'Yes, and Cauliff owned the property next to it.'

'Which means they both stood to make a buck on that fire.'

'Exactly.'

'Okay, let's watch the rest of the tapes just in case there is something else that might possibly have been tied to Jimmy Ryan's big payoff.'

Almost three hours later, they had found no other story on any of the stations that in any way could conceivably concern Jimmy Ryan. The destruction of the old mansion had been covered extensively on all the stations, of course.

They turned the tapes over to technical support to be copied for backup security. 'And run the six Vandermeer segments together,' Sclafani directed the technician.

They went back to Sclafani's office to review what they had learned. 'What have we got?' Brennan asked.

'Coincidence, which we both know is a dirty word, and the opinion of a ten-year-old girl that Daddy got upset while watching that broadcast. Maybe after a couple of beers, Daddy was just feeling down on his luck.'

'Lisa Ryan said that his story at the time was that
314

the "cancel the job" phone call related to extra work he'd already taken care of.'

'That's easy enough to check out, I guess.' Brennan got up. 'We've seen cases of homeless people accidentally setting fires in abandoned buildings,' he said thoughtfully, 'and other people losing their lives because of it.'

'Take it from the other angle,' Sclafani suggested. 'When a homeless person is known to be squatting in a building that burns down, it's easy to assume that's who caused the fire.'

'I think we both agree it's time to take a good look at exactly what happened on September 9th in the Vandermeer mansion.' George Brennan took out his notebook. 'I'll start digging on that end. Let's see. That's Twenty-eighth Street, on the east side of Seventh Avenue. The 13th Precinct would have the file.'

'I'm going out with bag lady Winnie Johnson's key again,' Sclafani said. 'We need to find the bank where she had that safe deposit box.'

'Unless it's too late.'

'Unless it's too late,' Sclafani agreed. 'If an eight-year-old kid from Wilmington is right, someone got off that boat before the explosion. My guess as of now is that the person he saw was Winifred Johnson. In which case, even without the key, she could have gotten into the box.'

'Do you realize that right now we're following up leads provided by a far-sighted eight-year-old boy and a ten-year-old girl who keeps a diary?' Brennan said with a sigh. 'Mother told me there'd be days like this.'

CHAPTER SEVENTY-FIVE

On Friday morning, Nell phoned the Old Woods Manor nursing home and inquired about Winifred Johnson's mother. She was switched to the nurse's desk on the second floor.

'She's really quite depressed,' the nurse told her. 'Winifred was a *very* dutiful daughter. She came up here for a visit every Saturday, and sometimes in the evenings during the week as well.'

Winifred the faithful daughter. Winifred the swimmer. Winifred the bag lady. Winifred the lover of Harry Reynolds. Which one *was* she, Nell wondered, or was she all four of those people? And was she now in South America or on one of those islands in the Caribbean that wouldn't send her back to the U.S. even if authorities located her there?

'Is there anything I can do for Mrs. Johnson?' she asked.

'I think the best thing you could do would be to pay her a visit,' the nurse said frankly. 'She wants to talk about her daughter, and I'm afraid the other guests here avoid her. She is a bit of a complainer, you know.'

'I had intended to come up to see her next week,' Nell said. *She wants to talk about her daughter*, she thought. Was it possible that Mrs. Johnson might be able to tell me something that could lead to Winifred's whereabouts, assuming she is still alive?

'But I'll come today instead,' she promised. 'I can be there around noon.'

She put the receiver down and went to the window. It was a gray, rainy morning, and when she had awakened, she had lain in bed for a long time, her eyes closed, reviewing everything that had happened in the last two weeks.

She had imagined Adam's face, painting it in scrupulous detail. On that last morning there had been no trace of the smile that had captivated her on their first meeting. He had been edgy and nervous, so anxious to get away that he had walked off without his jacket or briefcase.

The jacket with safe-deposit key number 332 in it.

I should turn the key over to the detectives, Nell thought, as she went into the bathroom and turned on the shower. I know I should. *But not until . . .* She did not finish the thought.

A possibility, both grotesque and bizarre, had been forming in her mind—a possibility that by keeping the key she might be able to confirm or refute.

Having the second key won't help them find the bank any faster anyhow, she reasoned, as she stepped under the steaming water.

She had almost confided to Dan what she was planning and why it was necessary, but last night had not been the time for that. That was the time to let him talk out his own grief and pain. In halting, broken sentences, he had told her about the accident that drove his mother away, about the long months in the hospital when he had kept praying that the door to his room would open and he would see her standing there. Then he had talked about how the devotion of his grandparents had helped him to heal both physically and

317

emotionally.

Finally he said, 'I know that once I'm able to move my mother to the family burial plot in Maryland, I'll start to have a feeling of peace about her. I won't wake up in the middle of the night wondering if she's out on the streets somewhere, cold or hungry or sick.'

I told him that I truly believe the people we love never really leave us, Nell thought as the pelting water coursed over her face. I told him about Mother and Daddy coming to say goodbye to me.

He asked me if Adam had said goodbye in the same way. I just shook my head. I didn't want to talk about Adam last night.

At ten o'clock she had gone into his kitchen and poked around, looking for the makings of dinner. 'You're obviously not one of those bachelors who's a gourmet cook,' she had told him with a smile.

She found eggs and cheese and a tomato, and was able to put together an omelet and toast and coffee. As they ate, he even had been able to joke a little. 'Are you able to make yourself invisible, Nell? I've been trying to figure out how you got past my doorman. He's worse than a prison guard. You practically have to give a blood sample to get in if you're not a tenant.'

'Somebody in the building is having a party. I joined a group of six or seven people, then when they got off on the fourth floor, I told the elevator operator I was visiting you. He let me off here and pointed to your apartment. I was afraid if I was announced, you either wouldn't answer the intercom or would turn me down.'

'Well, there your precognition was wrong. I would have said, "Come up, Nell. I need you."' He

318

gave her a steady look.

It was almost midnight when Dan had gone downstairs with her and put her in a cab. 'I won't be able to meet Mac at Bellevue until about noon,' he had told her. 'I'm scheduled for a couple of surgeries in the morning.'

Fifteen minutes later, when Nell arrived home, there was a message from him on her answering machine: 'Nell, I don't think I thanked you for coming to be with me tonight. It made me feel the way I would have felt as a kid if the hospital door had opened and the beautiful lady I loved was there. I know I have a hell of a nerve talking like this, and won't again for at least another six months, I promise. I do realize you've been widowed for only two weeks. It's just that I'm so thankful that you've come into my life.'

She had taken the tape out of the machine and put it in one of the dresser drawers.

Nell thought of the tape again as she stepped out of the shower this morning, toweled herself vigorously, dried her hair and dressed in light-blue gabardine slacks and a blue-and-white, man-tailored shirt.

She was tempted to go to the drawer, get out the tape and play it again. It was at least a hint of a future that might be happier. But she knew that the special, almost magical feeling hearing it had given her last night would not be there today.

In fact, she had a feeling of dread about the day ahead of her. She sensed that something terrible was going to happen. She had known it when she first opened her eyes this morning, after a fitful and dream-filled sleep. There was a catastrophe hovering in the air around her, in much the same way a tornado's spiraling black cloud hangs from the sky before touching ground and obliterating everything in its path.

She sensed all this, but felt powerless to prevent it, whatever it might be. She was *part* of it, an actor in an inevitable scene that had to be played out, that could not be avoided. Through her own experience over the years, and also because of Gert's influence, she had come to understand that what she was experiencing was precognition.

Precognition: The knowledge of a future event through extrasensory means.

Gert had explained it to her. It had happened to her a few times.

As Nell touched her lips with gloss, she tried to reason with herself. I thought it was precognition the other day when I experienced that sense of heat and burning and gasping for air. But when Dan's mother suffocated in that fire, that's what she must have been going through. Did I pick up some vibrations from her?

Only time would tell.

Once again, the questions that had haunted her dreams all through the night echoed in her mind. *Did* someone really get off that boat? If someone *did* escape that explosion, was it Winifred? Or was it perhaps a paid assassin who had been hiding in the engine room?

Or was it Adam?

It was a question she had to have answered. And if she was right, she knew how to find that answer.

CHAPTER SEVENTY-SIX

At noon, Dan Minor pushed open the door of the Medical Examiner's office on Thirtieth Street and First Avenue. Mac was waiting for him in the reception area.

'I'm sorry to be late,' Dan said.

'You're not,' Mac said. 'I'm always early. Nell said it's my way of getting the edge on people.' He clasped Dan's hand. 'I'm terribly sorry it turned out like this.'

Dan nodded. 'I know you are, and I appreciate your help.'

'Nell was shocked when I told her. I'm sure you'll hear from her.'

'I already did. She came over to keep me company last night.' A hint of a smile touched Dan's lips. 'After informing me that I had almost nothing in the cupboard, she even cooked dinner for me.'

'That sounds like Nell,' Cornelius MacDermott said. He nodded to the door past the reception room. 'A clerk back there has your mother's file ready for you to look at.'

They had photographed Quinny's face and nude body. So thin, Dan thought—she must have been anemic. It was clearly the same face as the computer-aged picture, but in death it seemed to him that a certain tranquility had returned to it. The high cheekbones and narrow nose and wide eyes were those of the young woman he remembered.

'The only distinguishing marks on her body were

321

some scars on her palms,' the clerk said. 'The examining physician attributed them to burns.'

'That would make sense,' Dan confirmed, his voice low and sad.

There was a photograph of the same snapshot he always carried.

'Where is that picture now?' he asked.

'They're keeping that as evidence. It's in the property room of the 10th Precinct.'

'Evidence! *Evidence of what?*'

'It's nothing to get upset about,' Mac said soothingly. 'She certainly didn't mean to burn that building down, but the way the experts figure it, September 9th was an unusually chilly night for that time of year. Quinny apparently threw some odds and ends in the fireplace, started a fire and went up to the bathroom. The damper wasn't open, and her stuff was too near the flames. In minutes the place was an inferno.'

'My mother may have died in that fire, but she did not set it,' Dan said positively. 'And let me tell you why.' He took a deep breath. 'Better yet, let me *show* you why.'

CHAPTER SEVENTY-SEVEN

Nell was just on her way out the door when Gert phoned. 'Nell, dear, you're still planning to drop off those boxes at the thrift shop tomorrow, aren't you?'

'Yes, I hadn't forgotten.'

'Now remember, if you need any help packing them, I'll be glad to come over.'

'Thanks, Aunt Gert, but they're boxed and ready to go,' Nell said. 'I've arranged for the car service I use to send over someone with a van. The driver will help me get the cartons to the shop and then unload them, so I'll be okay.'

Gert laughed apologetically. 'I should have known you'd have it all figured out already. You're so organized.'

'Don't say that, because I'm afraid it isn't so. I'm on top of this thing only because I wanted to rid this place of so many memories.'

'Oh, Nell, that reminds me: I was going through some photographs, trying to decide which ones to put in my new album, and—'

'Aunt Gert, I'm sorry, but I'm afraid I'm running late and need to get going. I'm due in White Plains in less than an hour.'

'Oh, my dear, I'm sorry. By all means, get going. Then I can count on seeing you tomorrow at the thrift shop?'

'Absolutely. The driver will be here at ten o'clock, so you can expect me by around ten-thirty.'

'That's fine, Nell. I'll let you go now. Bye, dear. See you tomorrow.'

God love her, Nell thought as she replaced the receiver. The stock of whatever phone company Aunt Gert uses will drop 20 percent the day she dies.

* * *

Before going to Mrs. Johnson's room, Nell stopped at the nurse's desk on the second floor. 'I'm Nell MacDermott, here to see Mrs. Johnson. We spoke this morning.'

The nurse, a pleasant-faced woman with graying hair, got up. 'I told her you were coming, Ms. MacDermott. I thought it would perk her up, and it did, but only for a while. Since then she has had a call from her landlord. Seems he wants the furniture out of her apartment, and that has her terribly upset. I'm afraid you may get the brunt of it.'

As they walked down the corridor, they passed a small dining room with three tables occupied by people being served luncheon. 'We have a main dining room downstairs, but some people think it's friendlier to have their breakfast and midday meals served on their own floor, and we try to accommodate them,' the nurse said.

'From what I've seen, there's almost nothing you don't do for the residents here,' Nell observed.

'We only fail them in one way: we can't make them happy. And, unfortunately, it's probably the one thing they need the most. It's understandable, of course. They're old. They hurt. They miss their husbands, or wives, or children, or friends. Some adjust very well to living here. Others don't, though, and it's painful to see them suffer. There's an old saying: 'As we get older, we get more so.' We find that the people who were naturally optimistic have the best chance of being relatively content.'

They were almost at Mrs. Johnson's room. 'I suspect Mrs. Johnson hasn't adjusted well,' Nell said.

'She knows this is as good as it gets, but, like anyone else, she'd prefer to be in her own home— and in her case, also running the show. You'll hear all about that, I'm sure.'

They stood at the partially open door leading to

Mrs. Johnson's apartment. The nurse tapped on it. 'Company, Mrs. Johnson.'

Without waiting for a reply, she pushed the door back. Nell followed her in.

Rhoda Johnson was in the bedroom of the small suite. She was lying on top of the bed, propped up on pillows, with an afghan thrown over her.

As they entered the bedroom, she opened her eyes. 'Nell MacDermott?' It was a question.

'Yes.' Nell was shocked to see the visible difference in the woman since her last visit.

'I want you to do me a favor. Winifred used to pick up a coffee cake for me at the bakery in the mall about a mile from here. Would you get one for me today? I can't eat the food here—it's tasteless.'

Oh, boy, Nell thought. 'I'd be glad to, Mrs. Johnson.'

'Have a nice visit,' the nurse said cheerfully.

Nell pulled up a chair and sat by the bed. 'You're not feeling that great today, are you, Mrs. Johnson?' she asked.

'I'm all right. But people around here aren't very friendly. You see, they know I didn't come from much, so they ignore me.'

'I don't know about that. The nurse who was with me just now was the one who suggested I drive up to visit with you today because you were feeling a bit low. And the lady who brought me up last week also seemed *very* fond of you.'

'They're okay. But I promise you that the people who work in room service and clean up the place, that sort of thing, are definitely not treating me the same since Winifred isn't around to slip them twenty-dollar bills.'

'That was generous of her.'

'A waste of money as it turns out. Wouldn't you think that now she's gone they'd have a little sympathy?'

Rhoda Johnson began to cry. 'It's always been like this . . . people taking advantage. I've been forty-two *years* in that apartment, and now the owner wants me out in two *weeks*. I have clothes in the closets; my mother's good china is there. Would you believe that in all these years, I never broke one single cup?'

'Mrs. Johnson, let me just ask the nurse something,' Nell said. 'I'll be right back.'

She was gone less than five minutes. 'Good news,' she reported. 'It's just as I expected. You're allowed to bring your own furniture here, if that's what you want to do. Why don't we plan for you to drive with me to your apartment next week, and you can select your favorite things to bring back here. I'll arrange to have them delivered.'

Rhoda Johnson looked at her suspiciously. 'Why are you doing this?'

'Because you've lost your daughter, and I am sorry,' Nell said. 'And if having your favorite things around you will give you comfort, I'd like to make that happen.'

'Maybe you think you owe me something because Winifred was on your husband's boat. If she'd stayed with Walters and Arsdale, she would have gone straight home after work, and she'd be alive today!'

Rhoda Johnson's face crumbled as tears spilled from her eyes. 'I miss Winifred so much. She never skipped coming to see me on Saturdays—not *once*. She didn't always make it in the evenings during the week, but Saturday was our day to visit, always.

The last time I saw her was the evening before she died.'

'That would be Thursday night, two weeks ago,' Nell said. 'Did you have a nice visit?'

'She was a bit upset. She said she wanted to stop at the bank, but she got there too late.'

Instinct made Nell ask the next question: 'Do you remember what time she got here that night?'

'It wasn't really night. It was Thursday evening, a little after five. I remember because I was having my dinner when she came, and I always have my dinner at five.'

Banks close at five o'clock, Nell thought. Winifred had plenty of time to get to one in Manhattan before she drove up to White Plains. She must have been using a bank near here.

Rhoda Johnson wiped her eyes with the back of her hand. 'I shouldn't go on so. I know I'm not going to be here that much longer. My heart's about as bad as it can get and keep going. I used to ask Winifred what she would do when something happened to me. You know what she always said?'

Nell waited.

'She said she'd quit her job and be on the first plane to nowhere. That was her little joke, I guess.' She sighed. 'I shouldn't hold you up, Nell. You've done me a lot of good coming here. Now you *did* promise to get me a coffee cake today, didn't you?'

*   *   *

The bakery was at a mall, about a ten-minute drive from the nursing home. Nell bought the coffee cake, then stood for a moment on the sidewalk outside the bakery. The rain had let up, but the

327

skies were heavily overcast. She could see a large bank, off at a right angle to the mall. It had its own circular driveway and separate parking lot. Why not? Nell thought as she headed to her car. It's a good place to start.

She drove to the bank, parked and went inside. A window at the far end had a metal sign on the counter: SAFE-DEPOSIT BOXES.

Nell walked over to the counter and opened her shoulder bag. She took out her wallet and extracted the small manila envelope she had found in the inner pocket of Adam's jacket.

She opened the clasp and let the key slide out onto the countertop. Before she could even ask if the key belonged to a safe-deposit box in this bank, the clerk smiled and handed her a signature card to sign.

'I'd like to speak to the manager,' Nell said quietly.

Arlene Barron, the manager, was a handsome African-American in her early forties. 'This key is tied to an ongoing criminal investigation,' Nell explained. 'I need to call the Manhattan district attorney's office immediately.'

She was told that both Sclafani and Brennan were out, but were expected back shortly. She left the message that she had found the location of the safe-deposit box for key number 332, and gave Barron's name and phone number.

'I'm sure they'll be up here with a search warrant, maybe even before you close today,' Nell told her.

'I understand.'

'Would it be violating security to tell me in whose name the box is registered?'

Barron hesitated. 'I don't know if . . .'

Nell interrupted her. 'Is it only registered to a woman, or is Harry Reynolds a cosignatory?'

'I really shouldn't divulge that information,' Arlene Barron said, as, almost imperceptibly, she nodded the affirmative.

'I thought so.' Nell got up to go. 'Please tell me one more thing. Has the box been opened since June 9th?'

'We don't keep those records.'

'Then if by any chance someone tries to get into that box before the police get here, you've got to stall them. If the box hasn't been cleaned out already, it may contain crucial evidence in a multiple homicide.'

She was at the door when Arlene Barron called to her, 'Ms. MacDermott, you forgot your package.'

The bag with the coffee cake was on the floor next to the chair in which she had been sitting. 'Thanks. I didn't even realize I'd brought it into the bank with me,' Nell said. 'I've got to deliver it to a lady in a nursing home. God help her, she's earned every bite of it.'

CHAPTER SEVENTY-EIGHT

When Sclafani and Brennan arrived at the 13th Precinct station house, they found Mac and Dan Minor there.

'Take a look at who's at the desk,' Brennan murmured to his partner. 'Congressman MacDermott. Wonder what he's up to?'

'There's a great way to find out.' Sclafani strode over to the desk. 'Hi, Rich,' he said in greeting to the sergeant, then with an expansive smile, he turned to Cornelius MacDermott. 'Sir, it's a pleasure to see you. I'm Detective Sclafani. Detective Brennan and I have been in constant touch with your granddaughter since the boating tragedy. She's been very helpful to us.'

'Nell didn't mention anything about you, but that shouldn't surprise me,' Mac commented. 'I raised her to be independent, and I guess I'm a world-class teacher.' He paused to shake hands with Sclafani. 'I'm here on a totally separate matter. Dr. Minor here needs information concerning his mother's death.'

Brennan had joined them. 'I'm sorry, Doctor,' he said to Dan. 'Was it recent?'

Mac answered for Dan. 'It was nine months ago. Dan's mother was a troubled woman whom he has been seeking for a long time. She suffocated in the fire at the Vandermeer mansion last September 9th.'

The two detectives looked at each other. Ten minutes later the four men were seated together at a long table in the station's private conference room. Captain John Murphy, the ranking officer on duty had joined them. The case file and the box with Dan Minor's mother's personal effects were on the table.

Captain Murphy extrapolated the most significant information from the file. 'Smoke was spotted coming from the lower floor of the Vandermeer mansion at about 7:34 in the evening, and an alarm was sounded. By the time the first fire equipment arrived some four and a half minutes later, much of the building was engulfed in flames, the fire apparently having traveled through a dumb-waiter shaft, which allowed it to spread quickly to the roof. Despite the danger, four FDNY firemen connected by a tether explored the first two floors, which were almost fully engaged. The hook and ladder company sent in additional personnel to search the third and fourth floors. They found the body of an adult Caucasian female in the bathroom on the fourth floor. She had taken refuge in the bathtub and had covered her face with a wet cloth. She was removed before the fire reached that floor. Despite intense efforts at CPR, she did not respond and was declared dead at 9:30 P.M. Cause of death, suffocation due to smoke inhalation.'

The captain glanced at Dan, who was listening attentively, his eyes downcast, his hands folded on the table.

'It may be some consolation to know that the fire never touched her. The intense heat and smoke, however, did kill her.'

'I appreciate that,' Dan said, 'but what I need to know is why she is being held responsible for setting the fire.'

'It began in what had been the library on the first floor. The window of that room blew out fairly quickly, and some papers landed on the street, including a human services or soup kitchen card as we call them. That was why your mother was misidentified for some time. It turned out that the card belonged to another homeless woman who claimed that one of her shopping bags had been stolen hours before.'

'Are you saying that there was *another* homeless

person in the building?'

'We have no reason to think so. There was certainly no other victim, and traces of some food and a bedroll were found in the library. We believe your mother must have been cooping in the Vandermeer mansion, started the fire accidentally—perhaps while trying to fix herself some dinner—and then went upstairs to use the bathroom. As it happens, it was the only one that still worked. She was trapped up there. If she *did* try to get out, the smoke was so dense she probably wouldn't have been able to find the staircase.'

'Now let me tell you something about my mother,' Dan said. 'She had a pathological fear of fire, and perhaps especially fire in an open fireplace. There is no *way* she ever would have started a fire in one.'

He saw the look of polite disbelief on the faces of Captain Murphy and the detectives. 'My father walked out on my mother when I was three years old. She went into a state of clinical depression that led to heavy, steady drinking. She controlled it during the day, but once I was in bed, she would drink until she had drunk herself into a stupor.'

Dan's voice faltered. 'I remember as a child that I used to worry about her. I'd wake up and tiptoe downstairs, clutching my blanket. Invariably she'd be asleep on the couch, an empty bottle next to her. She loved a fire then and used to read to me on that couch near the fireplace before I went to bed. One night when I went down to check on her, she was passed out on the floor right in front of the hearth. I shook the blanket out to cover her, and part of it went into the fire. When I tried to pull it away, the sleeve of my pajamas caught on fire.'

He stood up, took off his jacket and unbuttoned his shirtsleeve. 'I almost lost this arm,' he said as he rolled up the sleeve. 'I spent almost a year in the hospital, going through a series of skin grafts, and then a period of learning to use the arm again. The pain was awful. My mother was so guilt ridden and afraid of facing possible charges of negligence that, one day, after an all-night session at my hospital bed, she left and never came back. She couldn't stand seeing what had happened to me.

'We had no idea where she was, until seven years ago, when we saw her on a television documentary that was all about the homeless in New York. A private investigator we hired talked to some of the people in shelters here who knew her. They all had different stories about her, but on one point they all said the same thing: she panicked at the sight of an open flame.'

Dan's left arm was a solid mass of stretched, scarred flesh. He flexed his hand and extended his arm. 'It took a long time to get movement and control back into it,' he said. 'It's not a very pretty sight, but the kindness of those doctors and nurses when I was a kid is the reason I'm a pretty damn good pediatric surgeon today, and in charge of a burn unit.'

He rolled his shirtsleeve down and buttoned it. 'A few months ago I met a homeless woman named Lilly who knew my mother well. We talked about her at length. Lilly also brought up the subject of my mother's fear of fire.'

'You make a very strong case, Doctor,' Jack Sclafani said quietly. 'It is entirely possible that Karen Renfrew, the woman who claimed her soup kitchen card had been stolen, was the one who actually started the fire. The mansion was a very large house. She might have been totally unaware that your mother was also in it.'

'I think that's entirely possible. From what I understand, when my mother was in one of her darkly depressive moods, she tried to find a place where she'd be totally alone.'

Dan put on his jacket. 'I couldn't save my mother from herself,' he said. 'But I can save her reputation, such as it is. I want her name removed as a likely suspect in setting that fire.'

The phone rang. 'I told them to hold calls,' the captain muttered as he picked it up. He listened. 'It's for you, Jack.'

Sclafani took the receiver from him. 'Sclafani here,' he snapped.

When he hung up, he looked at Brennan. 'Nell MacDermott left a message a little over an hour ago. She's found the bank. It's in Westchester near the nursing home where Winifred Johnson's mother lives. She told them we'd be up with a search warrant.'

He paused. 'There's something else. I called North Dakota this morning to find out what's keeping our guy from getting back to us. He just picked up the call and left a message. He's compiled a full report on Adam Cauliff, and he's faxing it now.'

'What are you talking about?' Mac demanded. 'What is Nell up to, and why are you investigating Adam Cauliff?'

'As I said before, your granddaughter has been very helpful in our investigation, sir,' Sclafani replied. 'As for her husband, our contact in North Dakota has been digging into his background.

Apparently he's come up with some very disturbing information. Clearly there are things about Adam Cauliff that he wanted neither you nor your granddaughter to find out.'

CHAPTER SEVENTY-NINE

The rain began to fall again as Nell drove back to the city—a hard, driving, torrential rain that beat ferociously against the windshield.

The brake lights of the car ahead flashed glimpses of red, interspersed with sustained, brighter red, as the pace of the stream of traffic slowed almost to a standstill.

Nell gasped as a fender bender in the left lane sent one car veering into her lane, only inches away from her. She literally could have touched the passenger door.

Her mind had been racing with the events of the morning, but now she sternly willed herself to concentrate solely on her driving.

It was only when she drove into the garage in her building and had parked her car that she permitted herself to absorb the full impact of what she had learned.

Winifred had shared a safe-deposit box with Harry Reynolds.

Adam had a key to that box.

She hadn't figured out how to make sense of it, but there was a very good chance that Adam *was* 'Harry Reynolds.'

'You okay, Ms. MacDermott?' Manuel, the elevator operator looked at her solicitously.

335

'Fine, thanks, just a bit shaky. The driving is pretty rough out there.'

It was nearly three o'clock when she opened the door of her apartment and went in.

Sanctuary! Now she was almost frantic to be rid of Adam's possessions. No matter what else was found to be true, he and Winifred must have had a secret relationship of some sort. It might have been strictly a dishonest business relationship. It might have been what he had made her think was a romantic relationship. Although Nell still was not ready to believe that, it could have been true. No matter what the answer turned out to be, she wanted no reminder of Adam's presence left in the apartment.

I fell in love with love . . .

I never will again! Nell vowed silently.

You never will have to make that mistake again, she thought.

The blinking light on her answering machine indicated that there were messages. The first was from her grandfather: 'Nell, Dan and I were checking into the investigation of his mother's death. We happened to meet Detectives Sclafani and Brennan. You left a message for them, and now they seem to have some information about Adam. Unpleasant information, I'm afraid. They're coming to my office around five. Dan will be there. Please plan to join us.'

Next was a message from Dan: 'Nell, I'm worried about you. I'm carrying my cell phone. Please call me as soon as you can. The number is 917-555-1285.' She was about to turn off the machine when his voice came on again: 'Nell, I'll say it again. I need you.'

336

Nell smiled wistfully as she erased the messages. She went into the kitchen and opened the refrigerator. I had some nerve telling him that he had a poorly stocked kitchen, she thought as she surveyed the meager contents inside.

I'm not hungry, but I *do* want something. She settled for an apple, and as she bit into it, a memory from a long-ago history class struck her. Anne Boleyn on her way to the executioner's block had requested—or eaten—an apple.

Which was it? For some reason it suddenly seemed important to know the answer.

Let Aunt Gert be home, Nell prayed as she reached for the telephone.

Fortunately, Gert answered on the first ring. 'Nell, dear, I'm having one of those days I so enjoy. I'm putting photos in my album—the ones that I took of my psychic group at my parties. Do you know that Raoul Cumberland, who is so popular on that television show now, was at my house four years ago? I'd forgotten that. And—'

'Aunt Gert, I hate to cut you off, but this has been a crazy day for me,' Nell said. 'I have to ask you something. I'm bringing in five boxes of clothes tomorrow. That's a lot for you to be lifting and hanging and sorting. I'll be glad to dismiss the driver and stay and sort them with you.'

'Oh, aren't you sweet?' Gert laughed nervously. 'But that won't be necessary, dear.' She laughed again. 'I do have someone who's already volunteered to help. I promised her I wouldn't tell anybody, though. She simply doesn't want to be involved in any way with her clients' personal lives, even though—'

'Aunt Gert, Bonnie Wilson as much as told me

that she was going to volunteer to receive donations at the thrift shop.'

'*Did* she?' Gert asked, the relief in her voice mixed with surprise. 'Isn't that sweet of her?'

'Don't let on to Bonnie that I'm going to be there too,' Nell cautioned. 'See you tomorrow.'

'I'll bring my album,' Gert promised.

CHAPTER EIGHTY

Karen Renfrew liked to sit in Central Park, on a bench near Tavern on the Green. Her bundles around her, she enjoyed the sunshine, the comings and goings of the Rollerbladers, the joggers, the nannies pushing carriages, the tourists. She especially enjoyed the tourists, gaping as they took in the sights.

Her sights. *Her* New York. The best city in the whole world.

Karen had been in a hospital for a while after her mother died. 'For evaluation,' they said. Then they let her go. The landlady didn't want her back. 'You're nothing but trouble,' she said. 'You and all that junk you collect.'

But it *wasn't* junk. These were her things. Her things made her feel good. Her things were friends. Every single bag in her two carts—the one she pushed and the one she dragged—was important to her. And every single thing inside those bags was important.

Karen loved her things, her park, her city. Today, though, was not one of her favorite days. Today there was almost no one in the park. It was raining too hard. Karen pulled out her plastic wrap and put it over herself and her carts. She knew that when the cops drove by, they'd probably chase her. But until then she would enjoy the park.

She even liked it in the rain. In fact, she actually *liked* the rain. It was clean and friendly. Even when it fell as hard as this.

'Karen, we want to talk to you.'

She heard a gruff, masculine voice and looked out from under her plastic tarp.

There was a cop standing next to her carts. He was probably going to yell at her for refusing to go to the shelter. Or worse, he was going to force her to live in one of those dumps, with all those awful crazy people.

'What do you want?' she asked angrily, but she knew. She was going to have to go with him.

This cop wasn't mean like some of them. He even helped her with her things. At the street he lifted one of her shopping carts onto his van.

'Stop that!' she screamed. 'That's my stuff. Don't you touch it!'

'I know it is Karen, but we have to ask you a few questions at headquarters. Once we're done, I promise I'll drive you back here with all your things, or I'll drop you off somewhere else if you want. Trust me, Karen.'

'I've got a choice?' Karen asked bitterly as she watched to make sure the cop didn't drop any of her precious belongings.

CHAPTER EIGHTY-ONE

Nell dialed Bonnie Wilson's number. On the fourth ring the answering machine clicked on.

'If you want an appointment with internationally famous psychic Bonnie Wilson, please leave your name and phone number,' the tinny-sounding voice intoned.

'Bonnie, this is Nell MacDermott. I don't want to bother you,' she said, using an apologetic tone, 'but I feel it's very important that I see you again. I don't know if it's possible, but do you think you could channel Adam to me again? It's urgent that I talk with him. There's something I just have to know. I'll be at home, waiting for your call.'

The phone rang nearly an hour later. It was Bonnie. 'Nell, I'm sorry not to have called sooner, but I just got your message. I was with one of my new clients. Of course, you can come over immediately. I'm not sure if I can contact Adam, but I will try. I'll do my very best.'

'I'm sure you will,' Nell agreed, her voice carefully neutral.

CHAPTER EIGHTY-TWO

Jack Sclafani and George Brennan brought sandwiches in from the delicatessen and dropped them off at the squad office. Before they could break for lunch, there were a number of things that had to be taken care of. First they phoned the branch manager of the Westchester Exchange Bank. After that, they went before a judge to request a search warrant for safe-deposit box 332 at that bank. Finally, they asked the D.A. to give the assignment to open the box to other members of their squad.

They were anxious to know what might be lurking in that locked box, but they also didn't want to be away from the station if Karen Renfrew, the homeless woman whose soup kitchen card had been found at the Vandermeer mansion the night of the fire, had been located. If she was brought in, then they wanted to be around to question her.

It was three o'clock before they got to eat the sandwiches. Sitting in Jack's office, while they ate they also began reading the detailed report on Adam Cauliff that had come in from North Dakota.

'We ought to tell the D.A. to hire this guy in Bismarck,' Sclafani observed. 'He dug up more dirt in a couple of days than most gossip columnists dig up in a lifetime.'

'Pretty disturbing stuff too,' Brennan commented.

'From a broken home. A juvenile record that was expunged, but look what it was for. Shoplifting. Petty theft. Questioned in the death of an uncle when he was seventeen, but no charges were filed. Cauliff's mother inherited a chunk of money from the uncle. That was Cauliff's ticket to college.'

'How did our contact get all this stuff?'

'Good police work. Got hold of a retired sheriff with a long memory. Found a professor at the college who wasn't afraid to speak up. Keep reading.'

'Chronic liar. Braggart. Believed to have acquired advance knowledge of college final exams. Faked letters of reference for first job in Bismarck. His boss allowed him to resign. In his second job, he romanced the owner's wife. Fired. On another job, suspected of selling contents of sealed bids to rival firms.

'The report concludes, and I quote,' Sclafani read, 'His last employer in Bismarck said, "Adam Cauliff believed absolutely that he had a right to anything he wanted, be it a woman or a simple possession. I presented this file to a friend who is a psychiatrist. On the basis of the information I gave him, he concludes that Adam Cauliff has a serious personality disorder and is probably a full-fledged sociopath. Like many such people, he may be very intelligent and have ample surface charm. His general behavior may be acceptable, perhaps even impeccable. But if events turn against him, then at that point, he will do anything necessary to secure his personal aims. *Anything*. He appears to have a complete disregard for, and to be in conflict with, the normal social code by which most people conduct their lives."'

'Wow!' Brennan exclaimed after completing the report. 'How did a woman like Nell MacDermott get involved with a guy like this?'

'How do a lot of smart women get involved with guys like that? I'll tell you what I think,' Sclafani responded. 'It's because, if you're not a liar yourself, you have to get burned at least once before you understand that the Adam Cauliffs of this world are different from the rest of us. Dangerously so, sometimes.'

'The question now is, if somebody *did* get off

342

that boat, was it Adam, or was it Winifred Johnson?'

'Or, did *anybody* get off? Once they open that box, we'll know if one of them was there and cleaned it out.'

The phone rang. Sclafani picked it up. 'Good, we're on the way.' He looked at Brennan. 'They've found Karen Renfrew; she's at the 13th Precinct. Let's go.'

CHAPTER EIGHTY-THREE

Even her oversized golf umbrella could not keep Nell dry for the few steps across the sidewalk from the cab to the door of Bonnie Wilson's building. Once inside the outer vestibule, she closed the umbrella and dried her face with a handkerchief. Then, taking a deep breath, she pushed the button to Bonnie's apartment.

Bonnie did not wait for her to announce herself. 'Come right up, Nell.' As she was speaking, the buzzer unlocked the lobby door.

The elevator lumbered to the fifth floor. As she stepped out into the hall, Nell saw Bonnie standing in the door of her apartment. 'Come in, Nell.'

Behind her, the apartment was dimly lit. Even so, Nell gasped, feeling a sudden catch in her throat. The faint light around Bonnie was beginning to darken.

'Nell, you look so worried. Come in,' Bonnie urged.

Numbly, Nell obeyed. She knew that whatever happened in this place in the next little while was

343

inevitable. She had no choice, and she had virtually no control. The events ahead of her had to be played out to the end.

She stepped inside, and Bonnie closed the door behind her. Nell heard the click of double locks, then the slide of the dead bolt.

'They're doing some emergency work on the fire escape,' Bonnie explained, her voice soft. 'The superintendent has a key, and I don't want him or anyone else barging in while you're here.'

Nell began to follow Bonnie as she moved from the foyer. In the deathly quiet, their footsteps resounded on the bare wood. As she passed the mirror, Nell paused and stared into it.

Bonnie stopped and turned. 'What is it, Nell?'

They were standing side by side, their reflections gazing back at them. *Don't you see?* Nell wanted to shout. *Your aura is almost completely black, just like Winifred's was. You're going to die.*

Then, to her horror, as she watched, the darkness began to spread and encircle her as well.

Bonnie tugged at her arm. 'Nell, dear, come into the study,' she urged. 'It's time to talk to Adam.'

CHAPTER EIGHTY-FOUR

Dan had gone to the hospital to check on two postoperative patients, and it was four-thirty before he was able to get away. Once again he called Nell's apartment, but there still was no answer. Maybe Mac has heard from her, he thought.

Cornelius MacDermott reported that while he had not talked to his granddaughter, he *had* heard

344

from his sister. 'It's not bad enough that she sent Nell to some loony psychic, but now Gert is pulling the same stuff on *me*. She's worried because she has some kind of premonition that something bad is going to happen to Nell.'

'What do you think she means by that, Mac?'

'It means that she has nothing better to do than to sit around and fret. Look at the way it's raining. Gert's arthritis is probably kicking up, and she's turning her own discomfort into some kind of psychic warning. It's like she's channeling the pain for all the rest of us to enjoy. Dan, tell me I'm the sane one here. You should see the look that Liz is giving me. I think she believes in that nonsense too.'

'Mac, do you think there really is any reason to be concerned about Nell?' Dan asked sharply. Worry begets worry, he thought. This whole day has just been one unsettling thing after another.

'What's there to worry about? I told Gert to come over here to my office and listen to what those two detectives have to tell us about Adam Cauliff. Gert thought he was tops because he danced around opening doors for her, but according to what that Brennan told me, they've dug up a lot of dirt on that guy. They wouldn't tell me over the phone what all was in the report, but from the sound of it, seems like we're well rid of him.

'The detectives said they'd be here in about an hour. They were stopping at the 13th Precinct, where you and I were today. They said they'd located the woman whose soup kitchen card was found at the mansion fire, and she'd been taken there for questioning.'

'I'd like to know what she had to say to them.'

'I think you should know,' Mac said, his tone becoming gentler. 'Come on down now so you can hear everything firsthand. Then, when we hook up with Nell, we'll go out for an early dinner.'

'Just one more thing. Is it like Nell to ignore messages? I mean, do you think she's home and maybe is not picking up the phone because she doesn't feel well?'

'Good God, Dan, don't *you* get started.' But Dan could hear the concern in Cornelius MacDermott's voice. 'I'll call over to her doorman and see if he's seen her either coming or going.'

CHAPTER EIGHTY-FIVE

'I reported my bag with my good things stolen hours before that fire,' Karen Renfrew said angrily. She was with Captain Murphy and Detectives Sclafani and Brennan, seated in the same conference room in which they had met earlier with Cornelius MacDermott and Dan Minor.

'Who'd you report it to, Karen?' Sclafani asked.

'A cop who passed in a squad car. I waved him down. You know what he said?'

I can only imagine, Brennan thought.

'He said, "Lady, haven't you got enough junk in those carts without worrying if one bag fell off?" But I tell you, it didn't fall off. It was stolen.'

'Which probably means that whoever stole it was cooping in that mansion,' Captain Murphy said, 'and that person started the fire that killed Dr. Minor's mother. *That* means—'

Karen Renfrew interrupted the Captain. 'I can tell you just what that cop looked like. He was too fat, and he was in the squad car with another cop he called Arty.'

'We believe you, Karen,' Sclafani said soothingly. 'Where were you staying when your bag was stolen?'

'On One Hundredth Street. I had a nice doorway across the street from where they were fixing up that old apartment building.'

Suddenly alert, Sclafani asked, 'What is the avenue that One Hundredth Street crosses there, Karen?'

'Amsterdam Avenue. Why?'

'Yeah, what difference does that make?' Murphy asked.

'Maybe none. Or maybe *a lot*. We're following up something on a guy who was foreman on that job. According to his wife, he was extremely upset because of a change-of-work order that had canceled a job he was doing up there. We can't find, though, that any such thing ever happened—there's no trace of any order like that. So we figure maybe he was upset about something else. It also just happens that this all took place the same evening as the fire at the Vandermeer place, and while it could be pure coincidence, based again on what his wife told us, we've been looking for some way to connect him to both sites.'

George Brennan looked at his partner. There was no need to vocalize the rest of the connection they had just made. Jimmy Ryan had been working across the street from where Karen Renfrew was cooping. She was a wino. It wouldn't have been hard for him to have lifted one of her bags and

347

thrown it in the trunk of his car while she was sleeping. It would be a good way of planting phony proof that the mansion fire had been set by a squatter. It was a twist of fate that he grabbed the bag with her soup kitchen card, and that the card wasn't burned in the fire. The pieces of this puzzle were finally beginning to fall into place, and the picture they were getting was far from pretty.

If this line of reasoning panned out, Brennan thought with disgust, Jimmy Ryan was not only guilty of arson that resulted in a felony murder, but of stealing from a homeless woman who had a pathetic, compulsive need for the scraps and rags and trash he took from her.

CHAPTER EIGHTY-SIX

'Nell, I can sense that you are very troubled.'

The two women were seated at a table in the center of the room, and Bonnie was holding Nell's hands.

Bonnie's hands are ice cold, Nell thought.

'What is it you need to ask Adam?' Bonnie whispered.

Nell tried to withdraw her hands, but Bonnie gripped them even more tightly. She is frightened, Nell thought—and *desperate*. She doesn't know how much I know or suspect about Adam and the explosion.

'I need to ask Adam about Winifred,' Nell said, trying to keep her voice calm. 'I think she may still be alive.'

'Why do you think that?'

348

'Because a little boy who was on a ferry coming from the Statue of Liberty saw the explosion. He says he saw someone dive off the boat, someone dressed in a wet suit. I know Winifred was a strong swimmer, and I suspect it may have been her that the boy saw.'

'The child might have been wrong,' Bonnie said, her voice low.

Nell glanced about. The room was filled with shadows. The shades were drawn. The only sound she could hear, other than their own breathing, was the rain pelting on the windows.

'I don't think the child was wrong,' Nell said firmly. 'I think someone *did* escape from that boat before the explosion. I also think you know who it is.'

She felt a tremor run through Bonnie's body, convulsing her hands, and it was then that Nell was able to pull her own free.

'Bonnie, I've seen you on television. I believe you do have genuine psychic powers. I don't really understand what causes some people to have those special abilities, but I *do* know that I have had several psychic experiences myself—experiences that were very real but are not explainable as part of the rational world. I know that my Aunt Gert has had these experiences as well.

'But you're different from us. You have a rare gift, and I think you have been guilty of misusing it. I remember Gert told me years ago that a gift of psychic power must only be used for good. If it is abused, she said, the one who possesses it will be severely punished.'

Bonnie listened, her eyes fixed on Nell, her pupils darkening with every word she heard, her

349

complexion draining to alabaster white.

'You came to Gert, claiming that you had been contacted by Adam. I don't believe in channeling, but I was distraught enough at his death to want to try to be in touch with him myself. When my mother and father died, they came to say goodbye to me because they loved me. I thought Adam had not come to say goodbye because we had quarreled. So I wanted to be in touch with him; that way we could reconcile. I needed to part from him with love. That's why I wanted so much to believe in you.'

'Nell, I am sure that on the other side, Adam—'

'Hear me out, Bonnie. If you *did* channel to Adam, what you claim he said to me was untrue. I know now that he did *not* love me. A man who loves his wife does not have an affair with his assistant. He does not open a safe-deposit box with her under another name. I am *sure* that Adam didn't love me because that is precisely what he did.'

'You're wrong, Nell. Adam *did* love you.'

'No, I am not. And I'm also not a fool. I know you are helping either Adam or Winifred by trying to get the safe-deposit key that was inadvertently left in Adam's jacket.'

I've hit home, Nell thought. Bonnie Wilson was moving her head from side to side, not so much in denial as in despair.

'Only two people would have any use for that key—Adam or Winifred. I hope it is Winifred that you are working with, and that Adam is the one who is dead. I cringe to think that for more than three years I might have been living and breathing and eating and sleeping with someone who could

350

deliberately take three lives, and arrange a fire that took the life of a homeless woman.

'On a different, but important level, I cringe to think that I gave up the career I wanted all my life just to please a cheat and a thief—that Adam was both those things I know with certainty. I can only pray that he was not also a murderer.'

Nell reached into her pocket and took out the safe-deposit key. 'Bonnie, I believe that you know where Adam or Winifred is hiding. You may not realize that if you have assisted either of them in any way, then you have become an accessory to multiple murder. Take this key. Give it to whichever one is still alive. Let him or her think that it's safe to go to that bank in White Plains. It's your only chance for leniency.'

'What do you mean, "*think* that it's safe," Nell?'

She had not heard the footsteps approaching from behind. She turned and looked up in shock and horror.

Adam was standing over her.

CHAPTER EIGHTY-SEVEN

Dan Minor glanced at the window, hoping to see that the slashing rainfall was letting up. Unfortunately it was still pouring, beating against the glass, the rain creating a virtual waterfall. His grandmother used to tell him that when it rained like this, the angels were weeping. He found that an especially ominous thought today.

Where did Nell go? he kept asking himself.

They were all gathered in Mac's office. He was

there with Mac and Gert and Liz and the two detectives, who had just arrived.

Nell's doorman had confirmed that she arrived home at about three o'clock and went back out shortly after four. That meant she must have heard the message I left for her, he thought. Why didn't she call me back?

The elevator operator said she had seemed upset.

When Jack Sclafani and George Brennan had arrived, they were introduced to Liz and Gert. Then Sclafani took over. 'Let's start by talking about the homeless woman who reported the theft of one of her bags only hours before the mansion fire. We've been able to verify her story with the police officer she stopped that day. So we believe that she was not the one who set the fire at the Vandermeer mansion.

'I don't think we'll ever have absolute proof, but we believe very strongly that Winifred Johnson paid Jimmy Ryan, one of the people who lost his life in the boat explosion, to set that fire, and to make it look as if a homeless person had done it.'

'That means my mother—' Dan interrupted.

'That means that your mother has been cleared as a suspect.'

'Do you think Winifred Johnson was doing this on her own, or was she acting on instructions from Adam?' Mac asked.

'We assume it was all done for Adam Cauliff.'

'But I don't understand,' Gert said. 'How did he stand to benefit from the fire?'

'It was because he had bought the Kaplan property right next door to the old mansion. He was smart enough to know that it would increase

352

enormously in value if the mansion was gone and the property therefore no longer restricted by the building's landmark status. He then would approach Peter Lang, who bought the old Vandermeer property, and offer him a deal. He was also arrogant enough to think that he could force himself on the developer as architect for the project.'

'According to the widow, a man phoned Jimmy Ryan's home the night of the fire with instructions to cancel the job,' Brennan explained. 'That's one of the reasons we believe both Adam and Winifred were in on planning the fire together. They may just have learned that the Vandermeer mansion had been removed from landmark status that same day. Thus there was no longer any need to set the fire.'

'Well, it didn't do either one of them much good,' Liz commented. 'Since both of them were blown to bits on that boat.'

'We don't think so,' Brennan told them. Noting their astonished expressions, he said, 'A witness claimed to see someone in a wet suit dive off the boat an instant before the explosion. Two bodies have not been accounted for—those of Adam Cauliff and Winifred Johnson.'

'Thanks to some sleuthing by your granddaughter, Congressman,' Sclafani said, picking up the story, 'we have gained access to a safe-deposit box shared by a man and a woman who called themselves Harry and Rhoda Reynolds. The box contained doctored passports and various other forms of identification. We haven't seen the actual contents of the box, but copies of the pictures on the passports were faxed in to our offices. And while both the man and the woman are somewhat disguised, it is clear that they are pictures of Winifred Johnson and Adam Cauliff.'

'The box also contained nearly three hundred thousand dollars in cash and several million dollars worth of bearer bonds and other securities,' Detective Brennan added.

A long silence followed these disclosures, broken finally by Gert, who asked, 'How on earth could they accumulate that much money?'

'It's really not that hard with the kind of projects Walters and Arsdale handle. They have billings of nearly eight hundred million in their various jobs on their books right now. Also, we think this was something that Winifred and Adam had been planning for some time.'

Looking at the distress on Mac's face, Sclafani said, 'I'm afraid your granddaughter married a pretty despicable character, Congressman. It's a sorry history and it's all in this report. You can go over it at your leisure. I'm sorry for Ms. MacDermott. She's a fine woman and a very smart one. I know this will be a shock for her, but she's resilient, and in time she will get over it.'

'Will she be joining us?' Brennan asked. 'We'd like to thank her for all her help.'

'We don't know where Nell is,' Gert told him, her tone a mixture of distress and irritation, 'and no one will listen to me, but I'm worried sick about her. Something isn't right. I could tell when I talked to her on the phone earlier this afternoon that she was distracted. She didn't sound at all like herself. She said she'd just come back from Westchester. So why would she go running out again on a day like this?'

There *is* something wrong, Dan thought, agonized by his concern. Nell is in trouble.

Brennan and Sclafani looked at each other. 'You have no idea where she is?' Sclafani asked.

'That bothers you,' Mac snapped. 'Why?'

'Because Ms. MacDermott obviously found the other key to the safe-deposit box and was smart enough to investigate a bank near the nursing home where Winifred Johnson's mother is a resident. If she has figured out where either Winifred or Adam may be hiding, and tries to contact them, she is putting herself in grave danger. Anyone who, with cold deliberation, blows up a boat with several people on it, is capable of doing whatever it takes, including committing more murders, to avoid detection.'

'It *has* to be Winifred who swam away from the boat,' Gert said, her voice trembling. 'I mean, Bonnie Wilson channeled to Adam. He spoke to Nell from the other side, so he has to be dead.'

'He *what*?' Sclafani asked.

'Gert, for God sake!' Mac exploded.

'Mac, I know you don't believe in this, but Nell did. She was even following Adam's advice that she give his clothes to the thrift shop. I just confirmed that with her this afternoon. She's got them all packed up and is bringing them in tomorrow, and Bonnie Wilson even volunteered to help me unpack them. I told Nell that. Bonnie's been so helpful through all this. The only thing is, I was surprised that she either forgot or didn't tell me that she once had met Adam at one of my parties. I found a picture of the two of them together. I would have thought she might have mentioned that.'

355

'You say she told Ms. MacDermott to give Adam's clothes away, and then wanted to help unpack them,' Brennan exclaimed, jumping up. 'I'll bet anything she was trying to get at that key. She's in on this some way, whether she's in cahoots with Adam or with Winifred.'

'Dear God,' Liz Hanley said. 'I thought he actually had materialized.'

They stared at her.

'What do you mean, Liz?' Mac asked.

'I saw Adam's face appear in the mirror in Bonnie Wilson's apartment. I thought she must have channeled him, but maybe he really was there.'

That's where Nell went, Dan thought, to that Wilson woman's apartment. I'm sure of it.

Sick with dread, he looked around, seeing the sudden fear he felt reflected in the faces of everyone in the room.

CHAPTER EIGHTY-EIGHT

Adam was standing over her.

Despite the dim light, Nell could make him out. It was Adam, but one side of his face was blistered and peeling, and both his right hand and foot were heavily bandaged. She could also see his eyes, which were filled with rage.

'You found the key and you called the police,' he said hoarsely. 'After *all* my planning, after *three years* of putting up with that stupid, insipid woman, after nearly losing my own life because you gave her the wrong jacket and I had to search for her

356

damn pocketbook—after *all that*, plus the pain of scalding burns, I have *nothing.*'

He raised his left hand. He was grasping something heavy in it, but Nell could not make it out. She tried to get up, but he shoved her back with his bandaged hand. She saw a look of intense pain shoot across his face as she heard Bonnie scream, 'Adam. Don't. *Please don't!*'

Then a stunning, smashing pain exploded on the side of her head, and she felt herself falling, falling . . .

*　　　*　　　*

From far away Nell heard a strange sound, a mixture of moaning and sighing. Her head hurt so much. Her hair and face were wet and sticky. Gradually she realized that she was the one making the sound.

'My head hurts,' she whispered. Then she remembered: Adam was alive. He was here.

Someone was touching her? Who was it? What was happening?

'Tighter. Tie it tighter!' It was Adam's voice.

Her legs, why did they hurt? Nell wondered.

She managed to open her eyes enough to see that Bonnie was bending over her, weeping. In her hands she had a ball of heavy twine. She's tying up my legs, Nell thought.

'Her hands. Now do her hands.' It was Adam's voice again—harsh and cruel.

She was on a bed and had been rolled onto her stomach. Bonnie was pulling her hands behind her, wrapping the twine around them.

Nell tried to speak, but she could not make the

357

words that were in her mind reach her lips. *Don't do this, Bonnie*, she wanted to say. *You only have a few minutes of life left. Your aura is completely dark now. Don't go with more blood on your hands.*

Bonnie was pulling her wrists together, but then Nell felt her press her hand. She continued wrapping the twine, but more loosely now.

She wants to help me, Nell thought.

'Hurry up,' Adam snapped

Slowly, Nell turned her head. She could see a pile of crumpled newspapers on the floor. Adam was holding a candle against them. The first curl of flame sprang up. Oh God, he was setting the room on fire! She realized with stark, sudden clarity just what was happening.

'See how you like it, Nell,' Adam said. 'I want you to feel the pain, just like I did. And it was all because of you. It was *your* fault. Your fault that I didn't have the key. And then, looking like this, I couldn't even go to the bank and try to convince them to let me into the locked box. And all because of you and that stupid woman, bringing me the wrong jacket.'

'Adam, why . . . ?' Nell tried to speak.

'Why? Do you really have to ask me why? Don't you understand anything?' His rage now was tinged with disgust. 'I was never good enough for you, never good enough to mix with your precious grandfather's cronies. Don't you realize that when you ran for office, it would be all over for me? There were some things in my past that would have been a little embarrassing to a congressional candidate. If you hadn't insisted on being Mac's little girl, doing every little thing he wanted, I might have had a chance. But with you determined to run

358

for office, I knew it was over. Don't you understand what a feast the media would have had, looking into my background? I just couldn't let that happen.'

Adam was kneeling next to the bed now, his face close to hers. 'And so, Nell, you forced my hand. You and that simpering Jimmy Ryan, and Winifred with her wet, droopy eyes and her dry, cracked lips. Well, that's okay. It was time for me to go anyway. Time for me to make a whole new start.' He stood up and looked down at her. 'So what if I've only got a little left to start over with now—I'll make it. But *you* won't. Goodbye, Nell.'

'Adam, you can't kill her,' Bonnie shrieked, clutching his arm as the flames spread.

'Bonnie, you're either in this with me or you're not. It's your choice: you can stay here with Nell, or you can walk out that door with me.'

Just then the doorbell started to ring, its persistent, piercing sound reverberating through the small apartment. Smoke was filling the room as the wall behind the papers caught fire, and from the outside hallway a voice shouted, 'Police, open up.'

Adam ran into the foyer and looked at the front door. Then he turned back and looked at Nell. 'Hear them, Nell? They're trying to help you. Well, you know what? They won't get in here in time. I'm going to make sure of that.' He raced to the door and checked the double locks and the dead bolt. Coming back into the bedroom, he closed the door to that room behind him, turned the key in the lock, yanked the key out and, with his shoulder, shoved the dresser in front of the door. He pulled some newspapers that hadn't caught fire yet from the pile and threw the lighted candle on top of them.

'Quick, the fire escape,' he snapped.

The flames were leaping at the curtains. 'Open the window, damn you,' he shouted at Bonnie.

'They're working on the fire escape, Adam. We can't go out there. It's not safe,' Bonnie sobbed.

He was pushing Bonnie outside, onto the fire escape and into the pouring rain. Nell saw the wild look on Adam's face as he took the time to close the window behind him, sealing her in that room.

She was alone—just her and the heat. The unbearable heat. The mattress was burning. With strength born of desperation, Nell managed to slide off the bed, then to stand and steady herself enough so that she didn't fall. Supporting herself against the dresser, she managed to pull her hands free from the bonds that Bonnie had left loose. She shoved the dresser to one side.

The door was on fire. Nell tried to turn the handle. It was red hot. The blisters, the smoke— she had known this was going to happen. Blood was dripping in her eyes. There was no oxygen, only smoke. She couldn't breathe.

Someone was hammering at the door to the apartment. She could hear them. The door wouldn't open. The key was gone.

Too late, she thought as she slid to the floor and began to crawl. You're going to be too late.

CHAPTER EIGHTY-NINE

A thin trickle of smoke slid into the hallway. 'The place is on fire,' Sclafani yelled. As one, he and Brennan and Dan Minor kicked at the door. It refused to budge.

'I'll go to the roof,' Brennan shouted.

Sclafani turned and raced down the stairs, Dan at his heels. They reached the lobby and raced out into the street, running to the side of the building that held the fire escape. The rain pelted them as they rounded the corner.

'Good God, look!' Dan exclaimed.

On the fire escape above them there were two people, slipping and stumbling on the wet and treacherous steps.

Even in the dim light and through the driving rain, Jack saw the face of the man above and knew that they had cornered Adam Cauliff, the man Benjy Tucker had seen in the wet suit, and who had caused him so many terrible nightmares.

*   *   *

Inside the burning bedroom the smoke was overwhelming. Nell could see nothing as she crawled across the floor, gasping for the last remaining hint of air. She was choking on the smoke. The window. She had to find the window. Suddenly her head touched a solid object. The wall! She must have crossed the room—the window must be right there. She pulled herself to her knees and stretched her arms up to grip the windowsill.

All she felt, though, was heated metal. What was it? Was it a handle? A handle of the dresser. Dear God, she had gone around in a circle. She was at the door again.

I can't make it, she thought. I can't breathe.

She suddenly felt as if she were in the riptide again, being pulled down into a swirling vortex. She was beyond exhaustion. Unable to breathe. Desperately in need of sleep.

A voice came to her, only this time the voice that filled her head was not that of either of her parents—it was Dan, saying *Nell, I need you.*

Turn around, she told herself. Picture the window. It's straight ahead. Stay near the bed, then go to your right. Still hobbled by the cord around her legs, she crawled across the room.

I need you, Nell. I need you.

Choking and coughing, Nell plunged forward, willing herself to reach the window.

*   *   *

'Police! Stop!' Sclafani shouted to the couple on the fire escape above him. 'Put your hands up.'

Adam stopped and spun around as Bonnie tried to get past him. He grabbed her. 'Go back,' he shouted, as he pushed her back up the stairs.

At the third floor he slipped and grabbed the railing with his bandaged right hand. Shrieking with pain, he nonetheless forged ahead.

They made it past the window to Bonnie's apartment on the fifth floor, and reached the top landing on the sixth floor. Below them they heard the shattering of glass and saw smoke billowing up from the fire.

Adam looked up from the sixth-floor landing. The roof was six feet over their heads.

'It's useless, Adam!' Bonnie screamed.

Adam hoisted himself up onto the metal railing and reached up. His fingertips touched the edge of the roof. Too frantic to notice the terrible pain that came from putting pressure on his injured hand, he grasped the edge of the roof and tried to pull himself up.

Beneath him he heard a grinding sound, felt a sickening lurch, as the fire escape began to separate from the wall.

*   *   *

On the street below, Dan Minor could hear the sound of fire engines as they screamed their way down West End Avenue. He locked his fingers together, cupping Jack Sclafani's foot as the detective reached up and grasped the bottom rung of the fire escape. 'Drop the ladder,' Dan shouted as Sclafani began to climb to the second floor.

Moments later, Dan was scrambling up the treacherous fire escape. Above him he could see flames shooting from the fifth-floor window. Nell! he thought. Nell was in that inferno!

*   *   *

Nell hoisted herself up and stumbled as she reached the window. When she crashed against it, her shoulder broke the large single pane. Behind her she felt the rush of intense heat sucked outward, and beneath her she could feel the floor starting to give way. She thrust her body forward,

363

feeling the cool, damp air as it rushed up from below, allowing her finally to breathe again. She was only partially through the window, though, and she could feel herself sliding backward as the floor gave way beneath her feet. Her blistered hands grabbed the window frame. Shattered glass pierced her palms. The pain was too intense. She knew she couldn't hold on much longer. Behind her was the roar of the fire. There were sirens screaming below, and people yelling all around. Inside her head, though, there was only calm. Is this what it's like to die? she wondered.

*   *   *

Adam grasped the roof with his fingertips. With superhuman strength born of desperation, he began to pull himself up. Then he felt arms around his legs, dragging him down. It was Bonnie. He tried to kick free of her grasp, but it was no use. He could not hold on to the roof. He swayed and then fell back to the landing.

Snarling, he picked Bonnie up and lifted her over his head. The fire escape gyrated beneath them.

'Let her go, or I'll shoot,' Brennan shouted from the roof.

'That's exactly what I'm going to do,' Cauliff shouted back.

Racing up the steps, Sclafani saw what was about to happen. He's going to throw her over, he thought. He reached the top landing and tried to tackle Cauliff. He was too late. Bonnie fell screaming to the street below.

Adam vaulted back onto the railing and once

364

again reached up. This time his fingers barely grasped the edge of the roof before they lost their grip. For a perilous moment, he wavered, his arms flailing the air for balance.

Sclafani froze as he watched the man before him performing a deadly dance before he plunged down, falling without a sound until his body hit the pavement.

Just below Sclafani, Dan had reached the window that opened from Bonnie's bedroom. Seeing Nell at the edge of the inferno, grasping the window frame, he grabbed her wrists and held them in his own strong, sure fingers until a moment later Jack Sclafani was beside him, helping him to pull her free.

'We've got her!' Jack exclaimed. 'Come on. This thing is going to go.'

The fire escape was swaying wildly as they made their way down from the fifth-floor landing. Dan was half carrying, half dragging the now unconscious Nell.

When they reached the extension ladder, a fireman below yelled up to him, 'Give her to me and jump!'

Dan lowered Nell into the fireman's outstretched arms. Then he and Jack Sclafani bolted over the railing and dashed out of the way as six floors of metal fire escape collapsed and crumbled to the ground, covering the bodies of Adam Cauliff and Bonnie Wilson.

Tuesday, November 7
Election Day

CHAPTER NINETY

A new president was being chosen who would lead the United States of America for the next four years. A new senator would speak for the state of New York in the nation's most exclusive club. And at the end of the day, the city of New York would know if the congressional district over which Cornelius MacDermott had presided for nearly fifty years had chosen his granddaughter, Nell MacDermott, as their new representative.

Partially due to nostalgia, but also with a nod toward superstition, Nell had located her campaign headquarters in the Roosevelt Hotel, the scene of all her grandfather's triumphs. As the polls closed, and the results began to trickle in, they sat together in a suite on the hotel's tenth floor, their attention focused on the three television sets positioned on one side of the room—one for each of the major networks.

Gert MacDermott was with them, along with Liz Hanley and Lisa Ryan. Only Dan Minor was unaccounted for, and he had just called to say that he was on his way down from the hospital. Campaign aides wandered in and out of the room, nervously picking at the elaborate food and drink that had been laid out for all comers. Some of the aides were optimistic, some were fearful—it had been a particularly tough campaign.

Nell turned to her grandfather. 'Win or lose, Mac, I'm glad you made me run.'

'And why shouldn't you have run?' he responded gruffly. 'The party committee agreed with me—the

369

sins of the husband should not be visited on the wife. Although, being perfectly practical about it, if there had been a trial, you inevitably would have been dragged into it, and the media circus around it probably would have made your campaign impossible. With Adam and the rest dead, though, it was yesterday's news.'

Yesterday's news, Nell thought. Yesterday's news that Adam had betrayed her. Yesterday's news that he had cold-bloodedly made sure that anybody who could incriminate him, including Jimmy Ryan and Winifred Johnson, died on that boat. Yesterday's news that she had been married to a monster. I lived with Adam for three years. Did I always sense that at the core of our relationship there was something terribly wrong? I guess I should have.

The investigator from Bismarck has uncovered more disquieting information about Adam. He'd used the pseudonym Harry Reynolds on one of his questionable deals in North Dakota. He must have told that to Winifred.

Nell looked across the room. Lisa Ryan caught her eye and gave her an encouraging thumbs-up sign. At the start of the summer, Lisa had approached Nell, offering to help with the campaign. Nell had gladly taken her on, and had been more than pleased with the result. Lisa had worked tirelessly on the campaign, spending her evenings at headquarters, talking with voters on the phone, mailing out campaign literature.

Lisa's children had spent the summer at the shore with her neighbors, Brenda Curren and her husband. She had thought it better if they were out of the neighborhood until the talk about their father died down. It hadn't been too bad, though. Jimmy Ryan's name was in the police files, but he had received scant attention from the press.

'The children know their father made a terrible mistake,' Lisa said candidly when Nell first met with her. 'But they also know that his life was taken because he was going to face up to it. He wanted to atone. His last words to me were, 'I'm sorry,' and now I know what he meant. He deserves my forgiveness.'

It had been decided that if Nell were elected, Lisa would work in her New York office. I hope that comes to pass, Nell thought, as she shifted her focus back to the array of television sets.

The phone rang. Lisa answered it, then came over to Nell. 'It was Ada Kaplan. She's praying you win. She said you're a saint.'

Nell had sold the Kaplan property back to Ada for exactly what Adam had paid her for it.

Ada had then sold it to Peter Lang for three million dollars. 'Not a word to my son,' she'd told Nell. 'He gets what I promised him. The difference goes to the United Jewish Appeal. That money will be used to do good things for needy people.'

'You're neck and neck, Nell,' Mac said, fretting. 'It's tighter than I expected.'

'Mac, since when do you fidget while watching returns?' Nell asked, laughing.

'Since you got in a race. Look at that-they're calling it a toss-up!'

It was 9:30. A half hour later, Dan arrived. He immediately sat next to Nell and put his arm around her. 'Sorry to have taken so long getting here,' he said. 'There were a couple of emergencies. How are things going here? Shall I take your pulse?'

'Don't bother—I already know it's off the charts.'

At 10:30 the pundits started declaring a shift in Nell's favor. 'That's it! Keep it up,' Mac muttered.

At 11:30, Nell's opponent conceded. The cheer that went up among those gathered in the suite was thunderously echoed in the auditorium below. Nell stood surrounded by the people who mattered most in her life as the television monitor picked up the crowd in the Roosevelt's ballroom, celebrating Nell's victory. The crowd began to sing the song that had become associated with her campaign ever since the band first played it when she announced her candidacy. It was a turn-of-the-century favorite 'Wait 'Til the Sun Shines, Nellie.'

Wait 'til the sun shines, Nellie,
When the clouds go drifting by . . .
They have drifted by, Nell thought.
We will be happy, Nellie . . .
Sweethearts you and I . . .
'You bet we will,' Dan whispered.
So wait 'til the sun shines, Nellie, bye and bye.

The song ended, and the crowd roared its approval. In the ballroom, Nell's campaign manager grabbed the microphone. 'The sun is shining!' he yelled. 'We elected the president we wanted, the senator we wanted, and now, the congresswoman we wanted!' He began to chant: 'We want Nell! We want Nell!'

Hundreds of voices joined him in the chant.

'Come on, Congresswoman MacDermott. They're waiting for you,' Mac said, urging her toward the door.

He took her arm and steered her, while Dan and

Liz and Gert all fell in step behind them.

'Now, Nell, the first thing I'd do if I were you . . .' Mac began.